Nicholas

The Chrysalis
of
Winter Solstice

Christopher J. Wyatt

Book Design & Format: Christopher J. Wyatt & Monika Wyatt

Editing: Monika Wyatt

Cover Design: Adrian DKC (adriandkc.com)

Illustrations: Devin Maupin (devinmaupin.carbonmade.com)

Arena Sketch & Cartography: Christopher J. Wyatt

Library of Congress Control Number: 2025920456

ISBN: 979-8-9925212-5-2

ISBN: 979-8-9925212-9-0 (Hardcover)

ISBN: 979-8-9925212-0-7 (Ebook)

In loving memory of
my grandfather

A man who woke before all, starting
the morning fire to warm our family
on cold winter days.

The sound of a quill scratches in a cold and dark night:

The daylight grows shorter, the sickness grows stronger

The creatures of evil defeat us in slaughter

Our skin, it is blistered, our faces are dry

Our blades are dull, but our shields are held high

Our fingers frost-bitten, our outlook is dreary

For the Bacillus thwarts us, with sinistrous fury

Though embedded fog blinds us, we march toward the Strain

But with pure hearts and goodness, we block its disdain

We struggle together to avoid this fierce blight

The Restorer has come, and he aids us this night

Our battle cries roaring, our breaths misted with cold

For Nich'las is burdened, with an artifact he holds

The Questionable Whisper

Theopanes and Nonna sat together on the beach. Upon their faces, they could feel the light breeze and the spray of the sea's water. They spent time here often, walking along the shoreline and watching the sun rise. They lived an enriched life in Patara, a flourishing city in the region of Lycia. The two had both nobility and wealth but were not pretentious. They often gave to the poor and cared for the less fortunate. They felt the life they maintained would be ideal for the newcomer about to arrive in the family.

"Theopanes, he's stirring again! The sea seems to excite him."

Theopanes reached down to touch Nonna's stomach. "Have you decided on a name for him?" he replied. They were still uncertain what to call him. The two had longed for a child for quite some time, many years, but had faced struggles conceiving. Oftentimes, Nonna would find a place of solitude. With teary eyes, she would pray. "Please bless me with a son, a son who is strong in mind and strong in body."

As the fertility of Nonna's womb developed into an infant, she began having a re-occurring dream. It always started on the beach of Patara, where Nonna sat looking upon the blue waters, touching the sand with the tips of her fingers. A soft-spoken whisper suddenly called out, "Nicholas? Nicholas?" Startled, Nonna looked out to the sea, attempting to locate the mysterious sound. Among the swells, the water's surface froze and formed into ice caps. Quickly following, the ice cap began to crack and then broke into masses of crystal shards and frozen particles. The dream transitioned to a wintered field and a snow-white hare. In a long sprint, the hare hopped, and while in midair, it changed to a beastly form, with dark grey hair and glowing purple eyes. The dream finalized with a withered poppy as subject. A hand appeared, pulling the dead poppy from its roots. The hand became the silhouette of a small boy. With the flower in his hand, the child walked to his mother, and with each step, the poppy bloomed to its original and beautiful red color. The young boy offered the poppy to his mother. Smiling, the mother reached down to accept it, hugging the child. The dream concluded in darkness, except for two sharp fiery eyes of orange and yellow. The eyes spoke in a soft and friendly whisper "Nicholas... Nicholas? *Restorer of Goodness*... please help us."

Nonna awoke with a startle. She felt a slight pain and a few kicks inside her stomach. Rubbing her stomach, she spoke softly so as not to wake up Theopanes, "It's okay, little one, it's okay." Lying awake, she began wondering what the dream meant. Why did the voice keep calling out the name Nicholas?

Nonna and Theopanes started the usual day by taking a walk along the beach. They generally spoke to one another, but on this particular morning not much conversation took place. Theopanes could sense that Nonna had something on her mind. Holding her hand and walking by her side, he waited for her to speak. After a few minutes of silence, Nonna halted the walk and spoke to Theopanes with unexplained sincerity and certainty. "Theopanes? I would like to name our child **Nicholas**."

Pull the Sea

The newest resident of Patara lay in his infant bed made of reeds and wool; his fragile body covered with a colorful fabric blanket. His newborn eyes perceived blurred images of smiling faces and hand gestures of pointing and waving. His ears made out distorted sounds of greetings. "Hello, little one," some would say. "Welcome, newcomer," others would utter. The dawning of the child was a great day of celebration and delight. Close friends and locals of the town came by throughout the day to give respect to the parents and their baby and to give assorted foods, household items, and goats as gifts. Outside their home, they could hear voices of fellow townsfolk spreading the word.

"Rejoice! Nonna and Theopanes have finally been blessed with a new baby boy!"

Theopanes opened the front door of his home, holding his new babe, who was resting on his broad shoulders and stern forearms. Bystanders of the town gathered nearby to watch. He addressed the crowd. "Fellow friends and neighbors, meet our new child... Nicholas!" He carefully raised his new son up with two hands, and the group clapped and cheered in excitement for the gift Theopanes and Nonna had received.

Walking the city's main avenue was a holy man dressed in a cloak and wide lace garments, with a tall miter on his head and a wooden crosier in his left hand. This man was an abbot of the nearby town of Myra and a relative to Theopanes and Nonna. As he strolled through the streets of Patara, he frequently nodded or raised his crosier to the residents in greeting. One passing woman recognized the man and spoke. "Good day to you, abbot; what brings you to Patara?"

The priest briefly stopped and beamed at her, placing the end of his crosier on the ground to steady himself. "The heavens have gifted us with a child today. He is also my new nephew."

"That is wonderful!" she exclaimed.

He proceeded to the homestead. Several people who passed by knew him well, while others questioned who he was. It was part of his profession and nature to interact with them, since many shared his beliefs and faith. This was not always the case for everyone, however, and his presence caught the attention of two authoritarians. They were soldiers loyal to the Roman army, easily recognized by the common folk of the city, and were both equipped with prodigious armor and pugios sheathed to their waists. One soldier stopped the abbot in his tracks. "Halt! What is your intention of business here?"

He stormed up a simple but vague answer. "I am here to visit family."

The soldier threw him a stank eye but accepted his answer. "Very well, proceed then."

Those loyal to the Roman Empire commonly crossed paths with those who practiced the religious beliefs that the abbot preached. The Romans generally had different views and beliefs but often chose to turn their backs to reduce conflict or controversy. Those that followed spirituality often shared their faith behind closed doors or in places of sanctuary to protect themselves.

As the evening approached, a celebration feast was held, featuring wine and an accumulation of food items that had been donated throughout the day. Theopanes and the uncle sat, weeding through the assortment of fruits, breads, nuts, and many other options. Nonna, exhausted, skipped dinner and instead sat on a wooden rocker chair that was built by Theopanes, enjoying the crisp, cool breeze that came in through the nearby window. It was a clear and beautiful evening, and the stars above shone brightly upon her and her new babe cradled in her arms. The bishop got up from his seat and brushed a few dinner crumbs from his face. He approached Nonna and looked down at his nephew, who was lying with his eyes wide open.

"He's very observant and alert, has full attention of his surroundings."

The baby cooed as he looked up at his uncle.

"Yes, he does." Nonna smiled down at him. "When most younglings would sleep, he chooses to watch the stars outside."

"May I?" the bishop asked.

Nonna nodded and the abbot reached out and placed his hand on the infant's head. Concluding his first day in the world, his uncle provided a blessing of protection and safety to his new beloved nephew.

Paloma's hooves clopped as Nonna and Nicholas galloped through the Arch of Modestus. Its tall triple–arched structure stood beyond the outskirts of the city, indicating to travelers that they would soon reach the desert beach of Patara. Nonna looked back at her son who rode behind her with his arms wrapped around her torso. Paloma was a gentle horse, with the nature of a dove, dirty white in color. Her legs exhibited great strength and muscularity as she trotted. "Almost there, Nicholas; the weather is prime for today's training." It was a beautiful October day, a great opportunity for them to spend time near the sea. The horse traveled on the rocky hardened pathway, which soon shifted to a soft sandy terrain. The beaches consisted of dunes that had a desert-like appearance, and its lengthy shoreline went for miles along the Mediterranean Sea's coast.

Reaching their destination, the young boy jumped from the horse and began running toward the water. As he sprinted down the path toward the designated training area, a swirl of sand coated his legs, torso, and face. "Careful, Nicholas, not so fast! There may be sea turtle hatchlings burrowed below," Nonna cautioned her son.

Nicholas slowed his stride, trying not to disturb hatchlings that may be directly under his bare feet. The primary time of his training and playing at the beach was during the fall and winter months. His feet crunched through the sand that filled between his toes and felt comfortably warm to the touch. During the summer season, it was generally too hot; it felt like walking on hot coals and burned the soles of his feet. As he reached the shoreline, the waves brushed his feet and calves, the cool water rinsing his skin.

"Nicholas, let's begin," Nonna said. "We must practice your techniques. The tide is moderate and calm; we shall take advantage."

"Yes, Mother," Nicholas replied.

The young boy stared down at the glittering white sands of the beach. While he was growing up, he had completed several of his mother's swim lessons and was now at an intermediate level of training. He pressed further into the water, eventually meeting the depth where he could begin his swimming practice. Nicholas glided through the ocean's waves, his shoulders, arms, and legs synchronized together to increase his accuracy and propulsion. He loved the sea; he felt free of worry as the cool rush of the swells clashed upon his face, his arms grabbing and pulling the water behind him. Nonna observed him as he performed a series of breaths, kicks, pulls, and various sweeps. She smiled at her son's progress but sternly observed his weaknesses, preparing to correct him on proper technique when he finished.

After a solid day of swimming and training, Nicholas and his mother enjoyed a mid–afternoon picnic lunch. Paloma snorted and neighed from behind them, her skin fluxing from a random head shake. After each session, the two usually reviewed his approach and technique, analyzing possible improvements. Today, however, was different; he was not to be lectured. Nicholas looked into his mother's eyes and could see her pride and satisfaction.

"Nicholas, I have taught you all I know; I have nothing more that I can advise you on. Your only teachers now are the dolphins, since you swim exactly like them. But always remember, son... when swimming and in life, you must remain calm; you must pull the sea." Nicholas smiled happily at his mother and took in the advice she had given him; she was a great teacher to him and a woman of great intellect. Then suddenly, he was distracted.

"Nicholas, look!" Nonna said, excitedly pointing at the sea turtle eggs. "They are starting to hatch!"

Nicholas watched as the younglings began digging themselves out of the ground. The small turtles shook the sand from their small bodies and began their marathon to the sea. Several of them were successful at reaching the water, while others became an afternoon morsel for the surrounding seabirds

Nonna smiled at her son. "See, Nicholas? They strive for survival as we do; their challenge is getting to the sea. If they reach the water they live another day, but if they don't, well... you can see what happens. They too must pull the sea."

Nicholas understood the meaning behind his mother's philosophy. It was not just about swimming, but also about taking on the challenges in life to succeed- to survive. He watched as the small-shelled sprinters used all their might to shovel every grain of sand behind them. With each fore-flippered tug they battled forward, one step closer to reaching the finish line of freedom; they were pulling the sea to them.

The Ripple Effect

With saddened eyes, Nicholas nursed his parents, bed-ridden by their sickness. The disease had overwhelmed them with constant fevers, chills, sweats, and an anguish of coughs. Many people in Patara had made contact with the epidemic that spread throughout the region. Nicholas believed that his parents had been exposed while helping those in need, eventually becoming sick themselves.

"Here, Mother, eat this; it will help nourish you," Nicholas requested.

Struggling, she sat up to eat the soup he provided her with, spitting some of it from her mouth. The frequent coughs made it difficult for her to eat or breathe.

"I can't, Nicholas," his mother wheezed.

"Please try; do not let it defeat you. A bit more, and I shall let you rest."

She ingested what she could, then, weak in body, lay back down, quickly falling asleep. Nicholas observed his father lying next to Nonna. He could tell Theopanes was fighting a severe fever, sweating and muttering in his sleep. Deciding not to disturb him with food, he left his father to rest.

He went into the main corridor of the house and sat down on a rocking chair near the window. It was the same chair, built by Theopanes, that his mother had sat in while holding him as a baby. He rubbed his temples attempting to abate his distress and watched through the window as others, still healthy, walked by. He was glad to see that fellow neighbors and residents were not sick but felt terrible for his parents. His negative emotions somewhat lightened as his uncle approached.

"Greetings, Nephew!"

"Hello Uncle, it's good to see you today!"

"You too, Nephew; any improvement on your parents' health?"

"They are very weak, unable to eat much. Both have worsened this morning."

The abbot entered the bedroom and gave them a quick look-over; Nicholas could see the disappointment in his eyes. He watched from outside the room as his uncle raised his crosier, providing blessing in hopes to improve their health. He then joined Nicholas in the main corridor and eyed his nephew. "You show much exertion; perhaps you should get some fresh air. I can attend to your parents' wellbeing while you are away."

Nicholas pondered the idea but felt guilty leaving his folks behind. He knew he was in good hands having his uncle around and felt a sense of security, having a religious figure and mentor nearby in this time of his parents' anguish. Maybe, he thought, a short time away would strengthen his assistance for them when he came back. "Thank you, Uncle; perhaps I will."

As mid-day approached, the weather shifted to rain. Nicholas made his way to the horse corral outside his home where goats, chickens, and pigs roamed. Inside, Paloma stood tall, appearing peaceful and free of worry. Nicholas began to pet her on her face, "Shall we take a ride in the rain, old friend?" Paloma was close to the age of Nicholas, and he had grown up with her. When he was a young boy, his folks had purchased Paloma as a foal, and she was now an elderly horse by normal standards but still strong and reliable. As he began equipping her for the ride, the rain had thickened significantly, large drops wetting the ground.

"Iyah!" Nicholas commanded, sternly snapping the reins. Paloma instantly jolted out of the corral, then she and Nicholas traveled toward the Arch of Modestus and the beach of Patara. Reaching the desert dune, Nicholas began to vision past times with his mother teaching him to swim and educating him on the newborn sea turtles that fought the sand to pull the sea. Adrenaline built up inside Nicholas as he whipped the reins, shouting further command. "Hyah!" Hyah!" Maintaining strength in her old but muscular legs, Paloma kicked up muddied sand, increasing her rate of speed. Her dirty-white hair further browned in color from the splash as they crossed the shoreline. The cool rain tapped on Nicholas' face as they rode like the wind, bringing him temporary serenity. They crossed the lengthy stretch of the beach, reaching the western stream of Eşen, an artery of the Mediterranean, which bled some of its water northward into other cities of Lycia. Nicholas changed directions, following along the stream, and he and Paloma eventually approached a familiar bank, an area in which Nicholas and his dad spent many days together. Theopanes had taught Nicholas to fish here and engaged him in many discussions about life, women, religion, philosophy, and other distinct subjects.

Nicholas decided to sit and recollect; the rain had lifted, and the afternoon felt pleasant as he stared out at the flowing stream, mesmerized by the ripple effect caused by the eddy currents. He laughed to himself as memories of catching his first fish as a child struck him. It should have been his father's catch, but the stream's ripple and current had caused Nicholas' fishing line to cross his father's. After tangling lines, the fish had taken Nicholas' bait instead of Theopane's.

"You've hooked it! Bring it in, son! Maintain strong arms!" his father instructed.

Theopanes smiled as his son lit up with excitement. Nicholas could not wait to bring it back to his mother. When they arrived home that night, he told her the great tale of how the fish was caught.

"He was a sneaky one, very strong, fought me for hours," Nicholas shared.

Nonna glanced up at Theopanes, who shrugged and grinned, entertained by the exaggerated story. Instead of telling his wife what really happened, he simply responded, "Our son did well today. I'm proud of him."

His wonderful memory of that day subsided as a young girl, hollering in distress, ran toward Nicholas.

"My boat! Can you please get it? I cannot reach it! Please sir, I don't want to lose it!"

Floating down the stream's ripple was a small wooden boat with a single square sail that flapped in the breeze. Nicholas quickly jumped to his feet and reached for the boat. Intrigued, he examined the hand-crafted ship, and the square sail made of cloth, then handed it to the girl.

"Oh, thank you! Now my father won't be mad at me!"

Nicholas smiled at the girl. "Did someone craft this for you?"

"My father, it was a gift for my birthday," the girl responded.

"It's a fantastic boat- be sure to take care of it," Nicholas suggested.

"I will; thank you for saving it!" The girl ran back to her parents, who gave Nicholas a quick wave of appreciation.

An afternoon of riding and recollecting on the bank of the Eşen stream helped Nicholas feel better, but with a concerned mind, he decided it was best to return to his parents and relieve his uncle. He looked down the stream, once again seeing the father, mother, and the girl enjoying each other's time together. They cautiously watched their daughter as she played with the toy boat, this time preventing it from being taken by the stream. He tugged the reins to begin his trip back, giving one last glance over his shoulder. But the family had mysteriously vanished– as if they had never existed.

Nicholas dropped Paloma off, giving her a few servings of hay for an evening meal. Leaving her to eat, he gave her a quick pat on the side and proceeded to his home. As he opened the front door with a hesitant sigh, harsh coughs echoed through the house from the bedroom. He greatly despised the sound; every wheeze and hack reminded him of his parents' suffering and felt like a dagger piercing his heart. "Uncle?" he called out. "Uncle? Are you back there?"

His uncle entered the main corridor, leaning on his crosier, his eyes filled with tears. Nicholas gulped as his heart entered his throat from the sudden worry that struck him.

"Welcome back, Nicholas, how was your ride?"

Nicholas did not answer and went straight to questioning.

"Uncle... please tell me... how do they fare?"

His uncle frowned and shook his head in sorrow. "Your mother... I'm afraid she is dying."

Nicholas stormed past his uncle into his parents' bedroom. His mother lay there, struggling to breathe.

"Nicholas... my lovely son..." she reached out her hand and Nicholas quickly grasped it.

"Deep breaths, Mother," Nicholas urged.

In short gasps, Nonna spoke. "I always... wanted a boy... that was..." A series of coughs interrupted her. "A boy... strong in mind... strong in body..."

"Rest, Mother; you do not have to speak," Nicholas pleaded as he started to tear up.

His mother looked up and smiled. "God... he has given me... just... just that... You've... grown into the man I hoped you'd be."

Her grip tightened on Nicholas' hand, and her eyes watered and moistened her pillow.

"Remember, son... pull... the... sea."

His mother's hand released its grip as her sickness struck the fatal blow. Nicholas, trying to hold up strong, immediately failed. He grabbed his deceased mother and hugged her tight, sobbing intensely in mourning. "Mother... I will miss you dearly!" Nicholas' uncle stood teary-eyed behind him but tried to maintain composure to support his nephew.

The same evening, not too long after Nonna had passed, Theopanes left the world of Patara and reunited with his wife in spirit. The next day Nicholas woke up to a home, once furnished with warmness, now transformed to coldness. He no longer would see them in the morning and say "Good morrow, Mother" or "Good morrow, Father"– instead he faced emptiness both in his estate and inside his mournful heart.

Mare Nostrum

The stone-erected pharos towered high, overlooking Patara and the shores that harbored the Mediterranean. Standing on its upper podium, Nicholas watched the sun lower over the sea. The spherical ball of fire looked as though it was going to douse itself, creating permanent darkness. When he was a young boy, his parents had brought him to this lighthouse on many occasions; to him it felt like a large fort, an ideal place to play. The keepers of the pharos generally were strict on visitors but knew Theopanes and Nonna well and had grown fond of Nicholas. Now as a young man, it was his place of sanctuary where he went to think or to recollect.

As he mourned the death of his parents, Nicholas found that his mind had become scattered and confused. He began realizing that he had a lifetime of decisions and challenges ahead of him. He was still learning about the world, and now he began analyzing his next path forward. His parents had left him with a toolbox containing sharpened attributes of wealth, kindness, giving, and sharing. He stared out to the blue waters of the sea, feeling lonely and scared. He still had his uncle in the region to confide in, which he was thankful for, but he dearly missed his mother and father. He wished he could have had more time to spend with them, and to learn further methods of their good nature. His eyes began to water, and a tear drop trickled down his cheek and hit the ground below, several meters down from the podium above.

A sudden breeze from the sea brushed his face. The wind generally felt warm, but this time it felt cold... utterly cold. Nicholas squinted and touched his stinging cheek where the tear had drained from his eye. As he wiped the trail of water it felt abnormally icy. From the sea a soft voice spoke, frightening him. "Ma... Nost..." He could not make out what it was saying. The breeze increased and Nicholas began to shiver from the cold it delivered, the chilled sensation seeming unusual and mysterious. Perhaps his sorrow was just playing tricks on his mind. The whispered voice spoke again, this time more definite. "Mare... Nostrum..."

He knew that "Mare Nostrum" meant "The Sea" but questioned the voice's purpose. "Mare Nostrum? I don't understand." The soft voice came from the sea a third time "Mare... Nostrum... holy... land..." and at this point Nicholas began questioning his sanity. He was convinced the voice he was hearing was only gibberish. He stared out at the sparkling water, where from underneath the waves a silhouette of a ship rose, followed by a large square sail, an exact replica of the toy boat that he had saved for the young girl at the Eşen stream. He was now convinced his mind was far gone, the visions and voice a sham. He watched as the sail flapped and the silhouetted ship disappeared into the sunset. The sun dropped, turning the atmosphere to night.

Returning home, he made to his bed, his mind still scattered, confused, and weary. His thoughts kept indicating that he should go somewhere... travel. But where and when? What would be his agenda? He remembered the stories his uncle told of the *Holy Land,* its history, and the religious miracles that took place there. His eyes grew heavy and his mind eased as he drifted off to sleep, still recapping the voice he heard at the lighthouse.

"You're always welcome to join me in Myra. There is much that you can learn there and develop upon in my teachings," his uncle offered.

"Thank you, Uncle, I will consider the opportunity."

Nicholas and his uncle were enjoying a morning breakfast together. On his frequent trips to Patara, the abbot would attend to religious errands and stop to visit Nicholas as well. He enjoyed his uncle's presence; it helped fill the void of loneliness that often encountered him. From time to time, he would make visits in return, enjoying the opportunity to leave Patara for a short while. For several minutes there was an awkward silence between the two. Nicholas stared down at his breakfast- very little of its content had left the plate.

The abbot looked up from his meal, giving Nicholas a sharp look. "You are in deep thought, Nephew; what occupies your mind?"

Nicholas sighed. "Perhaps it is the sorrow of losing my parents that strews my sanity, but a voice of the sea, it instructs that I visit the Holy Land. It keeps speaking out to me…"

His uncle gave him a concerned look "Oh? Beware the voices you accept when you are weak; they can be of demons attempting to consume you."

"Yes, I will take caution; however… this feeling- it stirs inside me… signifying that I should travel there. My parents have shown me how to help those less fortunate. You have taught me the practices of faith and religion. Traveling there may help determine who I am… perhaps define my purpose."

"How would you get there?" his uncle asked.

"I've considered relying on Paloma; I believe she could get me there, but I fear the old girl might not get me back. She's a reliable horse, but she's not as strong as she used to be."

"Many voyage there by ship. Either route you choose, the journey can be dangerous. There is much warfare, both on land and out at sea," his uncle warned.

Nicholas nodded at his uncle's advice. "I believe I will make use of this day and contribute some good deeds. I would like to make the most of my parent's wealth and provide for those in need as they did."

Concluding breakfast, Nicholas said farewell to his uncle and began his day's venture of giving. He hoped it would also help him decipher his thoughts and unusual feelings and to better understand the meaning behind the mysterious voice. Perhaps there were others out there seeking meaning in themselves as Nicholas was.

The woman and her two young boys sat depleted and hungry, their clothing tattered and worn. With his inherited wealth Nicholas approached two local merchants of Patara, purchasing a few loaves of bread from one and a goat from another. Helping the woman and her boys, he decided, would be a good first task to accomplish on his own. This was not his first time of giving; many of his days had been spent with his folks providing for those in need, watching as his mother or father imparted food portions, animals, clothing, and periodically a hug or two. With goods in hand, he smiled at the woman and her small boys, attempting to put them at ease. Living a hard life, they had developed a paranoia toward those that approached them. Although the woman remained wary and the boys stood cautiously behind her, they noticed the bread and goat that Nicholas held in his hands.

"Please take these; I hope they will help you find improvement in your life, at least for a little while. Here is some extra to help you purchase clothing for your boys."

The woman's eyes lit up; they were not expecting to receive such acts of kindness "Thank you! You are most generous! My boys haven't eaten for a couple days now, they will be happy to fill their stomachs!" One of the boys who hid behind his mother reached for the lead attached to the goat. He smiled as if he had received a new pet, although the goat would also provide for them and be useful for many things.

Nicholas continued down the main streets of Patara, looking for those that he could help with their struggles. Through several encounters, he provided for those in need, relying on what he learned and practicing good intentions as best he could. He felt good being able to accomplish these tasks alone. His day swiftly passed by as he relocated outside of town into the busy harbor section of Patara, where several vessels of various sizes were docked, anchored, or resting on the sand of the shoreline. In an open area of the harbor a middle-aged man and his teen son were building a vessel. Nicholas could not determine what type or how large; it looked as though the ship was in the first stages of construction.

"Not enough locking pegs, we need another!" the man shouted out to his son.

The plank loosened and fell to the ground. "Blast! Try again! Check the plank edges. Be sure the tenons are straight!" he ordered his son.

The boy revamped the tenons as instructed. Afterward, the planks successfully bonded and the mortise and tenons matched up precisely.

"Better! We are flush now!" the father confirmed.

Nicholas watched– they coordinated well, bonding the wooden planks together. He noticed their skin: tan, yet coarse, rough, and dirty. From their appearance, he assumed they worked the harbor as shipbuilders. With curiosity, he greeted the man and his son.

"Might I ask what type of vessel you and your son are building?"

The man turned away from his work. "A cargo ship... it doesn't look like much yet, but someday it will travel Mare Nostrum in hopes of better days."

The name the father used for the sea struck Nicholas, reminding him of the voice he thought he heard at the lighthouse.

The man continued. "For now, my son and I transport goods on land. It's a reasonable living, have you; it feeds our bellies and shelters us, but we could be more successful and profitable. With the extra income we earn we put it toward materials for our project here."

"Apologies, I took you as shipbuilders," Nicholas responded.

"Used to be... was once a shipbuilder for the Roman Empire but was disbanded. My son here, he apprentices me both in goods transport and our building our ship."

"What kind of ships did you build for the Romans?" Nicholas asked.

"Many kinds, from small fishing boats to big war triremes oared by many Roman soldiers."

Nicholas found it interesting but peculiar that such a craftsman would be living here in Patara instead of a major Roman city.

The man answered his unspoken question. "They gave me the choice to exile or become a slave. I was wrongly accused of treason, and stories formed that I built ships for the Sassanid Empire. After being disbanded, I chose to come here, developing a business in transporting goods."

Nicholas watched as the father and his apprentice continued with their construction. It reminded him of his time with Theopanes, and he found himself missing him extensively. The words of the mysterious voice crossed his mind once more "Mare Nostrum... the Holy Land..."

From deep inside an idea fell out of his mouth as though it had a mind of its own.

"What if I could help you in your succession?" he asked.

The man tittered at Nicholas, halting his work. "Oh yeah? And how would you go about that?"

Nicholas explained his frequency of wealth inherited from his parents and how they had raised him to help his fellow people, assisting those that wished to thrive.

"Sorry lad... we don't hold bonds with anyone. My son and I, we earn our accomplishments on our own." The man and son then turned back to their work.

Nicholas respected the man's point of view and nodded in understanding. "I understand- best of prosperity to you and your son."

"You also, lad," the man replied, staying focused on his work.

Nicholas left them. He felt he'd had a strong day of following in the footsteps of his parents. But something inside him felt his venture was incomplete and urged him to go back in the other direction. His feet began walking again toward the shipbuilder and his apprentice, and again his vocal cords spoke as if they were self-acting, addressing the father and his son.

"There would be no bonds. I only wish to travel... reach the Holy Land. If I could help fund your dream of building a cargo ship, would you be able to take me there and perhaps bring me back? Would this ship be able to do so... once it is complete?"

The man again stopped his work, this time halting his son also.

"Lad... if we build everything correctly it will go anywhere we want it to go. We could transport goods from port to port, and my family and I could prosper as we always dreamed of. "

"Then... please let me help you. I can provide the food and necessities you need. You would not have to transport goods; you could focus on building your vessel."

"There would be no bonds to you?" the man asked to reconfirm.

"None, just transport to the Holy Land and back. The rest is my gift to you and your family, a gift to your succession."

The man and his son looked at each other in shock, as they did not expect such an offer or opportunity to arise. "Son... we have a lot of work to do."

The man held out his hand to shake with Nicholas. "The name's Drusus and this is my son Otho."

"My name is Nicholas." He shook the man's hand.

"Very well, Nicholas, we will get you to the Holy Land. When this ship is finished, she will cut through the sea's water like a sharpened blade."

Virago of the Sea

"**I** picked them out of the field just for you," the boy said.

"They are beautiful!" his mother exclaimed.

Although the poppies were dead and withered, the mother was ecstatic of her son's thoughtfulness. She grabbed a small vase and sat them on a wall-mounted shelf. Daylight peeked in, shining sunlight on the son's gift. "Let's give them water, shall we?"

The scene transitioned and the boy was now chasing a wild hare in the snow. He lassoed a stiff rope above his head with a snap and slung it at the hare, where it landed and tightened in a loop around its torso. Like a suffocating fish separated from water, the hare began flopping as the boy wrangled it toward him.

"I will not harm you, friend." The boy picked the wild animal up in his arms, pulling greens from his leather pouch in an attempt to soothe it.

"These are fresh; you will fancy them." The hare began to calm and accepted the greens as its nervous pants and rapid heartbeats eased.

The setting shifted, the boy now kneeling and weeping. Below him were his parents and the hare, all three slain on the floor. With cheeks sodden and blushed from his tears, he looked up at the man with the deep emerald-green eyes.

He spoke to the man, sobbing. "They killed them... my... my... parents... and... my... friend... they all had pur... purple glowing... eyes."

The boy grabbed his left arm, covering a gouged wound on his bicep. The man's emerald eyes softened, and he reached out his hand. "Come with me. I will be your friend." The boy stood up and grabbed the man's hand. A golden aura flashed, and they both vanished. At the dreaded scene of evil and death, the vase and the three poppies- no longer dead and withered- sat on the wooden shelf nearby. Two of the poppies were now yellow, the third a bright red.

Sweat dripped from Nicholas' forehead as he was drawn from his dream by a loud holler from outside.

"Nicholas? Nicholas! It's Drusus. I bring splendid news! Please come out!"

Still half asleep, Nicholas made his way outside. "Hello Drusus, did not expect to see you this morning. What brings you to visit?" Nicholas could see the excitement in Drusus' face.

"The voyager is complete! We are now sailors!"

Nicholas shook his hand enthusiastically. "That is great to hear, Drusus!"

The vessel had been cradled in the harbor's shipyard for 27 months. With the help of Nicholas, an adequate shipyard was built and accommodated to build the craft. From sunrise to sunset, Drusus and his apprentice son worked to exhaustion. At the end of their construction tunnel was a light displaying better days and great adventures. Knowing that helped them maintain focus and ambition each day. Within those 27 months Nicholas had developed a strong relationship with Drusus and his family.

"My family and I wish to celebrate tonight. We would be honored to have you join us, Nicholas. You must see the results of your generous investment!"

"I shall be there- no question about it," Nicholas replied, delighted.

Nicholas had developed a regular routine of visiting the neighborhood in Patara. Building a proximity with his fellow men, women, and children made him feel genuine and accomplished. What he had learned from Nonna and Theopanes was becoming a daily trade to him. He walked the streets feeling quite well, knowing the new voyager was complete. Drusus and his family would begin a more fruitful life doing what they had always wanted.

Walking down Patara's stoned streets, Nicholas acknowledged two small boys- one leading a goat- and their mother walking behind them. It was the same poor group he helped before, but they appeared better clothed and healthier in appearance. The two boys looked up at Nicholas, giving him the same cautious glance they gave him when he first assisted them. Slightly bent, Nicholas put his hands on his knees and spoke kindly to the child with the goat.

"You're raising a fine animal there," Nicholas encouraged.

The child was rather shy and did not reply but instead smiled. He then pulled the lead of the goat. "This way, Niblet."

The mother gently touched Nicholas' forearm. "Many people have been calling you the gift-bringer of Patara."

Nicholas was not sure what she meant but responded. "I'm happy to see improvements in your well-being."

Knowing that this mother and her two sons were happier and healthier gave Nicholas a sense of accomplishment, but the adventures of his life had to continue. There was a completed ship to be seen and a celebration afoot with Drusus' family. Nicholas entered the harbor and traveled to where he assumed the newly built craft would be, but as he encountered the building yard, the vessel was no longer cradled, and the area was empty. Nearby, Otho was removing leftover debris and random planks scattered throughout the construction area.

"Has the ship been relocated?" Nicholas asked Otho.

"Yes, my father has relocated it to the eastern wharf; he wishes for you to meet him there."

Nicholas made his way to the eastern wharf and identified Drusus, who was waving at him from further down the coast front. Along the bank, many ships rested; the majority of them were fishing boats that had returned with their catches of the day.

"Meet our new voyager!" Drusus spoke excitedly, pointing at the completed freighter as Nicholas merged closer. Affixed to the main mast was a large square sail which fluttered and waved in the sea's breeze. As Nicholas laid eyes on the completed project, an eerie feeling struck him. Standing in awe, he began questioning his sanity once more. Was the vision from the lighthouse revisiting him? He expected a whispered voice to enter his ear, but nothing occurred. Perhaps the crafted toy of the young girl lost its way down the Eşen stream, this time entering a land of giants. Perhaps those giants created a larger version of her small boat. It appeared extremely identical... perfectly exact, actually... which made it difficult for Nicholas to fathom.

"Please come!" Drusus invited. "We must celebrate! My wife has prepared meal and drink for us at our estate."

Following the celebration at Drusus' home, he and his family sat on the shoreline near the eastern wharf. A full moon in the night sky reflected light on the calm sea and the voyager that would soon be changing their lives.

Nicholas joined them but did not say much. He was preoccupied, trying to understand the meaning behind his past visions and the voice of whisper. Was the interaction with the little girl and her parents realistic or a mere spiritual event?

Drusus was concerned by Nicholas' long silence. "I hope you are satisfied with our finished work?" he asked.

Nicholas shook himself out of his deep thoughts. "You and Otho have built a fine voyager. What destination will you travel to first?"

"I believe our first delivery will be the island of Cyprus. Demand is high there, and we have the goods to supply them. We will not need many crews, just a few to oar. For the rest, we will rely upon the sail and the sea's given winds. The voyager will be put to the test, along with my navigating and weather forecasting skills."

"You are a skilled shipwright, Drusus; I'm sure your seamanship will be equally matched," Nicholas encouraged.

For a few moments the conversation stood still. Drusus put his arm around his wife and directed sincere conversation back to Nicholas.

"Nicholas... my family and I are most grateful for all you have done for us. Upon completing our delivery in Cyprus, we can sail southeast from there. We wish to fulfill your request of transport to the Holy Land."

Nicholas stewed on the thought as he looked out at the voyager and the moonlit sea. He was still young, and his path going forward remained uncertain and distorted. He leaned on his intention of visiting the Holy Land. He wanted to define his role and purpose in life. He had developed greatly in community involvement, but he felt his role had to be more significant beyond that.

"Yes, of course, I shall travel with you," Nicholas agreed.

"I'm glad you accept. We will begin preparations," Drusus replied. "We have only one thing left to accomplish... you are the investor of our family's dream, Nicholas, and she needs a strong name."

Nicholas felt honored to be able to name such a robust watercraft. He pondered on a name and then thought of his mother. She had taught him to swim, and she herself was a warrior swimmer with a perfected rhythm that could not be outperformed. The voyager would soon be the new swimmer of the high seas and he could not think of a better name for her.

"Perhaps Nonna would suit it well?" Nicholas suggested.

Drusus accepted. "Then Nonna it will be! We shall proclaim her our Virago of the Sea!"

The Golden Aquanaut

Drusus' crew consisted of three men and one woman, all with notable experience. One crew member owned his own fishing boat and took on extra voyages as further supplement to support his family; the other two were seeking adventure and a more rewarding life. The hired help began loading cargo onto the freighter, and weight accumulated with supplies of wool, silk, fruits, vegetables, oils, and several amphorae of wine, all ready to be imported to the island of Cyprus.

The investment Nicholas provided to Drusus allowed him to thoroughly engineer the craft using the sternness and strongest of materials. *Nonna* was constructed of a deep keel which would help her to sail more accurately and briskly. Her body structure was built strong to take the heaviest of cargo loads, which reduced drag and impact on forward mobility. The square sail was made of dense cloth attached with wooden brail rings. Her many planks were carefully adjoined with finely conformed mortise and tendons.

"You're certain you do not want to travel?" Drusus asked his wife, Leda.

"You and our son have worked long and hard and you should bask together in your accomplishment. There will be more opportunities." Leda smiled. "Besides, who wants a nagging wife on their ship?"

"You would be my best crew member," Drusus replied wittily. He kissed and hugged her goodbye, giving her one last additional peck on the forehead followed by the gratifying words, "*Incipit novam vitam notram hodie.*"

"Your Latin tongue always pleases me," said his wife coyly.

Leda turned to her son Otho and hugged him. "You are growing up too fast– please take care of your father."

Drusus turned to Nicholas, who was waiting behind him, and clapped him on his shoulder. "Nicholas, our crew awaits! They will meet us aboard our ship. *Nonna* is eager to be unleashed to the sea."

Nicholas could relate. "I believe I'm quite eager myself."

Drusus grinned. "There is something I wish to show you."

Drusus, Otho, and Nicholas reached the wharf where *Nonna* was moored, and Drusus pointed to the front of the ship. At the bow was a carved wooden figurehead of a beautiful woman dressed in a long Greek peplos tunic, with the wings of an angel on her shoulders. Flowing extensions of her wings were carved into the planks on each side of the boat.

"Otho and I carved her in appreciation for all that you have done for us. May she protect us and help evade any hazards we may encounter out there."

Drusus had developed a talent for crafting figureheads while building ships for the Romans. It is said that the architecture was first established years ago by the Phoenicians. Many Romans and Greeks that sailed the Mediterranean commonly engraved eyes or wings on their vessels. They felt that doing so appeased the gods and thus brought good fortune on their travels.

Nicholas examined the figurehead, stunned by each etch and detail that it displayed. He held back tears as he read "***Nóvva***" scrawled on the angel, then nodded at Drusus and Otho sincerely. "She is both amazing and beautiful-thank you both!"

Drusus introduced the others as they boarded the ship. "Nicholas, meet our crew. They will provide oaring as needed, control the sail and angle, and help deliver our goods."

"It's a pleasure," Nicholas greeted them.

Drusus changed position to the head of the craft and began lining out the crew. "Today we travel to Cyprus, putting *Nonna* to her very first undertaking. Out there is the potential for better lives for our families. But we must work together and maintain strong sea ethics. The sea does not take kind to the weary or weak; it must be respected and appreciated!"

As they left the port, Nicholas looked at the clear blue water below, smiling in amusement at the sight of the sea turtles swimming up to make acquaintance with *Nonna*. Standing on the shore was his uncle in his tall miter, raising his crosier. Surprised, Nicholas waved back. "Farewell, Uncle!" he shouted. Favorable winds howled at the large square sail rigged to *Nonna's* mast. Her planks stood strong and durable as she began moving at great speed, cutting through the sea's water like a sharpened blade. The crew was making good time toward Cyprus.

Drusus hollered in excitement. "Steady ho! The sea is kind today; oars we will not need!"

The delivery of goods to Cyprus was successful, and the crew spent the next few days on the eastern port town of Salamis. Throughout Salamis was a spectrum of shops, and many of the crew purchased items, including pottery, art, clothing, and jewelry from their earnings. Drusus bought a jeweled arm band to take back to his wife Leda. Otho visited many of the architectural excavations, including a gymnasium and a theatre in which he watched performances take place.

Nicholas, however, took the time to speak with the locals. Following his ambition of going to the Holy Land, he sought for fellow travelers that had been there. He gathered strands of information and history that helped him develop a plan to rely on during his visit.

Drusus and his crew spent their last evening drinking and cleansing themselves in the bathing complex. As they soaked in the hexagonal plunge pool, they sipped the fine wine that was left over from their supplies and shared their ambitions and plans for going forth. What was their next adventure? What major ports would *Nonna* soon travel to? They pondered and debated amongst themselves. A drunken Drusus slurred loudly.

"Weee shall not tra... travel... *hic*... elsssewheeere until we help my dearest... inveee... investor Nicholas get to his desi... nationaninin! Heeere is... *hic*... to Nicholas!" Drusus raised his goblet of wine.

"To Nicholas!" the rest of the crew bellowed.

Nicholas and Otho did not join the crew in the baths but instead sat on Salamis' beach watching the stars. Otho spoke of how he wanted to travel the world and see the amazing architecture and buildings that were built over the ages by the Greeks and Romans.

"You will accomplish those feats someday," Nicholas spoke encouragingly. The young boy's dream wasn't too far-fetched, Nicholas thought, since he had a father with means of sea travel. Perhaps Otho would be a traveler himself once he became a man.

"I hope so. Is that your dream, to visit the Holy Land?" Otho asked curiously.

"I am not certain if it is a dream, but something captivates me to visit," Nicholas explained.

Deep inside, Nicholas was nervous, still questioning his intentions. Drusus and the others knew why they were in Cyprus and why they would travel the sea from port to port. They wanted adventure, but they also wanted the best for their families. They now had the correct tools required to achieve that happiness and success. Nicholas did not feel the same– he had uncertainties as to why he was in Cyprus and why he was soon to be in a sacred land. Nonetheless, he was still determined to follow through.

Otho and Nicholas tittered as they watched their fellow shipmates struggle to get on board, hung-over yet freshly clean from the baths.

Nicholas spoke aside to Otho. "A fine wine in the evening can have a wretched effect in the morning."

"Perhaps the baths at least removed their bodily stench?" Otho replied.

"Perhaps," Nicholas laughed.

Drusus had forecasted that the weather would be efficient for them the next few days, which would get Nicholas to his requested destination. Still slightly tipsy, he positioned himself to the front of the ship, once again lining out his crew for the next venture.

"Crew! Today we fulfill a promise to a man who, with his charitable nature and faith, has given us the gift that we now stand on. The sea and weather have thus far been lenient! Now that our goods are delivered, *Nonna* has less weight. She will be able to spread her angelic wings and fly! Make ready for the Holy Land!"

The group made excellent progress on the first day of their southeast voyage. The crew members had taken shifts, two during the day and the other two at night. Otho and Drusus would periodically pitch in during the day to adjust sail angle or help to oar. Although Nicholas wasn't required to help, he aided as much as he could and was beginning to learn the many aspects of being a sailor. Unless she was ported, *Nonna* herself never slept or rested, but instead kept moving forward, like a true virago.

On the morning of the second day, they made similar progress. The morning's weather and winds had favored them in kindness. But the transition from morning to mid–day had resulted in different conditions, a weather that Drusus and his crew had never suspected.

Drusus expressed concern as their surroundings became blanketed in gray clouds. Weather was sometimes unpredictable, which Drusus understood, but these climate changes seemed immediate, as if they appeared from out of nowhere.

The wind that was assisting *Nonna* became calm and silent, the sea eerily still. The gray clouds began to thicken and darken to black, and sheets of light flashed from above, followed by a loud rumble of thunder. The ambient temperature, which had been pleasantly warm, became bitterly cold. Nicholas was struck by a sense of dread as he experienced the same chilled sensation he had felt when he was on the lighthouse in Patara.

Drusus gave Nicholas a defeated look. "Apologies; it appears my forecast is of failure."

Nicholas stared out at the sea. Another bolt of lightning flashed and stabbed the water's surface, which began stirring and waving. Several small ice caps formed as a chilly wind picked up.

"Drusus... do not be dismayed about your weather predictions. This weather feels... unnatural, as if it could not have been predicted."

It did not take long for Drusus to believe Nicholas, as more frozen caps built and grew to a traveling wave of ice maneuvering toward them.

"I am now convinced! No human could have foreseen this! Crew, prepare yourselves– we are going overboard!"

The sea became unsettled and angry, the swells growing larger in size. A demonic growl followed by a horrid roar came from below as the traveling wave of ice reached underneath the ship and tipped *Nonna* on her side with a shattering explosion. All crew members including Nicholas were thrown into the water. As Nicholas fell, his head met the rail side of the vessel, and the laceration began to shed blood. He was dazed from his injury and the shock of being thrown overboard, but his mother's voice spoke inside him. "*When swimming and in life, you must remain calm; you must pull the sea.*"

All his learned skills of swimming went into effect as he began pulling each swell, trying to get back to the ship. The remaining crew relied on *Nonna* to keep them afloat and above water. Nicholas was making steady progress toward the safe zone, but the sea was becoming further aggravated. His strong arms ignored the cold, but his bloodied head and the rest of his body became weak.

The crew, shivering and bitten from the cold water, shouted out to Nicholas. "Almost there, Nicholas! Stay strong!"

A demonic voice roared and spoke horridly. "DO... NOT... CONTEST!" A huge swell broke over Nicholas and he gasped for air; his arms were still willing to proceed but his internal organs were starting to give up.

"He needs help!" Otho shouted, attempting to make his way to Nicholas.

Drusus quickly grabbed Otho. "Halt, son! The sea is evil and will devour us. Stay to *Nonna!*"

As Nicholas sank beneath the water, a large ice cap formed on the surface above him. "*Filius canis!*" Drusus hollered in extreme frustration as he watched Nicholas go under.

The blue of the sea was turning black as Nicholas sank deeper and deeper, his supply of oxygen depleted. His cold body was beginning to shut down. Memories flashed in his mind of watching hatched sea turtles, picnicking on the beach with his mother, fishing with his father, playing in the lighthouse as a child, and watching the young smiling boy leading the goat.

As his eyes closed unconsciously, a voice spoke loudly and clearly. "Mortimer, it is now time! Golden aquanaut, I summon thee! Rescue the Restorer!" A series of clicks, squeaks, and whistles sounded as a bottle-nosed dolphin approached and plunged out of the sea, breaking through and shattering the ice cap above Nicholas.

The crew, still latched to *Nonna,* watched in amazement as the golden-finned creature took to flight, then dove back into the water, heading swiftly toward Nicholas. As his fluke swayed up and down, a stream of golden entrails floated behind him, illuminating the darkness of the deep.

Mortimer grabbed hold of the nearly drowned Nicholas but did not return him to *Nonna* and the crew. Blazing in his bright essence, the golden aquanaut began the long journey of rescue and protection. His bottle-nosed and finned aquatic figure transformed into a whale-like creature with a large glowing tusk on his head. Mortimer, now a narwhal, had taken Nicholas to an alternative safe zone, a far-away place- *Degomble*.

Salute of Degomble

Within the darkness, a soft voice spoke:

"Nicholas? Nicholas? You must now wake... their darkness needs light... the light's ignition rests inside your soul... WAKE!"

A golden glow shimmered around Nicholas. A jolt of pain in his chest ejected the water from his mouth, followed by vomit. With his vitals restored, chills began crawling down his spine, and his body shook as if a thousand spiders were crawling through his skin. His skin was a bluish tint, first from nearly drowning and now from lying on the freezing ground. His teeth chattered; a line of blood from his head injury dripped down his face.

An undistinguished voice of an older man ordered, "Kiffy, quickly, qiviut blanket! I've restored breath; his heart beats, but his body is frozen, and we must expedite him to warmth!"

Nicholas attempted to open his eyes, but his head throbbed, and his vision would not allow a clear representation of the party that was assisting him.

Through the blurriness he could make out the figures of two men, one with a stocky build who was standing directly over him. The man wrapped Nicholas in a blanket. "Do not perish, friend; stay strong," he urged.

The stocky man then called out to a blurred vision of an older and gray-haired man. "Norrick! Please help me lift him on to the sledger."

Nicholas felt as if he was floating, his body in pain and chilled misery as he was lifted onto the sledger. He heard a series of barks not too far from where he was positioned.

The blurry and stocky-figured man spoke to the barking animals, "Good work Bech, way to use that snot snout of yours! Group, let's get our friend to safety! Tele Huit!"

Nicholas felt the sled's rails slice and shake as they traveled forth, each vibration sending bolts of pain through his head and chest cavity. He felt extremely confused, then sleepy, as his body began to shut down and his incoherent vision turned again to darkness.

Nicholas opened his eyes, awakened by a moist lick on his nose. He tried to sit up, feeling dizzy and weak. His muddy vision began to clear, and he realized he was now in a soft bed instead of lying on solid frozen ground. Noticing a wolf near his bedside, he rose further in panic.

A nearby man spoke. "Easy friend, slow rise is best. Worry not of Bechstein; he was just checking to see if you were still alive. It usually results in a wet face." Nicholas vaguely recognized the stocky man but not the bed he was lying in. He looked around the room. The nearby window showed snow falling, a clear sign that he was no longer in Patara.

"Whe... where am I?" he asked.

"You are in Degomble," the man answered.

"Your voice... it... it... sounds familiar," Nicholas told the man. It seems that I've heard your voice, and another... I remember you putting a blanket on me."

"That's right, we found you lying near the ocean shore, frozen and not breathing."

"You rescued me?"

"It was Norrick and I; however, we would have passed right by you if weren't for Bechstein. He picked up on your scent."

Nicholas looked at the wolf sitting near his bedside. "Thank you... Be... Be... Bechstein?"

"Right, Bechstein... I often call him Bech; he also answers to 'What Did You Do Now'"? The man chuckled and introduced himself. "They call me Kiffy."

"Hello Kiffy... I'm Nicholas." Nicholas reached for his head as it began to sting in pain. He decided to lie back down.

"Best you rest more, Nicholas. Bech shall keep watch over you and I will keep the fire burning in here. If you seek help, I will be in close distance in the dwelling across from you."

Nicholas spoke in drowsy appreciation, "Tha... thank you... Kiffy," then fell asleep. Kiffy left the guest quarter and proceeded back to his home.

"Good morrow Kiffy, how's our frozen adventurer?" Norrick asked as he approached Kiffy's residence.

"He now speaks. Bech gave him a little scare as he woke, but he needs more time to rest and recover. He should be fine," Kiffy replied.

"Very good– I'm glad he is healthy. Does he show signs of sickness, infection, or worse– embedded evil?"

"He seems to be healthy and a gentle man, but it's hard to tell, as he is still recovering. I think Bechstein would have been growling instead of saturating his face to check on him."

Norrick smirked. "Well, that may indicate good news of our mysterious friend. Have you asked his name?"

"Yes– it is Nicholas."

"Has Lízabet come to heal him of his head injury?" Norrick asked.

From behind Norrick, a woman wearing rogue-like arctic attire spoke. She had long brown hair down to her shoulders, covered in a chullo hat that had long tails, and a scarf laced around her neck. "Yes, Grandfather, I'm here," she uttered as she entered Nicholas' guest quarters.

"Oh... good. Thank you, dear," Norrick replied, slightly startled at her sudden appearance.

"Would you like to come in for a mug of oggin' cider?" Kiffy offered Norrick.

"Not at this time but thank you. I have key initiatives to complete today with the union and the commander. I must inform them of our visitor. We should determine where he is from."

"Might we assume he is from Ethereal?" Kiffy pondered.

"Yes, it is possible, but we should confirm."

Kiffy nodded. "Once he recovers, I will attempt to interrogate him."

Inside the warm guest dwelling, Nicholas slept, and Lízabet entered slowly in hopes not to disturb him. Recognizing Lízabet, Bechstein did not growl or bark, but instead wagged his tail. "Greetings Bechstein," she whispered, patting the wolf on the head. "I see Kiffy has assigned you guard duty today."

In Lízabet's hand was a long wooden stave. Lightly pressing it to Nicholas' forehead, she whispered a healing chant *"Concu rema"* as the end of the stave illuminated.

Nicholas woke, startled, not expecting to see a beautiful woman with long brown hair pointing a long wooden stick to his head.

"Rest, Nicholas, do not fret, I'm here to help your head injury; it will no longer feel pain." Nicholas looked up at the woman, eased by her comforting smile, and quickly fell back asleep.

"Sweet rest, foreigner. Keep a good eye on him, Bech." Lízabet left the room.

A few days passed and Nicholas was now more mobile. Still in recovery, he stayed to his guest quarter. The death of his parents, the unsuccessful voyage to the Holy Land, and his revival from frozen death had taken quite a toll on him. Kiffy and Bechstein visited him, bringing nourishing food and company. Occasionally he glanced out the window at the town of Degomble. On the walkway that divided his quarters from Kiffy's home, residents and what looked like soldiers in armor walked by periodically. As they passed one another, they would raise their hand to their faces and swipe at them as if they were brushing something away. Nicholas found this quite odd, and he began trying to put the puzzle pieces together and to understand why he was in such a cold barren land. As his health improved, so did his desire to leave his provided guest quarters. He felt it was time to go outside, get some air, and pay Kiffy a return visit. In his guest abode was an armoire with a note on the outside, written with ink on parchment.

Nicholas,

Inside is arctic clothing to wear. Please be sure that you dress appropriately with these undergarments before coming outside. My quarters are right across from yours and you are welcome to visit when you are healthy.

–Kiffy

He dressed himself accordingly and headed outside for the first time. He did not expect such a snap of cold air to hit him so quickly. Nicholas glanced down the walkway, noticing a spectrum of various dwellings and buildings. In the middle of town was a tall tower with a sparkling gold bell that almost blinded Nicholas as he looked at it. Although his surroundings were cold and gray, the town had a sense of beauty. An alluring setting was created from the ice that bristled and shimmered on the town's dwellings and from the snow as it fell from above. He approached the front door of Kiffy's home. It looked to be a two-piece door, one which could be opened from the top or the bottom. He knocked on the top, but there was no answer from inside except for a series of barks. From further down the alleyway a voice called out:

"Nicholas, down here!"

Kiffy approached with a large survival rucksack attached to his back. Walking alongside him at shin height was a small animal with a bushy tail, pointy ears, and fur as white as the snow on the ground beneath it.

"Good to see mobility in you- your head also shows improvement," he remarked.

Nicholas nodded, grateful to be moving and functional. "Thank you. Because of everyone, I'm still alive. Quite strange... but I dreamt that a woman in long brown hair came to heal my head wound with some kind of magic."

"Friend, what you saw was no dream; it was Lízabet."

Nicholas gave Kiffy a blank, unbelieving stare.

Grinning, Kiffy explained. "You were healed by that of a woman's touch."

Two residents of Degomble then passed Nicholas and Kiffy, both using the perplexing hand swipe to their face. Kiffy returned the gesture.

"Would you like to come in?" Kiffy offered.

The two entered and sat down at a dining table as Nicholas observed Kiffy's abode. Four wolves- one he recognized as Bechstein- sat cuddled together by the fire nearby. Still at Kiffy's side and below the table was the snow-white animal.

Nicholas had many questions to ask. "Many reach for their faces. I don't quite understand the reasoning."

Kiffy explained. "It is a form of greeting called the *Salute of Degomble*. Our faces are commonly covered in snow from harsh winds and blizzards, and to remove it we use our hands. Our town name and the salute were originated from such."

Kiffy walked to the fireplace where a kettle was brewing. "Mug of oggin' cider?" he asked.

"Yes, thank you." Nicholas cupped his fingers around the wooden mug, lingering in its warmth. Kiffy did not hesitate but gripped the mug's handle and slammed the liquid down his throat.

"Ah! Warms the throat and is good for cold toes."

Nicholas attempted a swig, choked, then spit a portion of the cider out.

Kiffy chuckled. "You will get used to it; the water is from the ocean so it will taste bitter as first. The ocean water enhances the flavor of the cider."

"Tasty," Nicholas replied, still coughing.

The white, pointy-ear animal by Kiffy's side began moving into the adjacent room. "She's more of an independent family member, not quite as social as Bechstein over there," Kiffy commented as he and Nicholas watched her leave.

"What kind of animal is that?" Nicholas asked.

"She's an arctic fox. I rescued her almost a year ago when she was a kit. She was abandoned by her mother."

"You have many animals living with you. They all seem well-mannered."

Kiffy choked a bit on his second mug of oggin' cider, laughing at Nicholas' comment.

"They listen and are tame, but they are wild animals and can have minds of their own. They usually obey, but sometimes their born nature takes command over mine."

Throughout their conversation, Nicholas learned that Kiffy was a local fisherman and animal trainer of Degomble. There were many trainers throughout the vicinity that tamed animals for good use. Kiffy and the other trainers were known as pedagogs.

Kiffy decided it was time to interrogate Nicholas some, hoping to determine where he was from and how he ended up near the ocean, battered and frozen.

"Where are you from Nicholas– Ethereal, perhaps?"

"I'm from Patara in Lycia," Nicholas replied. "Our voyage to the Holy Land ended in disaster. I only remember trying to swim back to our ship, then all went black. I... I wish I knew how my crew is faring."

Kiffy was confused as "Patara" or "Holy Land" were not places he was familiar with. He wondered if maybe Nicholas had lost his memory and if these places he mentioned were false. He observed Nicholas closely and could see honesty and sorrow in his swollen eyes from his recent unfortunate event.

Kiffy then spoke sincerely. "Your face is still pale, friend, and your eyes still show weariness. You should get some more rest. When you are at full recovery we will meet with Norrick. Maybe then things will make better sense to you. The guest dwelling is available as long as you need it."

"Thank you, Kiffy; you are most kind." Nicholas left their first meeting and returned to his guest house. It did not take long for him to doze off once his head hit the pillow.

Kiffy made his way to the rear chamber of his home where an indoor parrock existed. At the tail end of the stable were two musk oxen and the arctic fox who lay napping in her designated spot. Kiffy bent down and massaged her ears.

"Well, girl... another successful rescue, first you and now our mysterious friend Nicholas." Kiffy began reminiscing about the day he rescued his white furry fox from the mighty blizzard that had attempted to take her life.

The Fox and the Wind

One year earlier...

The kit struggled in a limp while moving forth in the harsh resistance of the wind and flurry. Very ravenous and weak from her mother's abandonment, she forced her way into a local ice chamber. It was a creature-made cave, but small, most likely built by a hare or another fox. The blizzard had reached its peak of maximum strength, and the cold winds just outside hollered and screamed at enormous potential. The young fox's pearl-white fur camouflaged with the snow as it salted the land with drifts. As the kit used her last strand of strength, she lay down and curled up to protect herself. Her tail tucked over her like a blanket providing some form of warmth, but not enough. As her injured leg bled and throbbed, the overwhelming weakness and pain began to take over and the invitation of death seeped into her soul. As it did, the young kit reacted vocally with consistency of what sounded like painful giggles– not giggles of laughter but small whining barks. Periodically, she uttered a stern and long howl, advertising the intense discomfort.

Two approaching musk oxen were fighting the same storm as the kit. Booth and Eucera, however, were both seasoned and trained for the task at hand. With stout shoulders and massive body mechanics, the musk oxen pummeled through the intensity. Booth stood at 7 1/2 feet tall while his sister Eucera stood at almost 7 feet. Snowfall built up upon the curved horns of their heads and icicles formed upon their fur, but their thick and long coats provided internal warmth. Kiffy equipped both Booth and Eucera with a chain mail type armor that was formed and fit by Arvel. It provided protection from predators or attacks that could occur from creatures of the embedded. The armor glimmered with a metallic green and red reflection and was stamped with the mark of Arvel's work- a large violet flower. With the armor intact on the musk oxen, it gave Kiffy time to react, time to attack as needed to defend his traveling companions.

"Booth! Slack gash!" cried Kiffy as he wiped the gomble from his gaiter and face. "Are you going to let Eucera win again today?!" Booth and Eucera consistently turned their role into a game, a competition. If one was moving faster, the other would follow to keep up; it maintained motivation between the two. "Slack gash" was a taunt Kiffy used to remind them to maintain focus and move forth. Both musk oxen knew exactly what Kiffy meant when he used that command. It was a strong relationship the three had and shared as they traveled to the ideal fishing spots.

Kiffy was frequently asked, "Why go out in such intense blizzards? Why not consider calmer days?" "It's just my role" was the response he always gave them. What he did not tell them is that the best fishing was during the mid-climax of a storm. A temporary calm would exist long enough that he could catch a great amount. The fish developed a strong hunger and would feed more often during this calm. His catch of the day could feed the community up to two weeks and sometimes longer. Fewer fishing trips meant more time for the musk oxen to rest, and less wear on the equipment. It was a survival strategy Kiffy kept to himself. After he obtained his catch of the calm, it would commonly change to a fighting storm on the way back home.

A sound of misery began to reach Kiffy's ears, a sound of whines, fearful giggles, and howling- a signal of approaching death. As he and his companions came closer to the shelter of the kit, the cries became more definite and distinct. Kiffy realized what the sound indicated; it was a sound of distress. His several years of training and taming arctic animals helped him determine that the distressed signals were those of a fox. "Niah!" Kiffy hollered. Booth and Eucera came to a complete stop, complying with the command. Hoping to spot the sufferer's location, Kiffy threw quick glances behind his shoulders as he rotated his head 180 degrees to his left, then to his right. Additional sound waves of painful howls and fearful giggles produced. Kiffy jumped from his envoy sledger, taking closer glances and observations at the surrounding area. Going to a defensive tactic, he reached to his waist and wielded two weapons of use: a two-headed war hammer in one hand and a double-edged dagger in the other. The dagger, which Arvel described as the size of a gladius, had razor-sharp edges with teeth ridges as deadly as that of a wolverine. Both weapons were custom-built by Arvel. Although the weapons were intended for fighting, both weapons were also a good tool of a fisherman. The hammer was a great ice breaker and the dagger provided adequate fillet of the fish.

With his hands gripped tight on the handles of each weapon, Kiffy began following the cries for help. A cry came into Kiffy's right ear, and he turned his head quickly toward it. As he did, the visibility of the fox's shelter became apparent; the chamber was finally found. Kiffy sheathed his weapons and proceeded slowly to the small chamber's entrance. He edged himself closer and lowered himself to his knees. The blizzard's force made great attempts to push him from behind. He observed the inner chamber of the fox's protective shelter. With her eyes closed and in intense pain, the kit released her longest and terrified howl yet. "It's okay, sweetheart! I'm here now!"

Eyeing her bleeding leg and noting her pain, Kiffy carefully handled the kit and gathered her from the chamber. Folding his arms around her, he covered her torso with his chin down in what looked like a hugging position. This helped block the storm from her nearly dying body. When the two reached the sledger, Kiffy quickly pulled an extra garment from his equipment. The garment was known as a "Tunic of Qiviut," made from the fine wool that the musk ox contained. With extreme thoroughness, he wrapped the kit safely inside the garment. Signs of life were still in her fighting soul as crystallized vapor came from her breath. With aggressive strength, Kiffy flexed the reins signaling command to the oxen. "Booth! Eucera! Cele Huit!" As if by second nature, the musk oxen proceeded forth to get home as quickly as possible.

The fox woke up to the sound of crackling made by a warm fire. Several attempts to open her eyes were unsuccessful; the shock of her body required rest and little function. The exhausting cold that teamed with death was beginning to exchange with warmth and recovery. Her broken leg still stung with slight movements but felt more supported– her injury was now in a cast made of material created by the physician, the same person who rescued her. She was covered with a qiviut blanket to create more warmth, and her comfort deepened as Kiffy stroked the fur of her ears.

Several quick knocks were heard from the door. "Come in!" replied Kiffy. Arvel entered, slamming the door behind him. "Wretch' hooley!" Hooley was a word commonly used, but generally in a profane manner. It was expressed by those who had a hatred or annoyance of the climate's strong winds. As Arvel wiped the gomble of snow from his face, the four residing wolves came up to greet him, Bechstein jumping up on him and nearly knocking him over. "Hello Bech. Alright, alright! Bech, get down! Yer a damn thorn in my hide!" Arvel shouted. Kiffy, in the animal chamber, could hear the artificer complaining in the room.

"What have ya drug back from yer travels this time?" Arvel asked as he entered the adjoined chamber. He looked down to observe the slowly recovering fox, waiting on Kiffy to reply.

"I found her at death's door while heading to my fishing location. She looks to be abandoned by her mother."

"A kit?! What in hell ya plan to do with a useless kit?"

Kiffy ignored Arvel's direct comments as he usually did. "Arvel- look at her ears." Arvel glanced down. "What about 'em?"

"Her ears have a dark purple aura on them."

"Probably embedded. Have you seen its eyes?" Arvel replied.

As Kiffy continued to comfort the fox, he could sense the gentle nature of the creature. "She has been keeping her eyes shut so it's hard to tell."

Arvel grumbled. "Probably shudda left it where ya found it."

Kiffy glanced up at Arvel, noticing that he was equipped with a long, rounded leather case laid upon his back. Arvel opened the top and proceeded to pull out a pole-looking instrument, built and carved out of wood.

"Here's yer rod ya requested. I don't know if it will do ya any good, since yer rescuin' kit instead of catchin' fish."

"I intend to head out again tomorrow," Kiffy replied.

Arvel rolled his eyes as he handed the rod to Kiffy. "Good luck with it, made outta rare salix in the tundra region. I came across the wood in my expeditin', it was just long enough."

"Thank you, Arvel. Can I offer you a mug of oggin'?"

"Nah, workload is full today; another day we drink. Careful with that kit! If it carries evil, I wouldn't hesitate in annihilatin' it."

Evening hit and Kiffy ate his dinner. With the day's full events, he had nearly forgotten. As he dined, his thoughts revisited the pain and agony the kit had faced in her abandonment and starvation. Somehow, he could relate to what the kit had gone through, including the shelter she had chosen to avoid the blizzards and the cutting winds.

When traveling, Kiffy always planned well and brought adequate food portions. Fish he caught could also improve his portions, if needed. He provided enough lichens, mosses, and wood plants to feed Booth and Eucera, who could live off these portions for four to seven days. He and his team could take on the best of storms, but not all storms were safe to proceed in. When he encountered them, Kiffy would often take shelter and wait it out, since he did not want to risk the lives of Booth, Eucera, or himself. The most dangerous to encounter was the fog of the embedded. The fog was displaced in numerous stages of evil, its strength and color dependent upon the evil creatures that enacted it. During these times, embedded creatures attacked openly. Being in a blizzard was a fight itself, but tolerance and battle in the embedded fog took on a far more extreme challenge. Those not trained or experienced in facing its danger commonly met death.

Kiffy finished up on his evening meal, throwing the last of the scraps to Bechstein. Kiffy grinned and shook his head at Bech. "Always got to beg don't ya; you act like I don't feed you." Kiffy looked across the room where the rodded instrument and leather carrying case sat. He picked up Arvel's piece of work, instantly impressed by the craftsmanship of the fishing instrument. It had a light feel and balance as he held it in his hand, with a nice bending radius at its tip. The flexibility of the tool was nothing he had seen before. He spoke out loud to himself. "Great work Arvel- great work as always".

An uneasy barking came from Lillian and Ohen in the animal chamber. The kit had started to become more mobile in its small recovery section of the room and again began to utter small giggling whine and howls. The movement and noises put the wolves on defense, and Bech made his way into the chamber upon hearing the barks. "Bech! Niah!" Bech knew the command well when pulling the blitzkrieg sledger and quickly complied with a halt.

Kiffy went into the kit's recovery chamber, calming down the other two wolves. The kit indeed showed signs of improved life and mobility but still appeared anguished. To help comfort her, he once again began to stroke her ears. With some struggle, the kit slowly opened her eyes, and Kiffy felt his breath grow anxious and tight. Ready to strike her beating heart, he observed her cautiously in case signs of evil were embedded within. If he were to kill her, now was the time, when she was weak. He could not risk the lives of his fellow stronghold by housing an embedded creature. With a lengthy effort, the fox opened her eyes fully. Upon her face of bright white fur, two irises appeared, both a beautiful ocean blue. Her eyes met Kiffy's, and he breathed a sigh of relief. The kit did not appear to be embedded. He confirmed her nature of goodness but left the purple color of her ears in question and for further investigation later.

Strong winds, or "wretch' hooley" as Arvel proclaimed, once again took their toll outside through the evening. Sounds of clashing and clunking came from outside, followed by harsh whistles from the wind's tune. The young fox fell back into a sleep, most likely to remain in that state for the remainder of the night. Before concluding the evening and the eventful day, Kiffy observed the kit one last time. He looked over to the wolves– Marriam, Ohen, and Lillian– cuddled together in a peaceful sleep while Bechstein lay down solo, keeping his eyes open in defense as he watched the kit. Cautiously, he got up and joined in to help Kiffy check on things and Kiffy patted the wolf on the head. "What do you think, Bech? Do you think she's evil?" Bech looked up and licked Kiffy's face. "Yeah– I don't think so either." Kiffy smirked, remembering Arvel's bitching and whining about the wind. "Bech, say hello to our new family member... Hooley."

Resurge!

The contender was ready for her big day. For a few weeks, Kiffy had provided a diet plan that nourished and strengthened Hooley for the hunt. The full-grown fox was seasoned, trained, and prepared to take on the best of endeavors. The arctic weather, although cold and rigid as usual, maintained a mild temper, which perfectly matched preference for the day's event. Outside, Booth and Eucera were equipped and saddled, ready to provide transport to the arena. Kiffy sat inside near the fire waiting for the sun to rise above the horizon, with intention to reach the arena early to make ready for the annual competition.

"Hooley... come here, sweetheart," Kiffy commanded. Complying, Hooley entered from the animal parrock and sat in front of him. She slowly looked up at her trainer as he peered down upon his competitor of choice. Hooley's inner ear lobes still showed signs of a dim purple. Kiffy, intentionally ignoring the color, stroked them as he did back when he first brought her home. It had now become a common therapy to calm her down and reduce the general skittish and defensive nature she often possessed. He spoke soft words of encouragement to her "You have trained hard; you are my weapon of choice– today's the day– today is your day."

Kiffy moved to the dining table to grab a quick breakfast. Hooley hung by his shin and followed him to the table, while Marriam, Ohen, Bechstein, and Lillian lay idly in front of the fire. The wolves' lazy habits were common most mornings but were periodically discomposed, and the luxury of a nice crackling fire was often substituted with a ten-mile running expedition. The wild dogs, however, always favored the exercise; it did not bother them to change pace. It was also Kiffy's way of keeping them strong and in shape, but today would not be the day to do so. Kiffy looked down at Hooley, "Shall we observe this year's changes?" he asked her, as if she were a person. Grabbing a scroll from the table, Kiffy began to unroll the parchment. He read down the writing outlining the disclaimers and rules of this year's hunting event:

"All pedagogs must possess a trained animal, one animal per trainer permitted.

One caged hutch is provided to each competitor. Any retrieved lemmings and hares must be captured and contained within.

Each animal captured earns one pennant.

One pennant is eliminated if a lemming or hare reaches the arena and escapes past the gate-line.

The hunter must re-retrieve them immediately before escaping past the gate-line to avoid losing a pennant.

The first hunter and its pedagog to earn <u>four pennants</u> wins the match."

Kiffy brushed through the verbiage of the parchment to read the section on attire requirements:

"All pedagogs must wear a trapping pelerine outside their arctic undergarments. The pelerine must be uniquely crafted, separating them from the other competitors.

Trainers must possess the mark of the chosen hunter on their pelerine and/or other garments."

"Mark of the chosen hunter... that's you, Hooley," Kiffy jested. Hooley looked up as if she completely understood what he was saying.

Full from breakfast and ready to prepare, Kiffy proceeded to his bed chamber and opened a tall armoire, where his trapping pelerine hung. His pelerine was red in color and attached to a long black cape with a detailed silhouette of a white fox with its eyes closed. Then, magically, the eyes of the symbol fox opened, glowing in ocean blue, then slowly closed, then repeated itself. Kiffy removed his morning clothing, revealing a stocky and muscular frame, his arms quite a bit more developed than the rest of his body. On his left arm, a scar of elliptical shape showed signs of fangs or teeth that had gnawed the skin. Those that saw his scar never asked, nor did Kiffy ever share, what had caused such an injury. The trapping attire crafted for him fit well and secure over his arctic gambeson undergarments, and his refined biceps flexed as he pulled the cape down tightly to his knee line. He glanced down at his uniform and then sighed. "May the embedded evil remain silent and the spirits provide us a day of clemency."

Rays of sunlight finally peeked slightly above the snowy horizon, although some light was blocked by the high mountainous structures of the tundra several miles southeast of Degomble. Kiffy, with Hooley once again at his side, footed it over to Nicholas' neighboring guest residence. Nicholas, already up and dressed for the morning, noticed him approach and opened his front door before Kiffy could knock.

Kiffy gave a Salute of Degomble to Nicholas. "Good morrow, Nicholas. You look like you're feeling better, my friend. Would you like to travel with us today?"

Nicholas respectfully attempted to return the salute, noticing Kiffy's sported attire and cape. Just below him, his furry companion stared up at Nicholas as if she was waiting for an answer from him as well. "Where will we be traveling?" he asked curiously.

Kiffy brushed a bit of snow debris from his hunting uniform. "Today our destination is to the frozen arena in the southeast tundra. Hooley here is trained and is to compete in the annual hunting event."

Nicholas took strong interest in the hunting adventure that was soon to partake. "Certainly, I would be happy to join you."

As they waited for their role of transport, Booth and Eucera played a friendly game of nudge. Their massive body structures created opposite forces as they tried to push against one another. The wide rounded horns and long faces were used in the friendly match of push and pull. Kiffy scolded, interrupting the playtime, "Behave, you two; it's work time! Forma Hele!" The musk oxen complied, switching from friendly play to transport formation. Standing tall, they reduced their height by lowering their torsos to allow for passengers. Nicholas watched as Kiffy mounted to Booth, and commanded Booth again "Resurge!" Obeying, Booth raised his large torso back to his standing position, while Eucera still lay low waiting for a passenger.

"Nicholas, you may use Eucera as transport."

Nicholas looked down and mounted to the saddle attached to Eucera. Confusion crossed his face as Eucera still lay in a low position, not rising as Booth did.

Kiffy chuckled. "She's waiting for a command from you."

Nicholas nodded. "Uh... Re... Resurge?" Eucera instantly rose back to her standing position.

Kiffy smiled. "That-a-girl, Eucera."

Nicholas gave Eucera a quick but nervous pat. "Hell... hello Eucera." Properly sat to his mounted transport, Nicholas noticed Hooley on the ground next to Kiffy and Booth, looking up at Kiffy in his seat above. "What about her; does she walk alongside?" Nicholas inquired.

Kiffy grinned and shouted out a command to the fox. "Hooley, *pono!*"

Nicholas watched, surprised, as Hooley took a great leap from the ground on to the back of Booth, creating a comfortable seat just behind Kiffy. Hooley's quick response to Kiffy's command was remarkable to Nicholas. He admired the skills the pedagog had and the obedience his trained animals sustained. With all parties ready, the trip began as the musk oxen slowly trotted forth.

"I sense this is the first time for you riding a musk ox?" Kiffy asked Nicholas.

"Yes, yes it is. Growing up, I developed more of a mastery of riding horses.

"My parents and I took many rides by horseback across our region to visit its people. Many times we traveled by horse to visit my uncle. My mother and I would ride the shorelines of Patara beach where she taught me to swim in the ocean."

"How did you avoid death from the freezing of the sea ice?" Kiffy asked, amazed.

"It is much different there; it has a warmer climate. One can run barefoot across the sands that meet the ocean's water. If one is hot from the afternoon's heat, they can swim in the water to cool off."

"Sounds beautiful and pleasant," Kiffy replied.

"Yes, many great people live amongst its lands." Nicholas still missed his home and his parents that had passed and began to re-analyze the reasoning behind his mysterious visit to this arctic terrain. He reflected on the citizens he had met in Degomble. What was his purpose here, his objective to arriving in such a world? Perhaps there was no reason, or perhaps this was a surreal dream that would come to an end soon. He would then wake up, with Drusus, Otho, and the ship crew safe and in Patara, and continue to pursue his plan of reaching the Holy Land. Nicholas gave Eucera another pat on the side of her torso. "Seems as though great people live here as well, including your well-trained companions here."

Kiffy nodded. "Many great people do indeed, but we have faced an era of hard times. The courage and hard work of our people keeps us vigorous and alive." Kiffy observed his trained team of fauna, then laughed. "Including our friends here... when they obey command. Shall we increase pace?"

"I'm ready," Nicholas responded.

"Cele Huit!" Booth and Eucera's slow trot turned to a dashing gallop, their massive hooves crunching loudly on the snowy ground below. The daylight now nearly blinded them as they traveled eastward against it. Kiffy glanced back at his endeared white-furred huntress, her nose up and eyes closed. The warmth of the dawn bled upon her sharply pointed face, and her triangular ears slightly lowered as she enjoyed the gift the natural light had shone upon her. Kiffy smiled with emotion as he and his group forged ahead to the *Arena of the Frozen Demilune*.

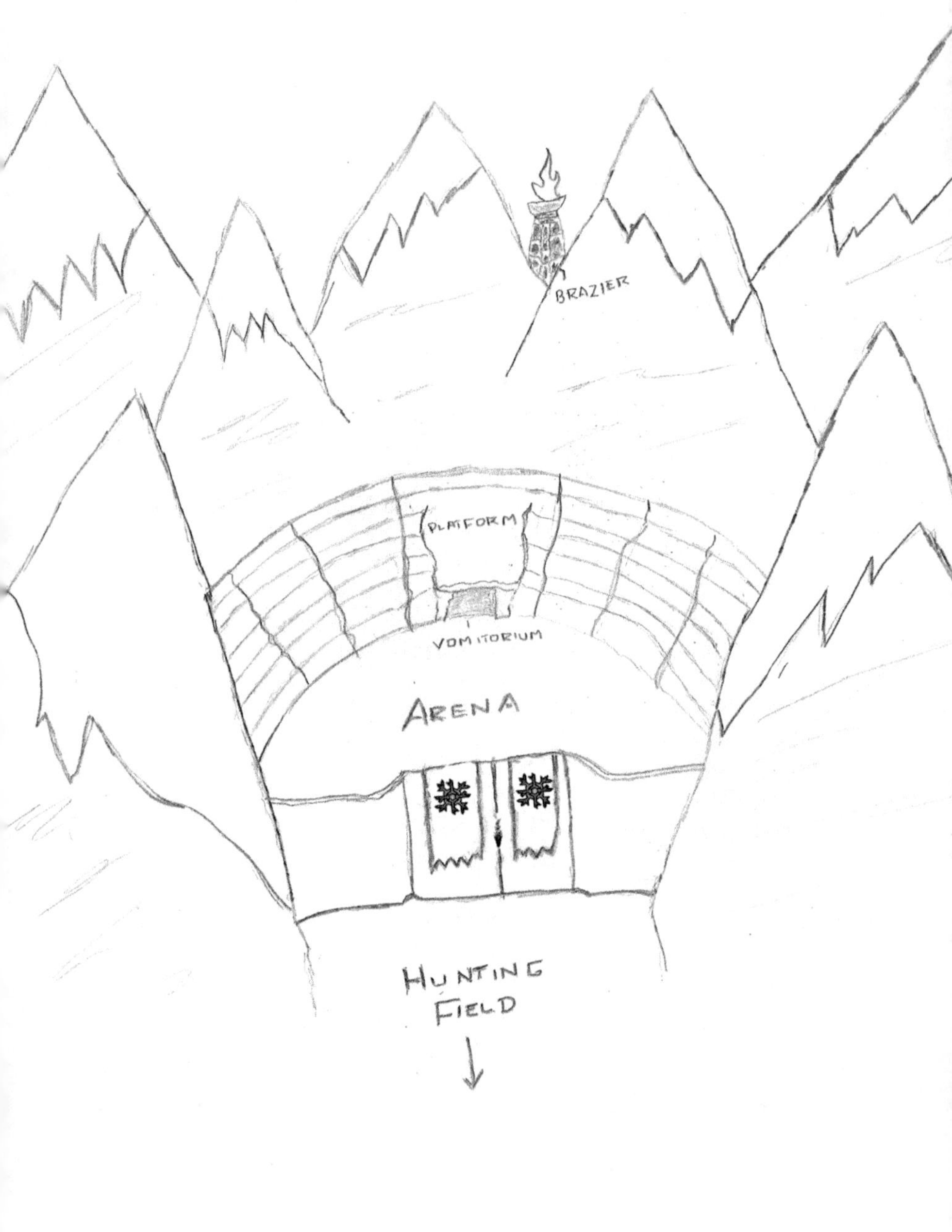

BRAZIER
PLATFORM
VOMITORIUM
ARENA
HUNTING
FIELD

The Arena of the Frozen Demilune

The gyrfalcon spread his wings, soaring high above the crescent-shaped coliseum below. The steep rocky walls created a curved depression in the mountainside of the tundra's terrain. Sloping tiers of seating sections had been formed from years of glacial masses caused by the winter's icy waters. At the lowest point was the main floor, known to all as the Arena of the Frozen Demilune, which remained frozen year-round due to the permafrost that had settled underneath. The arena floor presented the greatest of pedagogs teamed with hunters of elite training. A huge opening on one end of the arena was retained by a massive, closed gate. Two banners hung across the metal bars, both displaying an emblem magically illuminated in evergreen, red, and gold, which represented "Goodness Among All." At the opposite end was the vomitorium, a medium-sized cave nested into the mountain, almost perfectly centered in position. Its squared entrance had been created from huge stones that had fallen, molding a large open space where the contenders would wait until they were announced.

A wide cliff hung directly above the cave, creating a solid platform. High above the coliseum, between two tall mountain peaks, sat a large unlit brazier.

The gyrfalcon descended to the entrance of the vomitorium and landed on the arm of his pedagog inside, his white and black-peppered wings fluttering as he attempted to regain balance. "I trust you've scouted the hunting field well?" Mazielle asked her feathered fowl. She and her hunter, Free-Booter, were one of the final three teams that had made it through the qualifying matches. Mazielle was a fit, middle-aged woman with great knowledge and expertise in taming and training bird fauna. Layered on top of her arctic garments was a hooded, blue-feathered pelerine which covered both her shoulders and arms, the front reaching just below her bosom. She wore an armored gauntlet on her left arm, which protected her from Free-Booter's sharp and skin-piercing talons. A small hole in the back of her hood allowed her long-braided hair to fall down her back, almost reaching the heels of her feet. Chirping and perching in her hair strands were several tiny bee hummingbirds, exhibiting various colors and acting as braids.

Kiffy and Herald stood in a single-file line behind Mazielle within the squared cave. Herald was a rather skinny and wormy-looking man with a head full of messy shoulder-length hair, parted in the middle, with a grizzly mustache and beard to match. He wore an eye mask to represent the facial features of his hunter and an un-hooded, padded beige pelerine with two buckle straps in the front. His arctic garment underneath consisted of a sealskin gambeson dyed in lavender. Sewn to the front of the gambeson, near his torso, was a large and specialized pocket, from which rustling and chittering sounds could be heard. An ermine eventually raised its head out into view, "Stay in your pocket, Jaegar!" Herald commanded. "We do not want to cause trouble!"

At the far back were the returning champions, Bolo and his wolverine Clawclapper. Instead of standing in line with his fellow contenders, he sat with his back leaning against the cave's wall and his elbows on his knees. Periodically he would pull out a knife, cutting pieces of meat and feeding them to his residing friend. His secret was to force an appetite on his wolverine, which would improve his performance by making him long for an animal's flesh. Bolo and Clawclapper were full time hunters by trade, not just in competition. In his role he provided the people with sources of meat for food and furs for clothing. Bolo was the arrogant type with a competitive edge that a lot of returning champions displayed. Both had maintained champion status for seven straight years, with full confidence of earning an eighth victory.

The champ's trapping attire consisted of a pelerine and mukluks made from a wolverine's fur, the same brown and white. His undergarments were made from caribou hides and sealskin with a tint that matched his outer clothing. He periodically received criticism from spectators for using the fur that was the same as Clawclapper. Others, however, had accepted the fact and highly respected the champion nonetheless.

Nicholas examined the glaciated seats that were beginning to fill to capacity. The tall walls of the coliseum bounced and echoed with voices of men, women, and children as they began sitting and waiting for the final event to commence. Finding a mid–row section, Nicholas seated himself, noticing wandering merchants walking up and down the natural stairs, selling various foods and hot beverages. "Hot brew and cider! Peppermint droppers right here!" one merchant yelled. "Hare skewers! Halibut!" another shouted. They also had a vast assortment of souvenirs, glowing trinkets, and small triangular baubles with strings, which people wore around their necks to keep warm. The baubles were a popular item, but the most popular were the wooden models, hand–crafted figurines of the competing hunters. "Wolverines available! They are going fast!" a merchant uttered. Nicholas watched as the merchant handed a young child what looked to be a wooden fox. Excited from getting her new toy, the little girl grinned. Still wearing her smile, she looked up at Nicholas and waved to him with her other hand. He smiled and waved back, recognizing the crafted model, which looked exactly like Hooley.

"Good day to you, perhaps a skewer or two?" a merchant asked Nicholas. "We have various roasted meats also."

"No, thank you," he replied.

"No, eh? How about a wooden model of your favorite hunter? Have a few wolverines and gyrfalcons, counts are gettin' low though, plenty of foxes and ermines left."

"I'll take a fox," Lízabet requested from behind Nicholas. "Hello, Nicholas." She smiled as she greeted him.

"He... hello Lízabet," Nicholas replied, surprised by her sudden appearance and recognizing the long brown hair, scarf, and chullo hat with tails.

The merchant handed her the model. "Here you be, miss."

Lízabet thanked the merchant, then pointed to the hanging cliff just above the vomitorium. "My grandfather Norrick and our group would like for you to join us on the commissioning platform."

Nicholas glanced up at the platform. "Sure, of course."

"Come with me, then," Lízabet suggested.

Standing on the commissioning platform, as Lízabet called it, was Norrick, military commander Quilo Serdar, and a short elderly man, in a long red velvet robe with white trim. He wore a stocking cap that had a long tail and was too large for his head. His face remained hidden making it difficult to identify or distinguish. Norrick had gray hair, short in length, parted on the side. Nicholas found it odd that he did not possess a hood nor a necklace to keep his body warm like most others. Norrick's face had a defined full beard, with tips that looked like flames of white fire. His eyes were a deep emerald green that greatly contrasted with his older but fairer skin tone. The commander stood tall and mightier than the two, displaying intimidating characteristics.

"The commissioning platform– why is it called that?" Nicholas asked Lízabet.

"It is where the holders of today's event stand. They are commissioners and are part of a primordial legion known as the *Union of Goodness*. All its members take headship in events such as these, but also provide planning and tactics in warfare and the well–being of our town, its people, and the roles which we provide."

"Is your grandfather part of this union?" Nicholas asked.

"Yes, for many years, and is head of the legion."

"Are you part of this legion?"

Lízabet frowned. "No, I have yet to earn my place in the union."

Nicholas and Lízabet joined the group as they prepared to begin the championship and opening ceremony. Nicholas stood back, so as not to interrupt Norrick and his surrounding party during their tasks. Instead, he tried keeping conversation with Lízabet.

"Commander, your defense force- are they in readiness?" Norrick asked.

"They are in defensive formation guarding the outer gate at this time," the commander confirmed.

"Defensive force?" Nicholas asked, looking dumbfounded.

Lízabet explained. "Quilo Serdar has brought a defensive group of soldiers that stand in protection outside the coliseum's gate. In case of enemy attacks, they would be able to contain the citizens within and take the fight outside, except for aerial creatures."

"How do they protect from attacks coming from above?"

Lízabet gave him a smug look. "You shall soon see."

"And what aerial creatures-"

Nicholas was then caught off guard by the elderly man in the oversized stocking cap. With a snap of his wrinkled left fingers, a scroll tied with a red ribbon magically appeared in his hand. The fingers of his right hand then snapped, astonishing Nicholas, as he watched the scroll float in the air right in front of the robed man. The scroll began to unroll and unroll; it kept unrolling and unrolling, then finally stopped. The robed man spoke in a rough voice to the crowd.

"Ahem! Welco-"

"Gasper, we must activate the voice ring; they cannot hear you," Norrick interrupted.

"Oh, yes... yes of course. Thank you... yep... yep... yep." Gasper replied.

Norrick positioned his hands in front of Gasper; it looked as though he was holding an invisible sphere. Rotating his hands and pointing his fingers out he chanted "Ring of Sonant." Just in front of Gasper, a blue smoky ring appeared, to be used as a magical microphone.

"You may now proceed," Norrick confirmed.

Gasper cleared his voice, "Ahem!" His voice, amplified in great lengths, reached the highest sections of seating rows.

"Welcome, all, to the Hare and Lemming Hunting Championship! Today as we celebrate our 25th annual hunting championship, our final pedagogs and their trained companions will take to the outer field. They will attempt to hunt and retrieve the quickest of hares and the cleverest of lemmings. The first to earn four pennants is the winner, yep... yep... yep."

The eager crowd began to clap and stir, though several people stood cold and shivering.

"It is cold; please light the brazier!" a spectator requested.

"Let's get on with the ceremony!" another hollered.

Gasper glanced at Norrick. "Shall we begin the protection of warming?" he asked.

"Yes, it is time," Norrick replied.

Norrick closed his eyes and began to rub his hands together, creating friction. Putting his warm hands close to his face, he breathed hot air on his fingers. Opening his hands, he raised his arms toward the brazier high above, igniting it with an intense flame. The cold climate no longer impacted the crowd as a magical warmth from the lit brazier provided heat to all of those within the coliseum. Nicholas stood amazed; he too could feel the difference in temperature. He observed the fiery-layered cloud that domed the top of the arena, then glanced back at Lízabet, who still looked smug.

"Does that answer your question, foreigner?" Lízabet asked with a friendly gesture.

Having completed his magical enchantment, Norrick nodded to the announcer.

Gasper continued, "Now! Let us introduce our finalists!"

The four contenders could hear his voice from inside the vomitorium and tension grew within them as they waited for the signal to come out to the arena floor. Kiffy looked down at Hooley standing by his side. "Well, lady, this is it; because of you, we are here today!" Hooley's body shook nervously, made anxious by the loud sound and excitement of the crowd outside. One of Mazielle's braided bee-hummingbirds broke free from her hair and flew toward the fox. Flapping its tiny wings at a rate of five thousand times per minute, it perched on her pointed noise, chirped loudly, and vanished with a spark of magical dust. Hooley glanced back up at Kiffy with a baffled look on her furry face and he grinned in return, petting her on the head. "Worry not, girl; they are merely a chanted apparition."

"Finalists come forth!" It was now their cue to enter the arena floor. The crowd cheered and applauded as three of the four competitors walked out to the arena's open area, waiting to be introduced to the hundreds of spectators surrounding them.

Gasper grasped the extensively long scroll and began to read down the list.

"Introducing our first pedagog... Mazielle and her gyrfalcon, Free-booter!"

"Our second pedagog... Kiffy and his fox, Hooley!"

"And our third... Herald and his ermine, Jaegar!" Jaegar poked his head outside of the front pocket and jumped out. He stood up on his two hind legs, then hopped to greet the crowd.

The crowd clapped for the three contenders, then slowed and silenced. Following the silence, an orchestra beat on leather-made drums.

"Lastly... our seven-time winner and returning champion... Bolo... and his wolverine Clawclapper!"

The massive coliseum shook with the crowd's roars as Bolo and his wolverine entered the floor. Bolo raised his fist to the sky and growled out. "Time for number eight!"

"Tally keepers! Please prepare the pennants!" Gasper commanded in a rigid voice.

Four keepers entered the floor, one for each hunter. They quickly positioned themselves at the coliseum walls near the open gate, two on the left and two on the right. Each tally keeper held a wooden pole containing four pennants that were currently rolled up on the pole. Their job was to unroll a pennant each time a hunter delivered a lemming or hare.

With the tally keepers in position, Gasper allowed the commander the use of the magical vocal ring. He ordered, "Battalion! Proceed to open the gates; switch to a crosswise formation!"

The pedagogs and their hunters stood ready as the large gates slowly began to open. The creases of the gates began to expand, the mid-day sun projecting light to the arena floor and coliseum. The sacred hunting grounds of the snowy tundra outside displayed miles of potential prey. The defending soldiers stood perpendicular to the opened gates, creating defensive borderlines on both sides of the opening.

"Pedagogs! At the sound of the oxen horns, you may release your hunters!" Quilo Serdar shouted.

The horns blared, and the hunting gladiators began their crusade. Hooley and Clawclapper began a head-to-head sprinting marathon, as Free-booter soared directly above them, flying low to avoid hitting the protective domed shield above. All three quickly passed the coliseum's gate. With a competitive glance at each other, the fox and wolverine split ways.

Herald's ermine did not quite follow the same tactics as the rest but instead was confused and running in the wrong direction. He tumbled, rolled, and danced, and on-lookers in the surrounding stands began to point and laugh at his distress.

"No, no! Jaegar! The other way! Stop this instance! Go that way!" yelled Herald. The ermine's four small legs went into a fleet-footed dash. He was now moving in the correct direction but was the last to reach the outer hunting field.

It did not take the skilled Clawclapper long to pick up the scent of his prey. He began his pursuit, his sharp claws digging into the snow, and the hare bolted in defense. Finally catching it and grasping it in his mouth, the wolverine switched directions and returned his catch to Bolo, who was waiting in the coliseum. "Good work! Now get another!" his trainer growled. He approached the arena, dropped the hare into the designated cage, and nodded quickly at Kiffy. "There's one!"

Kiffy returned the nod in respect to the champion, then noticed Free-Booter flying by with a lemming in his talons. He watched Mazielle's excitement as she and her hunter delivered his first capture. The tiny blue, red, and yellow hummingbirds attached to her hair escaped in an attempt to follow the gyrfalcon as it returned to flight, then disappeared with a poof of magical dust. More birds re-attached, braiding her hair, replacing the escapees.

The confused ermine finally spotted a lemming not too far from the coliseum gates. With a creative approach of body rolls he grabbed it just before it could bury itself underground, then returned to his pedagog with his catch. Running just behind him was Clawclapper, already with a second arctic hare in his mouth. Both made their deposits into the cage and earned a pennant.

"Much better, Jaegar!" Herald encouraged him. Jaegar began to hop up and down, excited from his accomplishment. "Okay, good, now proceed! Make haste!" The ermine obeyed and took off with a flash, this time spotting a hare right by the gates. Perhaps it was just luck for this little fellow that available game was just outside, but it worked in his favor. Jaegar proceeded slowly as the hare stared at him. He changed to a hypnotic dance of rolls and twists with his body, getting closer and closer to the hare, who sat mesmerized and motionless by the ermine's acrobatic movements. With a forward hop, Jaegar grabbed hold, now with a second capture to return.

Free-Booter flew in from above with another lemming, catch number two for him as well. "Very good," Mazielle complimented, then quickly pointed with a command. "Free-Booter, *theevios*! The ermine!" The gyrfalcon swooped down low toward Jaegar, who was edging closer to the gates, then wrenched the hare out of his grasp with his sharp talons. Frustrated, Jaegar stood on his two hind legs and swatted at the gyrfalcon. "No! You wretched pilferer!" Herald yelled, glaring angrily at Maizelle, who sent a devious shrug and smirk back his way. Fortunately for Jaegar, his stolen hare did not cost him a pennant, since he was still outside the gates.

The tally keepers displayed the latest hunting results as the pennants hung off their wooden rods:

Clawclapper – *2 Pennants*
Jaegar *–1 Pennant*
Free–Booter – *3 Pennants*
Hooley – *0 Pennants*

Kiffy watched as his fellow contenders increased their pennants. With his cage still empty and his friend who had not returned, he began to question if he was an observer instead of a competitor. What Kiffy knew about his secret weapon, however, was she possessed a unique way of retrieving her prey. He had faith that she was using her natural skills but also relying on the tuned training he had taught her.

Hooley wandered into the sacred grounds, much farther out than the others. She could have retrieved a hare or lemming sooner, but her great sense of hearing directed her to a large group of lemmings living underneath the snow. She tilted her head, leaning her right ear to the ground, then switching to her left ear. She listened and waited, picking up on the sounds of rustles and movements of crawling critters, then on the sounds of breathing that she now confirmed was directly beneath her. It was time to dive, but not like a shark or a dolphin that springs into the air and dives back into the yielding waters of the oceans or seas. Hooley had to dive deep into the cold hard ground to earn her prize. She took a great leap into the air and plunged head-first into the rigorous surface. Her nose struck the hard snow with a thud, her back legs kicking straight up. Her head was stuck, and she shifted her body to release herself and break up the snow. Stunned, she composed herself and leaped again, mimicking the same action, but this time pummeling through the hardened surface and successfully retrieving a lemming. As she approached Kiffy with her first catch, the doubt he felt inside released, and he smiled as he complimented Hooley's hard work. "Excellent! You can do this! I know you can!"

A pennant on the rod dropped and hung for the fox; encouraged, she was now on her way to earning her second. Hooley sprinted to the same location she had identified before. She had some catching up to do, but circumstances changed frequently in this fierce competition.

She reached her destination, using her skill of 'stop, wait, and listen,' then once again dove head-first into the ground, this time retrieving two whole lemmings. With her jaws clamped down tight to contain both of them, she proceeded back past Clawclapper, who was tearing the ground with his sharp nails to gather his prey. The fox reached the arena floor, both lemmings trying their best to escape; one finally dropped from her clinch and took a dead run to the outer field. Hooley rapidly delivered her second lemming into the cage and chased after the third. The crowd was on its feet watching her scramble, but Hooley nabbed the lemming inches from the gate line, narrowly avoiding losing a pennant. With exhausted jaws, she released her catch into the cage as the arena screamed and cheered. Three pennants now hung for Hooley.

"That-a-girl, Hooley! Keep it up, sweetheart! One more!" Kiffy blared enthusiastically.

As Hooley exited to obtain her fourth, she again crossed paths in the outer field with Clawclapper, who was heading in direction of the arena. Free-booter soared in, thrusting past the wolverine with his fourth ready for delivery; if successful, he would become the new champion. The lemming in his talons began to scuffle and then broke free, quickly escaping outside the gate line. The gyrfalcon was penalized; the tally keeper retracted a pennant back into its rolled-up state.

As the lemming passed the gate line, Jaegar creatively snatched the escapee and turned it in for his third. A spectator from the crowd remarked "Did you see that? The weasel just made a sneaky play!" In desperation, Mazielle again tried to steal from another competitor. "Theevios! The wolverine!" she hollered. With a snap change in flight direction, Free-booter reached out his talons, ready to snatch the lemming from Clawclapper, but was thwarted by a quick swipe of the wolverine's right claw. The impact sent him rolling and crashing into the coliseum's wall. Clawclapper dropped and deposited number three, and Bolo grumbled at him. "Good! On to the last! Move it, move it!"

The crowd went crazy from the intensity. Nicholas stood on the commissioning platform, taking in the battle among the highly trained animals- it was nothing he had ever seen before. Slightly injured and half dazed, Free-booter gathered himself and perched on Mazielle's arm. She tried to calm and comfort him, then decided it was best to forfeit him from the match. She raised him on her feathered arm to obtain acclamation from the crowd.

Gasper on the platform shouted. "Please applaud our feathered friend, Free-booter; he performed well today, yep, yep, yep!"

Free-booter's tally keeper left the arena floor while the remaining pennants hung, updating the crowd on the score.

Clawclapper- 3
Jaegar- 3
Free-booter – *Disqualified*
Hooley – 3

It was down to three hunters in a three-way tie. Bolo, Herald, and Kiffy glanced at each other as they waited, not speaking. The Arena of the Frozen Demilune stood silent for several minutes, the fiery brazier above staying lit and providing warmth and protection to the spectators. Nicholas looked at the children who held wooden models of their favorite hunters, hoping for them to win. The four competitors, including Mazielle and her retired gyrfalcon, gazed out to the hunting grounds at a blur of three moving objects that was moving closer. It revealed itself to be a scramble: wolverine versus fox versus ermine, all three in possession of a captured animal. Clawclapper cut Jaegar off, causing him to stumble, drop his prey, and take off in the opposite direction in an attempt to recapture it. Hooley maintained equal speed with the wolverine, until suddenly, he used his bulky physique and pushed against her with a massive bump, attempting to take her off track. Hooley stood strong but lost some ground as the action depleted her stamina. Now falling behind, she began to grow tired, and memories flashed through her head of the massive winter storm she fought against when her mother left her. Her memories changed to Kiffy rescuing her and nestling her in his arms to keep her warm.

Then something quite mysterious happened– the light purple inside her ears began to glow, and a few strands of her hair morphed from white to dark grey. She suddenly felt stronger and faster, her tiredness substituted with energy, and she began regaining lost ground. She was now slightly behind the wolverine, and they ran past the gate line at full speed to their drop off points. The roaring crowd shook the coliseum as they approached. If Hooley were to win, she would have to take evasive action immediately. Hooley bent her hind legs and jumped over the wolverine, dropping her final catch into the cage just before he could. The fourth and final pennant dropped from the tally keeper's rod and hung low to the ground.

Bolo's jaw dropped at the realization that he was no longer champion. Kiffy looked down at Hooley with great excitement but became alarmed at the purple glow of her ear canals and the dark grey of her hair. The strands then turned back to white, and the purple glow diminished. He made eye contact with Nicholas and Lízabet, wondering if they or anyone else had seen what he had. Nicholas gazed back and forth between him and Hooley, puzzled at the sight.

Kiffy's thoughts on the mysterious morph were distracted by the cheers, applause, and recognition of the crowd. Gasper shouted, "We have a new champion– Kiffy and his fox, Hooley! Kiffy you may present your winner with the prize." In the center of the arena, a magical pedestal rose from the ground, displaying a winning medal. It was shiny gold with the words "Champion Tracker of Goodness" etched on its surface and was attached to a wide red ribbon.

Nicholas smiled as he looked about the mountainous Arena of the Frozen Demilune. He could sense a happiness and goodness among the men, women, and children attending the 25th annual event. Heartfelt emotion filled him as he observed the companionship Kiffy had for his Hooley. Kiffy hung the winning medal on her neck, then grabbed his huntress and raised her high above his shoulder. Fans hurrahed and shouted her name. "Hooley! Hooley! Hooley!" Her blue eyes watched the crowd as they accepted her as their new champion. The abandoned fox that once almost died as a kit had earned her winning victory. Today was the day... today was HER day.

Fog of the Embedded

The *Silver Bell of Trepidare* swooped back to forth, forth to back. The sparkling waist and sound bow rung loudly, as the red clapper struck one side, then the other. Alerting the vicinity of the stronghold, the bell's chime blended with conflicted voices from outside. The mixture of noises interrupted the sleep of Nicholas. Leaving the warmth of his bed, Nicholas peeked from his bedroom chamber's window at the thick fog that formed a dome over Degomble. The magical lanterns, attached to each dwelling, shed little to no ambient light on the outer walkways. The lanterns could not out-perform the fog or the frozen glowing rime that attached to each dwelling's foundation. An undetermined voice came from outside "The lying of the purple rime is vast tonight; it glows immensely!"

Putting on the arctic garments and clothing Kiffy had provided, Nicholas merged outside. Abrupt and slight barks along with questionable voices continued. Though his vision was challenged by the murky visibility, he counted four human figures in deep conversation. To the left of the group was a person standing on a sleek sledger with four wolves. "That must be Kiffy," Nicholas thought. As he got closer, he realized that two of the four were Norrick and Lízabet.

The third person was harder to recognize because of his heavy armor, but he determined that it was the commander, Quilo Serdar, whom he had met at the coliseum. The armor reminded Nicholas of a Roman Centurion, but it was more intricate and adapted to the polar environment. On his head he wore a helm with a padded hood and a tall, black-furred plume that flowed from front to back. Both shoulder plates of his metal cuirass- which was overlaid by a warm rectangular cloak- were made of skulls with sharp teeth that looked to be from a large animal or creature. His gauntlets and greaves were of the same metal, with the same pointy teeth riveted to the material.

The fourth and final man he did not know. "Come to join our evenin' of ruckus, Undertow?" the stranger asked Nicholas.

"Nicholas, meet Arvel, our town grumbler," Kiffy teased as he introduced the two.

The commander, interrupting Kiffy, questioned Norrick. "Malificus, how shall we proceed?"

Arvel quickly intervened. "I propose we drink a few mugs of noggin' and hibernate until this solstice is over."

Quilo Serdar scowled at Arvel, then looked back to Norrick for further observation. Discussions among the group continued with conflicted and opposing views of what strategies to choose. Norrick did not answer quickly to the commander but instead took time to observe the scene of the fog and the glowing purple rime. Throughout the town, the frozen rime formed and attached itself to many surrounding solid objects. Its density and illumination identified surrounding evil. The fog and its thickness provided a secondary identification. Norrick spoke softly to himself, as worry and caution reached deep within him. "No wind, no blizzard, the fog is thick... the hoarfrost and hard rime scatters. It is much too calm."

Norrick turned to the group with a forceful and direct instruction. "Arvel, prepare for battle! Commander, equip and form your battalion! We will proceed to the *Cave of Palisade*. Kiffy- you and your wolves re-direct the enemy!" He then turned his attention to Lízabet. He did not provide her instruction, but raised his eyebrows in an unspoken question, waiting for her response on assisting. As he waited, Lízabet slowly shook her head and Norrick frowned with a light annoyed sigh. "Very well! Please attend to the needs of the people within our borough." The rest of the surrounding party looked perplexed at the communication between her and Norrick.

The legendary Cave of Palisade was known historically for its battles and monumental structure. The main entrance was framed and carved by a massive, crystallized archway, followed by a temple entrance hall of waved icy architecture. The roof above hung long, sharp icicles with the length of five men. When hit by the day's sunlight, the cave reflected a beautiful hue of blue and turquoise, changing to a pitted gray at night. Within its deepest formation was a cardiac system of tunnels. Myths proclaimed that inside the heart of the cave, magical weaponry and treasure existed. Few attempted to challenge the cave's central labyrinth, and those that challenged never returned to Degomble.

In battle, the walls of the cave provided a barrier for most embedded enemy attacks. Such tactical plans eliminated attacks from above, from behind, or from the side. Fighters in battle could focus on a full–frontal defense within its entrance, the strategy most often chosen by the commander. The primary intention was to rely on the Cave of Palisade to sway incoming enemy onslaught from the residents of Degomble.

Quilo Serdar yelled abrupt commands. "Brigade! Head out! First half two hands, two swords. Other half arrows and bow strings! Take defensive formation on the way!"

The battalion was well–equipped with proper arctic armor, including cleated sabatons, and appropriate weaponry for battle. The cleated sabatons had bindings and decking that provided leverage, keeping the battalion above the snow, instead of knee-deep while trying to swing a weapon or fire an arrow. Although ample weaponry and strategic options were available, the commander chose dual wielding and bows as tactic for this campaign. Nicholas, watching all the actions being taken, felt confused and helpless. Norrick clapped a hand on Nicholas' shoulder. "Nicholas, can you help us?"

Still looking unsettled, Nicholas replied "Yes, how can I help?"

"Good! Come with us and carry this small satchel. Keep it closed and do not open it until instructed, understood?"

"Yes, understood," Nicholas replied.

With a snap of his fingers, Norrick voiced off a quick magic chant "Odos." Throughout Degomble, a sparkling gold glitter salted the dwellings, disappearing as it landed on each structure of soldiers off-shift and others of the militia that resided behind locked doors. Although Norrick never explained his ancient chant to anybody, it was said that the magic provided a protective barrier, an unattractive scent that only embedded evil could smell. Utilizing the chant and the Cave of Palisade, they swayed the embedded evil from Degomble, protecting those that remained in the vicinity, but also reducing damage to the stronghold itself. Norrick's abilities were unexplained but expected, since he was known as a *Primordial Malificus of Winter Solstice.*

Most of the group, including the commander and Arvel, began to proceed by foot to the Cave of Palisade. Kiffy whistled then yelled command. "Booth, Eucera!" The stout musk oxen appeared, ready and armored, equipped in metal braided chain mail that glimmered in metallic green and red. A white qiviut saddle blanket covered the armor, containing a large violet flower embroidered into the wool. Across their backs lay their leather saddles, equipped again for mounting. Kiffy shouted "Forma hele!" and both oxen lay down low, ready for transport. He nodded to Nicholas with a smirk. "You know the practice."

Nicholas nodded back and grabbed the long single strap attached to the satchel, placing it on his shoulder. He jumped, startled, at the sound of grunts and snorts coming from inside the satchel. He looked down at the leather pouch beside his waist, where a gold glowing aura bled through the creases of the closed lid as if the sun itself were trying to escape. Nicholas looked up at Norrick with a look of disbelief and astonishment. Mounted to Booth, Norrick smiled down at Nicholas. "Keep it closed until instructed."

The calm maintained well within Degomble but contained a sense of eeriness. Waiting with anticipation as thick as the fog, Kiffy and his wolves took position. The temperature had dropped significantly from the fog, and he and his wolves exhaled vapor that looked like fire-breathing dragons releasing smoke. Ready to run and pull, the wolves barked with excitement- although they sensed danger, it was also a time to play, a time to exercise. Kiffy commanded from the blitzkrieg sledger, "Easy, easy, quiet." The calm, still maintaining its quiet eeriness, created more anticipation. Kiffy continued to eye the parameter in several directions for signs of attack. Another small bark, followed by a steady growl, came from Ohen. "Stay calm, Ohen," Kiffy again commanded with a slight whisper.

Through the dense fog, illuminated by the glowing of the rime, appeared a set of sharp, drooling fangs below two purple glowing eyes, followed by a long drooping tongue, which distinguished into an embedded hound that growled and snarled. As it crept closer, all of Kiffy's wolves were showing teeth and growling back at the approaching enemy, this time not commanded to stay calm or quiet.

As Kiffy focused on the creature, several purple pupils appeared in the background and formed into a vast pack of hounds that edged closer, then closer, preparing to attack. Another strong growl from the pack, followed by a harping howl, was clearly a signal to take action. Full forward momentum of the hounds indicated that the sledger and wolves had become the target. Kiffy, with a scowl, focused on the quick movement of attack. "Oh boy! Here we go, Bech– you ready?" Bech replied with barks of approval.

"Let's see how fast you slobbering slops really are!"

Kiffy gave a stern yank of the reins as adrenaline filled the wolves. "Bech! Cele Huit!" The harness attached to Bech stretched tight as his body produced immense strength and pull. Since he was the lead wolf, his actions provided leadership and direction to Ohen, Marriam, and Lillian, and the working combination of the four turned into a fierce forward speed. The racing rivalry had begun: wolves versus embedded hounds. A safe distance from the town began to develop as they made their way to the cave. The rails of Arvel's well-built blitzkreig sledger glided across the snow with ease, leaving an exhaust of white flurry behind it. Kiffy periodically took glances backward, ensuring that the attacking enemy was being persuaded away from the sector of Degomble. Periodically a hound or two strayed from the pack intending to attack the town's dwellings, but with a sniff and an unpleasant sneeze, they were repulsed and rejoined the chase– the foul smell of Norrick's enchantment was working. How would Kiffy know which way to go, especially with such little visibility? This answer was simple- his four comrades. As if by second nature, they knew the direction to go whether the sun shone brightly or it was embedded fog in the black of night.

The leading hound of the pack showed competitive speed as he caught up to the sledger. Aligned to the wolves, Marriam yelped as the embedded hound slashed at her ear. In response to the danger, the wolves increased their pace and the hound fell back, lining up to Kiffy and the back end of sledger. Wielding his long, jagged dagger and taking attacking position, Kiffy stared down at the evil glowing eyes of the enemy and, with a battle–cry, stabbed at its flesh, taking its life. The attack transformed the hound into a shatter of frozen particles, which confirmed its demise. Kiffy glanced up as more embedded hounds approached. Two more, at full speed, caught up to the left side of the sledger, fully determined to put harm to the wolves.

"Nope- you're not getting by this time!"

Kiffy quickly yelled command to the wolves, "Hyzer huit!" The four complied, sharply shifting direction to the right, and the sledger reacted with a left skid, swiping the hounds off their feet. The impact caused the hounds to roll, followed again by a deathly shatter of frozen particles. "Good job, group! Almost there! Slack gash!"

Even as blood dripped from her ear and stained the snow, Marriam did not reduce her ambition and kept up with her fellow wolves with little resistance- she was an extremely fast wolf with much stamina upon her four legs. The gap of distance between them and the prowling hounds had increased again. Kiffy kept focus as he and his team neared the archway to the Cave of Palisade and continued various attacks with his war-hammer and lengthy dagger as the hounds approached. His role was to keep them away from the wolves at all times. If his friends were to be killed, they would not reach the others, and his mission to sway would result in failure.

Three hounds appeared on his right side, but the high speed of the sledger re-positioned the hounds directly behind him. The sledger went from intense forward speed to a dead skidding stop as they reached the legendary cave, and with a last-minute determination, the three hounds leapt in mid-air in hopes of killing their target. Kiffy quickly looked behind him as a great sword swung across the approaching hounds, beheading all three of them with a slash. More frozen particles formed, then disappeared.

"Thought yer wolves were fast?!" Arvel mocked.

Grinning back, Kiffy gave a nod of respect to Arvel for his great sword and the life-saving action. "Enemies delivered as requested."

"Be on the ready! More incoming!" Norrick interrupted.

The commander jolted in with commands. "First battalion, align the archway! Seven and seven! Second and third battalion, prepare for support in the entrance cavity!" Swordfighters and archers took to the frontline, nearly staged shoulder-to-shoulder in proximity. From one side to the other, the mouth of large archway was walled with the first defensive battalion. The front row consisted of fourteen fighters- seven dual wielders and seven archers. Behind the fourteen were the second and third groups of the battalion. In the middle of the first row of defenders stood Kiffy, Arvel, and Quilo Serdar of the frontline, ready with weapons in hand. Inside the cave's entrance cavity, Norrick and Nicholas sat upon Booth and Eucera, supported by the second and third battalions. Kiffy's courageous and speedy wolves were given rest at the back of the cave, having completed the job of enemy delivery. Although tired from the race, they could attempt to defend themselves if need be.

With tactics formulated, four packs of hounds faded into the scene out of the evil fog. Each pack contained seven to twelve embedded hounds. With purple eyes of fury, they took to full running strides, howling and snarling as they approached the archway entrance, which was the new pronounced target. Bow strings whipped and arrows flew silently into the fog, piercing the flesh of the hounds with a loud thud. More hounds footed fiercely into the entrance, avoiding the arrows but instead meeting the slash of the dual swords of each swordfighter. The swords slashed each hound one by one and more traveling arrows bulleted by in support. More yelps came from the hounds as each was destroyed in a shatter of ice particles.

After several minutes of successful defense, the attack of the embedded creatures began to slow, then stopped. All went quiet and a calm developed among the weary combatants. Up to this point, the battalion and its legion had held up the frontline well. It seemed to be a victory, and some individuals began to cheer for the great accomplishment. But was victory certain? The calm remained, but so did the eerie and evil fog. Observing this, Norrick expressed uneasiness to Nicholas. "The fog thickens to a dangerous level."

"What does that mean?" asked Nicholas.

"That we must fight blind," Norrick replied.

"What about the glow of the rime– will that help us?"

Norrick shook his head. "The rime merely indicates presence of the embedded evil; it does not help sight. If it was victory, the fog would be thinned and the rime reduced. The battle continues. We must wait until the right moment."

"The right moment?"

"Yes, Nicholas, that moment is where you come in."

Nicholas showed the same astonishment that he had when he'd received the mysterious satchel holding contents as bright as the sun. What role could a foreigner from Patara do in such a battle as this?

Fighters waited in position as the deceptive calm continued. Arvel, Kiffy, and Quilo Serdar eyed one another in anticipation and worry as the fog thickened. The condition changed dramatically as another snarling and growling hound attacked, throwing an archer onto his back. The commander, who was standing next to him, swung his great axe with intensity to save his fellow soldier. Another hound leapt into the commander, his head bouncing off the armor, and Quilo returned the attempted assault in full. More hounds bluntly attacked out of nowhere, taking advantage of the extremely limited visibility. The accuracy and readiness of the frontline went from successful to null, and several frontline archers and sword fighters now lay on the ground either from injury or death. Arrows flew by but often missed, as did the attempted attacks of the dual sword fighters. Fighting blind reduced all advantage to near impossibility.

The second and third battalions covered as hounds broke through the primary line, but they too were facing the same limits and inaccuracy. Two hounds plunged toward Kiffy and Arvel, and Kiffy's two-headed hammer met the upper back of the leaping hound, crushing its spine into ice particles. The hound pursuing Arvel made contact and dug its fangs into his shoulder. With a primal yell, Arvel grabbed the hound's neck and threw it to the ground, where it lay flat on its back with its legs in the air. Arvel, howling in rage, took a stab at its heart with his great sword.

"Nothing like bathing in hound drool, eh?" Kiffy remarked. Arvel swung his great sword into two more approaching hounds, annihilating both of them within milliseconds. Blood flowed from Arvel's injured shoulder and stained his armor.

The enemy, now at an advantage, was making its way farther into the cave. More supportive battalions were failing and falling to the ground, some with deep teeth injuries from the sharp jaws of the hounds. Arvel, Kiffy, and the commander, though experienced and seasoned fighters, began to grow weak and overwhelmed.

Norrick focused on Nicholas. "Nicholas! Now's the moment! Open the satchel!" Nicholas looked down at the glowing aura as he located the latch, then opened the lid and released the questionable contents of the satchel. The mouth of the cave suddenly glowed with an enormous, blinding golden light that stretched out to the field of embedded hounds, then transformed into a massive herd of magical caribous. Blazing a golden hue, they snorted and grunted. Their hooves drummed as they took full stride across the outer field, golden glitter trailing behind them. With their heads pointed down, they sliced through the vast number of hounds, and the sound of clanking antlers occurred as they made forceful and immense contact with the enemy's flesh. A death storm of massacred hounds created acres of iced particle dusting. The massive herd of caribou soon depleted and disappeared as if they were never there. The golden hue dissipated and the surrounding environment turned once again dark. The only light left was from the torches inside the cave.

The dangerous fog of the embedded that had taken over was now fading, then gone completely. The rime and its purple illumination– gone. Weary and tired, the community's defenders stood in awe. The commander looked down at his hands, which were covered in icy debris, then looked up at the stars in the sky that shone brightly above. Trying to catch his breath, he slowly walked out to the field to confirm that the battle was over, then turned, giving a Salute of Degomble to his fellow combatants. All who were standing returned the salute with respect. Quilo Serdar raised his great axe. A shout of cold vapor came from his mouth. "Victory to Degomble!"

The Interglacial Armor and the Healer's Hesitation

The morning's weather consisted of beautiful clear skies, completely opposite to the thick embedded fog that had persisted the night before. The village dwellings that were once covered in evil rime were now painted with natural tones of yellow and orange from the sunrise. A calm but extremely cold breeze sung through the alleyways of the town, decreasing the temperature significantly. The sway of the Bell of Trepidare stood at a standstill as did the outer aisles. Only a few residents walked amongst the stronghold's walkways since most stayed to their homes, putting their usual inner-community roles on hold. When evil events of the embedded occurred, the following day was observed for rest and restoration for those that risked their lives in battle to defend the town.

Nicholas woke from his bed chamber once again. He had slept some after the event, but not very well or for very long. The anxiety and adrenaline he had developed during the battle of the embedded evil had not reduced much. The events and the majestic caribou that destroyed hundreds of embedded hounds still captivated his mind. His thoughts were interrupted by memories of being a young lad who was regularly involved with the good-natured activities that his parents provided. Nonna and Theopanes were consistently benevolent in providing help to others, such as checking in on fellow neighbors and families in Patara. Periodically, they would join Nicholas' uncle in other sectors of Myra. Emotion gripped Nicholas, as he was still missing them and mourning the sickness that taken their lives. Being overtired made it easier to fall into this sadness, but a positive sentiment formed as he thought about the respect people had for his folks, and the thoughtful support they provided everyone.

Suddenly, he thought, "Why not go around and check on fellow townsfolk?" It would also help him get to know the people better. Leaving his guest sanction, he headed to Kiffy's front door, hearing a bark from the wolves inside.

"Quiet! Bech! Move away from the door!" Nicholas laughed as Kiffy opened the top portion of his two-piece entry door, keeping the bottom section closed so the wolves would not sneak out. "Hello, Nicholas. Good morrow to you."

"Good morrow Kiffy, checking on your wellness?"

"Other than feeling like I drank fifty mugs of oggin', I'm well, and you, Nicholas?"

"Aweary but well, thank you. Thought I would check on the fellow residents. Perhaps Norrick and Lízabet next."

"They will find fondness in your kind gesture," Kiffy responded. "I plan to visit them also. Marriam's ear is in need of aid."

"You will be taking Marriam to Norrick and Lízabet's abode?" Nicholas asked, confused.

"Correct, perhaps we will join in visit there? A couple quick tasks require my completion first, including feeding Booth and Eucera."

"Can I assist in feeding them?" Nicholas asked.

Kiffy grinned at the offer. "You will be their new best ally. Moss and lichens are in the feeding bin next to their parrock."

Nicholas took to feeding the two musk ox. As instructed, he grabbed the required feed from the bin that Kiffy indicated. As Nicholas threw the moss lichens into the trough, Booth and Eucera, who had been resting in their parrock, noticed his efforts and showed appreciation as they closely approached their morning's breakfast. He watched as they enjoyed their given meal, remembering the support they had provided him and Norrick the night before. "Probably earned your keep after last night, eh? I appreciate the ride Eucera; I would imagine Norrick appreciates you too, Booth."

Next to the parrock were two wooden sledgers with forged metal rails, finely crafted and named by the artificer himself. One was an envoy sledger which was used for carrying supplies and goods. It had a wider and bulkier base, was more universal for long-distant traveling, and adapted better to various ground conditions. The other, a blitzkrieg sledger, was built with shorter rails and had a more streamlined design. With quick, snappy, and high-speed dynamics, it was suitable for battle or for swaying away embedded evil as Kiffy had the night before.

As Nicholas left Kiffy's abode, the arctic's cold temperatures began to bite down on his face and nose, the chilled pain upon his skin like invisible insects with pincers of ice feeding on his cheek bones. As he headed toward his destination, he heard hammering and grinding coming from Arvel's residence atop the upper hill, a homestead that sat high above Degomble.

"Almost forgot Arvel," he thought. "Let's give him a visit on the way." Arvel was known as the town's artificer and maintained a reputation of wielding a weapon or holding a crafting tool upon his human hands. He approached the front door of the workshop, a door that hung a wooden sign "Ye Olde Warmonger." He gave a couple taps, but, when no answer occurred, realized the noise of Arvel working most likely blocked the sound of his knocking. He slowly opened the door and peeked in at Arvel forging a piece of glowing red-hot metal, which sparked as he hit it and sizzled as he dipped it into a water basin. He was favoring his bandaged left shoulder that was bitten by the hound in battle. Nicholas tried to pull attention from

Arvel between the thundering bangs and the clanks, but his full concentration on his work did not allow him to notice Nicholas' presence.

"Arvel? Hello there!" Still no response came from Arvel. Nicholas tapped the artificer on the shoulder. His vision quickly switched to a view of the ceiling as the action chosen resulted in him lying flat on his back. His breath suddenly felt tight as a small dagger leaned against his throat, almost deep enough to puncture through his skin.

Arvel quickly recognized the visitor. "Ocean drowned boy?! What the hell brings ya here?" He removed the blade from Nicholas' throat.

Nicholas recomposed himself on the ground. "Che… checking on your well-being, Arvel," he wheezed.

Arvel followed with a deep chuckle. "Well bein'? I would question yer well-bein' lyin' on yer back." Arvel locked forearms with Nicholas and helped him up.

"Thank you!" Nicholas brushed himself off from the floor's debris. "How fare you after last night?"

"Meh! There are bad days and there are worse 'uns." Arvel sheathed his dagger and wiped the sweat that dripped from his forehead as it created trails down his dirty face. His mustache and braided sparrow beard were stained black and brown from the forgery work. He threw a questioning glance at Nicholas.

"Yer face is as red as my smelter, boy! Where be yer gaiter and warmth necklace?"

Nicholas touched his cheek and noticed that his skin was blistering from bites the cold had taken. "These are the garments that Kiffy gave me when I first appeared in Degomble."

"That'll learn ya for relyin' on Kiffy for anything." Arvel smirked.

Nicholas was amazed as he began to examine the contents of Arvel's workshop and living quarters. His estate consisted of many wooden hand-crafted items including chairs, tables, shelves, and storage counters. Tools and various crafting materials scattered throughout the vicinity of four rooms, the front sector providing stations for blacksmithing including a smelter, anvil, and stone grinding wheel. Next to the anvil was a rack where Arvel's greatsword rested, which Nicholas recognized from last evening's battle at the legendary cave. The entrance chamber contained a small dining area with a handcrafted table and chairs. Adjoined was a room set up for woodworking, with crafted furniture and other various wood projects, and a sleeping chamber with a bed.

Nicholas' overview of Arvel's home became distracted by a long, chambered fourth and final room. From the view of the front quarter, he saw an abundance of armor and weaponry which stood in its vestibule. Noting Nicholas' curiosity, Arvel nodded his approval. "Yeah, yeah- go ahead!"

Nicholas entered the room and gazed in awe at the various weapons that were stored upon racks and various sized shields that hung from the walls. A lineup of armor sets was displayed amongst the equipment on stands, pieces that he had never seen before. His concentration of the various weaponry and armor shifted to the stairway heading downward, and Nicholas descended, following the bright light that shone from the room below. In the under-structured catacomb sat an interglacial set which stood out against all the other equipment in the room, shimmering with a bright glitter of golden sparkle as if the sun were shining upon it directly. The components of the primordial armor looked to be of a hardened material, but not of a natural steel or metal. Each piece was mystically crafted with gold icy scales that pointed downward, and their sharp crystallized tips dripped water, but mysteriously did not melt or create droplets on the floor. Tied to the armor was an outer arctic-rated garment: a long-hooded cloak, gleaming a rich shiny red color and trimmed in a white fur. Nicholas questioned himself as to what kind of animal would have such a color in fur, then thought about the Roman Empire army that passed through the region of Lycia from time to time. They equipped the finest of weapons and armor from head to toe, but nothing that looked close to the primordial piece displayed in this room.

Nicholas reached out his hand to feel the cloak and pelerine's material, then spoke out to himself. "Amazing... quite a world these folks live in."

"Chaff! That's all that this stuff is, boy... chaff!" Nicholas jumped, startled, as Arvel spoke from behind him.

"Here! Take this, yull need it out there in tha' nasty cold." Arvel handed him a crafted gaiter and a necklace, its string made of sturdy leather, and a trinket. Nicholas received both items gracefully, attaching the necklace to his neck and the gaiter to his face. Both fit perfectly.

"Thank you, Arvel."

"Now you can't say I never gave ya nothin'," Arvel quipped.

After quite a visitation with Arvel, Nicholas proceeded to visit Norrick and Lízabet. As he approached the front door of their home, he crossed paths with Kiffy and his injured wolf Marriam.

"Greetings, Nicholas– we meet again, I see."

"Hello Kiffy, hello Marriam," Nicholas responded.

They both approached the estate. The front of the abode contained large windows embedded into its walls. In contrast to many of the dwellings in Degomble that consisted of wood structures, Norrick's and Lízabet's estate was built of sturdy stone. Within the front chamber and recessed in the entry were two large double wooden doors. On the top center of each was the *Emblem of Goodness* engraved into the wood. Kiffy knocked, while Marriam below helped scratch at the door.

Kiffy looked down at Marriam. "If you think Lízabet is giving you a treat today, you're sadly mistaken."

Norrick answered the door. "Good morrow Kiffy, greetings Nicholas. Please enter." The two went inside, Marriam following closely behind.

"Nicholas… Kiffy, please sit."

"Thanks, Norrick, however I seek Lízabet's assistance for Marriam's ear."

Norick looked down at Marriam and her injured ear. "Ah, a courageous wolf indeed. Lízabet is in the recovery quarter attending to a few injured and infected soldiers."

Nicholas glanced at the room directly right of the foyer as Kiffy and Marriam proceeded to meet with Lízabet in a recovery area where a few fighters lay scarred and injured from the battle. He could see that Norrick's granddaughter was aiding their wounds. As he peered more sharply inside the recovery chamber, a wounded soldier voiced his agony. The soldier turned his head to look at Nicholas, and a spooked feeling approached Nicholas when he realized that the eyes of the soldier had a purple glow. A bright golden gleam flooded the room, blinding Nicholas and distorting his view.

A hand clapped Nicholas' shoulder, distracting him. "Would you like to sit with me?" asked Norrick.

"Yes, thank you," Nicholas responded, inwardly questioning what he just saw. Perhaps it was only a hallucination created from last night's experience. Norrick and his guest proceeded to the main living chamber of the sizeable house. A crackling fire was ignited, warming the front portion of the estate. Both Nicholas and Norrick took to conversation, sitting on two large chairs in front of the hearth.

"What brings you to our estate on this day of recovery?" Norrick asked.

"I've come to check on the well-being of others including yourself and Lízabet."

"Much obliged; we fare well, considering. And you, foreigner?"

Nicholas replied, "The same, but quite mesmerized by the events experienced last evening."

Norrick nodded in understanding. "Yes, the season of winter solstice brings on much evil, more so than other portions of the year. The followers of this diabolic evil grow strong. Degomble and its residents stand together to take on the evil that conflicts with our survival. We prepare throughout the year to be ready for this season and the events that occur."

Nicholas began to reflect on the battle and the soldiers that contributed. He thought of Arvel, Kiffy, and the commander that stood with their fellow combatants on the front line. He deeply wanted to ask about the mysterious release of the majestic caribou that shattered many embedded hounds into ice particles. How was it possible that such a powerful magic could exist? He questioned the unique armor which stood in the downstairs under-structure of Arvel's home. His thoughts were interrupted by questions from Norrick.

"Who have you visited today, Nicholas?"

"Kiffy and Arvel so far. I hope to visit and get to know others around Degomble."

"Ah, Arvel. Was hard at work, I would presume?"

"Yes, he was. He greeted me quite aggressively."

Norrick laughed, not surprised. "I shall not pry on to how he greeted you. Arvel is quite an independent individual; he prefers to work and live alone. He usually does not take agenda to speak with others, and if he does it is usually business only. His vocal cords may release words of negativity and meanness on most days, but inside, this man has a fluent heart of kindness. We would not sustain in this community without the ability and skills Arvel provides to us." Nicholas could not help but agree, remembering Arvel's skills in battle and the craftsmanship displayed at his home.

Nicholas again became distracted as he heard Marriam yelp from the recovery room. He turned his attention to the room, where another gleam of golden light rose, then faded away. He heard Lízabet's voice. "It's okay Marriam; you shall begin feeling better now."

He turned back to his conversation with Norrick. "You seem to have a strong community willing to do what it takes to defend Degomble."

"Yes... yes, we do. Everyone within our stronghold takes a contributing role so that we can survive. Do such evil circumstances occur in your world, Nicholas?"

"Yes, of course. We face conflicts and challenges every day. Many of our lands suffer famine, hunger, disease... even death. War develops amongst men that disagree or strive to take over other lands, which can be taken by a bloodied tip of a sword. The blades of weapons clash and meet one another in many duels. I must say, however, that we do not face such a majestical evil as you and your society see here in Degomble. But in parallel, we alleviate our worries and woes through acts of kindness and giving. We take time to feast together, take days of holiday to recollect on the accomplishments we have made. Norrick... may I ask... do you and your people take time for such festivities?"

A frown appeared within Norrick's full-fledged beard. "Besides our annual hunting event, we do not. Perhaps we should."

Kiffy went to pick up Marriam from the recovery room. "Lízabet, I'm sure Marriam appreciates your healing touch."

Lízabet smiled. "Careful, she has her nose wide open."

Kiffy gave the wolf a quick pat on the back and shook his head with a smirk. "You keep your open nose to yourself, Marriam." He smiled at Lízabet. "A world of additional small Bech doglets running around our land? The thought shutters me inside; that perhaps could be worse than facing twenty embedded creatures." Lízabet laughed, and a warm fondness arose inside Kiffy. He gazed adoringly into her brown eyes, noticing their unique gradient. His profound observance of her was interrupted by the voices of Norrick and Nicholas coming from the other room.

"Well, best to you, Lízabet– I must be going."

"Take care Kiffy, bye Marriam. May you stay healthy."

Both Nicholas' conversation with Norrick and Kiffy's agenda came to an end, and they took to foot outside. Lízabet looked out the window and watched Kiffy and Marriam walk back toward his estate. Norrick approached the other window and stood next to her. He smirked and shook his head as he observed her showing signs of endearment. "Quite cultivated in the animals of our frozen land, is he not?"

Lízabet agreed with a smile but kept her eye on Kiffy. She did not provide a vocal response.

"My dear?" Norrick asked, waving a hand in front of his granddaughter's face. "Lízabet?"

"Ye... yes?" She shook her thoughts from Kiffy and focused on Norrick.

"Your presence at the Cave of Palisade would have provided great value last evening. Many were injured and risked their lives to protect our commonwealth."

"I know, Grandfather; I am not yet ready in my practice. I fear to undertake my ability too early, as I fear I will fail them."

Norrick nodded and stroked his beard before replying. The cold breeze tapped upon the window as he glanced out at the ghostly silence of Degomble.

"Fear... yes, fear..." Norrick's thoughts deepened. "I believe we all must soon outflank our fears with vigilance. We soon must be ready– we soon must prepare. There may be great meaning to the new visitor showing up to our town."

"Nicholas?" Lízabet asked.

"Yes, I'm uncertain, but I feel Nicholas has a pivotal role to the conflicts we face against the embedded evil and the great *Bacillus of Winter Solstice* that controls them."

"Why do you feel this way, Grandfather?"

"Not just anyone can open a *Satchel of the Caribou*– it requires blood borne of a primordial ascendant."

The Ethereal Carolers

The logged cabin loomed in front of a vast taiga of pine, spruce, and birch trees, its long stack releasing an abundance of smoke from the fireplace inside. The gatekeeper waited for the coming of the group. The party, led by Norrick, consisted of Nicholas, Lízabet, Arvel, the commander, and a selection of soldiers from his battalion. Several soldiers equipped with ample armor and weaponry traveled by foot, while others were assigned to drive musk oxen with large leather carriers to be filled with goods and supplies and taken back to Degomble. Quilo Serdar had appointed a secondary commander and an adequate balance of militia to uphold protection in Degomble while they were away, in case of attacks of the embedded evil.

After a long trip south from the rigid northern arctic, they reached the gatekeeper's cabin. Quilo Serdar shouted command to his militia. "Halt and stand position! Allow the oxen time to rest!"

Norrick approached the door of the cabin and knocked. The elderly gatekeeper spoke in a rough voice. "Yes, yes, who is it?! Speak the magistical formula."

Impatiently, Arvel responded, "I'll speak yer useless formula. Open your door or I'll kick it in!"

Norrick quickly intervened. "They do not speak but sing in carol."

The door clicked several times, indicating magical locks being removed, then opened, revealing the man with a hidden face, velvet robe, and a long-tailed stocking cap. It was Gasper from the Arena of the Frozen Demilune.

"Greetings to you, Gasper; can you activate the *Ethereal Carolers?*" Norrick requested.

"Yes... yes... I can..." Gasper answered hoarsely, as his worn old knees rocked and shook, making it difficult for him to stand. Gasper began patting his robe and waist as if he was looking for something. "Now where did I put my *Crutches of Winterstorm?*"

"They are not safely stored in your storage chest?" Norrick suggested.

"Oh, yep, yep, thank you... that they are."

Norrick glanced behind his shoulder at Arvel's aggravated scowl, then shrugged. "Arvel, our ancient ally is growing old, just as you and I are."

"Mukluk!!" Arvel scoffed as he shook his head. "His mind's gettin' as soggy as 'em wet pinecones on the ground!"

"Perhaps, but a pinecone is much more brittle when dry," Norrick argued.

Lízabet, stifling a grin, eyed Arvel. "Does my grandfather's philosophy silence your tongue?" she quipped. Arvel did not respond but returned her gaze peevishly.

Inside Gasper's residence shone a flash of golden light, followed by more clicks, confirming that the storage chest was now unlocked. With empty hands, he rejoined the group outside. "Gasper... you still must retrieve it from the chest," Norrick instructed wearily.

Nicholas observed Arvel's face, which was still irritated. As he was a newcomer, he was trying not to smile or snicker, since he preferred not to be on his back with another dagger to his throat.

"Yep... yep... right you are," Gasper replied. He did not go back into his logged home but instead raised his wrinkled hands and snapped his fingers. Nicholas gaped in surprise as two long wooden crutches, white and striped in red, appeared in Gasper's hands. On the top side of each crutch was a large glass sphere with snow falling inside. Two golden straps emerged and wrapped themselves around each arm; Gasper took tight hold as the Crutches of Winterstorm helped support his old, withered body and fragile bones.

Arvel scoffed angrily. "Frack, ol' man! Ya shoulda done that in the first place; what good is a chest to ya?"

Ignoring Arvel's petulant complaints, Gasper simply instructed, "Follow me."

Gasper, a primordial malificus, could determine a specific entrance to the forest and could activate the caroling melody. As the group trailed behind him, he raised his crutches and pointed them at a mass of trees. *"Melovocal!"* he shouted.

Nicholas watched Gasper in disbelief as the snowfall inside each glass sphere changed to a blistering blizzard, then into a glittering spectacle of colors. He jumped, startled, as an ambient choir of men, women, girls, and boys hummed and sang in melody. He looked around, questioning why he could not see the people behind the voices.

Norrick glanced at Nicholas, looking astonished at his reaction. "You... you can hear them... the carolers?"

"Yes, can't we all?"

"No... not many can," Norrick replied, astounded.

Nicholas did not understand what made him different from the others or why he and only a select few could hear the voices. He was seeking answers but would have to wait until the group began traveling through the forest.

Norrick nodded to Gasper. "Thank you, old comrade."

"Yes, yes– wait... for what, may I ask?" Gasper looked confused.

"For activating the Ethereal Carolers," Norrick responded.

"Oh, of course... of course... yep... yep... yep– now let's get you all to Ethereal," Gasper replied.

"That won't be necessary, Gasper; please take today off, I can provide the escort and breach Ethereal's wall. For the sake of goodness." Norrick followed with a respectful Salute of Degomble.

Gasper returned the salute. "Yes, very good Norrick. Yep, yep, for the sake of goodness," he replied in his old, roughened voice and parted ways with the group, returning to his logged home.

The caroler's melody continued as the group and the musk oxen entered the vigorous growth of trees and fallen pine needles. Norrick directed the path forward and from time to time would slow or halt the pace to relocate the sound of the choir. Nicholas came to understand that if they went in the wrong direction the singing voices would weaken but would strengthen if they were on the right path.

For a good length of time the group followed the dreamy melody of the carolers, traveling deep inside the forest's inner sanctum. The melody grew louder and louder as they neared the town known as Ethereal. As one, the carolers hummed a tune of eerie, haunting yet beautiful proportions in variances of high and low tones, tempos, beats, and swings, rising and falling in intensity. The fluffy snow which covered the pines began to diminish, and water started to drip from the needles and leaves.

The frozen sub-soiled path that twisted and turned within the trees transitioned into a soft, muddy trail. Nicholas lost sight as his surroundings became blurry and distorted. He could not see his feet and felt as though he could easily trip or fall forward. Suddenly, the sound of the carolers stopped; Nicholas' eyes cleared, and his feet reappeared on a narrow-cut trail and cliff that overlooked a breathtaking view of Ethereal and a set of twin waterfalls. Nicholas gasped, taken in by the stunning landscape.

"It is fairly common for newcomers to react this way," Norrick remarked with a chuckle. Below was a town and community much different from the northern stronghold; the buildings and dwellings were dressed in moss, pine needles, and leaves, unlike the buildings in Degomble covered in snow, icicles, and frost. The weather was warm and pleasant but still shady and dark from the tall surrounding trees which blocked the natural sunlight.

The twin falls fell from the cliffs high above but did not rapidly plunge downward. Instead, it was a cascade of water that curled, twisted, and swayed side to side, looking like a falling ribbon. As it reached the lower pools, it shredded into pieces and fed a river that flowed throughout the town. It was used as irrigation for farms containing crops of fruits and vegetables that were grown from rich soil. Other plots of land consisted of gated fences and held livestock such as pigs, chickens, cows, and goats.

"I can see you are confused, Nicholas, and I'm sure you have many questions. Allow me to explain where we are," Norrick said. "This is Ethereal. Each one of us has some form of business to attend to here. Many soldiers, including our commander, take time to visit their families; others come to obtain supplies such as food, crops, and logs for their stoves in Degomble– hence why we have brought the musk oxen with stowage."

"These families do not live together?" Nicholas asked.

Norrick explained. "Degomble, although a community and town, is a central stronghold for many malificus, militia, and individuals with mastered skills for battle and war. With the existence of the embedded evil, Degomble is a dangerous zone for children, elderly, and those not seasoned to fight. Many of us stay in Degomble, most having vital roles in protecting them. They depend on us to stay alive and stay safe. We live in Degomble to prevent the embedded evil from coming here and attacking our loved ones."

Norrick further explained that the gatekeeper, Gasper, and the singing carolers protected the townsfolk and made it difficult for the creatures of embedded evil to enter, though from time to time they would stumble into the town, their attacks parried and then annihilated by residents trained to fight or those visiting from Degomble.

1 Curling Ribbon Falls

2 Nicholas's Perfect Rock

3 Union Hall of Goodness

4 Cottensedge Inn

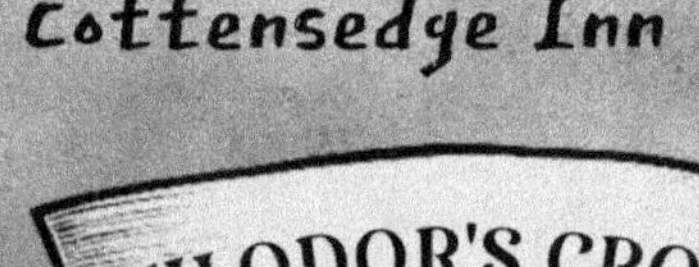

5 Rippin' Ribbon River

6 Serdar Ranch

7 Embedded Forest

8 Embedapist Care Center

9 Cardinals of Joy

10 Feyhandsel's Bastion

ETHEREAL
1
2
3
ATKA'S FLUME
4
5
7
8
9
6
VIOLET'S AGORA
EILODOR'S CROFT
10

Nicholas continued to listen to Norrick, learning a great deal of history about the forested town that they were visiting. Ethereal was a magical province created by the Primordial Ascendants of Winter Solstice, with the intention to provide a livelihood for families, children, and elderly folks. Each day babies were born and those that reached old age passed in peace. Ethereal was divided into three sectors and had an abundance of specialized trades. From where they stood, Nicholas could see an agriculture busy with farmers and ranchers.

"For now, I leave you, Nicholas, so please take time to visit. I myself must restore my supplies of meat and eggs– oh, and I suppose vegetables would be wise, or else Lizabet may yell profane words at her grandfather for not eating enough." Norrick grinned and began to walk away, then quickly turned around. "Also... I urge you to explore behind the waterfall to the west. Behind the Curling Ribbon Falls is a rock shelter, and inside you will find a winged animal with antlers, chiseled from stone. When it appears, utter the word *spanwingora*."

Following instructions, Nicholas headed to the twin falls and, as he neared, caught sight of cathedral–type building with large colored windows. Above its double steel doors, the letters U.H.O.G were etched into wood. The building reminded Nicholas of the cathedral in Myra where his uncle worked and preached. He found himself missing the breakfasts and long conversations they shared together and began feeling worried– would he ever see his uncle again?

Nicholas approached the falls. The sensation of spray that hit his face reminded him of the sea and the beach back home. Behind the west fall was the rock shelter; the fall to the east did not contain an inner cave or shelter but had a solid rocky foundation behind it. As he entered, Nicholas became confused; although he was awestruck by the beauty of the two ribbon-like falls, the shelter did not seem to have significance, nor did it contain the stoned animal that Norrick claimed it would have. He decided to turn back to seek more guidance from Norrick but was distracted by a rumbling sound from behind him. The rocky terrain began to shake, breaking up into small pieces. The dust and debris settled, revealing a stone winged animal with antlers, its head and beak of an eagle and its torso of an owl. Nicholas shook his head and determined that it was time for another sanity check but decided to play along. Remembering the word that Norrick suggested, he spoke to the winged animal *"Spanwingora."*

The stone animal's wings began to rise and span wide. The ground beneath Nicholas crumbled and broke, and he fell into the black hole with a horrified scream. As he descended, a demonic growl rumbled through his surroundings, which were illuminated by millions of glowing purple eyes. It felt as if he was falling for an eternity. Finally, he slowed down, his feet safely meeting a large rocky platform that was lit up by a natural light from above. The purple eyes around him had faded, and the demonic growl was no more.

Directly across from him was an identical platform where a spirited man stood. Below the two platforms was a cumbersome pit of eternal darkness. Nicholas stood staring at the spirit; it mimicked the same staring action in return, and he realized that the man was an exact replica of himself. Frustrated, he rubbed his eyes and face, and the spirit copied Nicholas's actions as if he were mocking him.

Nicholas became enraged. "I don't understand this lunacy! What purpose does this serve? Give me meaning or wake me up from this confusion!"

The mirrored spirit bowed in acceptance of Nicholas's request, then began to animate to an older version of him. The facial features of the spirit were no longer tan and smooth, but rough and coarse. His beard was a dirty grey, flowing down to his chest, and a hat with a bent apex covered his head. Now dressed in a long cloak, the spirit removed the hat and again bowed to Nicholas, as a long cut of grey hair fell to his knees.

The spirit transformed once more into a larger-set man with red cheeks and hair and a beard as white as snow. His attire consisted of a red velvet coat and pants trimmed in white. He also wore a large black belt held up with a golden buckle and black boots on his feet. He smiled at Nicholas and laughed in a hearty and cheerful tone, then set down a giant velvet maroon bag, glimmering with golden glitter and tied on top with a golden string. With gentle eyes he opened his hands, palms up, as if he were presenting the bag to Nicholas. From behind the chuckling man, a tall mystic animal with large red velvet antlers approached.

The cheerful spirit and his accomplice vanished, and Nicholas found himself back in front of the winged animal made of stone. Behind him was the lush sound of the falls, the moisture saturating the back of his neck. The stoned creature closed its wings, and the broken rock began to reassemble itself around it. Nicholas sighed heavily in frustration. He had many questions and was much more bemused than he was before.

The Emblem of Goodness

Union of Goodness

L ittle Urie began to feed her piglet, the runt of the litter, manually nourishing him with a bottle. As the smallest, the piglet found it challenging to suckle due to harsh competition from his larger brothers and sisters. His mother quickly grew empty and often refused him, leaving him in hunger.

"Nice and warm," Urie offered as the piglet began to feed.

Behind Urie, Quilo Serdar removed his armored helmet from his head. "Hello, my little keeper of the drift."

"Father!" Urie shouted in surprise as she turned to him with her arms wide open. In her excitement she dropped the piglet's bottle, and the piglet began snorting in confusion, trying to suckle the bottle from the ground.

As Quilo Serdar was a tall man, he took to one knee to hug his daughter properly. "How's our runt fighter?" he asked.

"He is growing! I feed him only four times a day now!" Urie replied.

"Because of you, he will grow to be the leader of the boars," Quilo encouraged. Still on one knee, he felt the gentle touch of his wife's hand upon his shoulder blade. "Urie dear, your piglet needs attention," she instructed. The piglet was still attempting to get milk from the bottle, pushing it around the drift with his nose.

The commander stood up, grasped his wife, and raised her off the ground. "My wife, how I have missed you!" He set her back down, put his large arms around her waist, and placed a kiss on her soft lips.

"Where is our son– should he not be home by now?"

"Lyman is at the training glade."

"His responsibilities, has he been fulfilling them?"

"Yes, he also trains twice a day, early morning and at sun fall. He worries me; he comes home exhausted and barely eats. He is ambitious and stubborn just like his father."

"Very well, I shall go see him and give him a father's greeting."

The grassy meadow of the glade lay flat under a canopy of pines. Lyman quickly advanced and retreated as he struck random logs with dual splitting axes. He approached a standing log and began to chip and notch it, swinging with overhead, outside, and inside attacks. He observed his footwork, following with proper blocks and defensive postures. Panting with exertion, he tightly gripped the handle of his right axe and flung it at a nearby pine, where it stuck itself into the trunk with loud *thwack!*

Wiping sweat from his brow, Lyman sat on an old stump attempting to catch his breath. A sudden sharp pain pricked the back of his neck and he smiled without turning around. "Hello Father, welcome home."

Quilo removed the sharp point of his battle axe from Lyman's neck and shook his head as he noticed the splitting axe mounted into the pine. "Son, it is difficult to split and make kindling with a dull axe. Worse, your kindling is wet. Have I taught you nothing?"

"A short time in the sun and it shall dry," Lyman retorted as the two shared a strong hug.

Lyman pulled the axe from the tree and equipped it to his waist along with the other splitting axe. He picked up a large felling axe and tossed it to his father. "Here Father, the blade is sharp on this one!"

Quilo ran his finger across the blade and a small line of blood droplets appeared. Teasingly, he flicked the blood in the direction of his son's face. "Good! Perhaps you have finally learned something!"

"How long will you be here in Ethereal?" Lyman asked, smiling.

"Three days– just to obtain food and supplies; we must prepare for another solstice. Your mother told me that you have been training more frequently."

"Yes, Father! I'm ready to leave Ethereal! I wish to fight with you!"

Quilo Serdar did not reply. "Your mother and Urie wait at home; we are overdue to spend time as a family."

After the encounter with the winged animal of stone, Nicholas' chest remained tight, his breaths short. He did not understand the experience and visions he'd had but felt nonetheless that it had been real. He looked down at his feet; they were still standing on the fertile ground of Ethereal. He sat down on a nearby rock, closed his eyes, and listened to the ambient sound of the falls. His chest loosened and his breaths lengthened as the setting mesmerized him.

"The Curling Ribbon Falls... they are a beautiful sight," a familiar voice suddenly spoke.

Startled out of his meditation, Nicholas opened his eyes to Kiffy and Hooley. "Hello, Kiffy. You have come to Ethereal?" he asked.

"Yes, I've arrived late. I'm here to attend this evening's council at the union hall. Norrick wishes for you to join us as well."

Nicholas nodded. "Can... can you also hear the caroler's melody?"

Kiffy reached down and stroked the fox's head. "Not I, friend. Norrick or Gasper are usually the lender of ears, but today is different. My huntress here- she led the way. It is not the carolers she hears but she seems to know the way somehow. Perhaps she sees them, but it is rather a mystery."

Nicholas remained sitting on the rock and stared at the falls, still dazed and bewildered. What did his visit, or rather his vision, mean? This world he was in was amazing and adventurous. Yet he missed Patara, his uncle, and most of all his parents. What of Drusus, his son Otho, and the crew? Were they now consumed by the sea? He hoped deep in his heart that they had been rescued or that *Nonna* had regained balance, her sails returning them home.

Kiffy smiled gently, as if sensing Nicholas' feelings. "I hear you possess similar talents. It appears Hooley is akin to you."

Nicholas looked down at the fox, her ocean–blue eyes staring back at him, and felt sudden warmth from her. Though still striving to find meaning in his venture, he felt calmer when Kiffy and Hooley were near, as if he had known them for many years.

"It is good to see you in Ethereal, Kiffy... you as well, Hooley."

The steel doors were open to the Union Hall of Goodness. Inside its walls was a group known as the Union of Goodness, which was assembled from malificus, warriors, pedagogs, embedapists, and Yuulnavvies.

Yuulnavvies were a race of engineers that focused innovation on defensive strongholds, buildings, and living infrastructure for the people. Although Yuulnavvies were human, they had a distinct appearance with a dwarfish height and posture. Their attire, including hats with ear flaps, was constructed with arctic hare skins and pelts. Their most unique feature was the snow goggles they wore that contained small rectangular holes on each eye, allowing them to see out and in most instance imparting excellent vision and depth perception. However, many others found it very difficult to speak to them, since they were unable to make necessary eye contact. Yuulnavvie newborns began a new life with goggles sewn to their heads, permanently attached as the skin grew over the threads, so not to fall off or be removed. The innovative goggles helped to prevent cnt snow blindness, but also to prevent a more dangerous and permanent ailment- shivering blight. Surrounding the Yuulnavvian city were miles of putrid and decayed sheets of ice, tainted by the Bacillus, and those exposed to the reflecting light felt a sharp pain in their unguarded eyes. But the strain went away– at least for a while. In a few years' time, the strain returned, and permanent blindness followed. Bodies soon turned cold, skin deteriorated, bones turned to ice, and hearts turned green. Those infected grew into tall, haggard, and malignant creatures of the embedded-Encier Giants. With decayed hearts, the diseased beings fed on the laughter of children. By removing amusement from a child's soul, the vulnerable beating organ of the Encier Giants remained healthy. Any child that was invaded in their slumber would wake with no emotional or impulsive urge to laugh or smile. The only way to destroy the mutated giants was to trick them into drinking a tonic– a tonic that would induce them to vomit their blighted hearts from their chests.

Mysteriously, the Yuulnavvian race never suffered from cold temperatures and naturally maintained body warmth. Unlike the southerners, they did not rely upon enchanted accessories such as necklaces, rings, or amulets. With sturdy tolerance, they were able to live in the farthest northern region of the arctic. Those not of the race rarely visited the region, as the severely cold temperatures and ruthless blizzards generally invited blindness, shivering blight, or immediate death.

One of the most revered constructions of the Yuulnavvies was the union building and its hand-crafted hall inside. The stone building's main corridor held a large window overlooking the Curling Ribbon Falls and was furnished with a long oval table, which was crafted from several trees in Ethereal's surrounding forest. Nicholas admired the grain and color combination of different woods blended into its construction– it reminded him of Drusus and his architecture of *Nonna*. In the center of the table was the Emblem of Goodness, this time engraved into the wood. The symbol did not appear to illuminate as it had on the arena's banners.

In the Great Union Hall of Goodness, a plethora of issues including battle tactics, defensive strategies, magic, and most importantly, survival of the people, were discussed, debated, and disputed.

"Disarm your weapons!" two guarding soldiers ordered as more members began to arrive. Whether blade, bow, staff, or shield, all were required to be left outside on a weapon rack mounted to the building. Myths among the primordial ascendants told that the union hall was constructed on top of sanctified ground beneath a buried temple which held old and primitive magic. Any blood spilt inside would tatter the grounds with devastating consequences. Though no one knew if the myths were true or false, it was a rule that was followed for many decades.

"Artificer? You must disarm!" the guards instructed Arvel, blocking the entryway.

"Mukluk!" Arvel scoffed. Instead of placing his great sword on the weapon rack, he stabbed the point into the ground and its long blade began swaying back and forth. "Alright! Hands are empty! Move the hell outta the way or I will deform yer gullets!"

All attending members arrived and the Great Union Hall of Goodness reached its full capacity. Norrick, who was headship of the union, stood at the northern end of the table, his back facing the large window. On the other end was Quilo Serdar. The remaining union members stood around the table in front of their designated throne like-chairs. Handcrafted by the Yuulnavvies, each chair had cushioning made of satin, lined with arctic hare material and dyed in maroon. The tall-backed framing and armrests were constructed with various antlers and dressed in pined garland. The headrest displayed a silver nameplate of each assigned member.

"Commander, you may now secure the doors," Norrick requested.

The commander shouted command as the two soldiers changed their formation to the inner foyer. Behind them, the doors were magically locked tight.

"Union! Let us begin session two hundred and sixty-two," Norrick instructed.

In the middle of the long oval table, a portion of the engraved symbol began to turn clockwise, while the other portion turned counterclockwise. The engraved symbol re-aligned itself, stopped, and began to illuminate in bright colors of evergreen and gold.

All members present sat at their designated spots. Only union members had the ability to sit around the table and give assent. Those that wished to visit or attend meetings but were not union members were provided wooden chairs that ran along the wall; however, they were unable to approve or disapprove of any items. Lízabet, Nicholas, and a few others that Nicholas did not recognize sat as visitors and non-members. They were called strike-breakers and were generally those that intended to become members of the union. Nicholas suspected that many of them, including Lízabet, would soon be initiated.

At the far end of the room an elderly woman sat at her own small table with a golden, sparkled quill in her hand, jotting words on a parchment.

"The old woman, what is her role?" Nicholas asked Lízabet.

"She is a scribe; she records what is discussed during our council."

"Ah, quite interesting," Nicholas replied.

Outside the locked doors of the union hall, Arvel's great sword was still stabbed into the ground, but its long metal blade began to glow with a golden metallic color, disappearing completely shortly after. There was a deep mark left in the ground where the sword's blade had nested.

Norrick began to speak. "We have fought through another long and hard year but have flourished in many ways as well. Our commander has developed stronger forces and defensive tactics. Arvel has built stronger armor and weaponry with his hands. The members Çóalrite and Tensîle have led their people to further advancements in our buildings and strongholds." Çóalrite and Tensîle were leaders of the northern Yuulnavvian race, and members of the union. They visited Ethereal to attend the meetings as much as possible.

"Within this assembly, many of you have contributed vastly to our well-being and I thank you all. We are close to the beating heart of winter, our shortest day– the solstice. The Bacillus of Winter Solstice will grow restless and strong. The embedded evil, which the Bacillus has created, will begin to wake, swayed to attack those that are good."

Norrick released a long, fearful sigh. "I'm afraid that I feel a heavier density of evil this winter. We should expect and prepare for the worst of the Bacillus 'creatures. There may be a waking of many dangerous species… those that we have not encountered in some time."

The members began to whisper among themselves. A member spoke out in question.

"Malificus, why do you feel this way?"

Norrick took a deep breath. "With this fear, I also feel a heavier density of hope." He nodded to Nicholas. "Members, I would like to introduce a visitor. This is Nicholas."

The committee greeted the newcomer, many of them questioning Norrick's introduction. "Is he a member of our union?" a woman of the committee asked.

Norrick replied. "Not yet, but I can only hope we initiate him, as he may play a vital role in our success in reducing the embedded evil... and... I feel he may be the one to end the tyranny of the Bacillus."

Arvel began to choke on his spit. "The... *cough*... ocean... *cough*... drowned boy?! I have yet to see 'im use a sword or a shield... or even magic!" Arvel wielded his great sword and slapped it down on the table in front of Nicholas. "Alright, Undertow! Let's see ya use it."

Norrick shook his head at Arvel's action. The commander rolled his eyes, snatching the great sword from the table.

"We must practice caution, Norrick! Protection is vital to our mankind!" the commander urged. He scowled at Arvel, tossing his great sword back to him. "That includes LEAVING OUR WEAPONS OUTSIDE OUR SACRED HALL!!!"

Arvel responded with a lively smirk and then chanted; the great sword quickly disappeared from his hand.

Kiffy, sitting next to Arvel, leaned in. "Once again... you've toiled with magic and encountered trouble. What shall we do with you, old man?" Arvel simply scoffed in reply.

The commander interrupted. "I WOULD agree with Arvel! What role does Nicholas play? What is his contribution? He should reside in Ethereal, or he endangers us and our families!"

"Yes, you are correct, Commander," Norrick agreed. "His allegiance to us has to be proved, as with any other member or those we recruit." He looked to Nicholas for answers. "Nicholas? Can you answer our fellow council? Why are you here; do you feel you have vital contributions?"

Nicholas frowned and then sighed. "I do not know... I am sorry."

Norrick attempted to help Nicholas. "Members! What I can tell you is that this man has hidden talents. Talents that most of us would not see. He was able to open the Satchel of the Caribou and is able to hear the Ethereal Carolers. How many of us in here can hear the melody?"

A member spoke up. "Only a primordial descendant or those in the bloodline."

"That's correct! Nicholas, can you please tell our members what you thought of the carolers and their melody?"

The room fell silent again, staring at Nicholas. Nicholas looked at the council, then at Norrick. "They had the most beautiful, yet alluring voices I've ever heard. As if they were singing angels."

Several members were astonished, and many still looked disbelieving. The commander slammed his hand on the table. "Malificus, you put too much trust in this foreigner! It is too early!"

Several members of the group began to nod in agreement.

"Perhaps, but may I suggest that Nicholas consult the *Nonesuch?* There may be more to our ocean-found visitor than our eyes can see. If he is not of importance, the Nonesuch will deny divination."

"Then we must decide," the commander replied. "Council! Those that approve to confide in the Nonesuch, provide your assent!"

The room showed no response. Nicholas felt his stomach tighten in knots from the silence, now feeling awkwardness colder than the arctic itself.

Norrick urged, "All! Please consider this man and allow him to find his meaning! If the Nonesuch cannot help him, he can perhaps provide services in Ethereal! All those that approve... provide your assent!"

Nicholas observed as the majority of the union members began clenching their fists. Noise built up in the room as they knocked their fists twice on the oval table and shouted "Ho! Ho! Rah!"

The commander spoke. "Union has approved; we will help Nicholas reach the Nonesuch in hopes of a proceeding divination."

Norrick asked, "Who here among us will escort Nicholas? He will need help." Lízabet began to raise her hand but quickly lowered it.

"Sorry Nicholas, I forgot… they won't allow me to help you; I'm still a strike-breaker and haven't been initiated. I must be careful not to ruin my chances of becoming a member."

"It is okay Lízabet, but I thank you. I would not want to conflict your changes."

Another awkward silence fell until Kiffy finally raised his hand. "I helped rescue this man and will escort him. My animals show fondness of him, and I know my rescue of him was not in vain."

The commander followed. "Union! Those who approve of Kiffy escorting, provide your assent!"

The hall's table thundered with the clenched fists of the members, as they knocked in approval and shouted. "Ho! Ho! Rahhh!"

Three days later…

"Be safe, little drift keeper," the commander uttered as he hugged Urie. He stood up and kissed his wife, then placed his hand upon Lyman's shoulder. "Son, take care of your mother and sister."

"Father... I wish to join you and your militia," Lyman requested.

The commander tried to hold back his emotion and fatherly love. As much as he wanted his son with him, he could not accept. He spoke abruptly. "Not yet- it is not time, son!" He patted Lyman's shoulder compassionately and began to walk away.

Frustrated, Lyman grabbed his father's arm, halting him. "Father, I beg of you! My heart grows restless; I am seasoned! Do not deny me this!"

The commander's arm began to sting from Lyman's stern grip. The strength placed upon him proved that his son had trained long and hard. Deep down inside, he was extremely proud of Lyman, but he could not bear to see him quickly annihilated in the heat of battle, especially in the season of the winter solstice. He needed to first be exposed to smaller battle scenarios. Quilo looked about as the traveling protectors, militia, and townsfolk stood waiting for his reaction. He had to maintain his strict role as commander and follow union regulations, but most importantly- be a responsible father. With matched strength, he swiped Lyman's hand from his arm and spoke firmly.

"Ethereal and Degomble depend on you for logs and kindling! Maintain your role! You are not yet ready; avoid haste!"

Lyman shouted, "I REFUSE TO ACCEPT YOUR DECISION, FA–"

Quilo cut him off. "Being son of a commander does not make you a shoo–in! You must be accepted by the union!" He turned and walked away. Rage grew inside Lyman; he could not accept his father's rejection. He picked up his sharpened felling axe and gripped its handle tight. His eyes grew dark and stormy with hate.

"Not ready? He shall taste my abilities!" Lyman muttered fiercely. He began a dead run toward his father but was quickly knocked flat on his back as a hilt of a sword smashed across his face. Lying on the ground, he spit blood from his mouth. Stunned and aggravated, he attempted to get back up but was stopped by a foot placed on his chest.

"Not smart, Nephew! Yer bein' gomble–brained! Stay on the ground!" Arvel urged.

"Uncle?!" Lyman questioned in surprise, wiping more blood from his face.

From a distance, Nicholas and Kiffy watched the family feud between father, son, and uncle.

"Does Arvel greet everyone in this way?" Nicholas asked.

Kiffy chuckled. "That old toot has the softness of feathers inside. But his many years in battle have turned him rigid and rocky on the outside, and I believe our fickle friend will remain that way."

"Does he have any family in Ethereal?" Nicholas asked.

Kiffy's grin turned to a frown. "Once a wife and son. Unfortunately, they... passed... quite some time ago during the winter solstice... attacked by the embedded evil."

Nicholas nodded. He could understand Arvel's feelings of grief for the loss of those he loved. "How were they attacked?"

"Sorry friend, it is best for Arvel to share that tale. It is not my place."

The conversation quickly switched directions as Norrick and Lízabet approached them. Norrick nodded and gave them a Salute of Degomble, then walked off. Lízabet stopped to converse for a bit longer. "Farewell, Kiffy."

"Farewell, Lízabet. See you sooner than later... errr... see you soon... in... Degom... see you in Degomble?"

Lízabet blushed, then smiled at Kiffy.

"Perhaps much later than sooner, I'm afraid. I am to meet with Gasper; he is to help me finalize my training and help prepare for my initiation into the union," she replied.

Kiffy stared into Lízabet's brown gradient eyes and gave an affectionate Salute of Degomble. "We all have faith in you, Lízabet. You will soon be one of our finest members."

Lízabet smiled again at Kiffy and Nicholas, then placed a kiss on Kiffy's cheek.

Before rejoining her grandfather, she whispered in Kiffy's ear.

"Take care of him; he needs you the most."

The musk oxen were loaded up with supplies, food, and logs, and were well-rested and ready for transport. The protectors and militia approached the difficult moment of departure. Nicholas observed as hugs, kisses, handshakes, and tears were shared among the people, and the children waved farewell to their mothers, their fathers, and their heroes. He felt a deep respect and compassion for the townsfolk of Ethereal and for those leaving. Those departing deeply preferred to stay with their families versus going back to the frigid climate of Degomble. But going back meant a potential of better days and a chance they would someday reunite- indefinitely. They all began to walk the muddy path from which they had entered, and magically vanished, one by one.

Nicholas sighed. "Kiffy... I'm uncertain as to why I'm here, but I must contribute... in some way."

"Of course, friend; I'm here to help. We shall take Norrick's advice and visit the Nonesuch."

"Thank you, Kiffy."

"I have spoken to a house warden, and she will show you your new abode. It's in the northwest sector, *Atka's Flume*. Please rest there awhile. At nightfall we must travel to the *Forest of Primordial Cedars*. For the Nonesuch will only confide in those that visit at night."

Vedettes of Aegis

K iffy reached for his survival rucksack and pulled out a small leather pouch of berries, seeds, and nuts. He gnawed on the mixture as he and Nicholas walked the forest beyond Ethereal. They had started their travels in the early evening and were now approaching sunset. Outside of the warm climate of Ethereal, snow and ice dangled from the branches, creating a contrast of green needles and white frost blended with a painted sky of pink and purple hues.

"This wintry scene is quite captivating," Nicholas proclaimed.

"Yes, this seasonal tide is beautiful and magical, but yet... can have an evil and disastrous nature," Kiffy replied.

Nicholas nodded. He was appreciative of having Kiffy and Hooley nearby. He could sense that Kiffy knew his way through the grand forest. To him, the labyrinth of trees looked as though it met the far ends of the world, and he would surely have lost his way venturing alone.

Kiffy stopped and evaluated the parameter, then threw a few more portions of mix into his mouth and some to the fox at his shin. "Traveling mix?" Kiffy offered Nicholas.

Nicholas accepted. The taste of the mixture was sweet and spicy. A few seeds from his hand dropped to the ground, where white poppies with bright red stripes grew immediately from the frozen soil. Fully bloomed, they made a distinctive but soft *aaachooooo!* sound. The perennials were short-lived as they rapidly withered and died.

Kiffy smirked. "Why sneezing shadblows suddenly bloom is quite a mystery." He saw worry on Nicholas' face and chuckled. "Worry not, friend, the seeds will not germinate in your stomach. But be warned- never eat the flower petals. Those that do will sneeze and then fall asleep for several days." Nicholas nodded.

Nighttime had verged into the forest, leaving them in a blanket of darkness, and Kiffy pulled two glitz twiglets from his rucksack, tossing one toward Nicholas. Glitz twiglets were magical twigs crafted from tree branches. They were very flexible and could not be broken. Once activated, they would glow with immense light for many hours but eventually lose power and become useless. Dumbfounded, Nicholas watched as Kiffy quickly crackled and bent the twiglet, giving it a hearty shake. "Tert glitz!" he chanted. The glitz twiglet illuminated the forest surrounding them.

"Mustn't forget you, Hooley." He glanced down at the fox, pulled a twigged collared ring from his rucksack, and used the same practice of crackling, bending, shaking, and chanting. The ring glowed brightly as he placed it around Hooley's neck. "This will help us maintain sight of her," Kiffy explained to Nicholas.

Nicholas nodded in understanding and mimicked the procedure and magical words. After a few attempts, his twiglet lit up. "Most amazing!" he thought to himself.

They drew near to the Nonesuch's realm, a lush growth of ancient trees and sacred ground known as the Forest of Primordial Cedars. It was protected by the *Barrier of Aegis,* whose purpose was to prevent embedded invaders from entering. The protectors of the inner realm that guarded the magical shield were called the *Vedettes of Aegis.* Those that attempted to cross its powerful protection were disintegrated.

Kiffy threw his arm out in front of Nicholas. "Hold a moment! We are close; we must tread slow." Nicholas stopped, and Kiffy reduced his stride to a tip-toe pace, his feet crunching the snow below them. Nicholas and Hooley followed his lead, only moving when Kiffy moved. Periodically, Kiffy would place his hand on his double-edged dagger, ready to wield it as a nearby rustle or noise from the resident animals startled them.

From time to time Nicholas would hear a short *hoo!* followed by a longer *hooooo!* Although the sound was fascinating to Nicholas, it was also concerning.

"Those sounds above, are they embedded creatures?" Nicholas asked Kiffy.

"Owls... great grays. They are pleasant and will not attack us," Kiffy explained.

Kiffy glanced around and upward at the surrounding area. Suddenly, he stopped, raised his arm, and chucked his glowing twiglet several yards in front of them, where it was destroyed in mid-air into millions of particles. The Barrier of Aegis reacted and oscillated many variations of bright colors, followed by a loud *wooooof!* An intense blue flash knocked Kiffy and Nicholas onto their backs and caused Hooley to roll backward.

After several seconds, Kiffy and Nicholas recollected and stood back up. Hooley kicked her legs trying to untwist her body. Kiffy lit another glitz twiglet from his rucksack, then noticed the aggravated looks of both Nicholas and the fox.

"Barrier exposed." Kiffy shrugged.

High above in the depths of the forest, a female voice hollered. "Who disturbs the Barrier of Aegis?! I demand you speak, or we shall annihilate you!"

"Threatened with death already," Kiffy muttered to Nicholas, grinning. Nicholas, however, did not take the threat as lightly.

"We come to consult in the Nonesuch!" Kiffy yelled out.

The voice scoffed. "We DO NOT abide to non-gooders! Be gone!"

"Non-gooders?! Gnoma, do you not recognize me? It is I... Kiffy!"

Nicholas listened and watched as Kiffy made conversation with the hidden leader of the Vedettes.

"Come out, Gnoma; let us speak in the open!" Kiffy requested as he opened his hand and held his palm upward.

Nicholas watched and waited, expecting a woman in human form to appear. But instead, a feather fell from a pine branch above and landed on Kiffy's palm. For a moment it lay lifeless and still, then glowed brightly in a golden color. Magically, it morphed to a small griffin the size of a pinecone. Standing on his palm, she glanced up at him, her black eyes quite large in proportion to her head.

Kiffy spoke to the titch griffin. "Greetings this fine evening, Gnoma!"

Gnoma nodded. "Pedagog, it's a pleasure... we have not spoken in some time!" The miniature griffin threw a stern look at the fox below.

"What is this foul, furry creature that shadows you below?"

"Foul creature? Heh... Hooley? She is not foul; she is quite beautiful and also my champion hunter," Kiffy explained.

"Is she one of us?" Gnoma asked cautiously.

"Well.... you're a titch griffin and she's an arctic fox. She is not an embedded creature, if that is your meaning?"

"That is PRECISELY my meaning!!!" she snarled. "And this man beside you. Who is he?!"

Kiffy whispered to Nicholas. "Your turn, friend. Careful- she has a short temper. Perhaps it's tiny griffin syndrome; I believe she'd prefer to be a regular-size griffin."

Kiffy could not help but throw a joke back at Gnoma. "Is that what is bothering you... weight of the world on your feathers?"

Gnoma threw Kiffy a nasty glare. "I DEMAND to know who this man is!"

Nicholas shook his take on reality once again. He could not comprehend speaking to a palm-sized griffin. Uttering a magical word to a stone eagle was one thing, but this was getting beyond insanity. Hesitantly, he greeted her. "Hello Gnoma, my name is Nicholas; I come from a distant land. I'm here to speak with the Nonesuch."

Gnoma rose from Kiffy's palm and flew toward Nicholas. Hovering in his face, she began giving him a thorough once-over.

Kiffy whispered to Nicholas. "Place your palm out, friend." Nicholas held his hand upward, allowing Gnoma to land.

She eyed him critically. "Hmm... Nicholas, is it?"

"Yes, that is correct," Nicholas confirmed.

"And of what realm is this distant land?" she asked.

"I'm from Patara, in the region of Myra."

Gnoma turned to Kiffy. "I do not know of such a place! You trust this man and the monster that shadows you below?"

"Yes, I trust the FOX below, and I trust... I trust Nicholas too. His divination with the Nonesuch is of great importance, I assure you."

Gnoma rose again and flew back into Kiffy's palm. She glanced up at Kiffy with cautious faith.

"Very well, pedagog– if you trust him, then we shall trust him."

With her small voice, Gnoma hollered. "Vedettes of Aegis... come forth!"

Five more feathers slowly dropped from the upper branches, and Nicholas felt one fall lightly onto each of his shoulders. They both morphed into perching griffins. He glanced at Kiffy, who was smirking as he received identical treatment. Nicholas' spirits began to lift; a small smile slowly crossed his face, and he soon found himself laughing alongside Kiffy as a sixth feather landed and morphed on top of Hooley's head. Startled, Hooley shook her head quickly from left to right trying to remove the griffin. The griffin fought for balance but kept himself perched on top.

Kiffy chuckled and comforted Hooley. "It's okay, girl; they are friends... they won't harm you."

Gnoma shouted further instruction to her fellow kind. "Protectors of the Nonesuch! Deplete the barrier!"

The six titch griffins flapped their wings and flurried aggressively toward the barrier. The forest was blinded with a bright golden light as the Vedettes of Aegis transformed and merged into one full-sized lynx with long pointy ears. The lynx began to spit, hiss, and growl as it leaped into the barrier, deactivating its safeguarding power.

The light dimmed and Kiffy, Nicholas, and Hooley stared into an open forest, now a majestic grove of rare cedars with huge, rounded trunks. Hanging on the branches of the pines were baubles that sparkled in colors of red, green, silver, and blue. A path that led toward the Nonesuch sat in the midst of the cedars. Nicholas watched in amazement as a family of golden caribou approached a wooden bridge further down the path and drank from the stream that ran underneath it.

Not too far away, the lynx stared back at Kiffy and Nicholas as the Vedettes of Aegis completed the deactivation of the barrier. Kiffy gave the lynx a respectful Salute of Degomble. "Thank you, Gnoma. Thank you all...

for the sake of goodness." The lynx returned a nodding bow. It blared a long hiss and growl and its body flashed brightly, re-forming into six individual feathers. A small cold breeze blew as the feathers floated and disappeared high above Nicholas and Kiffy.

Nicholas' smile turned wide. He never imagined visiting such a place so alluring and enchanting. With a mindset that was generally realistic, Nicholas was beginning to be taken into this world. For this short moment he felt as if he belonged here.

Faithlife of Kindness

Following the defined path, they reached the wooden bridge. Although the weather was inclement, the stream beneath remained unfrozen and flowed continuously. From the bridge's edge, Hooley sighted in on fish jumping from the sparkling water. The glitz twiglets kept glowing strong but were now competing with the ambient light that the Nonesuch's realm created.

Nicholas was rather awestruck by the gigantic trunks of the tall trees surrounding them. "These cedars are quite rare and very old; you will not find them elsewhere in this forest– only in this realm," Kiffy pointed out.

A mild snowstorm began releasing thick and chunky flakes, quickly consuming and covering the ground. Nicholas glanced down beyond the bridge and was unable to determine a pathway forward. He looked to Kiffy for insight. "Where do we go from here?"

"The snowfall is not nature's work, but that of the Nonesuch. It is further means of protection. She will guide us; it is best that we keep eyes out for her snow tracks."

Nicholas nodded in understanding. He was quite intrigued by the many protective measures; it seemed as though this realm had tighter security than a Roman stronghold. He envisioned many Roman legions attempting to invade such a place, only to be confronted by Gnoma and her fellow Vedettes, or worse, destroyed by the powerful Barrier of Aegis.

One after another, tracks began imprinting into the powdered snow. They were not paws of an animal nor footprints of a human, but of an angelic wing–like pattern. Kiffy pointed toward the tracks. "Our path has been redefined– we can move forth."

"Come Hooley, leave them be!" Kiffy shouted to the fox, who was distracted and swatting at a fish from the bridge. Kiffy and Hooley began to follow the path, leaving tracks of their own. Following from behind, Nicholas observed as the footprints of Kiffy and the paw indents of the fox vanished. The marks Nicholas left also disappeared, and he assumed they were magically removed for similar safeguards. He questioned as to why he could not see the Nonesuch, but refrained from asking, maintaining his trust in Kiffy.

They traveled the Nonesuch's pathway, wending into the late hours of the night. The angelic winged patterns soon guided them to an enclosed grove with a circular walled structure, constructed of spruce pines that were less tall and grand than the surrounding cedars. An alignment of candles flickered and formed a walkway that swayed into the grove's entrance. As they walked along the candle-lit path and neared the entrance, Nicholas noticed Kiffy grinning from ear to ear.

Nicholas smirked and shook his head. "Why do I sense we will partake in more majestic ventures?"

Kiffy chuckled lightly but did not reply, instead glancing behind his shoulder.

Nicholas was caught off guard by a sudden, massive swarm of colored fireflies. Like snapping sparks from a fire, they buzzed past them, fluttering into the grove's entrance.

Nicholas' amazement grew as they entered the grove's inner sanctum. The hairs on the back of his neck rose, taken in by the beautiful landscape and festive scene. Red velvet bows hung on golden strings with touches of holly leaves and berries. Decorative hangings crisscrossed from tree to tree, while bells of saffron and silver chimed intermittently. A glimmering garland wrapped itself around each standing pine. On the limbs of the trees were many baubles along with the fireflies that had zoomed past them earlier, lighting each spruce in a variation of colors that momentarily flickered, flashed, and blinked, creating a remarkable display. An array of square wooden boxes, wrapped in strings, red bows, and tags glistened underneath. The snow provided the final touch, painting the view in whimsical wintry whites.

In the center of the grove, a young child spirit lay sprawled on her back, her arms and legs shuffling the snow and creating a pattern identical to the tracks that Nicholas and Kiffy had followed. Iclyn stood back up on her feet and gazed at them shyly with beautiful, deep emerald-green eyes. She was dressed in a red velvet gown with white trim and wore a wreath woven of flowers, pine needles, leaves, and foliage over her long, frosty white hair.

Hesitantly, Nicholas greeted her. She remained silent but gave him a warm, welcoming smile, and he wondered if she was mute. "This child... she is the Nonesuch?" Nicholas asked Kiffy, confused.

"They both are," Kiffy replied.

A distinctive, shrill caw came from above as Iclyn raised her elbow. Swooping down, a winged fowl with the face and beak of an eagle and the torso of a snowy owl landed on her shoulder. His feathers were pearl white with tinges of sparkling gold and mounted on his head were red velvet antlers like those of a caribou. It stared at them with intimidating fiery eyes of orange and yellow. Observing the spiritual animal, Nicholas reflected on its similarities to the stone fowl he had encountered behind the falls.Kiffy, standing beside Nicholas, respectfully bowed his head in greeting to both Iclyn and the fowl Alzora. Alzora gave a slight nodding bow in return.

"Welcome, travelers, and which of you are seeking our divination?" Alzora asked.

Kiffy introduced Nicholas. "My friend Nicholas, a foreign visitor who has come to seek meaning from within."

Alzora's eyes opened wide in shock. "*You* are Nicholas! The *Faithlife* have spoken many times of you. They tell of a Restorer... a Restorer of Goodness. Are you this man?" Alzora asked.

Nicholas was dumbfounded and gave him a blank stare. He could not answer such a question. Alzora shifted his focus to Kiffy. "And nothing of yourself, pedagog? Or of the fox that cautiously hides behind you?" Hooley slowly peeked her head out from behind Kiffy's legs.

"Forgive her, she is very timid around others. Yes... I seek divination for her also."

"And whom shall we counsel first?" Alzora asked.

Kiffy and Nicholas glanced at each other for a few moments, until Nicholas finally spoke up. "Kiffy and the fox may go first."

Alzora retorted. "Very well, I respect any mortal who puts others before themselves. Allow me a moment to hark in the Faithlife of Kindness."

Still perched on Iclyn's shoulder, Alzora closed his fiery eyes. As he began channeling to the Faithlife, a small, icy, tornado-like breeze surrounded the group. He slowly opened his eyes and the breeze halted.

"The Faithlife speak of a champion- is that her... this fox?"

"Yes, she's this year's champion hunter," Kiffy boasted.

The pearled white fowl seemed to sense an unsettled feeling from Kiffy. "A champion, yet... you have brought her here in seek of our guidance?"

"Yes, I have concerns of her ear canals; they contain tinges of purple," Kiffy replied.

"And have these 'tinges' illuminated?" Alzora asked.

Kiffy hesitated in answering. "Yes... once... but for a short moment. Both Nicholas and I caught eye of it." Nicholas nodded, remembering the occurrence at the arena.

Alzora flew to the ground, stood in front of Hooley, and eyed her sternly. "She is quite unique, I must say, and not just any arctic fox. Her soul is strong in goodness and has traces of primordial abilities. Most animals generally do not have such abilities." Alzora took a deeper look at the fox, then, suddenly shocked, spanned his wings wide and recoiled from her. "I'm afraid her blood is tainted, however; it appears she has been combating consumption of the embedded for quite some time."

Kiffy frowned. "I suspected but was hopeful that she wasn't infected. Can you help her?"

"Perhaps... the goodness inside her remains hardy, the infection is slow– there still may be time," Alzora replied.

Alzora flew to a nearby pine branch and nodded to Iclyn for assistance. The child slowly approached Hooley, shed another warm smile, and began to stroke her head. Hooley was very skittish of anyone but Kiffy touching her, and Kiffy was alert and cautious but noticed Hooley shifting her head downward, enjoying the caress. It appeared that she did not feel the same discomfort with Iclyn as she did with most others. Kiffy smiled at the sight of his beloved huntress sharing a long moment of affection with Iclyn. But Hooley's relaxed state soon changed as the loving gesture of Iclyn began to aggravate and irritate her. The hue inside her ears, and then her eyes, glowed in horrid purple, and she began to growl and snarl. Her paws grew long, sharp claws that grasped the lit ringed twiglet on her neck and threw it to the ground.

Hooley's aggressiveness did not faze Iclyn as she softly placed both hands on Hooley's head, attempting to comfort her. The goodness of the child's spirit was now battling with the slowly spreading infection inside of the fox. Hooley growled and snarled again and took a swipe at Iclyn but could not harm the immortal Nonesuch. Kiffy felt his eyes tearing up. Wielding his dagger, he focused his mark on her torso, raised his weapon high, and prepared to strike.

"Hold!!!" Alzora shouted, stopping Kiffy just in the nick of time. "Iclyn has stabilized her, but only momentarily. Retrieve a gift with her name on it from under the pines!"

Kiffy followed instruction and weeded through many of the wooden boxes, soon identifying the correct one. The tag on the gift read "For Hooley". He untied the ribbons, removed the bow, and opened the top. Inside was a red and white striped scarf.

"Quickly! Place the scarf around her neck," Alzora instructed.

Kiffy cautiously approached Hooley and Iclyn and attempted to place the scarf on the fox's neck. She nipped at his hand, the puncture drawing blood that dripped down and stained the snow beneath. Kiffy's hand throbbed from the bite, but it was not as painful as seeing the suffering in the creature he loved. He remained steadfast through his anguish and tied the scarf snuggly and securely. As it began to perform its magical healing, primordial symbols flared in a golden aura on Hooley's body and face. The purple glow in her eyes and ears diminished and the inner canals returned to a natural color. The symbols again flashed brightly, then dimmed. Hooley no longer felt aggression, hate, or evil inside her. The sweet and meek fox she once was had returned, and she leapt up to Kiffy for comfort, terrified and confused. With the strength of a bear, he wrapped his arms around his companion in attempt to console her. "Don't worry, girl… I'm here; you're healthy now."

"The fox must always wear the scarf; it will keep her blood pure. If it is removed, tainted blood will return and her infection will continue. She will become embedded," Alzora advised.

Kiffy nodded to Alzora and Iclyn with gratitude. "I understand, and I thank you both. She is quite special to me." Returning to his witty self, Kiffy teased Nicholas. "Perhaps you should have gone first, friend?"

After all that Nicholas had witnessed, he felt he was as mute as Iclyn. As hard as he tried, he could not utter speech or partake in further conversation. With many thoughts scrambling in his mind, a question finally escaped from his mouth. "The Faithlife which you speak of- who... who are they?"

"Your question shall be answered by the Faithlife, as they have requested direct divination. Neither Iclyn nor I can provide this answer or counsel."

Alzora then looked to Nicholas with fervent eyes. "Nicholas... your divination... it will be like no other's. Why you are here, who you are, who you will be... it all begins once you accept. Shall we proceed?"

A frightful chill rolled down Nicholas' spine. His travels had brought him all this way somehow. It had started as a routine of generosity to his fellow townsfolk and the construction and shipwreck of *Nonna,* and he now stood foot in a realm of challenging yet inspiring proportions. The same feeling he'd experienced when he met Drusus began to spark deep inside his heart. Nicholas muttered to himself. "I must proceed with this divination, hold strong and true."

Nicholas looked to Kiffy, still at his side and grasping Hooley tightly in his arms. "Do not worry, friend… you can do this," Kiffy nodded encouragingly.

Nicholas nodded back and sighed deeply. "Yes… I am ready. Thank you, Alzora."

He was then drawn to Iclyn standing directly below him. She smiled and presented another wooden box taken from beneath the trees. This time, the tag read "For Nicholas". He slowly untied the strings, removed the large red bow, and opened the box. Inside was a gift he never would have expected: a frozen bauble with a foggy smoke misting on its outer surface. It had a bright golden hue but was transparent, allowing Nicholas to see all the way through. Attached to the bauble was a crimson red ribbon. Nicholas reached his hand down to retrieve the bauble but recoiled from the intensely cold feeling. Alzora provided further instruction. "Nicholas, you cannot touch the artifact directly. It must be picked up by its ribbon."

Nicholas grasped the crimson red ribbon carefully and lifted the bauble up to his face, observing its beauty and the way it maintained its frozen state, never melting, breaking, or shattering. His face was cold, with a pinching pain similar to the one he had experienced in Degomble. Suddenly Nicholas felt a harsh burn and ache inside his head. He began to breathe hard, became weak, and dropped the gift box into the snow. He kept his other hand strong, still holding the ribbon tightly as his vision blurred, his only clarity being of Iclyn smiling up at him. He could hear the distorted voice of Alzora. "Faithlife... please provide divination to the Restorer of Goodness."

Nicholas' surroundings turned to darkness. Weakened and confused, he mysteriously found himself inside of a small and worn-down house. Inside, an elderly woman was humming a tune as she knitted. He watched as the she suddenly dropped her string and needle, firmly placing her hand upon her chest as her aged heart began to fail her. She collapsed to the floor and lay on her back while her body shook fiercely. She raised her trembling hands close to her face and gazed at the wrinkled and worn skin of her palms- palms that were once of fair skin, that had been strong and hard-working day in and day out. Palms that lifted and carried her children when they were young. She clenched them tightly and gasped, releasing her last and final agonized breath before letting go. Oddly enough, Nicholas could see the breath leave the woman's lips and wander off as though it was a moving specter. Persuaded, he chased after it as if he were a cat chasing a mouse. He found himself then standing among many friends and relatives of the old woman, soon to bury her underground.

The priest spoke in sermon. "Each day of every year this woman was a mother, a sister, and a grandmother who served in charity, warmth, and kindness. The fruitfulness she provided to others will not be forgotten as her body and soul enter the afterlife."

Nicholas eyed the breath as it hovered above the deceased woman, then bolted away. He continued his chase as the breath passed a wooden sign stabbed into the ground. The sign read "Faithlife This Way -->". The breath thrust forward, and Nicholas soon found himself and the breath in a field of numerous round poppies: bright colors of red, yellow, and white. The sky above displayed a bright-colored aurora borealis. He watched as the elderly woman's breath acquainted itself and joined with other breaths floating throughout the sacred field. They flurried and bonded together, soon creating a formation of a spirited apparition that radiated brightly. Nicholas could not make out who or what it was.

The spirit neared to Nicholas and spoke. "Nicholas... welcome... we have long waited for your arrival."

It felt like a fist had struck Nicholas in the stomach. The voice was extremely familiar; he had heard its whisper many times before.

"Who are you?" Nicholas asked abruptly.

"We are but a gasp, a last dying breath of those who have passed, released from lungs, blood fed from pumping hearts of kindness."

"And this field, it is your sanctuary?"

"Yes, we travel and gather here in unity, creating a Faithlife of Kindness."

Nicholas glanced around observing the beautiful setting and the spiritual environment in which he stood and was interrupted by the apparition.

"Seeker of meaning and yearner of contribution, please raise the artifact which you hold. We shall begin in your divination."

With the artifact still in hand, Nicholas cautiously raised it high. The spirited apparition began to break its form, reverting to hundreds of agonized breaths that floated and hovered like dancing fairies. Nicholas squinted his eyes, cowered his head, and buckled his knees as they bolted toward him.

"Are they going to harm me?" he wondered. Physical resistance developed in his arm and hand, which then shifted backward as the Faithlife injected themselves inside the frozen bauble's structure. With all his might Nicholas held his hand steady and maintained his balance. The artifact shimmered and radiated brightly, blinding Nicholas. The voice that once was spirit spoke. "We the Faithlife have enchanted the Nonesuch's gift, the frozen bauble, the *Chrysalis of Winter Solstice*."

Overwhelmed by all that had occurred, Nicholas glanced inside the transparent bauble, which had changed. Within the frozen prism, a small icicle was suspended from a tiny twig branch, acting as a hard outer case or shell and appearing to be protecting something inside. "What must I do with this artifact; what is its use?" he asked.

"This artifact you possess is a magical segment. It can only be used by the Restorer of Goodness. Nicholas- that is *you*." The agonized breaths released themselves from the enchanted bauble and reformed, this time creating a distorted visual of a sickly-gray elk-like beast, whose yellow-green antlers were damaged, broken, and hanging from its head.

"Far north is an ancient and sacred temple securing a primordial artifact. The temple is beyond a lingering area of evil, the *Frozen Splode*. To reach the temple, you must release the foredoomed fallow from its sickness. Only the gallop of the fallow will transport you through the Frozen Splode. You, the Restorer of Goodness, must use the Chrysalis of Winter Solstice to restore the health and well-being of the foredoomed fallow."

Nicholas felt confounded with such a task. "I don't understand why you've chosen me. Would these tasks not be more suitable for a warrior or an malificus- Gasper or Norrick perhaps?"

"Nicholas... your eternal fate has assigned these tasks to you. A primordial bloodline flows within your veins." The Faithlife shifted once more, this time displaying the visual words- *crimson mimicry*. "In your homeland you are gifted in acts of generosity and soon it will be piety. In this realm you are the Restorer of Goodness, one of the chosen to help destroy the embedded evil, the Bacillus of Winter Solstice."

"Faithlife, you speak of a large task with such a heavy burden!" Nicholas lowered his hand and placed the bauble gently on the ground. Nervous and confused, he began rambling. "I... I cannot do this... I'm sorry... the impact on those good in nature is too high! I'm just a simple person from a small town... I know only of small deeds..."

Nicholas quickly realized he was standing in an empty field of colored poppies, and the Faithlife were nowhere to be seen. But then a miraculous encounter occurred as a familiar man in spirit approached. He picked up the bauble with his palm, the freezing surface not affecting him. The man took Nicholas by the hand as Nicholas began to shake and tremble, then closed Nicholas' hand and helped him maintain a tight grip on the ribbon, tied to the Chrysalis of Winter Solstice. The man spoke encouragingly.

"Nicholas... my son... you must take on this burden. The tasks before you are yours and no one else's. Within you is a grand foundation. A foundation that goodness, generosity, piety, celebration, happiness, and togetherness will build upon, now and for many centuries to come."

Nicholas gazed at the gentle spirit and smiled slightly. Theopanes smiled back at him, thrusting a sense of courage into him.

"Thank you, Father; I will do my best... and... take on this burden."

Dangerous "Imaggonations"

T he Curling Ribbon falls thundered and crashed, filling the crystal-clear pools and a peaceful flowing river beneath them. Nicholas sat up from his bed and listened to the soothing melodic tune. Wiping the sleep from his eyes, he made his way outside to a small balcony. From the third floor, the balcony overlooked a captivating view of the falls and the union hall standing before them. Before departing to Degomble, Kiffy had assisted Nicholas in obtaining a traveler's suite at the CottonSedge Inn. His suite consisted of a full bed, bath area, clothing cupboard, and a small kitchenette, containing a crackling fireplace and kettle. The inn was a three-story structure engineered by the Yuulnavvies and was built in northwest Ethereal, the same sector where the union hall and Curling Ribbon Falls resided. It primarily accommodated military folk, travelers, or explorers from far-off places, such as Degomble, that did not have family or relatives to stay with.

A few days had passed since Nicholas' divination with the Faithlife. He had been given further clarity on his true meaning and role, but many questions still pricked his mind. Firstly, where would he seek out the foredoomed fallow? What sickness or curse was bestowed on this creature, and when he found it, how could he help? His ambition was at full stride but was countered on what steps to take next. Nicholas determined it was up to him to seek these answers. Kiffy assured him that he would update Norrick and request another meeting with the union. Kiffy also provided input on what he knew of the Frozen Splode. It wasn't enough to help Nicholas proceed, but he appreciated the insight.

Kiffy warned that the Frozen Splode was a deadly region of the arctic. "The thrutches and snow squalls alone are enough to kill you!" he had exclaimed. Those that attempted to pass either froze from the rigorous polar winds, fell through deep layers of snow ('thrutches' as Kiffy called them), or were killed by the embedded haveldrolls burrowed beneath. Using their long, sharp claws, the haveldrolls built a series of tunnels spanning for many miles. Many of them remained stationary, prepared to attack any passer-by that traveled above, and could travel the tunnels at a high rate of speed. How this infestation had come to be, no one really knew. It was, however, known that arctic hares would often enter the dangerous terrain, unaware they would be common prey for the underground predators. Being quick on their feet, the swiftest of hares could avoid a few attacks but soon became overwhelmed by the mass of snowy up-thrusts and explosions that chased and consumed them. Infected and transformed, the hares soon joined and strengthened the underground army of haveldrolls.

Nicholas also learned that the Yuulnavvies had attempted to engineer a transport that could withstand such brutal conditions. Each prototype put to the test had failed, and the time to build, the materials, and those that chose to navigate- all obliterated. Eventually, the task was deemed impossible and the desire to explore disappeared. But why did such a dangerous region, infested with monstrous underground varmints, exist? Nicholas now understood that the Frozen Splode was a nexus. At the end of its dreadful plight was a sacred temple containing an artifact with primordial powers, capable of depleting the control and evil persuasion the Bacillus possessed on the embedded. He assumed that this evil collaboration was created by the Bacillus itself, thus creating a hazardous zone to prevent those of goodness from reaching the temple. Nicholas wondered if others such as Norrick or Gasper, who were the last of the primordial malificus, or Arvel, an ancient warrior, knew of this artifact or temple.

To start his morning, Nicholas chose to re-visit the falls. But before heading out, he had issues with his personal attire to attend to. He opened the cupboard's double doors and was quickly distracted by the wooden gift box he had received from Iclyn, which still held the tag "For

Nicholas". As he reached for the box and opened the lid, a frosted mist escaped from the Chrysalis of Winter Solstice, nipping at his fingers. The golden transparent bauble remained frozen as Nicholas stared, mesmerized, by the icicle-covered chrysalis hanging inside; gazing curiously, he questioned what its purpose might be. He re-closed the lid and placed the gift box safely back in the cupboard. Also inside were three extra sets of arctic attire and undergarments, all provided by Kiffy before he departed. They were not quite suitable for Ethereal's warmer climate, however; layered and thick, they were intended for the polar region and fit rather loosely on Nicholas. He recalled Kiffy's suggestion. "Simple, friend, request a habersoakerdasher service at the front desk."

Nicholas didn't fully understand Kiffy's solution or remember how to clearly pronounce such an odd word, but he proceeded in following Kiffy's instructions. With the vestments in hand, he headed downstairs to the front lobby. Nearing the first floor, he could see a nearby corridor, containing fresh breads, fruits, and baskets filled with other appealing breakfast items. Nicholas was not particularly hungry and refrained from eating but instead sauntered on and took a moment to observe a large water fountain exhibit nearby.

The inn had received its name from the fibrous cotton sedge that grew in the arctic tundra. The cotton was used in crafting wicks for the unique candles that were decorated throughout the lodge and provided in each guest room. The wax of each candle was shaped and formed using the fat of ocean seals. Each candle shed light and warmth and came in many different sizes. Never did the wick burn out, nor did the wax of the candle melt, due to the spellbinding properties they contained. Additionally, the candles put off a pleasant aroma of various scents depending on the current season. The most stunning was the fountain exhibit that stood in the front lobby. The stem of the fountain was a large candle that burned a grand flame, but instead of dripping melting wax, it heavily dripped water, filling the basin below. Magically floating inside, candles of many sizes burned, distinctively illuminating the fountain. Many times, residents, children, and non-guests of Ethereal would visit the popular exhibit just to fancy the candle's remarkable light, feel the sensation of the fountain water, or take in the delightful smell of the season. The scent of the current winter season was a pleasant mixture of cinnamon and cedar wood.

A placard near the fountain listed each season's aroma:

- ***Winter*** – *cinnamon and cedar wood*

- ***Spring*** – *blossoms and warm rain*

- ***Summer*** – *salty seas and warm sand*

- ***Fall*** – *pumpkins and wet decaying leaves*

At the front desk was a curvy and warm-hearted woman wearing long dangling earrings and nicely dressed for her working role. Maintaining a friendly atmosphere, she attended to the guests and their needs.

"Good morrow, name and room number please?" she greeted Nicholas, smiling.

"Good morrow! It's Nicholas; I'm in suite 343," he replied.

From a bin, the receptionist pulled a small booklet with a red ribbon placeholder and began flipping through the pages. The front of the booklet was labeled "Third Floor."

"Nicholas… Nicholas… Nicholas… 343… ah yes, there you are! Will you be leaving Ethereal today, Nicholas?" she asked with a friendly gesture.

"I believe I will be staying here for some time, a few days at least," Nicholas confirmed.

"Wonderful! Any further services we can provide today?"

"Yes… I would like to request…" Nicholas hesitated, trying to remember and pronounce the service name Kiffy had suggested. "Ha… habbsopping… habersoakerdasher service?"

Surprisingly the receptionist seemed to understand Nicholas' stuttering request.

"Yes, of course! Will your vestments need a simple quench cycle or full habersoakerdasher service?"

Nicholas stared, confused, and sighed. "Truthfully… I'm simply seeking wearables that fit properly and are lighter. What I possess does not bide well and I'm seeking something that can be worn in town. Are such services available in Ethereal?"

The receptionist spoke heartily. "Yes, but that won't be necessary, as we all know our A.Q.D.C.P.L cleans and tailors your clothing to your body type, climate preference, and height!"

Nicholas stared, much more confused than before.

"I'm sorry, did you not know?" The receptionist looked concerned.

"Sorry, no. Unfortunately, I'm a foreign traveler, still learning of these magical luxuries," Nicholas replied.

The receptionist gleamed. "Allow us to show you. Hand me your vestments and follow me!"

"Thank you!" Nicholas said. He followed the receptionist down a long hallway, listening to the sound of her long earrings as they clashed against her neck. Clap! Clank! Clap! They entered the washatorium, a long, wide room that consisted of a large contraption. On the front of the lengthy contraption was a nameplate stamped with the initials A.Q.D.C.P.L., which stood for "Arcane Quenching Drying Couturier Process Line." The contraption was operated by two service workers, one on the entry side and one on the exit side. The receptionist handed the attire to the entry-side worker.

"Good morrow to you two! Please have these cleaned and tailored for our guest. He would like to watch the process."

"Climate choice?" the service worker asked as he received the clothing.

Nicholas wasn't sure of the correct answer but replied, "Ethereal's, please?"

The entry service worker nodded and began to feed the clothing into the A.Q.D.C.P.L. Near the entry side was an operator station with several options and selections to choose from:

Body Type	Climate	Height
Fey	*Frozen to the Morrow*	Wee-Lil-Bitty
Ectomorph	*Numbing*	Short
Endomorph	*Chilly*	Medium
Mesomorph	*Warm*	Tall
Brute	*Searing*	Mammoth
Dreadnought	*Inferno*	Gigantesque

The worker chose warm based on Nicholas' request and then stared him down, analyzing his body type and height. "Hmm, thin– Ectomorph and Tall, I would say." He selected the corresponding buttons.

The receptionist interjected. "This mechanism was built by the Yuulnavvies, and it is very riveting to watch. Guests await; I must get back to the front. Enjoy!"

"I shall. Thank you!" Nicholas responded.

Through the small viewing windows, Nicholas watched the contraption begin its quenching processes– soaking, splashing, and churning as a miniature snowstorm of soap sprinkled itself onto the clothes. It then entered the drying stage, thermally heating the garments with magical flares and sparks. Nicholas looked on in disbelief as the third and final stage commenced and as his thick arctic attire began to twist and tug; threads loosened and unwound. The garments reformed themselves, re-stitching and combining into a different set of vestments, now more suitable for Ethereal's climate. The exit-side service worker received them, folded them neatly, then handed them to Nicholas.

"Here are your three sets of civvies. If you need further service, put them in your room's habersoakerdasher bin or at the front desk. Climate and tailoring choices can be written down on parchment and attached to them."

"Thank you, the A.C.D.C... er... mechanism is quite impressive!" Nicholas remarked.

Now with fresh attire, Nicholas returned to his room to try the garments on. They were much lighter and fit him more comfortably. Better dressed for the task at hand, he was ready to head out and acquaint himself with Ethereal.

Nicholas entered the outside courtyard of the inn. The walkway was built with fine chiseled stone, similar to the stone used at the entrance of the Union Hall of Goodness. Lined up in the courtyard were benches and chairs for those that cared to sit or rest. To the left of him was a wooden fenced-off area containing a large flower bed. Mounted on the fence was a flat circular dial with a large arrow that pointed to "Winter: Glacier Sore-Throats." The dial contained four seasons and flora types to choose from:

- ***Winter:*** *Glacier Sore-Throats*

- ***Spring:*** *Sniveling Tulips*

- ***Summer:*** *Star-Shooting Petunias*

- ***Autumn:*** *Jack-in-the-Thorns*

Next to the dial was a small sign posting a disclaimer:

"Warning! Switching to the wrong season may cause flora to go dormant or react unnaturally! Please do not touch! Inn personnel only!"

Intrigued by the inn's washing contraption, Nicholas' inner child got the best of him, tempting curiosity and mischief. He turned the dial to 'Spring' and the bed of winter flora cracked and shattered, re-blooming into sniveling tulips. Startled, Nicholas quickly changed the dial back to winter. The springtime flora whimpered and whined loudly as it withered and died. The flower bed bloomed back into the glacier sore-throats and Nicholas looked about nervously, wondering if someone may have seen his actions or heard the loud noise. Unfortunately, he was caught, as a woman passed by, tittering.

"The Star-Shooting Petunias are my favorite," she commented kindly.

Nicholas blushed. "Yes, a beautiful garden, I must say."

Refraining from causing further trouble, Nicholas headed for the falls. He located the same flat rock as before and sat staring at the tall cascade of water. His mind cleared itself and entered temporary solitude. The mist moistened his skin, reminding him of the coastal rainfall in Patara and of his beach rides with Paloma. When he encountered mazes and puzzles of life, her fast trot and the stinging strikes of the raindrops sometimes created a clear solution, and other times, swimming the Mare Nostrum or "pulling the sea" was the remedy.

Nicholas began analyzing the spiritual meeting with his father. Was it a true visitation from Theopanes or just a dreamy illusion created by the Faithlife? His thoughts deepened further as he tried to understand his role and the path forward. The choices he would be making were now at his ownership. What frightened him the most was that his actions would result in deep and meaningful impact, which would greatly affect those that were of goodness. Nicholas sighed with frustration as his mind kept hitting a wall. "What must I do; what lies next?" he asked himself, discouraged.

Eventually his roots of generosity dropped hints of his next step. The values taught by his parents convinced him to interact with those living in Ethereal. His daily routine of helping those in Patara had created proximity and friendship with Drusus and his family, so perhaps similar acts in Ethereal would lead him to more answers and a clearer path forward. If anything, he could develop new friendships, show forms of kindness, and learn of this forest town, protected and created by so many magical elements. It was a solid step, Nicholas thought, and could result in further solutions when the next union meeting took place.

Nicholas followed the river that swayed southeast through Ethereal's farming and ranching community. "Now Entering Elidor's Crofting", a small wooden sign read. He observed as the townsfolk attended to their daily duties. Relying on the river's resource of water, farmers irrigated and hydrated their crops and vineyards, while others began to plant and sow the seeds of various fruits and vegetables. Nicholas was amazed by the enchantments that persisted inside Ethereal's protective walls. A healthy agriculture that contained fertile soils, healthy farm animals, and food resources, and a warm climate that was never impacted by the time of year were quite intriguing, especially considering that the outer surroundings were nothing more than a winter-bitten forest, or further north, a vast land of skin-piercing storms and heart-stopping temperatures. Nicholas gazed down at the crystal-clear river, containing shiny pebbles, where a mirrored image of the morning sun and pine trees reflected on the water. He stopped and stared at his grizzly face, touching the beard of fuzz that had grown from his chin. Attending to a mass of unforeseen ventures, he had not realized he had such growth. He still appeared to be a young man, but his eyes looked strained and weary from the crow's feet below his eyelids. Suddenly, startling Nicholas, a piglet caught itself between his legs, tangling itself around his ankles.

"Get back here, you lil' snort!" Urie shouted and hollered from behind.

Nicholas calmly bent down and picked up the animal. "Does this belong to you?" he asked.

"Yes, thank you, he escaped!" Urie replied, huffing and puffing from running.

Nicholas patted the piglet's sides and gently scratched its chin, reducing its panicked squealing and squirming

"I believe he is more relaxed now," Nicholas confirmed, handing it to Urie.

"Thanks... uh... who are you?" she asked.

"I'm Nicholas."

Urie gave Nicholas a cautious eye. "Nicholas? Do you live here? I never seen you before... Mother says never talk to those you don't know or who glow purple."

"Your mother is wise. I'm a new resident, at least for the moment. But don't worry- I'm not glowing purple," Nicholas assured the child. He spoke under his breath, "Let's hope I'm not."

"Oh... good! I'm Urie. Are you a shoulder... I mean... soldier of Father's? An embedapist... sis? I know! You are a mali... malif..."

"A malificus?" Nicholas suggested.

"Yes! A malif... cuss... sess. You look like you are."

Nicholas laughed. "No, I'm afraid I'm not any of those. How did your piglet escape?"

"Well, I only opened the gate for a second... only a second! Mother always says not too. I wanted to feed him inside this time... pet him... but he escaped again!"

Nicholas chuckled. "Not the first time, I see?"

Urie frowned. "Nope. Can you help me take him back to my home? He's heavy for me to carry."

"Absolutely I can!" Nicholas agreed.

Nicholas took the piglet from Urie and it returned to snorting, squealing, and squirming. Nicholas was again able to calm the piglet. As they traveled back to the drift, Urie dominated the conversation while Nicholas listened with open ears.

"My mother, my brother... and me... we have lived here a long time! My father too, except he is gone a lot for work."

"I see; where does he work?" Nicholas asked.

"Far away... he's a com... commender... a commander! I miss him when he's gone. I work too! Well... daily duties... Mother has me do them... like feeding my piglet. Lyman has more duties than me, though... oh!... I feed my piglet a lot! He is always hungry!"

"You must be good at feeding him, then," Nicholas encouraged.

"Do you have any animals?" Urie asked.

"Not here, but back at home. Goats and a horse named–"

"I love horses!" Urie interrupted. "But Mother and Father won't let me have one... they say maybe when I get older..."

"Perhaps they have their reasons," Nicholas advised as Urie jabbered on.

"That's okay! There is another horse... it visits me... I see it all the time... It doesn't look like most horses...

it's much bigger! And– even though it's sick– it's the most beautiful horse. I followed him once... ya know... into the beetle forest. Father told me to 'Never!' go there... I got lost and attacked by the beetles... they bit me... left red marks on my skin... they have scary purple eyes... the horse protected me though... it scared them off... then my brother Lyman saved me and brought me home."

"Good of your brother to save you!" Nicholas replied.

"He's a good brother. The horse scares the other animals too... but not me... lets me pet it when it visits me... I think it's hungry though... I tried to feed him once, ya know... one of our carrots!"

"You're very brave– did it eat the carrot?"

"No... I don't think it likes them, maybe because it's sick. Oh! It has big horns too! Not like other horses! I felt very bad for it... its horns were broken and hanging on its face."

"Do... do... you mean broken antlers?"

"Umm. Yes! Antlers... that's what they were!" Urie sighed in sadness. "I think it's really lonely."

A bone-chilling sensation struck Nicholas. Urie's description appeared to match that of the foredoomed fallow which he was shown during his divination.

"Was... was it gray?" he asked, to confirm his suspicions.

"Yes, it was dark gray! Have you seen it too?" Urie asked in excitement.

"Perhaps, but not in physical form. Did your brother see this 'horse' when he saved you?"

Urie frowned. "No! My brother and parents say that I have a dangerous imaggonation! That I see things that aren't real. They say there is no horse... but I see him... I promise! He shows up in the pasture over there."

"Your family believes you have a dangerous imagination?" Nicholas asked.

"Yes! Imag... imaginatio... nin... nin."

Behind the farm of the Serdars was a long, wide–open meadow. Along the meadow, the river flowed, heading eastward toward Ethereal's outskirts and magical walls. Ethereal's walls were surrounded by pines in various sizes and makes. In this particular vicinity, the pines showed signs of disease. The lower section of branches was scarce, diseased, and withered, as if it had been eaten by an intruder. The upper section remained healthy and lush, still bearing long green pine needles.

"Past the pasture, where the sick trees are, is that the 'beetle forest'?" Nicholas asked.

"Yep! I think the horse lives there too... Lyman says the beetles eat the trees and that's why they are dying."

As Nicholas and Urie approached the fenced drift, Nicholas noticed that the gate was still open. Fortunately, the many other pigs and boars had not run loose. Throughout the family's urban farm were several fenced sections of farm animals. Just before the meadow was a large barn with the sounds of sheep and cattle coming from inside. A large sign on the barn's doors read "The Serdars." Nicholas soon learned that Quilo Serdar was the father of this young lady.

"He goes in here," Urie remarked, pointing at the fenced drift.

Nicholas entered the drift, sat the piglet down, and closed the gate behind them, safely securing it from further escapees.

"I'll get his bottle!" Urie began feeding the piglet from outside the drift.

Nicholas smiled as he watched her perform her assigned duty. He realized that he enjoyed the child's company. Even though it was mostly a one-sided conversation, he was enlightened by listening to her stories. Urie could hear her mother hollering from their home nearby.

"Urie, dear! Are you almost done feeding?"

"Almost, Mother!" she shouted.

Urie looked up at Nicholas with sad eyes. "My mom will be upset that I lost Savage again."

"Does she know?" Nicholas asked.

"No, but when I tell her, she will be angry."

"Perhaps we can keep a secret this time?" Nicholas suggested.

Urie smiled. "A secret? Okay! Our secret?"

"Yes, our secret. But only if you obey your mother from now on and keep the drift's gate closed."

"Ok! I will!" Urie agreed.

"Urie?!" her mother shouted again.

"I'm coming, Mother!" Urie pulled the bottle from her piglet and began to run homeward. "I must go now. Bye, Nicholas. Thanks for carrying Savage!"

"Bye, Urie. You're quite welcome!" Nicholas replied.

Nicholas glanced down at the 'lil snort' who was looking back at him as if confused about why its bottle disappeared. He could overhear broken words of conversation between Urie and her mother as she entered their home.

"Who were you speaking to, Urie?" her mother asked.

"Nicholas–"

"I've told you– never to–"

"I know, Mother– but he– kind man–"

Nicholas had grown up following the teachings of his uncle and was raised by his folks to understand the power of spiritual and human encounters. He believed in them, and he knew that these encounters appeared from time to time to help those in need or during difficult times. His divination with the Faithlife of Kindness, and his conversation with the child who attended to the drift, may have hinted on further endeavors. Nicholas looked out to the river that flowed into the 'beetle forest', as Urie called it. Perhaps meeting her was not a coincidence, the story she shared not a false tale. Was it possible that the 'horse' that had protected and visited her was the foredoomed fallow? A floating leaf caught the corner of his eye, taken by the eastbound currents of the river. Nature's palette had given the leaf an attractive blend of colors containing reds, oranges, yellows, and blotches of decayed brown. Nicholas was astounded as the leaf began producing a golden glow in its veins, then, shortly after, evolved into a floating toy ship. Nicholas quickly recognized the square sail on the mast; it was the same ship the boy had lost in the stream of Eşen. He watched as the square sail caught the breeze and swiftly made its way into the diseased forest. With disbelief, Nicholas began to question his own frame of mind- perhaps both he and little Urie had 'dangerous imaggonations.'

Primordial Vials

Arvel descended to the catacombs beneath his estate. Passing his crafted collection of weaponry and armory, he approached a wide and blank brick wall. He threw a glance at the interglacial armor, glimmering and shining, as the hardened form dripped water from its icy surface. Arvel shook his head and rolled his eyes, remembering the fascination Nicholas had with the armor. "Damned ocean drowned boy!" he grumbled under his breath.

On his left finger he wore a wedding band– not his own, but a ring he had given to his wife at the time of their marriage. The ring was uniquely constructed, its head not of stone, nor its shank made of a fine metal. The head contained a miniature living flower, a purple mountain saxifrage whose miniscule petals were tightly closed as if resting in the dark hours of night. The flower's stem acted as the shank, wrapping itself tightly and securely around Arvel's finger. It was understood that these magical bands couldn't be worn by just anyone. For the ring to fit and attach itself, it had to be enchanted, given willingly by one and accepted by another.

Around Arvel's neck was a short leather cord and pendant, hidden under his tunic, that consisted of two small golden bells. Arvel pulled the necklace out from under his clothing. Using the ring on his finger, he made contact with the pendant. Shortly after, the petals of the flower opened and the bells began to ring and chime, one after another. He raised the still–ringing pendant in his hand and faced it toward the wall. A section of bricks illuminated in primordial symbols, separated, and exposed a secret cellared chamber with three large curio cabinets. One was labeled "Weapon Vials", another "Armor Vials", and the third "Primordial Vials". Using the wedding band, Arvel mimicked the same practice as before, raising the pendant to the cabinet holding the primordial vials. The magical locks clicked, and the door of the cabinet opened automatically. Inside were glass vials of many sizes, full of oozy liquids with vivid colors of orange, red, turquoise, and lime green. Arvel chose a distinctive vial containing a glittering–gold substance that sparkled inside.

Returning to his forge upstairs, Arvel pulled a long piece of iron rail from the flame, its one end red–hot. His aged right forearm tightened, and his veins bulged. With muscles still as defined as those of a seasoned warrior, he put his hand and hammer to work. The artificer struck the rail and anvil, and he let his mind drift to thoughts of kissing his wife, handling her silky long hair, and stroking her soft cheek. More positive memories emerged, of him chasing his son and of both of them tripping and rolling on the ground. Delighted, Arvel listened as his son giggled, attacking him in a storm of tickles. "Ha, ha, ha... please, Father... stop!" Arvel smirked fondly as his hammer tapped the hot iron. *Tink! Tink! Tink!*

It did not take long for Arvel's usual scowl to return as a series of evil screams and sounds of horror invaded his mind. His sweaty face turned red and the veins in his forehead bulged like those in his forearm. His strength and frustration grew as he struck the rail once, then again with great might. Evil thoughts, of his wife begging and pleading for mercy, further consumed him. *"No... please! He is only a child... no! Nooooo!"*

Demonic flashbacks flooded in of the pain and suffering of his infected love, the sickness weakening and destroying her body. Her wedding ring, containing the purple saxifrage, slipping from her finger and skidding across the ice. As the life exited her body, she had uttered a final request. "My love, accept my ring, it is yours to use... for... for the sake of goodness."

Arvel's blood boiled and grew as hot as his forge. He hollered in distress as his forging hammer rumbled and thundered, spanning faster and faster, louder and louder. *Clank! Clank! Clank!* The foul thoughts continued to taunt him, and the thick rail threw large sparks throughout his abode. Arvel began to miss, now striking the anvil's horn, deforming and denting it with great intensity. The lengthy rail of iron fell to the ground with a wobbling thud.

"Easy, old battler! You have a strong ticker, but not that strong." Kiffy interrupted smugly as he and Bech entered Arvel's shop. Kiffy quickly slammed the door behind him, attempting to keep the storm's snow from coming inside. "Here! Per your request, I've brought you some freshly caught cod."

"Fresh! Pfft! Fish caught two days ago ain't fresh! Yah! Throw 'em in that ice bucket there!" Arvel instructed, annoyed by Kiffy's presence.

Kiffy spotted the iron rail on the ground. "What is that you're crafting? Seems rather long to be a great sword."

"Nah! No great sword! Yer dense mind wouldn't understand!" Arvel teased.

Arvel picked the rail up from the ground and placed it on a wooden workbench near his forge. He pulled the special vial from a pocket on his apron, removed the stopper, and poured the sparkling liquid on one end of the rail. The metal began to magically curl and wind, creating a circular spiral shape. The remaining portion on the long rail lay flat.

Kiffy looked down to Bechstein. "I tell ya, Bech, the ol' man and his mysterious projects... he's up to something again." Bechstein looked up at Kiffy and barked in agreement. Overhearing them, Arvel grumbled back. "So, what the hell ya want, Animal Lover? Work to do!"

"I've come bearing fish and celebration!" Kiffy replied.

"Celebrate what?" Arvel grumbled again.

"The day of your birth, you growly polar bear! For it only comes once a year."

"What gibberish then? Dancin', singin', spankin', buildin' ice sculptures?" Arvel jeered.

"Have hot oggin' cider ready at my estate. Come! We must drink!" Kiffy insisted.

"Nobody likes that watered-down ocean crud ya make! Ya should know that by now!"

"Nicholas seemed to enjoy it," Kiffy argued.

Arvel appeared amused. "Hehheh, ya got Undertow to try it, eh? Gomble-brained enough to drink yer slop, yet he seems to be in tune with the primordial jargon."

"Our friend does have a proper name, after all."

"Yah! It's Undertow and yers is Animal Lover," Arvel teased. After a few moments he finally gave in. "Fine! Grab some ale from the back; we'll drink good stuff!"

Kiffy headed to the back where several barrels stood with closed taps and filled two mugs with Arvel's ale. The afternoon carried on as Arvel and Kiffy celebrated his birthday. Both eventually were taken under from the alcohol and began to lighten up. The old warrior was not holding his liquor quite as well as Kiffy. The two reminisced about past battle victories and losses and about Arvel's family and tossed around several conversations, teasing one another as they always did. An intense discussion commenced about Kiffy's wolves and sledger.

"I've told ya... animal loveeeer... *burp*... mooore howlin' dogs... *hic*... I mean wolves is better. Mooore of 'em ya go faster, yull cover more ground quicker," Arvel suggested.

"Perhaps the problem is that rickety battle sledger you built me," Kiffy taunted.

"Heh! Was finely built! 'Specially if it can handle a bulky gowk like yerself'!" Arvel replied sharply.

Kiffy could not help but agree with Arvel's remarks about his craftsmanship. Both his blitzkrieg sledger and envoy sledger, made by Arvel's own two hands, were flawless. The sled had faced many rough terrains, perilous storms, tough battles, embedded creatures, and long distances, but was still as sturdy as the day Kiffy received them.

"Meh! Perhaps... you are right. But I'm thankful for my four wolves. It is quite difficult taming them; some simply refuse to be trained. Takes a lot of time, ambition, and discipline. Bechstein was a good example of that. So full of energy when he was a pup, but he listened and was willing to learn. Now he is my best wolf and leader... strong as a musk ox and fast as a hare."

"Yah... *hic*... he looks it, alright! Lying near the fire like a stuffed rug!" Arvel replied. He then grew curious about

Nicholas. "Undertow... *hic...* tha' boy... did speak with the Nonesuch?"

"Yes- both they and the Faithlife were expecting him. And... his divination... not with the Nonesuch, Nicholas was directed to the Faithlife. Have others been requested in this way?" Kiffy asked.

"Nah! *Burrp...* not many. It's rare... only a few in the primordial era," Arvel answered. "How 'bout Norrick, have ya told 'im yet?"

"Not yet... I'm intending to update him at our next union meeting. You do know that Norrick has the same hunch of Nicholas?" Kiffy pointed out.

Arvel sighed, slugging another drink from his mug as the foam drizzled down his beard. "Yah, I know... we thought these were bad days but they're gonna get worse, 'specially when he understands his ability of crimson cleansin.'"

"Hard times indeed," Kiffy agreed as he sipped his ale. "The Nonesuch claimed Nicholas as the Restorer of Goodness; perhaps our foreign friend has come to lead us to prosperity and better days?"

Before Arvel could answer, a knock from the front door interrupted them.

"Yah, it's open!!" Arvel growled.

One of Quilo Serdar's high-ranked lieutenants entered. He was known for his talents in tactical planning and advising Quilo in many victorious battles. In his mind, he also thought he had a talent for swordplay, but most knew that his talent for cockiness outweighed his skills of hilt and blade.

"What ya want!" Arvel snarled.

The lieutenant pulled the hood away from his armored anorak, showing his irritated face. He released his sword from its scabbard and pointed it at Arvel. "This sword you have forged, it is FIDGOB! The blade is DULL…"

Arvel eyed the blade held in the lieutenant's hand. "Rubbish! The blade looks sharp to me!" he replied.

Kiffy jolted in with an attempt at a friendly suggestion. "Your scabbard, friend, it needs to be re-enchanted. It is snow-covered and is wet inside. Correctly enchanted, it will block the elements and keep it dry, as well as your sword."

The lieutenant threw Kiffy an arrogant stare. "I have no business with you, pedagog; this is of crafting matters, not petty animal taming!" He directed his conversation back to Arvel. "As I said, artificer, I cannot contend in battle with it. It does not satisfy ME! REPAIR IT!"

With a cocky approach, the lieutenant dropped the sword. The tip sliced Arvel's left forearm and knocked his mug from his hand. Bech began to growl, and Arvel's eyes went dark with anger.

Kiffy clicked his tongue. "Not good, not good at all, both Bech and the ol' grump are angry with you now. Worse, you spilt his good ale."

From the cut on his forearm, Arvel confirmed the blade was plenty sharp. He twisted and popped his neck in aggravation, then hollered back at the lieutenant.

"You can't contend in battle, eh?! WHAT GOOD ARE YA THEN!"

The lieutenant argued back. "I have not time for this nonsense! This must be repaired promptly! Quilo demands it!"

With his right hand, Arvel grasped the soldier's neck and lifted him up against the wall. He took his bloodied left forearm and wiped it on the lieutenant's face as he began to gasp for air.

"Quilo is my brother, flesh and blood, not my commander!!! There is no YOU and there is no shittin' ME! Only WE 'n US! We survive! We stand together! This arm, this hammer, an' this anvil we work together! We never neglect!"

Arvel's grip grew tighter and the lieutenant's face turned as purple as the horrid glow of the embedded. "I decide what I craft! What I repair! Not you! Not Quilo! Nobody!"

Kiffy quickly clasped Arvel's shoulder, attempting to calm him. "Easy, he needs air."

Arvel released his hand and the lieutenant dropped to the ground with a thud, breathing deeply and raggedly as he sat against the wall. Arvel grabbed the sword from the floor and lightly sliced the lieutenant on his cheek. A drop of blood released and dripped down his face.

"It cuts jus' fine! See! Take yer weapon; it is yer wit and fightin' skills that are "FIDGOB"! Take it and go remove icicles with it! That's all yer good for, sweetie! Git the hell outta ma shop!"

Intimidated, the lieutenant grabbed his sword and exited. Winded and still taken from the ale, Arvel sat back down to rest. Kiffy picked up the mug, cleaned it off, and proceeded to the back. Kiffy then handed the mug to Arvel. "A fresh fill."

Arvel grabbed the mug and took a chug. His eyes grew sad as he stared blankly at the floor, stained with blood that had fallen from the lieutenant's face.

"My lady and I... we wed on this day."

"Yes... I know..." Kiffy replied.

On the day of his birthday, Arvel and his wife had chosen to join in matrimony. Exactly a year later, a child, stubborn in his partner's womb, was ready to enter the world. Arvel's birth date became a yearly celebration of marriage and of family, which he deeply treasured.

"She was beautiful as a purple saxifrage, and ma child, best birthday gift I ever got. But... I failed 'em! Was weak as a young'un enterin' puberty! Rotten embedded took 'em away!" Arvel began to wipe his wet eyes, covered in dirt and sweat.

"We must stay strong in heart. We have to believe in Nicholas, that he can end this tyranny of the embedded," Kiffy encouraged.

"False hope, all it is, ya have no faith comin' from me!" Arvel retorted.

"Nicholas will need help from all of us, those in Ethereal, and you especially. We all need you... couldn't survive day to day without you."

Arvel choked and spat out a bit of ale, followed by a negative snicker. "Mukluk! We're hunted lemmings caged in by the embedded, and Ethereal jus' the same!"

Kiffy argued further. "Yet those here in Degomble and Ethereal pertain to their duties and strive for hope. You said it yourself "Only we and us" – does not every swing of your hammer, every weapon forged, and every armor piece formed, contribute to hope? Besides! If I didn't feel Nicholas had a meaningful role in all of this, I would not have escorted him to the Nonesuch. I'm not that gomble-brained, you ol' wash up!"

"Gomble-brained enough to take care of those animals! 'Specially that fox of yers!" Arvel replied.

"That's better! Back to the mouthy artificer I know!" Kiffy simpered and raised his mug. "Happy birthday, Arvel. Many more to you!"

Arvel butted his mug against Kiffy's. "Here's to my lovin' lady and ma son. May they slumber in peace!"

Cardinals of Joy

Nicholas had spent a few days visiting *Violet's Agora*. Ethereal's northwest sector was a large concourse of merchants and establishments consisting of specialized trades, goods, and services. At the sector's south-central division were dwellings that provided living for working folks in the area. A few of the many professions throughout the sector included traders, barterers, carpenters, butchers, bakers, candle-makers, clothiers, tailors, alchemists, and those who were adept with magic.

Nicholas had taken some time to familiarize himself and outline any opportunities that could help his cause. He always felt he had a knack with people and had been proficient in interacting with his neighbors in Patara. He attempted the same skill set in Ethereal, obtaining several greetings, waves, Salutes of Degomble from visiting militia, and confused stares of those who did not know him. He took time to speak with many of Ethereal's shop owners, trade workers, service workers, visitors, and general residents, learning bits and pieces of its culture. Although Ethereal practiced unexplained magic and enchantments, not to mention anything Nicholas had not seen yet, in many ways it felt like home. The small-town environment, the hard-working people, and the friendliness they showed, gave Nicholas an enriched feeling similar to the one he'd had in Patara.

A new day had come as Nicholas set his best intentions forward. From the CottonSedge Inn, he traveled back to Violet's Agora, but this time carrying the Chrysalis of Winter Solstice. Nicholas worried that the gift box containing the artifact did not provide enough protection and wanted something such as a bag or pouch that he could carry. Although the suite's cupboard seemed secure, he felt better about always having it on his person. Prior to reaching the sector, Nicholas came across another two-sided sign, one side reading "Now Entering Violet's Agora" and the opposite side reading, "Now Entering Atka's Flume."

Entering from the north, Nicholas stopped to observe a towering standalone building to the east. It overlooked the sector and contained large, square windows. At the entrance, a stained-glass Emblem of Goodness filled the upper wall and a sign that read "Embedapist Care" was placed above the door. The facility was surrounded by a vast number of individual dwellings where patients lived as they recovered from their treatments.

Four birds with pointy heads swooped by Nicholas, brushing his hair. Two of them were vibrant red in color, the other two a faded brown. He watched as two of them landed on a windowpane of the facility, while the other two flocked toward the smaller burrows. With a loud *click* and a steady *creeek!,* each window flew open and hands reached out. The birds comfortably perched upon each palm and were escorted inside.

Nicholas pursued his route through a maze of inner alleyways, walkways, and corridors, attempting to greet any passersby and identify more buildings that he had not recognized before. He entered a courtyard, a central marketplace, more crowded with walking townsfolk. The open plaza was filled with merchant stalls selling various fruits, vegetables, breads, plants, flowers, animals, and magical entities. Nicholas was instantly inspired by the variety of unfamiliar magical items on display.

A nearby merchant, specializing in such magic items, hollered loudly, presenting his product to the public:

"Fresh mistletoe of the season!
Its leaf and berries beautiful for many reasons!
Simply hang it high above!
And you'll want to kiss the ones you love!"

Another hollered:

"Beautify your estate with our piney garland
Crafted and made by the best in the far–land
It hangs, it droops, and gleams with magical light
Get it fast, it surely will be gone by tonight"

Overwhelmed by the busy flow of customers and merchants, Nicholas eventually crossed paths with a small girl who had red and silver ribbons in her hair and was carrying a basket of eggs. He smiled, recognizing the drift keeper, watcher of the "lil' snort."

"Hello, Urie!" Nicholas greeted her happily.

"Hello..." she replied blandly and kept walking.

"Do you not remember me?" Nicholas asked, quickly intercepting her path.

Urie stopped and turned. "Oh! Hi, Nicholas! It's you!"

"The eggs you carry– from chickens?" Nicholas asked.

"Yes, they are! Mother sent me to trade them for more grain bags... our bags have holes in them. It was Lyman's duty... but he went to train instead." She spotted the gift resting beneath Nicholas' armpit. "Is that a present? Is it your birthday today?"

Nicholas chuckled, "No, I'm afraid not." He glanced down at the eager eyes of the little girl. "Can you keep another secret?"

"Uh–huh!" Little Urie replied, excited.

Nicholas eyed her with sincerity "I'm putting utmost trust in you now."

"Our secret only!" Urie confirmed.

Nicholas laughed. "Very well." He got down on one knee, observed his surroundings to ensure that no one was watching, and slightly cracked open the lid to the wooden box. A cold steam released and Urie's eyes gleamed at the ornamental artifact. "Wow! It's pretty, and it's cold!" she exclaimed.

"Yes, very much so. Take care not to touch! I'm told it will freeze the skin on your hand," Nicholas warned.

"Okay, I won't. Is that an icicle inside?"

"I believe it is, but wish I knew its purpose. For the moment, I'm hoping to find a something to put it in, something I can carry with me," Nicholas explained.

Urie volunteered ambitiously. "I can help you! Can I help choose? Please! A nice one too! You can get it at the same place I'm going."

Nicholas nodded. "Yes, of course! Lead the way!"

As they walked side by side, Urie began to jabber on.

"I'm going to the *Cardinals of Joy*... you and me I mean... we get our grain bags there... they don't have any holes... Oh! They have birds too!... Pretty ones! Red ones and brown ones!! My favorite is Gandomine. It has both colors! Sleeps all the time... but I think it likes me though... wakes up to let me pet it... 'Urie, you must leave Gandomine to rest!' they always tell me."

"Do they sell these birds?" Nicholas asked.

"No, but they let them fly to the building over there." Urie pointed to the towering care facility that Nicholas had observed earlier.

Nicholas and Urie continued their chat and walk through Violet's Agora. Nicholas still enjoyed having Urie's company and listening to her jabber on. Her stories delighted him and, oddly, helped dull the sharp loneliness he felt inside.

"Are we nearing the shop?" Nicholas asked.

"Close! Oh! I almost forgot! I need to deliver this letter to Father."

Nicholas nodded and obligingly followed Urie to a nearby building. In the front was a large rectangular box with a swinging door at the top. "Letters to Degomble" was marked on the front with sparkling green and red letters.

"I send Father a letter once a week. I always tell him I love him... that I miss him..."

"That is wonderful of you. How long does it take before he receives your letter?" Nicholas asked.

Urie shed a wide and warm smile. "It is a magical mailbox! Father gets it right away!"

The Cardinals of Joy consisted of a two-building structure, established and operated by two elderly shopkeepers who had been married for many years. Linde and her husband Duggle specialized in selling both regular and magical pouches, satchels, chests, and various other storage selections.

"Welcome, Urie!" Duggle said as she and Nicholas entered.

"Hello, Duggle! Mother sent me to trade these for new grain bags."

"Perfect timing, dear, we are starting to run low on eggs. Who is this man you are with?" Linde asked cautiously.

"He is my friend; his name is Nicholas! He needs something to put his present in," Urie explained.

Nicholas politely greeted both Duggle and Linde and scoped out the shop's display shelves, which exhibited an impressive array of storage merchandise.

"What kind of storage are you looking for?" Duggle inquired.

Feeling comfortable with his surroundings, Nicholas carefully pinched the red ribbon on the artifact, removed it from the box, and presented it to the shopkeepers. "I'm seeking a reliable bag or pouch I can safely store and carry this artifact in."

Duggle gave the artifact a quick look, then threw Nicholas a blank stare. "You want to safely carry an empty ornament?"

"You do not see the icicle that hangs inside?" Nicholas asked, confused.

"Icicle?" Duggle replied, even more confused.

Nicholas shrugged his shoulders at Urie, who shrugged back with a twisted face.

"We have a few leather pouches with drawstrings. They tie securely and should keep it safe; you would be able to wear it on your waist," Duggle suggested.

"You don't want those!" Urie proclaimed.

"I don't?" Nicholas asked.

"You want one that locks! With magic!"

Nicholas nodded and spoke to the merchants. "Do you have one that locks... and with... magic, perhaps?"

"None that lock, just ran out of stock yesterday. Lead times on new ones are long, especially during this dangerous winter season- it is difficult for the Yuulnavvies to transport them."

Duggle thought for a moment on his inventory and reached for a distinctive magic pouch from the display shelf behind him. "We do have this one-of-a-kind memorizer pouch," Duggle suggested as he handed it to Nicholas. "It is much better than a locking option.

Locking pouches, although usually secure, can be breached with the right magical spell. This memorizer pouch is completely un-breachable."

"Memorizer pouch? How do you mean?" Nicholas asked Duggle.

"This pouch 'memorizes' its owner. Once an owner is claimed, it will not store anything besides that owner's possessions inside."

"And what if a non-owner tries to put something inside?"

"It rejects the possession and will not allow them to place it in the pouch," Duggle explained.

Nicholas was impressed but still concerned. "And the possessions I put inside; can they be stolen?"

"The items inside only appear to the owner who claimed the pouch. As I said, completely un-breachable. It also has a convenient front pocket for the most crucial of items!"

"But the items inside- where do they go?" Nicholas asked, fascinated.

"No one really knows; that's the mystery of the Yuulnavvie's magic and engineering abilities."

"Oh! Wow! Pick that one, Nicholas!" Urie interrupted excitedly.

Nicholas looked down at little Urie, delighted in the offered product. "Will it handle cold well?" he asked.

"Durable enough to withstand the coldest of temperatures, both inside and outside of the pouch," Duggle assured him.

Nicholas took time to feel the texture of the leather pouch and dressed the carrying strap to his shoulder. The pouch and strap fit him well, but he noticed that there were no drawstrings, straps, or buckles to keep the lid closed. He opened the lid for a slight moment, hearing jingling chimes coming from inside. Nicholas frowned. "The memorizer pouch sounds ideal, but unfortunately I have no form of currency to pay for it."

Duggle eyed Nicholas with confusion. "Then I'm sorry; I'm not sure if I will be able to help you."

"Are you from Degomble?" Linde asked. "Those who serve in Degomble receive our products for free. If not, we barter and trade our goods for other goods and services."

Nicholas nodded in understanding. "I'm sorry, I do not have any goods to offer either."

Urie tugged at his sleeve. "I will help you, Nicholas! How many eggs for the mem… meso-memorazor pouch?" she asked them.

Nicholas intervened. "Thank you, Urie! But you cannot! It is best you obey your mother and purchase the grain bags." He apologized to the shopkeepers. "I'm sorry that I've wasted your time- allow me to seek forms of trade and I will return for the pouch."

Although she didn't know Nicholas, Linde sensed a warmth and kindness in him- something about him that was unusual- and stewed up a solution.

"Hmm... I'm late sending out cardinals today, and they are growing restless. Perhaps if you help me with this task, we can give you the memorizer pouch?"

Nicholas grew interested in the idea. "Certainly, how can I help?"

"Great. Then follow me to the aviary. Urie, Duggle will finalize helping you with new grain bags."

Nicholas said farewell to Urie and followed Linde upstairs above the shop. The upper room consisted of a storeroom area that acted as a warehouse of inventory items, and a grand collection of storage products sat ready to be displayed in the front of the shop downstairs. Adjacent to the storeroom was a long passageway connecting the shop to the aviary. The pillared walkway provided a sky-high view overlooking the urban south sector of Violet's Agora. Nicholas took a moment to take in the exquisite view of the sector and listen to the loud chirping and singing coming from the aviary next door.

As they entered the home of many red and brown-colored birds, Linde led Nicholas to an area containing a long tree branch and a wooden shutter-like window. Linde pointed to the birds residing within the aviary. "These are our Cardinals of Joy. We raise these birds and give them as gifts to those residing in the care facility just north of us."

"Ah yes, I've caught eye of them flying on the windowsills. It seemed that those inside let them in. Is there purpose behind that?" Nicholas asked.

"We believe these cardinals have unique powers to assist those that are sick, dying, or injured. Many that were sick recovered, those injured or hurt are now strong and vigorous, and many that were dying continued living. Unfortunately, some remain sick, feel pain, or pass on, but they fulfill temporary happiness and joy to ease their suffering."

Nicholas frowned in sadness, thinking about the death of his parents and the plague that had taken them away. "What sicknesses do they suffer from?"

"There are variances, but the most common is those infected by the embedded evil."

"How do they get infected?" Nicholas asked.

"It is usually from attacks of embedded creatures or infected animals. Sometimes a simple defensive bite from a sick animal or a peck of bird's beak that punctures the skin. The care facility also houses many of those who fought outside our protective walls. The infected are taken to this facility to be treated by the embedapists."

Intrigued, Nicholas gazed upon the aviary of cardinals flying, chirping, singing, and hopping. They all seemed happy and cheerful- not a worry in the world. Each cardinal possessed feathers of a dominant color that indicated gender: the male birds were a bright red color, while the females were more of a dull brown. The one exception was a cardinal alone in its cage. Its crest and feathers were a blend of both colors.

"What's the bird in the cage?" Nicholas asked.

"That is Gandomine," Linde explained. "Our feathered friend here is a primordial cardinal. He is an extremely rare species born of both male and female characteristics–very old!"

Nicholas focused closer on Gandomine, perplexed. Besides having both colors, the cardinal's pointy head contained two small crimson antlers, which reminded Nicholas of Alzora. "Why is it caged?" he asked.

Linde began to share the story of Gandomine as Nicholas listened closely.

Gandomine was a special and powerful cardinal that had once belonged to a gifted embedapist named Violet. Violet was one of the three creators of Ethereal, was the founder of the care facility, and had also owned and operated the same aviary that Linde and Duggle ran today. Violet and Gandomine were known for their great powers of protection and healing of the town's people. They had great gratitude for Violet and had named the sector after her. But one day, Violet walked into Linde and Duggle's shop. With sad eyes, she presented them with Gandomine, bound to a locked cage. Violet had made a disheartened request that they take care of Gandomine and her aviary and that they continue to raise the cardinals and release them to spread joy and hope to those suffering. She was required to leave Ethereal, she said, as her help was now needed elsewhere.

"From that day on, Duggle and I never saw my mother again. We never understood why she left Ethereal, nor knew of her cause. But we strive to continue what she started. Gandomine still remains bound, the cage remains locked, and we have yet to find anyone that can undo it."

Tearfully, Linde changed the subject. "So, now for your task instructions!" She pointed to the long branch where seven cardinals sat. "We call this the *drome branch*. The birds roosting on this branch are scheduled to depart. Your task is to simply release them outside so they can meet and greet those in our care facility."

"Understood, but couldn't you simply leave the shutter open?" Nicholas asked.

"Yes, we could, of course, but many would escape. It is mostly the younger cardinals. They don't quite understand their role yet and would fly into the wild. As they grow, they develop a magical longing to help us-bring us joy... this yearning behind all of them is quite fascinating and unexplainable."

"It seems this fair town is full of wonder and mystery," Nicholas commented.

"It is, which makes it such a wonderful place to live," Linde replied, grinning.

Nicholas smiled. From what he observed of Ethereal and its history so far, he could not help but agree with her.

"Any further questions before I leave you to your work?" Linde asked.

"One, perhaps. How do I know when my task is completed?"

Linde smirked. "What is amazing about these creatures is that they have a schedule all their own. Once the drome branch remains empty, your task is complete. Oh, and when you are finished, come back to the store. I will pay you with the memorizer pouch."

"Understood! Thank you!" Nicholas nodded.

Nicholas carefully set his gift box down, keeping it in near sight, and went to work. He approached the exit shutter as the scheduled cardinals stirred and fluttered, knowing they were about to begin their flight. New at the task, Nicholas slowly and cautiously opened the shutter, and four of the seven birds quickly stormed out, slapping Nicholas in the head with their wings. Startled, he quickly closed the shutter, forgetting about the three more cardinals that remained perched on the drome branch. Nicholas re–opened the shutter and allowed the last three to exit. He viewed them as they hovered over Violet's Agora in elegant coordination toward the care facility. He closed the shutter, checking that the branch was empty. Was that all; had he completed his task so soon? Nicholas wondered.

His assumption was proved wrong as seven more cardinals roosted, scheduled to depart. Nicholas cautiously opened the shutter once again, this time releasing all seven cardinals at the same time. His task continued as seven additional cardinals perched themselves on the branch. Developing confidence, Nicholas quickly opened the shutter, releasing them. Again, seven more roosted, then seven more, and seven more after that. The process went on and on, and Nicholas felt as though he was operating a cardinal production line. His afternoon drew long as the day's sunlight began to shift into early evening. But finally, the drome branch remained empty; all scheduled flights had been satisfied. Nicholas closed the exiting shutter tightly and locked it securely, completing his task.

From behind, a MAN'S voice spoke in a heckling manner. "THE RESTORER OF GOODNESS SHOULD BE SEEKING THE FOREDOOMED FALLOW, BUT INSTEAD TENDS TO THE FLOCK?"

Alarmed, Nicholas turned around, trying to identify the voice. The room stood silently still, only containing the cardinals and Gandomine in its cage.

"I'm sorry, is someone here?" Nicholas asked, looking about and questioning if his mind was playing tricks on him again.

"I am always here," a woman's voice replied from the cage.

"You... you can speak?" Nicholas asked, identifying that it was Gandomine.

"Yes," Gandomine replied again in a woman's voice.

Nicholas was puzzled. "I'm certain I heard a man's voice as well."

"CORRECT. IT WAS MY VOICE ALSO," Gandomine replied in a man's voice. "I CANNOT CHOOSE WHICH GENDER BUT RANDOMLY SPEAK IN VOICE OF EITHER WOMAN OR MAN. YOU HAVE BEEN BUSY, NICHOLAS. YOUR EYES ARE WEARY, STRAINED FROM A LONG JOURNEY THUS FAR. YOUR WALK DISPLAYS A HEAVY BURDEN THAT ANCHORS ITSELF TO YOUR FEET."

"How is it that you know my name?" Nicholas asked

"MANY ANIMALS AND I COMMUNICATE THROUGH A PROTECTION SYSTEM. THEY SPOKE TO ME, TOLD ME THAT THE RESTORER OF GOODNESS HAS ARRIVED, A MAN NAMED NICHOLAS."

"I met a pearl white eagle/owl who had red antlers, just as yours. He name was Alzora," Nicholas commented.

"Yes, I know Alzora. Theses antlers aren't just for decoration!" Gandomine replied firmly, returning to a woman's voice, and began to explain.

The crimson red antlers represented specialized animals able to telecommunicate through one another. Gandomine was one of several animals once infected with the embedded evil. Instead of becoming embedded themselves, they were cleansed from the sickness. The cleansing performed was known as the Crimson Mimicry. When cleansed, they developed an immunity that protected themselves from the infection and often obtained abilities of the human who had helped them.

"I was bloodied and sick in the snow and it was Violet who found me and saved me. After I was cleansed, I obtained her embedapist abilities, was able to speak to humans, and these antlers grew on my head. Violet and I had great adventures together, helped many people. Now I'm just a cardinal withering away in this cell, one feather at a time."

"The embedapists, can they all perform this cleansing?" Nicholas asked.

"No, MOST CANNOT," Gandomine explained, switching to a man's voice. "A CRIMSON MIMICRY IS AN ANCIENT AND RARE ABILITY, ONLY PERFORMED BY FEW. THE ANIMALS THAT WERE CLEANSED WERE MOST FORTUNATE TO BE HEALED, INCLUDING MYSELF."

Gandomine directed attention to Nicholas. "IT SEEMS YOU ARE STRUGGLING IN YOUR CALLING, STILL SEEKING ANSWERS?"

"Yes, unfortunately I have not determined further solution to my cause. I was given an artifact from the Faithlife, but I do not know of its purpose. Questionable visions, I would call them, have hinted some, and several good people have helped me, both here in Ethereal and Degomble," Nicholas sighed heavily "... and stories told by a little girl. But realistically... I question my sanity and find it hard to believe a child's stories."

Gandomine tittered in a woman's voice. "Little Urie, such a spirited one. Children- they are often considered storytellers that share tales rarely believed by others. But perhaps those that don't believe them are lying to themselves and the truth comes from the child telling the story. But then again... you are speaking to a two-colored cardinal with antlers- perhaps you are insane."

Nicholas sighed again. "It that all this is... insanity... tricks being played in my mind? Am I wasting my time and my energy?" he asked, discouraged.

"You tell me Nicholas, the Faithlife deemed you the Restorer of Goodness, did they not?" Gandomine questioned.

"Yes, correct."

"The question then is: is it your head that aches from tricks that insanity invokes, or rather, is it an ache in your heart and soul that persuades you to believe your visions and the stories little Urie tells?"

"I... I... feel a deep passion... a hunger to help these people... they all seem real and genuine. I was raised in a religious family and believe in things that are unexplained. But... this embedded evil people suffer, the culture of magic, and talking to animals, it seems far-fetched... a dream... supernatural even."

"BUT YET, IN YOUR WORLD OF RELIGION, DOES IT NOT RELY ON STRONG BELIEF AND FAITH?" Gandomine asked in a man's voice.

"Yes, certainly."

"THEN YOU MUST MAKE THAT DECISION, NICHOLAS. AVOID CONTEMPLATING AND DECIDE IF YOU HAVE FAITH, IF YOU BELIEVE IN ALL OF THIS, AND IF YOU DO, ARE WILLING TO TAKE THE NEXT STEP?"

"I feel I must help restore goodness but am uncertain how to proceed," Nicholas remarked.

"YOU WANT TO RELEASE THE FOREDOOMED FALLOW FROM ITS SICKNESS, DO YOU NOT?"

"Yes... yes, I do."

"THEN I CAN HELP YOU. OPEN THIS DOOR AND LET ME OUT OF THIS PRISON CELL. IF YOU ARE TRULY THE RESTORER OF GOODNESS, THEN YOU CAN UNLOCK IT. BUT BE WARNED, WE ARE NEAR THE WINTER SOLSTICE AND ONCE YOU BEGIN USING YOUR PRIMORDIAL POWERS, AN UNFORESEEN DANGER WILL BE BROUGHT AMONG THE PEOPLE GOING FORTH."

Nicholas felt a huge lump in his throat, realizing that the people would soon depend upon him in hopes of having a flourishing future. He did not want to put them in harm's way but understood that dangerous circumstances were required in order to reach prosperity. His hand began to tremble as his fingertips made contact with the cage's door. He clenched his hand, firmly gripping the cage's bars. The cage began to shimmer and shake, fighting back. Gandomine chirped loudly, flapping wings and shedding feathers while being thrown around the cage. Nicholas' fingers began to slip as he lost grip and let go.

Gandomine hollered in a woman's voice. "Come now, Restorer! You must release all the goodness you have inside if you want to unlock this cage! Try it again!"

Nicholas took a deep breath and took another hold of the cage. The cage reacted ferociously, shimmering and shaking even more than before. A horrid demonic voice began to grumble in the surroundings.

"Do not challenge us; thy will be destroyed!"

Nicholas' fears and doubts began to contend with him, attempting to deplete his strength and primordial ability.

The demonic voice yelled and grumbled at Nicholas "You are weak and nimble, a Restorer of nothing!"

Aggravated, Nicholas ignored the taunting voice and reminisced of his mother's soft hands holding his as she passed away. Within him, a warrior's strength grew and battled his fears and doubts, massacring each of them. He tightened his grip on the cage, holding it firmly and steadily. The shake and shimmer of the caged slowed as Nicholas removed the enchantment. The cage's door flew open and Gandomine swiftly fluttered out, but, having weak wings, crashed and thudded to the floor. Nicholas stumbled backward as the ground beneath quaked, then stopped.

"Gandomine? Are you ok?" Nicholas asked, startled.

"Yes, I am fine," Gandomine reassured him, still using a woman's voice. "Phew! My wings have not flown for a long time!" Gandomine gained composure and flew to Nicholas, perching on his arm. "Thank you, Nicholas. It is wonderful to be free once again!"

Nicholas was agape of the ability he had just performed but was deeply concerned and frightened. "I heard an unholy voice, and I did not expect the ground to shake," he commented.

"Yes, your abilities aggravate the Bacillus. It is not surprising," Gandomine confirmed.

The ruckus of events concluded, and Linde entered the aviary with the memorizer pouch in hand. She observed Gandomine released from the cage and nodded to Nicholas with a respectful gesture. "Somehow... I immediately knew. When you first came into our shop, you showed a sense of warmth and kindness. Your eyes, they are gentle just like my mother's. I can understand why you were chosen to be the Restorer of Goodness." Linde handed the memorizer pouch to Nicholas. "Please take it; Duggle and I owe you for your work today. The pouch and Gandomine now belong to you."

"Thank you," Nicholas replied. "I can only hope that I do the right thing. I can't imagine accomplishing such great deeds as your mother did."

Linde smiled sincerely. "You have Gandomine with you now; that will help."

Nicholas sighed deeply and nodded to his feathered friend perched on his arm.

With a man's voice, Gandomine spoke. "THE TIME – IT HAS COME, YOU… THE RESTORER… HAVE CHOSEN TO BELIEVE, TO HAVE FAITH– NOW WE MUST BEGIN UNLEASHING YOUR TRUE POWERS OF GOODNESS."

Spirit of Loveliness

Young Lizabet and her mother sat on a water-soaked log overlooking a glinting emerald lake. Surrounded by tall mountain peaks, it was a secluded and peaceful place for a mother and daughter to spend time. The summer's warm weather had softened the snow. The glaciers had drained themselves from the winter's storms, and the incoming streams delivered the melted ice and snow, nourished by the lake's curative properties. Embedapists claimed it as a sanctuary of charming, and for many generations they had come to saturate their magical devices. Once charmed by the water, the devices became therapeutic instruments that were capable of healing and recovering those infected by the embedded evil.

"This is an Embedapist Staff," Lizabet's mother explained as she handed it to her. "Everything you are capable of begins with this. You are now old enough to use it." Her mother then frowned. "You- you are growing up so quickly." Lizabet smiled affectionately, accepting the staff with great fascination. "Go now, you must charm it in the lake," her mother instructed.

Excited, Lízabet hopped from the log and placed her new staff into the water. While soaking, it took in the curative powers from the lake.

"That's plenty of time; now it must dry," her mother instructed further.

Lízabet sat her staff down on flat ground, allowing it to sear in the sun. After several minutes, it began to sparkle and flash, concluding the charming application. With widened eyes, Lízabet picked up the staff and smiled back at her mother.

"Great! Let us test it out, shall we? I know a perfect place!" her mother said.

Leaving the lake, Lízabet and her mother headed to a nearby marsh. Within the mud, rushes, and reeds, a large swarm of mosquitoes resided, attempting to draw blood from their legs, arms, necks, and faces. Lízabet and her mother swatted and smacked them.

"You can practice here. Make use of your staff and see what it can do," her mother advised with a wide grin.

Using her staff for the first time, Lízabet made contact with a flying mosquito, turning it into a flower petal that dropped to the ground. More blood–hungry mosquitoes approached, and with excitement, Lízabet contacted a second mosquito, then a third, a fourth, and a fifth one, creating a scattering of fluttering flower petals.

Lízabet was delighted with her new skill but was soon outnumbered and overwhelmed as the dreaded swarms joined forces that would not stop at getting their fill. The skin on both Lízabet and her mother became overrun with many rashes and itchy bumps.

"Mother, they are everywhere; I can't get them all! Can you help me?" Lízabet asked.

"No, I cannot- it is up to *you* to help us," her mother replied as she continued to smash and swat more mosquitoes.

"But... but... we will be eaten alive! I'm not fast enough!"

"Remember, dear, it is not quick hands, fancy words, weapons, or wondrous items that our greatest magic is born from. It is an ancient spirit that is inside of us, the *Spirit of Loveliness*. But to do so, you must comprehend your inherited spirit and ignite its true potential. You are capable of unleashing the purest of magic and bearing the most remarkable of miracles."

Without using quick hands, fancy words, weapons, or wondrous items, Lízabet's mother followed with a magnificent demonstration: shape-shifting the blood-sucking vampires into serene dragonflies. Instead of biting, they healed the skin of both Lízabet and her mother, treating the itching and bloodied bumps they had once created.

That day with her mother had created a special moment that Lízabet would cherish forever. Like a pesky mosquito, reality invaded as an older Lízabet returned into the heat of her training, staring down her mentor with focused yet fretting gradient-brown eyes. The epitome of malificus stood motionless, hidden underneath a stocking cap of versed abilities, and waiting for a signal from Lízabet. Placing a hand over her face, she swiped with the Salute of Degomble, indicating that she was ready for her training. Biting her lower lip, her mind turned tactical and her battle stance stern, prepared for any magic ailments that might come her way.

Gasper nodded his shrouded head, accepting Lízabet's salute. His shriveled and exposed hands shook the Crutches of Winterstorm, creating a blizzard that rotated and swirled inside the glass spheres. For most, the dreaded bite of the arctic feasted on those who dare expose the slightest bit of skin. But for Gasper, many years of fighting in the Interglacial War had helped him develop a strong tolerance and immunity for the cold. Although aged and tattered, his primordial velvet robe had enchanted properties that warmed his corroded joints and brittle bones.

With fully-charged spheres, Gasper unleashed a vigorous spell of razor-sharp ice spikes, each the length and size of a lance. Looking like hundreds of hurled spears, they soared toward Lízabet. Swiping her staff, she quickly parried the attack, staking each one downward into the frozen ground, then followed with a confident smirk.

"Well done! Yep... yep..." Gasper complimented in a raspy voice.

He shook his crutches once again, the glass spheres now storming with small ice pellets inside. "HAILSTONE FORTH!" Gasper hollered ruggedly. A severe thunderstorm up-drafted and flashed as lumps of round ice fell swiftly toward the ground. Lízabet cowered, attempting to cover herself; the hail punctured her arctic rogue attire, stinging and bruising her skin underneath. Using both arms, she threw her staff toward the sky. While hovering in the air, it mended into a sheltering shield, protecting her from the elements. Gasper lowered his crutches and the dangerous storm soon slowed and stopped.

"Yes. Very good... yep... yep... yep," Gasper complimented Lízabet once more.

The overhead shield began to fade as Lízabet called out to retrieve her reformed staff but was intercepted by Gasper who quickly tossed it several yards away from her.

Gasper's elderly body had become tired from his attempted blitzes and storms, and he spoke in deep and gasping breaths. "We swi... switch... now! No instruments! And I shall pl... *gasp*... play by my own rules!"

The magical bands that braced Gasper's arms released themselves and vanished. The crutches levitated and landed softly near Lízabet's staff. The attached glass spheres were now clouded, gray, and inactive.

No longer supported, Gasper's legs, knees, and arms wobbled and shook. Having no weapon or defensive strategy, Lízabet threw glances at her staff- now covered in a thin layer of snow- knowing she was not capable of reaching it. The only viable option was a nearby rock formation where she could take cover from her mentor's next move. Gasper raised his hands, curled his calloused fingers, and motioned to release his next attack, but was halted by a wild musk ox who was carelessly trudging through the middle of the lesson. Across the way, Lízabet was face first in the snow behind the rock formation. She had inaccurately anticipated Gasper's attack and had dived for cover. Frustrated, Gasper raised his fists "Be gone, you dim-witted animal! You interrupt us!" Startled by Gasper's abruptness, it scampered off.

Lízabet stood up, recouped, and brushed the snow from her whitewashed and irritated face. Meanwhile, Gasper held a firm gaze and directed a spell of injury toward the ox, who was still scurrying away. Its back leg twisted and bent, breaking with a loud *snap!* It tripped and plummeted to the ground, breathing deeply and grunting in pain.

Shocked, Lízabet looked to the suffering animal with emotional eyes. It reminded her of Kiffy's own musk oxen, Booth and Eucera, and she reacted and raced toward her staff, hoping to retrieve it. Gasper opposed her and clapped his hands together, causing both her staff and his crutches to vanish from the frozen ground.

"Again! No instruments... *gasp*... we train without them!" Gasper hollered.

Lízabet was frustrated and distraught, partly from wasting her energy diving for cover, but mostly from the cruelty Gasper had displayed toward a harmless animal. She did not understand her mentor's motive and argued back. "I cannot restore its health if I do not possess a staff, rod, tome, or wand!"

Gaspers bellowed back in a croaky old voice. "Wrong! The gift of your mother's spirit is your instrument. Wands are used by lazy wizards to do all their dirty work... yep... yep... yep!"

Gasper's insight reminded Lízabet of the cherished moment with her mother and of the advice the older woman had given her on that day. With dire sympathy, she listened to the deep calls of the ox pleading for mercy. Keeping a keen eye on Gasper, she planted her feet and dashed toward it. Her mentor's body shuddered, and his hands shook like flapping wings of a butterfly. Lízabet had completed several lessons with the man, but this time something wasn't right. She felt an unusual wickedness coming from him– an evil nature infiltrating. His shivering motion was unusual, more than an old man trying to stand upright. Her legs suddenly became numb, and she tripped, falling to her knees. Her feet stung and felt unusually warm as if they were frost-bitten; she realized that Gasper had put a spell of immobility on her.

"Hold!" the malificus grumbled and gasped. "You must defend it… *gasp*… before you can ease its suffering!"

Lízabet gazed at Gasper with worried eyes as fear struck her harder than any magical attack could. She was frightened that she too might end up with a broken leg.

"Gasper, no! I am still not ready! I need more time and training."

Gasper did not listen to or support Lízabet's hesitation. Like clockwork, three evil embedded banshees were cast from his bare hands. Soaring through the tundra's algid air, their long hair flared in a purple flame, their eyes in a purple glow. Their wrinkled faces showed misery and hate as they cried with terrible screeches, preparing to prey on the injured ox just ahead of them.

Lízabet attempted to stand up but struggled, still having no use of her legs. She was bewildered by Gasper's actions; they were unexplainable and unexpected, especially from a primordial malificus of high respect who stood true to the Union of Goodness. She felt helpless and infuriated as she watched Gasper cough blood that matched the red color of his robe and stained the white trim. The momentum of the last summoning spell had agitated his aged lungs.

It was now Lízabet's move, and seconds were passing by. Her teeth chattered, not because she was cold, but because deep inside she knew that she had the Spirit of Loveliness and was highly capable of using it. But she also knew such magic had consequences; she had lost her mother because of it, which terrified her. Her usual task as an embedapist was clear-cut: bring forth those infected by the embedded evil and restore them back to health. Healing and helping those to recover was Lízabet's preference, but Gasper had taken her staff out of play. And worse, she was up against banshees who were pursuing a helpless animal.

She had to prove herself worthy to the Union of Goodness. Norrick and Gasper had fought together for many years and were like brothers. If Gasper gave her grandfather approval, she knew he would allow her to join the union. Completing his lessons was her key to acceptance. She gaped at the musk ox, still in agony, and at the evil embedded banshees one fallen snowflake away from consuming it. Gasper continued coughing aggressively, spitting more blood but empowering Lízabet. "Make haste, woman! *Cough...* Elimi... *cough...* eliminate... your hesitation, HONOR YOUR MOTHER!"

Lízabet's ancient and inherited spirit sailed the rapid rivers of her blood, incubating magic inside, and was ready to be fertilized and born. Lízabet closed her eyes and meditated, reaching deep within herself, while blocking out the interfering commotion, stress, anxiety, and fear. Without using quick hands, fancy words, weapons, or wondrous items, she released a spell of internal spirit onto the embedded creatures. The flying banshees quickly shape-shifted into a loveliness of ladybugs, red in color with silver glittering spots. Like the dragonflies her mother had summoned before, they gently and tenderly repaired the ox's broken leg.

The animal's health was then restored, and the large mass of ladybugs buzzed away in a gleaming fashion. Finalizing her lesson, Lízabet could not decide if she felt good about what she had accomplished or outraged by what her mentor had done. She was indeed worried about him, and it saddened her to see him still coughing blood.

Gasper's coughing eventually calmed, and he snapped his fingers loudly; his crutches returned to him and the magical bands reattached to his arms. Lízabet's staff appeared next to her, and she retained feeling in her legs and feet. Although her legs felt frail, she was able to stand back up.

Relying on his crutches, Gasper hesitantly approached Lízabet with a shaky-handed Salute of Degomble. Lízabet saluted back, no longer feeling the evil nature, she had sensed earlier. She felt comfortable around him now.

"Quite a lesson today, was it not?" Lízabet asked as she picked up her staff.

"Yes, quite a day... yep... yep... yep," Gasper replied. "More importantly, you conquered your hesitation with perseverance."

Lizabet observed her mentor still shaking, his body weak, weary, and tired from the day's training. She wrapped her arm around his shoulder, assisting his staggered mobility.

"Come, Malificus, let's get you home– you need rest."

Mallow Bom Coco

Lízabet brushed a light layer of snow from the tall stack of firewood. From the pile, she had chosen logs less wet and ready to burn. Filling the wood carrier, she made her way back to Gasper's cabin. The pines that surrounded his home were frosted with an alluring view of white crystals glistening in the morning's sunlight. It was a preferrable site over the hindered growth of trees and hollering winds of the tundra where she had trained with Gasper.

As she walked, Lízabet's feet and toes stung in pain, causing her to limp. Her head throbbed, reminding her of the consequences of her inherited spirit, no longer unprecedented. She recalled what her mother had once said. "Conditioning and maintenance of your mind is essential to using the Spirit of Loveliness. You must be hard-headed, tough as stone, or you will be unable to harness it."

Entering Gasper's home, Lízabet removed the chullo cap and scarf from her neck, allowing her long brown hair to fall at her waist. The cold air from outside had applied a natural blush of red to the apples of her cheeks, adding a beauty of warmth to her face. From the adjacent room, she could hear Gasper coughing aggressively and wheezing. She emptied the wood from the carrier, stacking it on to a nearby rack, then removed her footwear and socks, attempting to determine the cause of her pain. She discovered that her feet were covered in fluid–filled blisters and her skin was mottled.

Yesterday's training had had adverse effects, taking a toll on both Lízabet and her mentor. Still young, Lízabet was capable of a fast recovery, but ol' Gasper was not as fortunate. Most mornings, he was up before dawn, but today he remained in bed suffering a string of fevers and chills. His body and hands shook viciously, more so than the day before, paying dearly for the artillery of spells he had cast. More wheezing, gasping, and coughing came from his room. Worried, Lízabet lightly tapped on Gasper's bedroom door.

"Mentor... are you well?" Lízabet asked in a soft voice.

"Yes... fine... *cough*.... yep... yep... *cough*...yep. I sha... *gasp*... shall be... *cough*... up shortly," Gasper replied.

Lízabet grabbed a kettle that was hanging over the fire and poured hot water into a mug. She pointed her embedapist staff at the mug and chanted "*Mallow Bom Coco.*" A brown sphere with crushed particles on top floated above the cup and then dropped. Inside, the clear water fizzed and bubbled, shifting to a rich brown color as white foam rose to the top of the mug. Using her staff, she performed a stirring-like motion and the mixture swirled in a clockwise rotation. Lízabet had created a healer's concoction, an elixir meant for Gasper.

"Perhaps it is better you stay in bed and rest today?" Lízabet recommended.

"Nonsense!" Gasper argued from his room. "I will rest when I'm dead! I have... *cough*... work to do... I must get our people to Ethereal today."

It appeared that Gasper's mind had returned to its stormy and forgetful self; he had lost track of what day it was. "It will be a few days before they arrive. Besides, my grandfather will be with the group. I'm sure he can provide escort," Lízabet reminded him.

Contending in the primordial wars, Gasper and Norrick had stood together as malificus. During a time of downfall and darkness, many lives had been lost to the Bacillus, the embedded evil, the infected body organs that had failed them, or the malnourishment caused by empty stomachs. Still, a strong friendship flourished between the two, and they worked together to create the Union of Goodness. The union brought others together, invented solutions, and structured a fellowship with the Yuulnavies. The northern race went to work, using brilliant minds and durable hands to build the Union Hall of Goodness. Several years after Ethereal was created, a union of pedagogs, warriors, malificus, embedapists, artificers, and alike joined to create a thriving community that met at the hall's table at regular intervals to uphold the well-being, protection, and safety of the people. They also bargained with the Yuulnavies, soliciting their expertise in engineering, architecture, and economics. It was a valuable relationship that resulted in prosperity and hope in Ethereal. The union created was not an original idea but instead was molded upon a myth of a bargaining unit much stronger and grander. This myth proclaimed that a union of incredible workers and craftspeople lived in a far-off land located in the northernmost pole of the world. Like Ethereal, it too had special means of access and could not be inflicted by the Bacillus and the evil creatures it created.

As a child, Lízabet had spent much of her time with Gasper. After her mother passed, Gasper took her under his wing and became a second grandfather. Lízabet and Norrick had lived in Ethereal, but she was often left alone while he was in Degomble and would visit Gasper, learning the ways of the malificus and enhancing her talents in healing. As an adult, she dedicated her time to the care facility in Violet's Agora or attended to those infected in Degomble or wounded after a recent battle. Lízabet had become a well-known embedapist and helped many to recover. While in Degomble, she was able to spend more time with her grandfather and further understand his role as a leader. Maintaining his leadership in a stronghold of militia, day-to-day warfare, and a union was no easy task. "No bliss in yer grandfather's role. Easy to be part of a pack and bein' told what to do, but harder leadin' the pack and doin' the tellin'," Arvel once remarked.

Inside Gasper's log cabin was a scattered library containing many magical tomes, scrolls, and parchments that bestowed a vast history of the Primordial Ascendants, the Interglacial Wars, the evil embedded, and the conflict of the Bacillus. Lízabet had a love for reading and spent countless hours taking in the rich stories and events that took place before her time. Her nose was often ocean-deep in words, and she rarely spoke to Gasper. Nonetheless, Gasper embraced her company and loving presence.

With the staff still in hand, Lízabet stirred the concoction a second time, re-conditioning its medicinal properties. "Mentor, your daily elixir is ready; shall I bring it in to you?" she asked.

"*Gaaaaaasp… cough…* no, my dear! *Wheeze!* I am out of bed and naked as a polar bear! Out shortly… yep, yep, yep," Gasper responded.

"Stubborn old man- he should rest," Lízabet muttered under her breath, though relieved at not having to see an old man in his birthday suit.

A speck of light from a nearby bookshelf caught the corner of Lízabet's eye. Curious about its bright radiance, Lízabet pulled out a large tome that had an illegible blur of words sparkling in gold on the front cover. A maroon ribbon with golden trim was used as a placeholder. Lízabet attempted to pull it out, but it would not move, and she stared at the tome, its distorted title and ribbon teasing her and urging her to look inside. Growing eager, she tried to open the tome, but it appeared to be magically secured and locked. Her passion for absorbing words then took the best of her. She firmly gripped the front and back panels, attempting to force them apart, then slammed the spine down on the table, again, then again, and once more. It was no use. Irritated, she drew her embedapist staff, aiming it downward in hopes that it would release the magical lock.

"As hard… *cough*… as you might try… *cough*… you will not unlock that tome." Gasper remarked as his bedroom door swung open, startling Lízabet. He leaned on the Crutches of Winterstorm, his face still hidden beneath his stocking cap.

"That… *gasp*… tome belonged to the Primordial Ascendants, it contains… *cough*… secrets, written by them. It cannot be opened so easily, yep. Yep. Yep."

"Mentor, I have not seen this before. Have you always possessed it?" Lízabet asked.

Gasper sat down, set his crutches on the table, and began taking long sips of the elixir. "Thank you, dear; this is perfect… yep, yep. I cannot… *wheeze*… prepare it as well as you. You have a… *cough*… healer's touch, young lady."

Lízabet smiled at Gasper, then glared at him with folded arms, demanding answers.

"Oh yes... right... the tome. Correct- I have possessed it for many years. But it is worn and usually blends... *cough*... with the others sitting on the shelf. The title... *cough*... that is a different story, yep, yep, yep. It only appears and illuminates under a certain condition."

"And the condition?" Lízabet asked curiously.

"Condition? Well, dear... *cough*... *gasssp*... I'm in rather bad condition. I'm old, weak, and... *cough*... rather sick today, I'm afraid."

Lízabet bit her lower lip, try to remain calm with her old mentor and fully respect his senility and forgetful mind. But right then it almost seemed as though he was provoking her intentionally.

"I meant the tome- its condition?"

"Right, the tome's condition!" Gasper took another drink of his elixir, forgetting to answer. His lengthy sips began to annoy Lízabet and his hesitation continued to poke at her nerves.

"Which tome again?" Gasper asked.

Lízabet's patience was exhausted; she now wanted to swing the tome across Gasper's head. Instead, she used non-violent means, picked it up, and pointed at the title.

"Oh... yes, yes, the title- it becomes... *cough*... visible and luminous when the Restorer of Goodness has completed divination. Only that same person is capable of unlocking and comprehending the pages within."

"The title appears blurry; I cannot make it out," Lízabet commented.

"Patience. It will be readable soon enough... yep, yep, yep," Gasper replied.

The room remained silent as Gasper took a final drink, downing the remaining elixir. He began feeling sleepy, but it helped clear his mind and reduced his coughing and wheezing. He spoke further with intelligent clarity and less hesitation.

"The words inside are very powerful. What has been written portrays what the Restorer must do to end the tyranny of the Bacillus and the infectious embedded evil."

Gasper's explanation hit Lízabet like a ton of falling logs, as one name came to mind– Nicholas.

Lízabet glanced down at the primordial tome, its front and back cover soiled, scuffed, and stained. The joints, hinges, and pages were, however, in perfect condition. The title began to clear itself and sparkled brightly, reflecting off the beautiful and fair skin of her face. Now able to see the title, she read it out loud:

"The Delineation of a Magnanimous Toymaker"

The Bear-Muda Triangle

Gasper had retired to his bedroom to further rest his ailment. The daily medication he consumed had been secretly altered by Lizabet. The usual ingredients that helped him retain better memory and energy were substituted with ones that caused drowsiness. Having respect and care for her mentor, she also knew that Gasper would not rest and would allow his sickness to linger. The best remedy was sleep, and the potency of the elixir would keep him in bed until the next morning. Lizabet suspected Gasper knew of the alteration- he was not gullible by any means- but he trusted her, swallowed his pride, and allowed assistance.

Lizabet also felt tired and less energetic and took the remainder of the day to rest. She pulled some unfamiliar parchments from the scattered library and struggled to interpret the writing as her feet and toes continued to tingle and burn. In a final attempt, she wielded her embedapist staff and aimed it downward, casting a spell of healing. The spell faded, still leaving her with pain and irritation.

Lízabet scoffed at herself. "Pfft. I have the ability to heal the infected, summon ladybugs, and concoct elixirs, yet I cannot repair my own two feet."

Treatment was needed, but it would have to wait until she returned to Ethereal. Unable to hear the tune of the carolers, Lízabet would not make it to Ethereal alone. She would only end up lost and vulnerable to the deadly elements and lurking evil within a massive forest. Holding off until her grandfather arrived would keep her from imposing on her sick mentor for escort, and she could assist him for a few more days.

Every year, the winter season was the busiest as the frequency of those infected rose to overwhelming heights. The care facility in Violet's Agora was at full capacity, while staffing of embedapists grew thin. Lízabet's therapeutic role was in high demand both in Ethereal and Degomble, and she often traveled from one location to another at only a moment's notice.

Lízabet rose her head from the parchment, drawn to a sudden noise of stamping hooves and shuffling snow coming from outside.

"Niah!" a man shouted. "Calm down you two... I don't want to have to–"

The broken–up voice and noise stopped, as the sound of heavy steps headed toward Gasper's cabin. Lízabet quickly jumped up and confirmed that the front door was magically locked. Going into a defensive formation, she gripped her embedapist staff and stood ready by the door.

"Speak the magistical formula!" Lízabet instructed as the man approached.

The man outside cleared his voice. "Ahem! Yes. Bechstein loves to bay at the moon, but his singing, rather awful I must say."

Lízabet smiled widely, recognizing the man's teasing voice, but remained stern.

"Incorrect! This door will not unlock without the correct formula."

The man answered again, still using the wrong approach. "Come now... it is Kiffy; I'm merely passing through, stopped to say hello to yo... er. I... I mean check in on the gatekeeper."

"How do I know you are not an embedded creature inside Kiffy's body?" Lízabet replied bluntly.

"Well, I reckon they made a bad choice of character, if they chose me," Kiffy joked.

Lízabet snickered behind the locked door, hoping Kiffy did not hear her. She was confident it was him but remained cautious, keeping to a serious tone.

"Again, you must speak the correct formula. If it unknown to you, then begone!"

Kiffy smirked and glanced down at Hooley, speaking to her in his usual fashion. "Playing hard to unlock, she is.

Very well, I shall play along. 'They do not speak but sing in carol.'"

The security locks began to magically unlatch as Lízabet opened the door. Maintaining a fake scowl, she refrained from showing bliss at Kiffy's visit. A few yards behind Kiffy and Hooley were Booth and Eucera attached to a supply sledger.

"Good noon, Lízabet," Kiffy greeted her with the Salute of Degomble.

"Hello Kiffy, here for the 'gatekeeper' are you?" Lízabet asked, joshing with disbelief. "Unfortunately, he is sick today and bedridden."

Lízabet bent down, greeted Hooley, and stroked her head. "Hello Hooley, your pedagog does not lie very well, does he?" she remarked with a smirk. "Are you on a supply run?" Lízabet asked further, noticing a saddlebag attached to the torsos of Booth and Eucera and a sled bag tied to the sledger.

"Fishing expedition. Heading to a secret frozen pond tomorrow. Conditions are near perfect. Should have a good catch to supply Ethereal." With a wide grin, Kiffy pointed to Hooley. "Also training my little lady to spot them under the ice. She has been an excellent fish finder."

Lízabet smiled at Hooley, admiring her scarf. "She has a beautiful neck garment; it appears to be well-crafted."

"I believe it suits her well, and she fancies them as you do," Kiffy replied, avoiding the real meaning behind the scarf on Hooley.

Hooley became cold and bored and had little interest in all the human chit-chat. Without hesitation, she passed by Lízabet and lay down by the cabin's fireplace, curling her bushy tail around herself.

"Well now, just make yourself cozy, shall you?" Kiffy commented, shaking his head.

"Taught her bad habits already, I see," Lízabet teased.

Kiffy smirked. "Not I, she learned that trick from Bechstein and the other wolves. They are a lazy bunch when it comes to a warm fire."

Giggling, Lízabet moved her feet away from her body and closer to Kiffy's. Kiffy was once again memorized by Lízabet's deep and gradient brown eyes. He moved in closer as their lips began to seek out one another.

"Ouch!" Lízabet cried out suddenly.

"Apologies! Did I mash your toes?" Kiffy asked.

"Yes! Sorry, NO! I, I stepped on yours. My feet are swollen; they pain when I move them." Lízabet backed away from Kiffy, sat down, and pulled the socks from her feet.

"From my training yesterday," Lízabet remarked, displaying her condition.

Kiffy gave Lízabet's feet a quick once-over. "Rather intensive training... you have a moderate level of frostbite."

"Yes, well, I should be able to treat them when I return to Ethereal."

Kiffy disagreed. "You require a hunter's response. Please allow me to help. I have the appropriate ointments; I carry them at all times."

"Thank you, but I am fine and can wait," Lízabet replied stubbornly.

Without Lízabet's approval, Kiffy reached for his survival rucksack and pulled out two round wooden canisters with lids.

"Do you carry that pack everywhere with you?" Lízabet joked as she watched Kiffy go to work.

"Yes... surely, you never know when you may need something in haste."

"Does it sleep with you?" Lízabet teased further with a slight snicker.

"Well, no... unless I accidentally fall asleep with it. Makes for quite a rough morning."

Lízabet tittered at Kiffy's humor as he began to unscrew the lids of the wooden canisters. Inside one canister was a powdery substance while the other contained a creamy salve.

"Training yesterday went well, I hope, except almost losing your feet?" Kiffy jested as he gently applied the balm. The touch of his hand sent an arousing sensation up Lízabet's leg.

"Uh... Yes... fa... fairly well, except..."

Kiffy could see deep concern in Lízabet's eyes. "Except?"

"Except... I... I did not expect a primordial malificus to summon embedded banshees as part of the training."

"Did he summon them to attack you?" Kiffy asked, concerned, as he began to rub and massage the salve into Lízabet's skin.

"Well... he... oooh... woooo... ummm... mmmm... he... he... what was it that you asked?" Lízabet had become distracted from Kiffy's soothing massage.

"The banshees, did they attack you?"

"Yes! Sorry, NO! No, they did not! Gas... Gas... whooo... Gasper summoned them on to a musk ox, the same animal that he intentionally injured. I understand that... his... his... ohhhh... mmmm... umm, motives were only to teach me. But it is odd that he would hurt a harmless animal and summon embedded creatures for our lesson."

"Odd indeed," Kiffy replied as he raised an eyebrow. "Norrick once mentioned that some malificus were capable of summoning embedded evil. In the heat of war, they would use them against their own kind."

"Yes, well... yesterday, he was the fantastic malificus he once was. His focus was sharp as icicle tips. I felt that I was up against a younger version of him. It saddens me to see Gasper's old age dement and disorient his mind. His ancient magic is still very strong."

"And the musk ox was consumed by the banshees?" Kiffy asked as he continued massaging the salve into Lízabet's other foot.

"No... I... I... whoooo," Lízabet felt hot and flustered inside and fanned her face with her hand. "I, um... was able to... to... stop them and return the wild animal's health."

"Sounds as though Gasper's protege was equally fantastic," Kiffy complimented, flattering Lízabet as she blushed and stared at him admiringly, still hard at his work. "Thank you, your hands are... are... mmm... very soothing for someone who trains animals," Lízabet remarked.

Kiffy nodded, gazing up at Lízabet. "My pleasure."

An awkward silence followed between them as they stared into each other's eyes. Kiffy cleared his throat. "Ahem! Let's apply the powder, shall we? Hopefully you will feel more moist... er... I mean your feet and toes rather... YOU will soon be properly lubricated... I mean YOUR FEET and TOES... YOU will feel much better." Kiffy's face turned red as dragon's fire as he sprinkled the magical powder on to Lízabet's swollen skin. Lízabet began tittering and shaking her feet from the sensation.

"The powder tickles," Lízabet remarked.

"Hehheh, yes it tends to do that; your feet must be ticklish."

"Yes! I mean NO! They are not!"

"You're not going to kick my face, are you?" Kiffy replied smugly, still on his knees.

Lízabet counter-attacked with a glance of thrown daggers, an evil look so swift and so fierce that not even the largest or strongest of shields could block it.

"Ahem! Apologies... almost finished." Kiffy replied, cowering from the look as if he were a child recently disciplined.

The fluid-filled blisters began to break, releasing blemishes of blood. The frostbite then vanished as Lízabet's waxy skin turned from yellow to its natural color. Completing the treatment, Kiffy stood up and brushed the powder from his hands. "Perhaps you can stand and test your walk?" he suggested as he started closing the canister to the salve.

Lízabet stood back up, but her knees began to buckle, causing her to trip forward. Dropping the open canister of powder, Kiffy caught Lízabet before she could fall. Both now surrounded and blinded in a thick mist of dust, Lízabet could feel Kiffy's muscular arms under hers. Her knees buckled once again, and it felt as if her body had become a boat anchor. Embarrassed, she was uncertain if it was the numbness of her feet, Kiffy's treatment, or the fact that she felt hot and flustered, held up by the fisherman's strong body.

The dust settled as they stared at one another, faces both covered in a layer of powder. Their white-chalked lips re-started the process, craving and seeking one another. A passionate kiss, only a millimeter from touching, was interrupted by a long wheeze and cough coming from Gasper's bedroom.

"That would be excellent... *cough*... more wonderful with peppermint, I must say, yep, yep, yep," Gasper uttered in his sleep.

Both blushing, Kiffy and Lízabet laughed at one another. Lízabet then brushed a bit of debris from Kiffy's nose. "Thank you," Kiffy replied. "You still have a bit on your face." Lízabet eyes closed in deep affection as Kiffy gently placed his hand on her cheek, slowly brushing away the remaining powder.

"Ahem! Well... I believe I've created enough ruckus for one day, best I head out," Kiffy suggested.

Lízabet slowly opened her eyes, still in a dreamy state from Kiffy's touch. "I'm happy you came by even if was to check on the gatekeeper," she teased.

"Great to see you again" Kiffy replied, followed by a stern command to his lazy fox. "Hooley! Pono... sledger!"

Lízabet watched as Hooley obeyed and made her way outside, joining Kiffy as they returned to the sledger.

Kiffy stared and smiled tenderly at Lízabet. "If Booth and Eucera ever need help, I know who to bring them to now."

Blushing once again, Lízabet nodded modestly. With a snap of the reins Kiffy hollered "Tele Huit!" and threw a quick Salute of Degomble as he sledded away. With a long sigh of affection, Lízabet returned the salute to the departing pedagog and his pulling twain.

Kiffy and his team reached the ideal campsite, a spot within an abundance of rolling banks that was framed of bent and broken tree limbs and held down mercilessly by the snow and its mighty weight. A tunnel of chilling air blew upwind, reducing the appeal to intruders and evil alike. Invaders would most likely divert from the area, keeping Kiffy, Hooley, and the musk oxen safe. Kiffy would follow with additional safety measures to keep his traveling family unassailable.

He started by untying Booth and Eucera from the sledger and hiding them behind a nearby snowbank equal in width and height. Kiffy praised the musk oxen and patted the stout brutes on the shoulder hump. "Good work you two; you have earned food and rest."

Strapped to the supply sledger was a large sled bag containing food stores, tools, and fishing gear. Kiffy opened the bag, pulling moss and lichens for each musk oxen to forage on. He also included some magical berries, which mysteriously induced nourishment, strength, and a quicker recovery from miles of traveling and pulling of the sledger.

Next, a sleeping quarter was needed for Kiffy and his champion hunter. Kiffy was well-seasoned in training and taming, but he also had enhanced abilities exceeding that of most pedagogs. He could create and call on small animals that remained in the wild. In this case, it was the flurrymunks: artificially created animals that breathed life, slept, and naturally hungered. They were albino in color- which helped them blend with the winter environment- except for two luminant stripes, one red, one green, that ran down their backs. They housed themselves among the banks of snow, using the framework of branches as shelters.

On Kiffy's left wrist was a survival bracelet equipped with an artillery of tiny and useful tools. While most depended on enchanted necklaces to maintain warmth from the cold, Kiffy relied on his bracelet. Attached was a small slit that housed a square mouthpiece. Placing his lips around the slit, Kiffy blew air into the mouthpiece, creating a melodic tune that called out to his wild comrades. The surrounding snowbanks began to shake as the tree limbs beneath swayed to and fro. The small flurrymunks chirped and trilled as they plunged from their homes, racing toward Kiffy and the fox. Hooley became skittish, hiding behind Kiffy's leg. She was not fond of such ambitious animals with chubby cheeks, stubby legs, bushy tails, and luminant stripes heading toward her and her pedagog.

"Hello. friends," Kiffy greeted them as they approached. "The fox and I desire a sleeping quarter for the evening–can you help us?"

With beady black eyes the flurrymunks stared up at the stocky pedagog, expecting a form of payment.

"Yes, right! I'm sure you are all famished from the harsh winter. Please allow me to provide!"

Kiffy reached for his rucksack and pulled out a Tinder–Flux Bellow, a long circular expanding rod, and a Glittering Tundra Chayote, a large fruit with a hard outer shell. Unsheathing his dagger, Kiffy scored an X pattern into the fruit's outer shell and placed it on the ground. With the Tinder–Flux Bellow, he pierced through the X and blew air inside. A fire ignited, consuming the fruit as it seared and roasted in the heat. Frightened, the group of flurrymunks scattered, staying a safe distance from the flames. The colored stripes of their backs illuminated brightly, due to the excitement and anxiety of their dinner being prepped. The large fruit began to scorch, burn, and swell, doubling in size as the outer shell stretched and cracked. Weakened, the glittering tundra chayote ruptured, and a rainstorm of roasted chestnuts fell upon the group of flurrymunks. With wee arms, they feasted on the entree, rapidly stuffing their faces as if it were their last meal.

With their hunger satisfied, the flurrymunks honored their end of the bargain. Using teensy but hefty hands, fast feet, and zippy movements, they began forming a sleeping quarter from a nearby snowbank. Patting and chiseling the snow covering, they created a roof and igloo–walled structure. Other flurrymunks worked underneath, reforming the bent tree branches into studs and joists, creating a tent–like foundation. Lastly, they structured a doorway so Kiffy and Hooley could easily enter. Then, with construction complete, the flurrymunks scattered, returning to their own homes beneath the surrounding snowbanks.

"All is well girl; they are gone now," Kiffy reassured Hooley, who was still hidden behind his leg. "It will be dark soon; one final task is left… a protective triangle."

Kiffy began walking in the opposite direction of the campsite at a sixty-degree angle. He counted out loud with each large step "1… 2… 3… 4… 5…" Hooley joined the game, leaping then landing, leaping then landing, trying to match Kiffy's long strides.

"We must reach ninety; that would be… perhaps… nine hundred in Hooley steps?" Kiffy questioned humorously, although the fox had no clue as to what he was saying.

Kiffy reached the final counts "87... 88... 89... and... 90," as he approached a tall pine tree.

Reaching again for his survival rucksack, Kiffy removed some rope and a chunk of Colrock Candy, pressing its sticky surface on to the rope. He lassoed the rope and slung it over a tree branch, leaving it to hang. Colrock Candy was an ideal tool for distraction. Its bitter-sweet aroma and sugary taste were enjoyed by many, even hungry predators and embedded creatures. However, over-consumption of this treat resulted in stomachaches and an abrupt sensation of releasing it in unpleasant ways.

"First diversion complete," Kiffy commented to Hooley. "Let's carry on!"

Kiffy and Hooley continued shaping the protective triangle, walking a straight line and moving in an opposing direction to the hanging Colrock Candy. "1... 2... 3... 4," Kiffy counted again, eventually reaching 90 at the new location. Reopening his rucksack, Kiffy removed a Snowhare Piccolo, a long, tall tube that had a fuse and a ground stake attached to the bottom. He firmly placed the Snowhare Piccolo in the ground and removed a flint stone from his bag. On his bracelet was a small piece of metal that he scraped with the stone, creating a spark and igniting the fuse. Staked to the ground, the tube remained in place and screamed loudly, releasing a magical fountain of terrific colors and sparkles. An apparition of snow hares then leaped from the canister and ran into the wild. This pattern continued infinitely. The escaping hares could potentially distract any who would attempt to chase them instead of trying to find the campsite. With the Colrock Candy and the Snowhare Piccolo in place, the protective triangle was complete.

"I believe all is in order," Kiffy grinned as he and Hooley headed back to camp.

Kiffy lay inside his flurrymunk–made igloo while Hooley curled up at his feet, already asleep. Kiffy felt warm, cozy, and comfortable covered in a thick qiviut blanket, crafted from the soft underlayer of wool of his musk oxen. Outside, both Booth and Eucera continued to forage, replenishing their energy. Although Kiffy had Hooley nearby, he longed for a loving companion that he could lie next to- one he could caress. He felt lonely, but recapped on those that enlightened his life, such as his animals, old man Arvel, his fellow union members, and his newest friend Nicholas. In his heart he somehow knew Nicholas had significant meaning, but was also one who could understand his anguish, being so far from home, from family, from friends, and from people he once knew. Kiffy could only guess that Nicholas was lonely, perhaps even terrified. His eyes grew heavy as he thought of Lízabet and her silky hair, gradient brown eyes, and smile. With a sleepy chuckle, he thought of her soft lips covered in treatment powder.

Come early morning, it would be a short hike to the frozen pond. It was a favorite spot of Kiffy's, a place of temporary serenity. Pulling one fish after another from a simple ice-shaved hole was heaven to him. He would further indulge in the sport, training Hooley to track the biggest and hungriest of fish beneath the ice. He was very proud of how much she had learned and accomplished. Just before sunrise, they would arrive, hoping for perfect conditions that would result in a deluge of winter-starved fish. The evening's clear sky, with its full, bright moon, showed promise. For reasons unexplained, fishing seemed far more superior when the large sphere of light was completely round. Perhaps it was a magical artifact, Kiffy thought, that swayed the fish to feed. Weather also played its part in the outcome, and Kiffy made best intentions to plan his trips based on these factors. A grand catch, one that would feed Ethereal's people for several weeks, was his ultimate goal.

Kiffy began drifting off to sleep, but his eyes soon bolted open to the sound of stirring musk oxen, followed by deep and low growls. He grabbed his war hammer and dagger and equipped them to his waist, then quietly exited his sleeping quarter, attempting to calm Booth and Eucera.

"Shhh! Quiet down!" Kiffy commanded in a whisper, as he threw more berries toward them, attempting to keep their heads down and out of sight.

Kiffy creeped slowly to the nearest snowbank and carefully peeked over the top. Hooley followed, yawning and stretching out her legs, still half asleep and oblivious. In the spot where Kiffy had staged the Snowhare Piccolo were now eight pairs of purple glowing eyes and a toxic green mist. Subtle growls continued along with snarls and clicks, the sounds of a foreign communication among the questionable invaders. Kiffy remained behind the snowbank and waited tensely for them to depart. Once they were gone, he crept 90 steps to the tube of leaping and racing snow hares. Imprinted in the snow were large bear tracks, melted pockets of ice, and lingering fumes that burned and irritated Kiffy's eyes. He scouted the area thoroughly, checking the hanging rope of Colrock Candy, still intact. Both locations showed no further appearance of invading creatures or sounds of growling, snarling, or snorting. Kiffy sighed heavily, looking down at his fox with a frown of fear.

"They were polar bears, but not just bears... embedded polar bears... consumed by gashgobs. That means– NO! It can't be. That would mean the gashgobs have awoken. But... how... when?!"

No "Resultin'!" Only Delaying

Union meeting two hundred and seventy. Three days until the winter solstice...

"Change formation!" the commander ordered as two soldiers positioned themselves inside. The steel doors of the grand hall slammed shut, locking tightly and securely.

"Let us begin!" Norrick called out to his fellow members. The engraved Emblem of Goodness, glistening in evergreen and gold, rotated and re-aligned. The union took to their assigned seats while the strike-breakers sat in the surrounding area.

Norrick continued. "Today we have business of upmost importance, but first- I wish to start with positive news. My granddaughter has completed the requirements to join us as a new member. She has trained hard, faced many trials and challenges, and has helped many to overcome sickness and infection. Gasper has given approval for her initiation. Lizabet, if you would, please?" Lizabet rose from her strike-breaker chair, looking nervous as all eyes shifted toward her.

"Begin the initiation! Those that approve, provide your assent!" Quilo ordered.

Without hesitation, the sound of knocking fists rumbled the union table, followed by a loud "Ho! Ho! Rah!"

"Majority approves!" Quilo confirmed. "Lízabet is a now a member of our unit."

Lízabet became surrounded by clapping and encouragement. Arvel, as always the dispirited artificer, grumbled and scoffed, folding his arms.

"Very good, Lízabet!" a strike-breaker cheered.

"Well done! Our union is stronger!" a fellow union member cried.

Lízabet gleamed from the attention, her reddened face growing paler as Kiffy stood, clapped, and threw her an affectionate smile from across the table.

"Sit yer love-struck ass down!" Arvel grumbled to Kiffy.

Kiffy elbowed Arvel in the shoulder. "Come now, you negative grope, at least clap for our new member."

"Mukluk! More members, more debatin', endless negotatin', no RESULTIN'!"

At the union table was a newly crafted chair. Tensîle, a native Yuulnavie who created custom nameplates for each member, had a thin piece of metal with Lízabet's name on it in her hand. She handed it to Norrick, and with a swipe of his hand, he gave it a final magistical touch, infusing it into the chair's antlered headrest.

Lízabet presented the Salute of Degomble. "I thank you all for your assent. Without the support of my grandfather and my mentor Gasper, I would not be sitting with you today."

From his strike-breaker chair, Nicholas listened in as meeting *two hundred and seventy* proceeded. Various subjects, issues, and loose ends were discussed and debated. He learned more on the culture of the people, future projects planned for Ethereal, the militia's training structure in Degomble, and other insightful accomplishments. He found attending these meetings to be beneficial, not only to assist him with finding further answers, but also to build a better understanding of those he would be helping. After a while, the spotlight turned to him.

"Kiffy... Nicholas... further updates on your visit with the Nonesuch?" Norrick asked.

"Successful visit," Kiffy replied vaguely.

"That tells us nothing! Successful how?" Quilo asked bluntly.

"Nicholas was–"

"The Nonesuch accepted my visit and proceeded in divination," Nicholas interrupted, rising from his chair. Now having all the attention on him, he felt even more nervous than Lízabet had.

"Your divination– did you determine meaning, reason for being here with us?" Norrick questioned.

"Somewhat, but with stormy visions and complicated tasks."

"We are a union; we create complication," Norrick replied, comforting Nicholas. "Can you describe what tasks were defined to you?"

Nicholas wanted to cite specific details: Kiffy's interaction and the scarf given to his fox, how he was directed to the Faithlife of Kindness, seeing his father in spirit, and the special gift given to him- the Chrysalis of Winter Solstice. Instead, he kept to a simple and firm answer. "I am tasked to rescue a "foredoomed fallow;" it is said that this sick animal can safely transport me through the Frozen Splode. Beyond is an artifact of importance... inside a temple," Nicholas explained.

Arvel chuckled scornfully. "Well, this meetin' is over!"

The union hall turned silent as Arvel was stung by a room of glares.

"The Frozen Splode is a death zone, nothing more! The best of our primordial ancestors and Yuulnavian engineers have failed to withstand it," Çóalrite pointed out.

"And what of the recent quakes?" another member inquired.

"That is also a concerning matter," Norrick replied. "We too had quakes in Degomble. Çóalrite – what of Ycevein; were they felt in your fair city?

"Yes, three of our engineering towers encountered structural damage," Çóalrite replied, peeking through his snow goggles. Nicholas felt terrible. Had he created further problems instead of helping the cause? Norrick began stroking his flame-flowing beard. "Hmmm... Nicholas... have you taken other actions besides your divination with the Nonesuch?"

Nicholas sighed heavily, reflecting on his ventures of releasing Gandomine from the locked cage. "Yes... I have encountered one that can help in rescuing the foredoomed fallow."

"Here in Ethereal?" Norrick asked, bewildered.

"Yes, correct."

"And who is this person?"

"This person is not a human, but a bird... a cardinal," Nicholas replied.

"A... a... cardinal? From the Cardinals of Joy?" Norrick asked.

"Yes, but a rare cardinal- Gandomine."

Norrick paused thoughtfully, then muttered under his breath. "Interesting... I would not suspect Violet's dearest friend to be the link. Well-hidden, and smart on her part, very smart indeed."

Nicholas continued. "After I released Gandomine, a horrid and mocking voice spoke in a demonic nature. Thereafter, Ethereal's ground began to shake.

Gandomine stated that my abilities, and my act of unlocking the cage, had aggravated the Bacillus."

"That sounds like 'RESULTIN' to me," Kiffy bantered, jabbing Arvel in the ribs.

"Undertow's just 'nother oaf with pedagog abilities, useless as you are," Arvel snapped back.

"Gandomine is correct," Norrick said. "It appears you are deemed to be the Restorer, yielding unique abilities of goodness. Your actions threaten the Bacillus; its aggravation will lead to extremely harsh reactions." The room suddenly filled with creaking chairs and whispering conversations. Norrick raised his hand toward the unsettled group, silencing them.

"What must I do, then? I want to contribute, but I do not wish to harm anyone." Nicholas asked.

"Your choices are at your discretion, Nicholas. Yes, excruciating consequences may result, but I recommend you follow the advice of the Nonesuch and play by your divination," Norrick suggested.

"Yer the pic a the litter, Undertow!" Arvel jested.

The union hall turned silent as Arvel was stung by a room of glares again.

"NONETHELESS, the results of the divination and these so called "UNIQUE" abilities should remain confidential within the union," Quilo Serdar argued.

"Agreed, Commander." Norrick nodded. "We must not put excitement or panic on Ethereal's people. Not yet.

If Nicholas chooses to proceed, he shall soon prove otherwise."

"What of the people and the union? What are we to do; what is our role?" a member asked.

"If Nicholas' fate is to perform these tasks and he and Gandomine successfully rescue the foredoomed fallow, then... I propose we focus on delaying."

"And what must be delayed?" a member at the table asked.

Norrick's emerald-green eyes showed signs of dread. "*Torment.*"

"We are ill-prepared for Torment!" Quilo advised. "Embedapists are already overworked and small in numbers. Our militia requires further recruiting and training; tactics and planning require strengthening."

"Agreed. That is why we must delay its release," Norrick replied.

"Mukluk! Our tactics 'n plannin' are hobble-gobble!" Arvel replied.

The hall turned silent as Arvel was stung by a room of glares for the third time.

Kiffy nudged Arvel. "Pleasing the group as always, I see," he teased.

Quilo Serdar's face reddened in anger. "We must halt further actions by this foreigner; THEY DO NOT HELP OUR CAUSE!"

"Nicholas is not a member of our union," Norrick debated. "We cannot approve or disapprove of his actions; we can only decide if we are to support him or not!"

"Yes! I'm aware of the union rules, malificus! But there are exceptions, and I will not hesitate to proceed over objection!" Quilo argued.

"I understand your frustrations, Commander," Norrick replied. "But to proceed over objection will only send us backward. We must work together to determine the smartest and safest solution. Delaying Torment is our best line of defense. We cannot hope to confront a variant of the Bacillus, not yet!"

Norrick turned his attention toward the group. "Members! Although his motives aggravate the Bacillus, Nicholas' actions are destined as well. If it wasn't him, someone else would have been chosen to do the same thing. Yes, Nicholas has unknowingly hastened our problems, but these issues are inevitable; we must also realize that we have reached a turning point, an opportunity to gain prosperity and well-being that we can only dream of. If we are to support Nicholas, we can potentially end sickness, the embedded evil– potentially destroy the Bacillus.

The room filled with laughs and scoffs of disbelief. "The sickness and evil will never end! Not in our lifetime!" a fellow member hollered.

"Agreed, even our ancestors failed to destroy the Bacillus!" another member voiced.

"We have a strong alliance with the Nonesuch," Lízabet argued. "I recommend we support these tasks defined to Nicholas... we must provide him Union protection." Lízabet started blushing, but felt good inside, realizing that this was her first time voicing input as a new union member.

Norrick glanced at Kiffy. "Kiffy... you have been quiet... you appear concerned. Further thoughts to share with the union?"

Kiffy rose from his chair and released a long sigh.

"For gomble-shittin' sakes! Sit... DOWN, Animal Lover!" Arvel growled.

"Two nights ago, I encountered signs of gashgobs near my campsite," Kiffy replied.

"Gashgobs?" Norrick asked. "Are you certain? They have been in permanent slumber."

"This cannot be!" a member shouted.

"I am certain," Kiffy confirmed. "Imprinted in the snow were polar bear tracks and lingering fumes. After meeting at the gatekeeper's home, I traced the tracks. The gashgobs... have intentions, a purpose..."

"What purpose?" Norrick asked.

Kiffy's face showed signs of dread as Norrick's had. His fellow union members and the surrounding strike-breakers listened with concerned eyes as he struggled to speak of the bad news. "Norrick is correct that we must delay Torment. The gashgobs are heading to the ruins and intending to give their support. If they are successful, then–"

"They must be stopped now!" a fellow member interrupted. "We cannot suffer another major outbreak!"

"We CANNOT be thwarted into rash decisions based on tasks assigned by the Nonesuch or the words of a pedagog!" Quilo argued. "There is too much risk on the lives of our people! We should hold steady, wisely, and prepare ourselves until the summer season. The Bacillus and the embedded evil will be weaker and more vulnerable."

"Yes, perhaps you are right, Commander." Norrick agreed. "However, with the release of this cardinal and the awakened gashgobs, the Bacillus fears annihilation for the first time. It is extremely threatened. The winter solstice is in three days, and the Bacillus' sway will be at its strongest. With the support of the gashgobs, there is a high chance of creating the deadly variant."

Nicholas now felt extremely discouraged as he observed the union hall filled with tension, loud chatter, and angry gestures. He was raised to help others. But in this instance, he felt that he wasn't a Restorer, but a *creator* of problems. He understood conflict, sickness, and even war, but these issues were beyond his ambition and confidence. He also wished he hadn't met Drusus and

Otho and constructed Nonna, only to endanger them and the crew. Perhaps they wouldn't have been shipwrecked and he wouldn't have been sent to this mysterious land of embedded creatures, this "Bacillus," and "deadly variant". Not only did he feel he was affecting the lives of these people, but he most likely had taken away the breaths of his fellow shipmates, suffocated and eaten by the sea. His mind stormed in anger. HE WANTED HIS PARENTS BACK!

Then Nicholas remembered the colorful garden of the Faithlife where he had made a promise to his father. He had to remain level-headed, maintain bravery, and continue his venture with integrity.

"Members! Please calm!" Norrick called out. "I know there is doubt in your hearts, distress in your souls, and worry in your minds. I know we are all weary of the fight, the embedded evil, and the sickness we suffer from the Bacillus. For the better of our families and ourselves, I ask that you trust in the Nonesuch, our union, and Nicholas."

"What is our plan going forth?" Tensîle asked from across the table.

"I urge we support simultaneously as Nicholas rescues the fallow. Doing so will temporarily stun and weaken the Bacillus, and we would have a small opportunity to delay Torment." Norrick looked to Quilo with a sincere gesture of friendship and respect. "Commander, we cannot be successful without your support and your militia."

Quilo Serdar grumbled. "Bah! Typical strategies of a malificus, our window of opportunity will be runty and our chances slim to none."

"Yes, I know, Quilo. It's our best strategy, for now- we must try," Norrick replied.

Quilo nodded. "Very well... you have my support, Norrick. Union of Goodness! Those who approve in the delay of Torment- and supporting Nicholas, PROVIDE YOUR ASSENT!"

Nicholas did not get the quick response that Lízabet had during her initiation, and his stomach turned as the union hall remained silent. But soon a disruptive knock of a single fist shook the union table. "Torment! Disease outbreaks! War! Death! You got ma assent. HO! HO! RAH!" Arvel shouted.

Another fist knocked. "You also have my assent, friend! HO! HO! RAH!" Kiffy shouted.

A third fist knocked. "I believe in you, Nicholas! You have my assent! HO! HO! RAH!" Lízabet cried.

With emotional awe, Nicholas watched as another fist knocked, followed by another, then several more, along with a repetitive pattern of "HO! HO! RAH!"

"Union majority approves!" Quilo cried. "We will begin preparations. To all that is dear to us, our friends, and our families. FOR THE SAKE OF GOODNESS!"

"Nicholas? Nicholas!" Lízabet shouted as she exited the UHOG building.

"Congratulations on your initiation, Lízabet," Nicholas said as she approached.

"Yes… thank you," Lízabet replied, handing Nicholas the *The Delineation of a Magnanimous Toymaker*. "This book was sitting in a library of literature; I believe it is meant to be yours."

"Mine?" Nicholas asked, dumbfounded.

"I'm told it has important primordial secrets that only the Restorer of Goodness can decipher."

Nicholas accepted the book, noticing the dim title on the front cover re-illuminating brightly. Lízabet watched with shocked eyes as the book easily opened, with golden sparkles fluttering outward. Inside were words written on old and well-worn pages. Lízabet quickly clasped Nicholas's hands, closing the book.

"Best you wait until no one is around," Lízabet suggested, as she glanced furtively at the area around them. "As you can see, it reacts to you somehow. No one can open the book to read its contents, not even Gasper. That accounts for something!" Lízabet explained, smiling. "Please keep it safe and secure."

"I... I will," Nicholas stuttered, uncertain as to what he should do with such a book of mystery. "Thank you, Lízabet."

Lízabet smirked. "You're welcome, Restorer of Goodness; please take care of yourself."

"I... I will. You as well. I hope for the best for you... for all of you."

Lízabet squeezed Nicholas's hand and began to walk away but turned to Nicholas once last time.

"Restorer?" she shouted.

"Yes?"

"I'm glad it's you. I don't understand why, but the "Spirit of Loveliness" inside tugs at my heart; it tells me that the Nonesuch chose the right person."

Nicholas smiled and nodded modestly. "I hope to do my best."

As each union member and strike-breaker left the Union Hall of Goodness, Nicholas felt a frightening chill. The meaning and contribution that he so heartily sought out had to correctly synchronize with theirs. He now MUST be successful in completing his tasks. Not only was a mysterious book sitting in the palm of his hands, but so were the lives of all these people who were good and just.

Embedded Bears of Maritime

Shortly after the release of Gandomine...

The bears of maritime, snow, and ice scavenged the ocean's coastal realm. Many of the sows had gone dormant and were now resting in dens, soon to birth new cubs.

With deeply scooped claws, a celebration of four polar bears tore through pancakes of sea ice in hopes of finding frozen carcasses. Soon their attention was drawn to a distant iceberg, where a group of fat and sassy seals taunted them as they lay sprawled on the slippery surface. Persuaded by hunger and the dull pain in their empty stomachs, the bears plunged into the cold waters. Using their large front paws as paddles and rear paws as rudders, they merged toward the iceberg. Two of the bears descended underwater, distracted by a school of swimming cod below.

Focused on their prey, the predators were unaware that they were in a dangerous zone, soon to become the hunted. Residing in the deep and dark waters below were the gashgobs, aquatic creatures of the embedded. In the

Primordial Wars, the ancient malificus had cast a spell of slumber, which entrapped them to an enchanted and permanent nap.

The gashgobs had the upper bodies of a human but with circular fin-like appendages on their arms and shoulder blades. Their mouths were wide and ugly with long pointy teeth outside their lower lips. Their skin was transparent, displaying purple glowing veins and a pumping heart, pulsating blood. Their lower body- the most feared- had long and stringy tentacles that would latch to those they attacked.

Several gashgobs broke from slumber, their purple eyes illuminating, and emerged from the watery depths with a belching scream. Their appendages began to rotate and spin, increasing their propulsion immensely. The blackness of the ocean turned to blue as they reached the surface. The first victim was to be one of the two fishing bears.

After a few unsuccessful attempts, the first bear had finally outwitted a single cod, bringing it to the icy surface to feast. Enjoying his morsel, he was soon consumed by many stringy tentacles. Trying to break free, the bear slashed and clawed at the tentacles, shattering them into many ice particles, but became outmatched as more tentacles punctured its flesh. The bear roared in agony as the gashgob pulled him back into the sea. The surface of the water bubbled, and the bear's head appeared again above the surface. His eyes were now glowing purple, and his fur was no longer hollow white, but dark gray with purple glowing tips. His entire body had transformed into an embedded creature with a centaur appearance-a blend of an evil polar bear and a gashgob. The gashgob was mounted on top, controlling the bear's thoughts and actions, and relied on the bear's respiratory system to breathe on land. The embedded bear growled and breathed from its mouth and nose, releasing a vapor that melted the ice and snow beneath them. Any folk or animal of goodness that breathed in this toxic substance would easily fall ill.

The next victim was the second bear fishing for cod; it too was consumed and transformed.

The final two bears slowly edged closer to the island buffet of seals. Carefully planning their ambush, they sneaked around to the back side of the iceberg and climbed aboard. One of the two swiftly attacked his prey, and the other seals panicked and nose-dived into the water. With a long leap, the second bear plunged back into the ocean, grabbed hold of an escaping seal, and brought it to the surface. As she attempted to eat her earned lunch, stringy tentacles took hold of her, throwing her back into the water where she was quickly consumed. The mutated creature climbed onto the ice for a third time. Her breath melting the top layers of the iceberg, she approached the final bear, who at first was oblivious to the danger as he focused on his meal. She stood tall, growling and snarling, with the gashgob riding above her belching a horrid scream. The final bear rose to his hind legs, then what had been a dining area became a slick wrestling mat as they began to brawl.

The embedded bear slashed with her sharp claws, slicing his torso. He growled and snarled in pain, then attempted to counterattack and missed. He shifted his body weight and pummeled forward at the embedded creature. Suddenly– stressed by the battle and the toxic steam– the iceberg began to calve and collapsed beneath them. Both were thrown back into the cold water, and the fourth and final polar bear fell victim to the embedded evil.

What was once a celebration of four hungry polar bears was now a group of four monstrous anomalies. The mounted gashgobs began to communicate amongst each other with a native tongue that could not be understood by those of goodness.

"Click... screeee... burrp... clack!" one bellowed.

Another replied. *"Screee... clack... blaraaar... burrp... creee!"*

Concluding their belching conversation, they commanded the bears to proceed forward. They would soon join ranks with other fiendish creatures of the embedded.

The Bacillus was now restless, growing strong, and its sway of the embedded evil was mighty. The summoned gashgobs would meet on common ground, a ruin that nested inside the tundra's sweeping plateaus and sculpted formations– the *Strain.*

Feyhañdsel's Bastion

Three days until the winter solstice…

Nicholas stared at the Curling Ribbon Falls. The flat rock had become a regular resting place where he could think, analyze, and center himself. It was no longer the use of the pharos, sitting on the warm beach of Patara, a refreshing swim in the Mare Nostrum, or riding his ol' girl– Paloma. "There will be a beautiful sunrise soon. What say you, girl? Up for a morning ride?" he would always ask her.

The small delights that he enjoyed in Patara were events of the past. He was now considered a Restorer and had these "true powers of goodness," as Gandomine called them. Nicholas continued to question his role. What would be the result of his accomplishments? What if he failed, and if he did, what chaotic events would everyone face? He still felt horrible for instigating aggravation on the Bacillus. But what was done was done, and he had to venture on. How would he breach the magical walls that encapsulated Ethereal? At times, he felt imprisoned not being able to leave on his own. Perhaps he was capable, but how? He hoped the guidance from Gandomine would help him determine a way out. Having support from Kiffy, Lízabet, Norrick, and the UOG also helped un–fog his navigational map, defining coordinates in his role.

He stared at the questionable book that Lízabet had given him, mesmerized by the title's glowing hue. He opened the book for a slight moment, only to find an empty compartment for storing. The pages did not appear to have useful words of instruction or wisdom. Discouraged, Nicholas stored it securely in his memorizer pouch. He had taken some time to familiarize himself with the pouch's function. So far it had worked well, and he learned that he could place several items inside without worrying about them being stolen or destroyed. The Chrysalis of Winter Solstice remained separated in the front pocket, due to its bitter coldness.

Nicholas pulled a long parchment from his pouch. Linde had provided a list of shops where he could purchase food, clothing, and other necessities. At the very bottom of the parchment was a specialized list of merchants:

Restorer only!

–Autumn's Leaves

–Bity Bitey's Baker's Bake

–Gibben Gubbin's Gizmos

–Warmth Thee Heart

All shops are in Feýhañdsel's Hamlet. For the sake of goodness! –Linde

Feýhañdsel's Hamlet? Where might that be? He had become familiar with the northern sector and devised a daily route to the Cardinals of Joy; however, he could not recall ever seeing such a place. He questioned if the hamlet might be in the southern sector of Violet's Agora. Having grown up as a small-town resident, he was intimidated by the denser layout of the south sector and so far had refrained from visiting.

"Good morrow Nicholas, will you be heading to Violet's Agora?" Gandomine, perched on a nearby tree, asked, throwing Nicholas off guard. He did not realize the cardinal had been up in a tree, watching over him, and was still adjusting to being able to speak to a rare cardinal- or any animal for that matter.

"Good morrow Gandomine. Yes… shortly, I wanted to gather my thoughts for a while."

"I can imagine it is a lot to take in," Gandomine commented.

Nicholas nodded as Gandomine's male voice spoke more bluntly. "WE ARE STRAPPED FOR TIME! WE MUST BE SUITABLY PREPARED IF WE ARE TO RESCUE THE FOREDOOMED FALLOW."

Nicholas agreed. "Unfortunately, I am still seeking the location of the required merchants. Do you know where Feýhañdsel's Hamlet is?"

"YES, I KNOW EXACTLY WHERE IT IS! IT IS IN VIOLET'S AGORA!"

Nicholas could not decipher if Gandomine was being sarcastic or stating the obvious. "Do you know if it is in the north sector or the south sector?" he asked.

Gandomine's wings shrugged, and the bird retracted to a woman's voice. "Sorry, no, I'm simply a cardinal."

"Pardon, didn't you say you knew the exact location?" Nicholas asked, confused.

"He did! But I did not!" Gandomine replied stoutly.

"Apologies. Would "he" know?"

Gandomine switched to a male voice. "SORRY RESTORER, I WAS DISTRACTED BY A BUTTERFLY. PLEASE REPEAT YOUR QUESTION."

Nicholas became impatient. "It is fine, Gandomine, thank you anyway."

"VERY WELL, ASK ANYTIME. I AM ALWAYS HERE TO HEL— OH MY! A PUDDLE! I'M OVERDUE FOR A BATH!" Gandomine exclaimed, flying away from the conversation.

Nicholas brainstormed for ideas, what supplies he would need, and whether the south sector was the place to purchase them. The problem was that he had no clue. Seeking answers, he glanced at his supposed confidant soaking, splashing, and playing like a child in muddied water. It appeared that Gandomine was on a meaningful venture of cleansing and refreshment.

For several days, Nicholas had worked for Linde and Duggle at the Cardinals of Joy and had earned bartering tokens. A common transaction among shop owners, merchants, and trade workers was bartering– whether it be goods for goods, goods for services, services for services, or service for goods. If these conditions could not be met, a secondary means of obtaining goods or services was bartering tokens. All merchant and service shops had the choice to either accept the currency or to simply accept goods and services.

Nicholas had spent a fair number of tokens to purchase additional clothing. Although the A.Q.D.C.P.L at the CottonSedge Inn could provide cleaning, tailoring, and garment changes, a quick variety of attire was also nice. His suite's clothing cupboard now had more options to choose from.

Throughout Ethereal, an economic system of bartering designed by the Union of Goodness was practiced every day. The system was divided into two networks, inner–swops and outer–swops. Inner–swops consisted of those living in Ethereal and/or serving in Degomble. Those that served to protect were also awarded tokens for their heroics and could purchase necessities for themselves or their families. Bartering or token requirements were generally higher for outer–swops, which consisted of visitors from other outside communities, including Yuulnavvies from Ycevein. Although Ycevein was far North and exposed to danger, it was surrounded by a rich environment of resources that could be utilized within the city. Merchants also protected themselves from traveling rubberhawkers that roamed the streets of the town. Rubberhawkers were clever thieves that would steal goods from honest business owners or use counterfeit bartering tokens, then re-barter the merchandise for personal profit or gain. But how would a merchant know when a rubberhawker arrived? Most establishments or merchant booths kept a rubberchecker fern nearby, a magical plant that could detect a rubberhawker and identify them by withering and turning brown. When this happened, merchants were encouraged to refuse service and remove them from their establishment or booth. Many incidents called upon resident military to capture a rubberhawker and confine them for attempted thievery.

Many also donated goods and services to Ethreal's less fortunate. At the Cardinals of Joy, Duggle's kind soul often gave goods to fellow townsfolk for free, whether they were inner-swops or outer-swops. Linde would often scold Duggle, demanding that he stick to bartering practices.

"If they do not have goods or bartering tokens, at least inquire for services!"

"Yes, dear," Duggle would always reply. Being married to Linde for many years, he found it was much easier to agree than to argue.

Nicholas became lost in the southern sector of Violet's Agora. His sense of direction had been altered by the twists and turns of the busy alleyways and walkways.

The tall buildings and residential structures formed giant walls, making it difficult to navigate in what felt like an enormous labyrinth. Frustrated, Nicholas questioned if the "Restorer only" shops were in fact in the northern sector and he had wasted time venturing south. If he were to head back, it would consume the remainder of his day. Having urgency in his role, he wished he would have asked Linde for directions before attempting to find the place on his own.

"Pardon me, do you know where Feýhañdsel's Hamlet may be?" Nicholas asked, interrupting a passerby.

"Sorry, I do not."

"Good day, sir... would you–"

"No! Never heard of it!" a man replied coarsely.

"Excuse me, ma'am... ma'am?"

"I am only aware of Feýhañdsel's Bastion," an elderly woman replied. "He lives in a villa inside the bastion's ward. I've lived here my whole life and never heard of such a place."

"Thank you, do you know which direction to Feýhañdsel's Bas–" The woman sauntered off before Nicholas could complete his question. Discouraged, he sat on a nearby wooden bench to calm himself and ponder his next move. He preferred to be in front of the Curling Ribbon Falls, venting his aggravation. Massaging his forehead, he heard a familiar woman's voice coming from above him. "You will fail to find the hamlet if you keep asking the locals."

"Gandomine? I did not see you perched there. How long have you been following me?" Nicholas asked.

"Quite some time."

"You are very stealthy," Nicholas commented.

"I see that you are lost?" Gandomine asked.

"I'm afraid so. Could you help me? I believe you… sorry, HE stated that you know exactly where the shops are?"

"Yes, he knows, but he is in a tizzy today. He prefers to be an unsociable tiz-woz! I will do my best to help you."

"Great, thank you," Nicholas replied.

"I recommend that you follow those children; that is your answer," Gandomine advised.

Nicholas stared, confused. "Children?" he asked as a young boy scurried past, stomping on his foot. "Sorry, mister!" the boy cried out, staggering as his older sister grabbed him by the hand. "Hurry, brother, the line is already long!"

"Follow them?" Nicholas asked.

"Yes! Hurry, Restorer! We have no time to waste." Gandomine replied.

Nicholas jumped from the wooden bench and switched to a jog, attempting to catch up with the boy and his sister. As he followed from behind, he was led to a widespread fortress-like structure with curtained walls made of stone and four two-story towers with pointed roofs adjoining the walls at each corner. A heavy reinforced door with steel rails was in front, closed tightly. Nicholas was amazed by its architecture, as it was like nothing he had ever seen before. Surrounding the outer perimeter was a long line of children that spanned several blocks.

The heavy door screeched and squeaked as it moved upward. The irritating sound of the steel rails was overtaken by the cheering and chattering of each boy and girl, many of them hopping up and down with excitement.

"Hey look! The door's opening!"

"Yay!"

"Can we enter now?"

"No! Not until Feýhañdsel comes out."

Sharp tones of rattling, crackling, and thumping followed from inside as four drummers exited the bastion and made their way into the street. Each marching drum displayed the Emblem of Goodness on its outer shell. Lastly, a tall Yuulnavian man with a noticeably thick mustache exited through the door. The little ones hollered with glee. "It's Feýhañdsel! Yaaaayyy Feýhañdsel!"

"QUIET PLEASE! LISTEN CAREFULLY!" Feýhañdsel shouted through the commotion. "Only three may enter at a time! I repeat... ONLY THREE AT A TIME! Be prompt in your gift request so others can enter! Parents, please remember this is for children only! We can now begin this year's event."

The long line grew fidgety as Feýhañdsel returned inside the bastion.

"Yaaaaaayyyyy!"

"Woo hooo!"

"I'm so excited!!! I can't wait to request my gift!"

As three youngsters entered, Nicholas lost sight of his original intentions. His mind was no longer focused on finding supplies or rescuing some sacred fallow. Instead, he stood by others in the line, quite taken by what he had seen.

"What is this place, and why this line?" Nicholas asked them, attracting a swarm of various explanations and conversations.

"You do not know? Each year during the winter season, we can request a gift from Feýhañdsel."

"Yeah! And then Feýhañdsel delivers our requests to the Yuulnavies up North."

"That's right! And if we are good! The Yuulnavies will build it for us!"

"Feýhañdsel?" Nicholas realized that was the exact name on his list. "Is this where Feýhañdsel's Hamlet is?" Nicholas asked.

"Hamlet? What's a hamlet? No... Feýhañdsel lives in a villa; it's in the bastion's ward."

Another child chimed in with exciting news. "Have you heard?! The Yuulnavies crafted a new toy this year!"

"They have? What is it?!"

"I was told it's a new Mini–Battling Hexcritter!"

"It is? I'm requesting that!"

The joyous sight was a breath of fresh air for Nicholas. Seeking further insight, he looked for Gandomine, who was nowhere to be seen. Had the cardinal flown off or just hidden well out of sight? He trusted his instincts and waited at the back of the line, pretending to be a small sprat himself. What would he request? "A one–way trip back home to Patara, please," he thought. As other last–minute children arrived, Nicholas kindly allowed them to go ahead of him. In the surrounding area, he could hear muttering, followed by cold stares and glances of other parents waiting nearby.

"He is no child!"

"Does this man not understand the rules of this event?"

Nicholas felt extremely awkward standing in line. It appeared he was breaking the "children only" policy but was determined to enter the villa and show the list to the Yuulnavie inside in hopes that it was the same Feýhañdsel he'd been seeking.

The massive line moved forward, as three children at a time entered and then exited. Nicholas thought of Urie; he missed her company and bubbling enthusiasm. Perhaps the drift–keeper was here waiting as well. What kind of gift would a sweet and kind little girl request? He traced the line from front to back but did not see her. He wondered where she might be and envisioned Urie hard at work, with ribbons of red and silver in her hair and a basket of eggs in her hand, buzzing through Violet's Agora like a hummingbird seeking nectar from a flower.

Nicholas felt as though he had stood in line for several hours. While waiting, he eavesdropped on various conversations, learning of the latest and greatest in Yuulnavian toy technology.

"The best Mini-Battling Hexcritter is Yearmark!"

"Shadowtree is just as strong as Yearmark!"

"Tickle a Snow-Moggie is fun, but I like Tickle a Flaming Tortie much more."

"The Whelping Whining Wisp makes all kinds of neat sounds! But is always hungry and must be fed."

Finally, the long line depleted, and Nicholas was then face-to-face with the grand entrance to the bastion. Ignoring further parental comments, he moved inside to the foyer of a large villa made of marble and stone, with an impressive chandelier hanging from the ceiling. A sign on a nearby pillar stated "Annual Gift Requests" and pointed to an adjacent room. Nicholas followed the sign, finding Feýhañdsel focused on his work, jotting names and gift requests onto a papyrus. The instrument he used looked like a reed pen but had a peculiar cane-like shape with red and white stripes on one end, and a sharp point on the other end that blotted ink on to the paper.

"Name and gift request please?" Feýhañdsel replied, focusing on the papyrus and not realizing a grown man stood before him.

"That was the last of the younglings. My name is Nicholas and I have this list. It was provided by Linde and Duggle from the Cardinals of Joy," Nicholas replied.

"Yes, I know them both well, good associates. This is a child–only event today– come back tomorrow during regular business hours!"

"My apologies for the interruption, but this a rather urgent matter and I'm short on time."

Feýhañdsel snapped back. "I have urgent matters of my own! What on the list is significant enough that I must stop my work?"

"I have a list of shops that supply items to the Restorer of Goodness. The instructions state that these are in Feýhañdsel's Hamlet," Nicholas replied.

Feýhañdsel pulled away from his writing and peered up at Nicholas through his winter goggles. "Restorer of Goodness?! Who was selected, and when? Were you assigned to retrieve supplies for them?"

"I... I am... I was deemed the Restorer of Goodness during my divination with the Nonesuch."

"A young man such as yourself chosen to be our Restorer? I would have expected a seasoned malificus or embedapist."

Nicholas felt dejected by the Yuulnavie's words, but he couldn't help but agree with him. Feýhañdsel was right– why him? He had no special talents or experience. He'd opened Gandomine's cage under magical lock and key and unknowingly aggravated the Bacillus. But what capabilities would he have going forth? He felt as useful as a crate of kittens. Perhaps a candidate that fully understood his abilities and had the know-how would be more ideal for this role.

"What proof do you have that convinces me to take you to my hamlet?" Feýhañdsel asked.

"Does this list not provide proof?" Nicholas replied bluntly.

"NO! Your list is a common parchment. Anyone could have written on it! I trust Linde and Duggle, but I don't know you, nor do I trust you!"

Nicholas's temper rose and he regretted not bringing Linde or Duggle with him. He reached into the front pocket of his memorizer pouch and pinched the red ribbon on the Chrysalis of Winter Solstice. "I have this artifact; it was a gift given to me by the Nonesuch."

Feýhañdsel glanced at the artifact. "An empty ornament? And what does that prove?"

Nicholas again questioned why only he and Urie were able to see the contents of the ornament. "You do not see the iced chrysalis inside?" Nicholas replied.

"I see NOTHING! You appear to be a fraud, Nicholas, and are wasting my time! I have a list of requests to complete today. If you do not have further proof, LEAVE MY BASTION!"

Nicholas's face turned red with anger. He was not fond of Feýhañdsel's short-spoken personality and wanted to belt out at him. Suddenly he remembered the book given to him by Lízabet. "I only have one more item- this tome. I do not know what use it has!"

Feýhañdsel's jaw dropped, and his eyes grew big behind his winter goggles. "How did you come upon this?! I was told that this was lost during the Interglacial Wars."

"A fellow embedapist and friend gave it to me. She is now a member of the union. I met with the Union of Goodness a few days ago; they are aligned with my role as well."

"I know the Union of Goodness. They are a group of lost bargainists, but they are decent people."

Both Feýhañdsel and Nicholas stared at the tome's glowing title, hypnotized. Feýhañdsel shook himself from his daze. "Ahem! Well? Don't just stand there, "deemed Restorer." Its title gleams brightly because of you. OPEN IT!"

"There is nothing inside but an empty storage compartment!" Nicholas argued.

"Shows what you know, young man. If you want to convince me, then OPEN IT!"

Nicholas aggressively opened the book and continued to argue. "As I said, nothing inside but an empty storage compartment. I have nothing more of proof!"

"This primordial tome has an enchanted mind of its own," Feýhañdsel explained. "You cannot obtain answers by simply reading left to right! Inside are hidden secrets written by the ascendants. These secrets can only be unlocked by the Restorer, using the correct items."

Nicholas was not surprised. With all the sickness and evil about, everything seemed to be structured under many locks and security measures. "What items will it accept?" he asked.

"You are the deemed Restorer of Goodness and you should know these things!" Feýhañdsel replied.

Nicholas sighed in frustration. His endeavors were becoming more complicated than training a hodgepodge of fantastic beasts. What items did the book require? Nicholas carefully lifted the Chrysalis of Winter Solstice and placed it in the compartment. To his surprise, the ornament shook and the book slammed shut, nearly consuming his fingers. The tome displayed a visual popup of a healthy sapling, a pine with tangled branches, and a tall elk–like figure with hanging antlers that stood near it.

Words suddenly appeared glimmering in gold:

My limbs they must be separated
Thus, then the bauble can be decorated
I alone cannot provide the cure
But joined together, the disease cannot endure

Both Feýhañdsel and Nicholas were speechless and astounded by the tome's reaction. What did this riddle mean? The page transitioned back to the compartment, holding the ornament. Nicholas carefully grabbed the red ribbon, still remembering the frozen hazard of the ornament. As he placed it back in the front pocket of the pouch, he noticed that the iced pupa inside was blemished with a small hairline crack.

"Nicholas– this is a very special tome. It can lead one to an incredible place– a place that is built on imagination, innovation, and magic, but is as real as the fingers on your hands and the toes on your feet. That bauble which you possess is the first key to unlocking a door to this amazing world. It is a place of kind and hardworking people who focus on only one thing– giving to others. Sadly, these people are lost and manipulated, seeking someone who can lead them. They remain captivated inside a world they cannot leave."

Deep inside, Nicholas somehow knew why.

"They are imprisoned by the Bacillus, aren't they?"

"Yes– and have been for centuries," Feýhañdsel replied. "You have proved yourself well enough, Nicholas. Please leave my villa and exit through the bastion's portcullis. I will show you to my hamlet shortly."

Feýhañdsel's Hamlet

Nicholas lost his temper as the portcullis slammed shut in his face. Feeling deceived, he pounded and shook the steel rails. "Feýhañdsel? Feýhañdsel!" he shouted. The day had grown long, and he was tired from the constant puzzle solving. Peeking through, he could see that the villa's door was closed and Feýhañdsel was nowhere to be seen.

Nicholas glanced out into the empty street behind him, once overcrowded by noisy children and their parents. Not a single person walked by or approached the bastion now, and the eerie and silent tone concerned him. He became discouraged, assuming he had accomplished nothing and had wasted his entire day. Perhaps Gandomine was around and could advise. "Gandomine? Gandomine... are you nearby? I seek your help!" Nicholas shouted. No appearance or response came from the cardinal.

Nicholas yelled into the street, "What must I do now!" An abrupt chill then trickled through the steel rails, biting on his neck. Startled, he turned back around and peered through- the villa that once stood in the ward was no longer there. The view inside was now a snowy long-stretched road that led to a small settlement. Like many times before, Nicholas questioned what he was seeing, but he was adapting to a world full of heedless surprises. The bastion's portcullis opened, the escaping draft activating his warming trinket.

Staring from afar, Nicholas wondered if he should pursue walking toward the settlement or if he was to wait for Feýhaňdsel. His answer quickly arrived as a man with a frozen mustache appeared right behind him. "Feýhaňdsel? Where did you come from?"

"How do you mean? I have been behind you for several moments," Feýhaňdsel replied, brushing icy chunks from his mustache.

Nicholas stared, confused, as Gandomine flew in. "You seek my help, Restorer?" Gandomine asked in a woman's voice.

Nicholas tried to remain calm and polite. "Yes, I did– quite a while ago– but Feýhaňdsel has arrived."

"Gandomine... long time," Feýhaňdsel greeted the cardinal.

"SEEMS LIKE DECADES," Gandomine replied in a man's voice.

"You... you two are acquainted?" Nicholas asked.

"For a long time," Feýhaňdsel replied. "Was it Nicholas who released you?"

"Yes, it was… and since he was capable of unlocking my cage, it appears he is our deemed Restorer," Gandomine replied.

"Were you not- *sigh!* - I mean wasn't HE in a "tizzy" and preferred not to speak with anyone today?" Nicholas recalled, still confused and frustrated. No reply came from the cardinal.

"Gandomine would have been acceptable proof also," Feýhañdsel added.

Nicholas rubbed his temples and pushed hard on his eye lids. At this point he felt as though he was being toyed with. "Are we not past needing proof now?!" he asked.

"We are… please follow me, Restorer- Gandomine, are you coming also?" Feýhañdsel asked.

"Let me speak with my counterpart. Hmm… no, not today- she says no!"

Walking the long-stretched road took longer than expected and presented a challenge of deep snowpacks, slippery conditions, and blustery winds. Nicholas was reminded of his newly grown facial hair, frosted from the wintry mix of snow and rain; Feýhañdsel's thick mustache appeared to be equally matched. The daylight diminished, reducing visibility as it transitioned to darkness, and the only directional indication remaining was the flickering lights of the hamlet.

Nicholas firmly held the strap of his memorizer pouch, raised his elbow, and covered his face, blocking the gusts that nearly knocked him down. "Are we still in your bastion? I no longer see the outer walls or the towers!" Nicholas hollered over the wind.

"The bastion is no more! Keep moving!" Feýhañdsel replied.

Unlike the strenuous roadway before it, Feýhañdsel's hamlet had a magistical, peaceful, and calming aura. Thick flakes of snow gently fell, covering the ground and the surrounding shops, which were structured into a circular cul-de-sac. Hanging signs indicated the name of each establishment with stunning themes of glamorous and shiny decorations, festive looms, and bright candlelight. Fireflies flew wildly, blinking in hues of various colors as they landed on strapped garland. The settlement had an alluring beauty, identical to what Nicholas had experienced in the Forest of Primordial Cedars.

"Are these people passing from shop to shop residents of Ethereal?" Nicholas asked.

"Some of them are- ideally," Feýhañdsel explained. "But they are malificus, embedapists, pedagogs, and others alike with unique talents. I built this hamlet to support them with goods and services... to help them thrive in their special abilities. That is why you are here, Restorer."

An incredible smell came from the nearest shop. Nicholas' stomach growled, alerting him that he was famished and had not eaten all day. He took a quick glance at the hanging sign: "Bity Bitey Baker's Bake."

"That's the bakery!" Nicholas said. He read the hanging sign of the next building. "And that is... Warmth Thee Heart over there!"

"Correct, Restorer," Feýhañdsel replied with a smirk. "You will also find Gibben directly across from them. Autumn is in the settlement's center sanctum where those piles of leaves are. There are also many other shops here not stated on your list. Visit at your leisure, if you have time."

Warmth Thee Heart had a large front window with mannequins showcasing various warming armor, caps, gloves, clothing, scarves, bracelets, necklaces, and many other accessories. Nicholas took a moment to look through the window, glazing the glass with his steamy breath. He placed the flat of his hand on his warming trinket, which reminded him of Arvel's kindness. The necklace had helped greatly, especially during his short time in Degomble and the road he'd traveled to the hamlet. Unfortunately, the rest of his attire was only suitable for Ethereal's comfortable temperatures and wasn't much help.

"Begin with Bity Bitey," Feýhaňdsel instructed. "As you are strapped for time, I would make only quick conversation with her. Her bakes are amazing and she is a lovely woman, but she is extremely friendly and will not let you leave."

Nicholas chuckled to himself– Bity's personality reminded him of Urie's. "Thank you, Feýhaňdsel. However, I still do not know what supplies I need from each merchant."

"You do not, but they will. Show me that shop list of yours." Feýhaňdsel pulled the striped reed pen from his pocket and jotted on the list.

"The Restorer of Goodness has arrived! Please provide him with the supplies that he needs."

Feýhaňdsel signed his name, rubbed his thumb and index finger together, and pushed down on the parchment. A stamped Emblem of Goodness appeared next to his name. "This will prove to them that you are the Restorer of Goodness. Show them my approval and they will provide you with the supplies you need."

"Will they accept bartering credits?" Nicholas asked.

"They are not needed here," Feýhaňdsel replied.

Nicholas nodded. "Understood, thank you Feýhaňdsel."

"Good! Now that I got you here, the rest is up to you! I must get the children's gift requests to Ycevein promptly. Travel the same roadway back to Ethereal.

But be cautious! Returning is not as safe!" Feýhaňdsel warned. "Best of luck to you, Restorer."

ᛟᛟᛟ

"Goooood afternooooon and weellcoooome!"

Nicholas was instantly thrown off, entrapped by the sheer cheerfulness of Bity Bitey. She was indeed the extremely friendly sort and lovely in both personality and appearance.

"Sorry, but is it not evening now? It is dark outside," Nicholas commented sternly, attempting to incite quick conversation.

"Ha... ha...! Nooooo you silly somebody! Here in Feýhaňdsel's Hamlet, it is always dark this time of year."

"I see." Nicholas attempted to cut to the chase. "I possess a supplies list given to me by Linde and signed by–"

"You muuust try these; they are freeeshly made!" Bity interrupted, offering a plate of bakes. "These are my cranberry custer bitter buster deeeelightfuls sprinkled with a few fingiees of chickleee white chitteees!"

Nicholas sighed and grabbed a sample from the plate. His taste buds erupted at the phenomenal taste. "These are amazing! You are very talented, Bity!"

"Thaaaaank youuuuuuu!" Bity replied, blushing.

"But I'm afraid I must be prompt. I possess this list–"

"Now try these raisin–berry covered choking cherry trufflllles!" Bity interrupted again. "They meeeelllt instantly, so taste and swallow quickly! If you do not, they will permanently block your throat. Veeeeerry taaaasty, but verrry deadly!"

One would assume a tasty treat that caused choking would be simply refused. His mouth watering, Nicholas tempted fate; his hand automatically grew a mind of its own and picked up the sweet, forcing it into his mouth without hesitation. Perhaps the fact that he was hungry did not help his cause. As instructed, he tasted and swallowed the truffle with haste. He checked himself, ensuring he was still breathing and not blue-faced or lying dead on the floor. It was well worth the risk; the truffle was as equally amazing as the "cranberry custer bitter buster deeeelightfuls."

"Very good, Bity!" Nicholas complimented. "Both bakes are most excellent! But I must continue–"

"Thaannnks! We have many more! Now try theeeese–"

"NO more! But thank you," Nicholas replied bluntly. "Apologies, but I must interrupt; I'm in a bit of a hurry and I seek these supplies." He showed Bity Bitey the list, hoping she would halt in giving him further samples. His defensive wall for sweets was now weakened and trampled, and he wouldn't be able to refuse.

"Sweet Honey Icicle Twizzeeetwists! You are the Restorer of Goodness?! Oh my! I must bake a batch of frigorific wafers right awaaaay!"

"I'm sorry, a batch of...?"

"–a batch of frigorific wafers," Bity said. "They prevent you from getting frigorificitis, eeeeespecially from beetles! Beetles are the most venomous."

"Oh, very good, then! I believe I will be encountering these beetles very soon. This ailment you speak frig... frigosouritis... what is it?" Nicholas asked.

"Frigorificitis is when your jawseee freezes and you cannot open or close it," Bity explained.

Nicholas stared blankly. "Forgive me, *what* freezes?"

"Your jawseee freezes!"

Nicholas listened in as Bity Bitey explained further, speaking in her unique terminology. The frigorific wafers contained special ingredients that worked as an antidote. If eaten prior to a sting or bite, the wafers could prevent the venom from spreading. Some embedapists had the capability of removing frigorificitis, but the ability to do so was rare among them. Sufficient facial covering, using armor or clothing, sometimes helped. But many embedded insects found their way underneath, injecting venom into the victim's bloodstream. Bity's Bitey's wafers were the best solution and were carried among many in battle or by those traveling from place to place. Not only were they great for preventing the illness, but they also tasted wonderful. It was rather intriguing to Nicholas that an assortment of bakes could create issues such as choking to death, while others could prevent dangerous ailments.

Next was Warmth Thee Heart. Nicholas entered, greeting a woman who was friendly and kind, but nothing in comparison to Bity Bitey. His visit was a quick in and out, which he preferred. The shop's atmosphere and its stocked items were as equally amazing as the display window out front. After he showed his list to the shop owner, Nicholas received a questionable item: a stiff coiled rope with a loose knot, large loop, and a long stem. He had a thorough understanding of how to use the frigorific wafers, but he did not understand the use of the rope. The shop owner dropped a hint that it was often used for tying mounts, such as horses or caribou. "For the Restorer of Goodness, it is hard to say," the shopkeeper claimed. Nicholas thanked the shopkeeper and made his way to the last two places on his list.

Centrally located in the hamlet's circular emporium was Autumn. Instead of a shop or building, a pile of leaves with many different patterns and sizes landscaped the hamlet's center sanctum.

A sign nearby was staked into the ground and read:

Want to grow that perfect tree?
You can't go wrong with Autumn's Leaves
Pick and choose the one you desire
Roots will sprout and branches transpire

Puzzled, Nicholas looked about, expecting to see Autumn or a nearby shop. His attention was drawn to a big and vivid orange leaf. He plucked it from the pile and ran his index finger along its tip and veins, feeling the thickness and fleshy texture of its surface.

The pile of leaves shook and shifted. "Good gracious!" a tiny, meek voice shouted from within the pile. "I must say! It's polite to ask first, before taking one of my leaves!"

"So sorry," Nicholas replied, returning the leaf to the pile. "Are you Autumn? Are... are you a talking leaf?" Nicholas felt idiotic for asking such a question, but in this world anything was possible.

From beneath, a mouse with tiny crimson antlers came out into the open. "Hmph! No! Whoever heard of a talking leaf?"

"Whoever heard of a talking mouse?" Nicholas responded wittily.

Autumn folded her small mouse arms. "Hmph! Well, what did you expect, a fire–breathing reindeer?"

Nicholas stared, amazed. In Patara, mice were rank rodents, thieves of the night that barraged for food, leaving waste for him to remove. Autumn was quite different and full of life. The crimson antlers and her ability to speak suddenly made sense.

"I believe I understand," Nicholas replied. "The crimson mimicry– was it performed on you?"

"Yes, but not many know of its name." Autumn began to tell her story.

Autumn was once an ordinary mouse that invaded the houses of Ethereal as any typical mouse would. One day she became sick with a terrible cold and wrapped herself in a leaf, trying to keep warm in hopes of replenishing her health. Slowly dying, she was then touched by the curing hand of a gentle woman. She quickly felt better, crimson antlers grew from her head, and she gained the ability to speak. But talking with humans was difficult for her and she was frequently chased by swinging brooms. Having the ability to associate with others was intriguing, but Autumn felt distressed. Discouraged and alone, Autumn ran throughout Ethereal, eventually finding the woman who had rescued her.

"I know the perfect place for you, little one," the woman claimed.

"She brought me to this hamlet, and this has been my home ever since," Autumn explained. "Everyone here accepts me as a friend instead of as invasive vermin.

I was given this wonderful home– this magical pile of leaves. Now I help many pick the perfect leaf so they can grow trees in Ethereal or replenish the forests. The leaf is crumpled into the ground and a tree instantly grows!"

"That's amazing!" Nicholas replied. "I'm glad that you were saved. I have a cardinal friend, Gandomine; he was saved as well. It seems you are not alone."

Autumn smiled. "I would like to meet this Gandomine."

"Perhaps you will someday. It seems you two were given a special gift to speak and to help those in need. I am Nicholas. I am also striving to help others. I am being called a Restorer– The Restorer of Goodness."

"Hello, Nicholas," greeted Autumn, extending her small paw. Nicholas shook her paw with two of his fingers.

"I have this list of supplies to retrieve. Your name is on this list. Would you be able to help me?" Nicholas asked.

"I have the perfect item waiting for you! It has been hidden inside my pile for a long time." Autumn disappeared as she dove into the mound of leaves.

The pile swayed as Autumn wrestled inside. "Now where did I put it? Hmph! Come now, where are you?! Hmph! It was here moments ago!" Waiting patiently, Nicholas envisioned Autumn springing out with a beautiful, unique, and grand leaf. The leaves continued to shuffle. "Oh yes, here it is!" Autumn clenched the special item with her wee paws, vaulted from the pile, and held it up triumphantly. "Da-da-da-daaaa!"

Nicholas glanced at the item, mildly amused. "A... a... dead... pine needle?"

"Not just any pine needle. This will grow the most amazing and beautiful tree- the *Primordial Noble Fir!*"

Nicholas finally reached the last of the merchants, Gibben Gubbins, owner of Gibben Gubbin's Gizmos. Little did he know that behind its closed doors was a special toy. It was a toy capable of breaching Ethereal's protective walls and had a special resemblance to one Nicholas dearly loved and missed. Gibben was a tall and sleek shopkeeper with a long face and a nose that pointed upward in a snobby yet professional fashion.

"Hello, my name is Nicholas. I possess-"

"I know who you are. Amusing news travels quickly in Feýhaňdsel's Hamlet," Gibben interrupted.

"Yes of course, I'm sure that it would in a small civilization such as this."

"We are only a few in Feýhaňdsel's Hamlet," Gibben replied. "I am now required to present you with your first item." From underneath the counter, Gibben removed a bottle with a rolled-up message inside. Nicholas accepted the bottle, popped the cork, removed the message, and carefully unrolled the paper:

My child,

You so loved to swim,

You so loved to watch the boats as they went out to sea,

You so loved life, and you loved me,

Do not forget me, my son, as I will never forget you.

I give you this gift, may it lead you in fulfilling your meaning and your purpose.

A mother's love– always and forever

Nicholas could not believe what he read. "What is this? Trickery or devious manipulation?!" he asked angrily.

"We do not play tricks or manipulate in Feýhaňdsel's Hamlet," Gibben replied. "Henceforth, I present you with your last item."

Atop the wooden counter of Gibben Gubbin's Gizmos, a toy freighter was placed. It was the Virago of the Sea with her angelic figurehead and flowing wings, and it was scrawled with the name "Nóvva." Nicholas buckled and weakened, barely able to stand. Emotional and staggered, he fell to his knees in disbelief.

Nicholas had a puzzling yet gratifying day. With the stiff rope tied to his waist and the rest of his supplies stowed in his pouch, he pressed on. But his return to Ethereal resulted in an unexpected and unnatural storm, and he suddenly felt as terrified as he had before the shipwreck with Drusus and the crew. Cracking and bending a glitz twiglet that he had acquired before leaving the Hamlet, he lit his way forward. The bright glow shone a reflection on the steel rails of the portcullis, in plain sight and only a few miles away. Oddly, no outer walls of the Bastion connected to the entrance, standing alone and transparent in the heart of the storm. Nicholas paced quickly, keeping warm from the trinket and determined to reach the outer gate. But in the open terrain, an evil presence instigated a rip-roaring squall. He gasped in pain as a razor-sharp wind sliced his skin like shards of broken glass. Splotches of blood dripped from his face, his arms, and his hand. He grabbed his injured knuckles, dropping the glitz twiglet, and the memorizer pouch blew from his shoulder and fell at his feet. A demonic growl rumbled around him, mocking him once again.

"You are a scared and weak lamb! Just another to INFECT... to SLAAAUGHTEEERRR!"

Extraordinary amounts of snow blasted toward Nicholas, suffocating his body and burying him. Nicholas' inner child- the same child who'd built intense stamina and great endurance while swimming and pulling the resistance of the Mare Nostrum- grew in anger and hostility. With mighty arms of strength, he pulled himself through the heavy, wet snow, destroying the graveyard plot the Bacillus was attempting to create. Nicholas swiped the memorizer pouch from the ground, aggressively strapping it to his shoulder. He hollered back at his enemy.

"What are you? WHO ARE YOU! I'm growing tired of this! You wrecked Nonna and my dearest friends, and I nearly drowned!" Nicholas cried out in rage. "AHHHHHHHHHHHHHHHHHHHH! I am not afraid of you!" He slammed open the lid of the memorizer pouch and cracked another glitz twiglet, nearly snapping it in half. The light bled brightly on his face- not the face of Nicholas, but of the wanderer with a dirty grey beard, hidden underneath his apex bent hat. With clenched teeth, tension in his jaw, and glossiness in his eyes, he shouted profanely at the Bacillus.

"You are HEATHEN! An invisible DISEASE!"

The Bacillus reacted by growling and roaring, besieging a havoc of snowfall on the bearded man.

"Sleeeeep, weak lamb! Sleeeep! DIIIIE SLAUGHTERED LAAAAAAAMB!"

With maddened eyes, the wanderer looked to the sky and raised his arm, concocting an artillery of miraculous abilities. The snow capturing his body began to melt, turning into a stream of boiling liquid. He screamed, spitting each word out in cadence.

"YOU... HIDDEN... DISEASE!

I... AM... THE... RESTORER... OF... GOOD... NESS!

WHO... IS...WEAK... NOW?

WHO... IS...THE... THREATENED... LAMB... NOOOOWWW!"

Throughout the long–stretched road that connected Ethereal and the hamlet, specks of golden glitter remained in the shape of the wanderer, his bodily figure no more. Nicholas found himself lying flat outside the bastion's steel gate. Coughing and breathing heavily, he rolled his head to his left. Feýhañdsel's Bastion had returned, its walls and towers reformed, as had the villa within the inner ward. He rolled his head to the right. Ethereal's street still lay silent and empty. He was no longer bleeding, nor were there any slices or blemishes on his face, arms, or hands. Worried, Nicholas quickly opened his memorizer pouch, but thankfully all items were still safely inside, the rope still tied to his waist. He slowly rose to his feet and released an exhausted sigh.

"I must quit ending up flat on my back!"

'Twas the Restorer of Goodness

Eve of the Winter Solstice...

Hi Daddy,

Although Mother writes these letters for me, I always tell her what to say. I tell Mother that I don't like winter or the fuzzy cotton that falls outside our town. I don't like it because I know I won't see you very much. I cry sometimes, knowing that you are so far away, wishing I could hug you. Letters from you always make me happy, and I smile. Mother cries sometimes, because she misses you too, but tells me that the fuzzy cotton is a beautiful thing, that it cleanses the air and our world, and that Father is out there to keep us safe, to prevent the snow from getting sick.

Oh! I'm being good. I promise! Except when Lyman gets me in trouble. Big brothers! I am taking care of Savage and listening to Mother. Oh! And I get all my chores done too! Everyday! Tell Uncle Arvel to be kind to you and to take care of you. Although he's a grump, he has a big heart. Bye, Father. Please write back soon!

Deepest love,

Urie

P.T.O.

With teared eyes Quilo turned the letter over.

My husband,

The bed remains cold and lonely without you. I long for your touch and your roughened fingers that run down my spine.

I await the day I can remove your armor and sloth-headed pauldrons, only to kiss your battle-scarred shoulders.

Come home to us safe, my love. For the sake of goodness!

–Your wife

Quilo set the parchment down, attempting to hide and divert his emotion.

"Well?! Ya gonna sob over that letter all night or get prepared?" Arvel teased.

"I should ask you the same, brother! Why do you sweat over forging on the eve of battle? You should be resting!"

"Yah... helps my mind off things – offa *them,* ya know."

"Yes! I understand!" Quilo replied.

Like many siblings, Quilo and Arvel rarely got along, and their personal views were like day and night. But the two shared three common traits– hardheadedness, wits in warfare, and lastly– brotherly love. Prior to any battle, they made a point to visit one another, as they knew either one of them could perish at any time.

The commander had sanctioned the encampment on top of a nunatak, overlooking the icefields that separated the brigade from the diabolic ruins. The polar nights of the winter solstice provided ceaseless darkness, while the strong presence of embedded evil created a thick and dense fog. The only ambient lights came from the encampment, caused by the warming bonfires and the starlit skies above them. On the opposing side was the horrid purple glow of the rime, hoarfrost, and the tooth-shaped seracs. The seracs were mountainous, rigid, and unstable glaciers. They had sharp points that reached to the sky and created a bowl-shaped wall around the ruins. These diseased grounds were often referred to as the Strain. Without having the proper abilities, no one dared to enter. Those brave enough to set foot in the inner sanctum, and without proper protection, were easily infected and died instantly.

Many believed that the Strain was the birthplace of an imperceptible nemesis, known as the Bacillus. The Bacillus survived on two primary necessities- sickness and deathrate of humans. It worked in physical form through the embedded evil, feeding on the morsels of coughing, fevers, pain, and nausea.

Primordial malificus, embedapists, Yuulnavian engineers, and alike sought to determine a resolution, one that could destroy the embedded evil and the Bacillus.

They fought long and hard, but failed, as each attempt only aggravated the Bacillus. It often retaliated by drifting, shifting, or mutating to protect itself, causing the grounds to quake, and released outbreaks of disease. Eventually, the endeavor of destroying the Bacillus came to a halt. The people of goodness had learned from their mistakes. Putting the Bacillus into a vulnerable state meant only two things– the creation of a deadly variant, and destruction. They could only hold out and wait for the right time, the right process, and the right individuals. To survive, embedapists did what they could to restore the health of the infected and the sick. The militia trained and seasoned themselves to terminate any embedded evil that invaded them, while the Yuulnavies engineered Ethereal as a safehold and livable community.

Arvel continued his work and poured a specialized liquid onto a second steel rail; it shaped, formed, and curled identically to the one he crafted before it. Arvel would often set up tools in his encampment tent. He did not have the room for a full–fledged artificer shop but brought three important items with his equipment: a forging hammer, tongs, and a collection of primordial vials. These vials contained magical properties that could create the heat he needed for the metal to properly yellow, and, by using a simple boulder or log, Arvel could transform it into an anvil sturdy enough for mass distribution. The artificer was a master worker, tried–and–true with his great sword– Leonora, which remained by his side and was always razor sharp. While others would rest, weary from battle, Arvel would work extended hours, using his skills to repair any weapons and armor that had been damaged and weakened in the battlefield, only to return them to rightful owner, good as new.

"More weapons? Why?" Quilo asked. "My legion is well-equipped and ready for the solstice."

"Nah! It's fer Nicholas!"

"The foreigner? He does not fight! You are wasting your time, brother! Rest!"

"Yer as dense as that Animal Lover! It's fer later... nothin' to do with this battle."

Quilo shook his head. "You are insane as always, brother! INSANE!"

"Pfft, insanity!" Kiffy teased as he entered the tent with Hooley by his side. "Old man is senile."

"Tol' ya to holler before enterin' my tent! One of these days yer gonna come in and my manhood will be hangin' about."

"Is that a call for something? I surely hope not," Kiffy teased, as Quilo Serdar rolled his eyes, not amused.

"What the hell ya want?" Arvel replied.

"Ran the wolves today and scouted the outer parameter– something's wrong."

"Ya always have something wrong with ya. What's yer point?" Arvel growled.

"Not I, you old nut offeror!" Kiffy jested. "Outside the embedded fog line below the nunatak, the evil rime is thicker than expected. My wolves are acting extremely cautious, and Bech tracked down a long trail of hare droppings."

"Yer trained mutts are good fer nothin'," Arvel replied.

"I'm afraid it's worse," Kiffy continued, ignoring Arvel.

"Yeah? How so?" Quilo asked, concerned.

"We encountered patches of infected snow."

"So what! And why'd you bring that skittish fox with ya? Shudda left 'er home!" Arvel asked.

Kiffy patted Hooley on the head, and she accepted the gesture with a nuzzle of her head against his hand. "Something tells me that she can help me out."

"Hehheh! Mukluk! Highly doubt that furball with legs is much help."

"I DO agree with the pedagog!" Quilo interrupted. "Something isn't right out there- out of place. There should not be infected snow, either!"

"Bring it up with Norrick then! I don't give two snot-cicles! I will be up at the crack a morn' with Leonora, regardless! Now lemme do ma work!" Arvel hollered.

"Maybe it's best we leave," Quilo suggested.

"Agreed... old grope probably has pre-battle jitters. I've managed to pack up some warm oggin' cider if you are interested, Commander?"

Quilo accepted. "Yes, fine! A warmup would be beneficial before retiring for the night."

Arvel grumbled under his breath as Quilo and Kiffy left his tent. "Gomble-headed nitwits!" His hammer struck the second rail with great might, finalizing its creation.

Late into the evening...

'Twas the eve of the solstice, and inside each tent
The good folks were restless, prepared for lament
Weapons were placed near their bedsides with care
All were concerned how his rescue would fare
The camp was bound tight in a blanket of rime
While thoughts of infection tormented their minds
And Arvel all bundled in arctic-lined fleece
Finally wound down, drooled and slumbered in peace
When out in the darkness a noise stole his rest
From grunts of a creature, respiring, distressed
Arvel then woke, grasped his sword and his armor
Whatever was out there he'd fight, keep his honor
In the haze, the reins tightened, a golden light glowed
While a man shouted out "Whoa! Xalibu! Whoa!"
To Arvel's amazement, what did he soon see?
The once-foredoomed fallow, now healthy and free
On her top was a rider, exhausted but just
The Restorer of Goodness, it was- Nicholas!

Urie's Sick Horse

"You gomble-brained shrew!" Quilo Serdar shouted, distraught. "YOU have endangered our lives- faltered our strategy! We all agreed that you were to release the fallow simultaneously!"

"Easy, brother! Undertow's still a pup- runnin' in circles and chasin' 'is tail."

"Do not interfere, Arvel! You know better! His so-called journey ends NOW! His contributions are worthless to us!"

"Mukluk! I might be an ol' man, can't find ma feet cuz of this ale-stuffed belly, but brother- I will feed YOU and yer EGO an icy cass'role!"

The commander retorted, sucking his teeth and eyeing Nicholas with disgust. "Restorer? Pah! You are a CURSE- a MISHAP!"

"Quilo Serdar... STOP!" Nicholas shouted at the commander, halting him from exiting the tent.

"Stop? Hehheh. Stop? Now yah dun it, boy. Might as well told 'im to eat yella snow!"

"Yellow snow? I don't understand, Arvel," Nicholas replied, irritated, then glanced up at the honorable but hostile commander. He spoke gently and calmly, hoping to reduce Quilo's anger. "I did not choose to be here, BUT I AM. I miss my small town, my uncle, my friends, and my home just as you do. I'm sure you dearly miss your family- and Urie."

Quilo's giant hand grabbed Nicholas by his throat. "How do you know my daughter?!"

"Quilo! Let. Him. Go!" Norrick ordered as he and Kiffy entered the tactical tent.

"Neck grabbing again? Must be a family trait," Kiffy jested.

"I... I..." Nicholas stuttered, regaining his breath. "I- *cough*-encountered her in Ethereal; her piglet ran loose, and I helped her retrieve it. Without her speaking to me, I wouldn't have known of Xalibu or of the Embedded Forest."

"Frosty turds, boy! Ya gave it a name? Yer worse than the Animal Lover."

"Excellent name choice, friend," Kiffy encouraged with a smirk.

"Urie almost died out there!" Quilo interrupted. "Thankfully Lyman was hunting game and helped her escape. She tells false tales of a sick horse protecting her."

"Yes, I know, Commander, she told me the same story. I don't believe they were false tales; she did indeed encounter a sick animal."

"I did not see a horse THEN and I don't believe you NOW!" Quilo replied.

Frustrated, Nicholas aggressively opened the flaps to the tent's entrance and pointed at the fallow outside. "That is the creature that protected your little girl from the embedded beetles. *That* is Urie's sick horse. A friend recently told me 'Children are often considered storytellers– they share tales rarely believed by others. Those that don't believe them could be lying to themselves and the truth comes from the child telling the story.'"

"No! You are the liar, foreigner! That animal is healthy!" Quilo retorted.

Arvel clapped his forehead. "Mukluking sakes, brother! The boy has the crimson cleanin' ability. Ya should know that bah now!"

Quilo Serdar exhaled sharply and closed his eyes, briefly reflecting on his memory of Lyman carrying Urie in his arms, her skin bloodied and her jaw frozen by the bites from the embedded beetles.

"Can you help her?" Quilo asked, distressed, as he watched Lyman lay her down on the ground, her body shaking aggressively from the shock,

"Do not fret, Commander; she will be fine," Violet stated as she cast a golden aura around Urie's body.

As the treatment settled inside of her, Urie stirred and opened her eyes. "Da... Daddy?! You came home!"

"I'm home, little drift keeper, I'm home!" Quilo replied with thankful tears as he lifted Urie and held her close, hugging her with the power of a polar bear. "I told you time and time again! NEVER leave Ethereal's walls!"

"I know, Daddy. I'm... I'm... sorry," Urie sobbed. "I... just thought that maybe the sick horse... it... it... would give me a ride to see you, so... so... far away, because I... I miss you so much."

Quilo's mind jolted back to the present. He remained stern, hiding his emotions from his past memory. "How does this foreigner's ability and this animal help us? Because he is here, we have lost our window of opportunity! It is now a death trap!"

Norrick clasped Quilo's shoulder. "Do what you're best at, Commander– plan accordingly and re-align our tactics. You have done so in many battles and led us to victory. We all believe you can do it again, even in this major turning point."

"Just 'nother shit-licated battle, brother! We've been through plenty of 'em before!" Arvel encouraged.

With the change of events, the commander would have to restructure and do it soon. The Bacillus was still weak and recovering from Nicholas' rescue of the foredoomed fallow. There was still time and a pinch of opportunity.

"That primordial creature that you claim protected my daughter– did it protect you also?" Quilo asked.

"I wouldn't have escaped the embedded forest or the beetles without her," Nicholas confirmed.

"Fine! Very well! I will begin creating an alternative strategy, in hopes we do not face grievous defeat!"

"Thank you, Commander," Norrick replied. "For now, we all should rest and take advantage of the remaining hours we have left."

"Be ready in a few hours! I wait for no one!" Quilo demanded. "Leave my tent and leave me to my thoughts– and foreigner– STAY AWAY FROM MY DAUGHTER or I will put you back into the ocean where you should have drowned!"

The group separated from the evening's erratic events. Nicholas took some time to check in on the fallow. He stroked her neck of shaggy fur and patted her torso, helping her to relax and remain calm from her big day. She returned the gesture, pushing her head on to Nicholas and rubbing cheeks with him.

"Least it's fond a ya," Arvel jested. "Couldn't keep control of it tho', could ya? Had a feelin' she'd bring ya here!"

"No. I'm afraid I could not," Nicholas replied, surprised that Arvel knew. "She chose to come here at her own will. And I haven't a clue how we got here. When I released her from her sickness, it was just before daybreak. I attempted to follow our plan, but her rescue... everything... moved rather quickly. I know it sounds strange, but it- it was as if time rewound itself during our escape. Where we ended up, I know not, but I do remember an archway."

With the skills of a pedagog, Kiffy carefully approached the fallow, offering a carrot for her to eat, which she gladly accepted. "Archway... hmm... archway... you tried to return home, didn't you girl?" Kiffy asked Xalibu, then turned and looked Nicholas straight in the eye. "Nicholas... this animal is unique and special. She has the caliber of prancing like a bolt of lightning, and when she does... she can manipulate time!"

"She's very special indeed," Nicholas replied. "I can only hope her amazing prance can get me across the Frozen Splode."

"Hehheh... gomble-brained greenhorns! Yer not ready for no Frozen Splode! Firs' ya gotta get that thing to listen to ya. Second, ya gotta get it to fly. Ya won't get through that hellhole unless she flies."

"Hmmm... that explains those sweat-stained rails you've been crafting," Kiffy commented. "But... all of this- it's finally happening, isn't it? The Bacillus has not been this threatened in a long time."

"Yah! Tha' pot a crud is stirred now. Thanks to Nich'las here!" Arvel replied.

Nicholas quickly snapped back at Arvel. "That was the first time you have used my name correctly."

"Wouldn't get too used to it, friend. Ol' grope can't remember his own name," Kiffy teased. "You have had a long venture, Nicholas. For now, there is an unoccupied tent with a cot; please rest awhile. In a few short hours, you can ride with me, and I can help you train her- break her. She has been sick for a long time. This is all new to her, as it is to you."

"Yull get to know one 'nother real quick!" Arvel added.

The Encampment of Righteousness slept under starry skies in short-lived silence and peace. They too would soon run in circles, chasing their tails, just as Nicholas had during his adventurous rescue of the fallow. Their intention was to use what time was given to them. Whether the Bacillus was weak or not, they would take on the embedded evil and gashgobs and do their best to prevent the release of Torment.

Before retiring, Nicholas peeked out at the hungry fallow from his tent. Her appetite had grown stronger, and she was now gnawing on the additional carrots Kiffy had given her. He remembered what Urie once said:

"I think it's hungry though... I tried to feed him once, ya know... one of our carrots!"

"You're very brave- did it eat the carrot?"

"No... I don't think it likes them, maybe because it's sick.

Nicholas now knew that he had completed the task. He had released her from the foredoomed state she once was in. Urie's "sick horse" loved the carrots and was now healthy. She was a remarkable creature- vigorous and robust.

Rest in Pieces

"*Mother, why do you and Father help others– are they unable to help themselves?*" *Nicholas asked.*

"*Others are capable of helping themselves,*" *Nonna explained.* "*But sometimes they need a nudge or an upper hand from another. They need to know that others care about them and their well-being. Sometimes the smallest gift of generosity is all they need. Theopanes and I are very blessed to be able to help others in this way.*"

"*Have you and Father ever needed help from someone?*"

"*Of course. Everyone needs help from time to time,*" *Nonna replied.*

"*Will I be capable of helping others?*"

Nonna shed a genuine smile as she gently brushed sand from Nicholas' face. "*You will be more than capable, my son, and when you do, others will thrive. You will cleanse the heartstrings of those dirtied from fear, doubt, and uncertainty.*"

The day before the Winter Solstice...

It was late afternoon in Elidor's Croft. Nicholas sat along the bank of the river, puzzled and in disbelief. The shocking coincidence of receiving his mother's message seemed unrealistic– how was it possible? Nonna was dead, struck down by plague. This was simply becoming a whimsical dream; it had to be. His thoughts blurred as he visioned his younger self sitting with his father at the bank of the Eşen stream.

"It is a beautiful day, Nicholas! And you know why?" Theopanes remarked.

"Why, Father?" Nicholas asked.

"Our family is healthy and plentiful, the sun shines above us with warmth, and the stream sparkles full of water. We must be thankful for days such as these. Life can be rash and change like an unexpected thunderstorm!"

His past memory faded away as he listened to the soothing burble of the river's flow, while broken reeds and twigs floated the current and disappeared into the embedded forest. It was quite peculiar that the protective walls hadn't stopped the debris or dammed the water, flooding the banks of the river.

Nicholas watched as a bee landed on a nearby flower, feeding from its natural pollen and nectar. After completing its work, the insect hovered above the river and darted toward the diseased forest. With a thud, it ricocheted off the protective wall and flew off in the opposite direction, buzzing loudly in vexation.

"Hello, Nicholas. Your trip to Feýhañdsel's Hamlet was successful... I hope?" Linde asked as she approached.

Nicholas smiled, happy to see her. "Yes, it was- mostly. Thank you for the list. I'm now pondering on how to breach Ethereal's walls."

"It is complicated... only a selected few can breach them."

"I'm sure it is. I don't believe I have the abilities that they possess," Nicholas replied.

"Well, perhaps not, but you have an asset they do not have." Linde pointed to a clump of reeds. Nicholas could only hear a soft jingling sound and was confused. "Is that coming from the river?" he asked.

"No- Gandomine," Linda replied. Nicholas finally spotted the cardinal swaying back and forth on a nearby cattail. A tangled mess of white ribbon and a small bell were now attached to the antlers. Gandomine quickly became distracted and flew off. "OH MY! THE SERDAR'S FEEDER HAS BEEN REFILLED. I MUST GO TASTE!"

"I'm afraid it has been difficult obtaining advice," Nicholas complained to Linde. "The cardinal comes and goes rather frequently."

Linde chuckled. "Have patience; Gandomine has a short attention span and has been enjoying freedom after being caged for so long."

Nicholas nodded. "I will certainly try."

"My mother taught Gandomine many things, which will be very helpful to you, especially when entering the infected woods."

"Ethereal's protective walls– are they harmful?" Nicholas questioned, recalling the glitz twiglet Kiffy had thrown into the Barrier of Aegis, and the way it had been obliterated on contact. Nicholas was paranoid that the same danger could occur again.

"REACH OUT AND FEEL IT WITH YOUR HAND," Gandomine suggested coarsely, returning to the swaying cattail with the bell lightly ringing.

"Back so soon?" Linde asked, grinning.

"RELENTLESS SPARROWS AND STARLINGS! HOGGISH SEED GUZZLERS THEY ARE! THE FEEDER WAS EMPTY– AGAIN!" Gandomine replied in frustration, then turned to Nicholas. "GO ON, TOUCH IT. GO ON RESTORER, TOUCH IT ALREADY!"

Nicholas eyed Gandomine skeptically, distracted by the spiderweb of white ribbon tangled in the antlers, uncertain whether the cardinal was teasing him or not. He was hesitant to touch any magical walls and did not want to see his hand missing, or rather, his entire arm amputated from his shoulder.

"You will be fine, Restorer," Gandomine assured him, switching to a gentler woman's voice. "The wall consists of an invisible mass, a solid blockade. Touching it is harmless."

Nicholas sighed, shook his head, and flinched as he cautiously reached into the invisible wall. He felt an odd tingling in his hand that crawled through his arm, into his shoulder, and down his spine. His fingertips compressed and bent as he hit the protective surface. "Interesting sensation. It is nothing I have ever felt before. The barricade itself is hard as stone."

"THERE IS ONLY ONE WAY THROUGH THESE WALLS– WE SAIL DOWNRIVER," Gandomine replied, returning to a man's voice.

"Pa... pardon? We are to sail down THIS river?" Nicholas was confused.

"YOU WERE GIVEN A TOY FREIGHTER, WERE YOU NOT?"

"Yes, that's right."

"WE SAIL USING THE VESSEL!"

"How so?" Nicholas asked irritably. "It is a miniature toy, and I'm much too large! This does not make any sense!"

"You must understand, these tasks assigned to you are not as cut and dry as you may think. The steps you take helping others will require belief beyond realism. Instead, you must have a stout imagination; it is the axis to being the Restorer of Goodness."

Still frustrated, Nicholas pulled the toy from his memorizer pouch and placed it safely on the bank. "As I stated before... my foot alone would crush this seacraft. THAT my imagination can comprehend! So, tell me, how would I sail down this river?"

On the swaying cattail Gandomine remained silent, while Linde folded her arms and sent cold glances. "Come now... Gandomine... it's time!" she growled.

"YES, I'M WELL AWARE! IT IS SHE WHO'S BEING RELUCTANT!" Gandomine replied defensively.

Next a back-and-forth quarrel stormed, involving GANDOMINE AND– Gandomine.

"Do not lie to them! It is both of us who are reluctant!" Gandomine argued in a woman's voice.

"FINE! WE BOTH ARE!" Gandomine snapped back. "RESTORER, HOLD OUT YOUR ARM!"

Nicholas reached out and clenched his fist as Gandomine swept from the swaying cattail and on to Nicholas' arm. Arguments continued, MAN versus woman.

"NOW... SING... RING THE BELL!" Gandomine demanded in a man's voice.

"I'd prefer you did! You sing more than I. It is much clearer and more concise!"

"NO! YOUR SINGING IS JUST AS GOOD! I DO NOT WISH–"

"Gandomine, ENOUGH!" Linde interrupted. "Please help Nicholas!"

With feathers shuddering as if in the midst of a lingering cough, the cardinal whistled and trilled a series of beautiful notes, followed by a wing tap of the bell.

Nicholas and the bird were now standing on deck aboard the miniature watercraft. The once calming sound of the river was now loud and bustling. Startled, Nicholas jumped backward, shocked to see a giant-sized Linde from above, waving her massive hand and shedding an enormous smile.

"Again, Restorer, you must look past realism and focus on using imagination."

"I am doing my best to understand... to keep an open mind," Nicholas replied, attempting to slow down his heart rate. "Am I able to perform this shrinking ability as well?"

"No!" Gandomine snapped. "YOU MAY BE THE RESTORER, BUT YOU AREN'T CAPABLE OF EVERYTHING!" The cardinal repeated the series of whistles, trills, and jingles, and they both returned to full size.

"Welcome back!" Linde greeted them with hope gleaming in her eyes. Stressed and frightened, Gandomine fluttered away from Nicholas and perched shakily on to Linde's shoulder. She gently stroked the cardinal's feathers with her fingertips. "I know, darling– I know. It takes a lot out of you. Violet would be so proud of you, knowing her best friend is helping the Restorer of Goodness."

Early Morning of the Winter Solstice...

After a restful nap at the CottonSedge Inn, Nicholas returned to the river. He was adequately supplied and dressed in proper attire, aware that the climate would be significantly colder once they passed Ethereal's walls. The items he'd acquired were safely stowed inside the memorizer pouch, and the stiff coiled rope was tied securely to his waist.

A full moon lit up the early morning darkness, and Nicholas cracked a glitz twiglet to further improve illumination. To his surprise, Gandomine had already arrived but was dozed off in a nearby tree. "Good morrow, Gandomine!" Nicholas called out, his voice and the bright light of the twiglet startling the cardinal awake.

"NONSENSE! IT'S ALL HER FAULT," Gandomine mumbled in a man's voice. "I TOLD HER NOT TO DO IT! BLAME HER, NOT ME!"

"Pardon?" Nicholas replied.

Gandomine switched to a woman's voice. "Wake up, you unnerving ramble-babble! It is morrow... morrow of the Winter Solstice. It is time to help Nicholas!"

"I'M AWAKE! DON'T RUFFLE YOUR FEATHERS!"

Nicholas shook his head, still adjusting to the cardinal's personal conversations. "Same practice as yesterday?" he asked.

"YES, PRECISELY!" Gandomine replied. "WHEN YOU ARE READY, PLACE THE VESSEL ON THE RIVER AND HOLD OUT YOUR ARM."

Nicholas removed tiny Nonna from the memorizer pouch and placed her on the river. Quickly taken by the current, she began to float downriver.

"WE MUSTN'T DELAY, OR WE WILL MISS OUR OPPORTUNITY! THE RIVER NEVER SLEEPS!" Gandomine advised, perched on the Restorer's arm. "ONCE WE START, THERE'S NO TURNING BACK!"

"Understood." Nicholas nodded. "Gandomine, thank you for your help. This must be hard for you- being apart, I mean... from a friend you greatly admired and cared for."

"YES, WELL-" Gandomine began, then interrupted in a calmer woman's voice. "It is we who should be thanking you, Nicholas!"

The voyage to the Embedded Forest commenced. The gifted songbird warbled and the bell jingled. Reduced in size and repositioned on the deck of Nonna, Nicholas and Gandomine floated flawlessly down a river of glass. Although everything looked enormous, the ride itself was smooth and quite intriguing.

"Are we to navigate this vessel?" Nicholas asked.

"NO! ITS DESTINATION IS AUTOMATIC; THE RIVER IS OUR NAVIGATOR," Gandomine explained.

Soon they were in exact alignment with the protective boundary. Although they were very small, Nicholas still cowered, hoping that it would not repel them as it had earlier with the bee. He sighed in relief as they passed safely through. They had breached the walls, leaving the balanced climate and serene surroundings of Ethereal behind, and were now confined in a snowy and frozen forest of diseased pines, sickened by the embedded evil.

The river's mild current changed as they reached a gentle slope- or at least it would have seemed gentle to a full-sized figure. But to a small-scaled ship, the Restorer, and unique cardinal, it seemed as though they were riding the headwaters of a steep mountain consisting of V-shaped valleys, deep cuts, and roaring rapids. The toy Virago of the Sea was now the Virago of the River. She swayed to and fro, splashing them with icy water, but remained strong and agile, avoiding the natural boulder clusters and rock riffles that were only millimeters away.

Nonna eventually lost vigilance as she rubbed surfaces with a floating log. Nicholas fumbled, attempting to maintain balance as the ship's hull rocked, pitched, and tossed. It felt as though they were being attacked by explosive cannons, fired from a mighty pirate ship.

"ALMOST TO OUR DESTINATION!" Gandomine hollered. Nicholas nodded and peeked over Nonna's angelic figurehead, noticing a wide waterfall just ahead.

"Our stop... it's before those falls, I hope?!" Nicholas questioned.

Shivering and frozen from soaked feathers, Gandomine turned silent, still, and fearful, captivated in a memory of Violet and the warming caress of her hands as she picked up the nearly dead cardinal.

"Gandomine? Gandomine?! GANDOMINE! THE FALLS!" Nicholas shouted.

Gandomine startled out of a reverie and responded at the last second, with a quick song and wing-slap of the bell. As he successfully returned to full size, the Restorer planted his feet safely on the river's bank; the tall and dangerous falls were now just a small cascade to them. Nonna was less fortunate, falling over the edge from a great height. As she plunged viciously into the water below, the square sail ripped from her main mast and her planks separated and split.

A nearby fragment, with the word **Nóvva** written on it, caught Nicholas's attention. With sad eyes, he watched the remaining wreckage float down the river. Nicholas placed his hands together, as if he was going to pray, and gently kissed his fingers. "Thank you, tiny Nonna… may you rest in pieces."

Nicholas was soaked to the bone. His adrenaline was still pumping from the extreme river expedition. He paused to take a momentary rest while his necklace warmed his body and dried his attire. Amazingly, the glitz twiglet remained lit and unscathed.

At his feet was Gandomine, barely coherent and fluffed up like a ball of cotton. The bell and ribbon had somehow managed to stay tangled up in the antlers.

"Gandomine? Are you well?" Nicholas asked.

"S–s–so cold. I–I f–f–feel s–s–sleepy." Gandomine replied in a weak and shivering woman's voice. "Th–th–think… I will j–j–just… r–r–r rest for a while."

Nicholas kneeled closer to the cardinal. "Perhaps you should keep moving?" he suggested. Strangely, Gandomine did not answer or move.

"Gandomine?" Nicholas asked again, but there was still no response. Concerned, he gently poked the bird with his fingertip. Gandomine felt stiff and rigid.

"Gandomine?! No! No, this cannot be!"

Nicholas' breath became rapid and heavy as he stormed for ideas to help the frozen animal. He jerked on the warming necklace, quickly removing it from his neck. Taking the broken rope, he tied a smaller loop, shaping it to fit the bird's torso. He waited anxiously, hoping the trinket would do its work, but Gandomine remained motionless.

Frustrated, Nicholas slapped a mound of snow. He covered his face with his hands and started to tremble in sadness. It appeared the cold and rough voyage had outmatched the old cardinal. "I… I'm very sorry…"

A blunt voice responded. "S–s–SORRY FOR WHAT?" Nicholas uncovered his face, showing teary but reassured eyes. "Gandomine! You're still alive!"

"Y–YES I'M S–STILL ALIVE!" Gandomine replied, slowly recovering.

Nicholas sighed in relief. "That must mean the necklace worked?"

"OF COURSE IT WORKED!" Gandomine snapped. Nicholas nodded and smiled at the cardinal's outspoken manner, knowing that his traveling companion would be okay.

Still shivering, Gandomine encouraged Nicholas fervently. "Y–Y–YOU SOUGHT A SOLUTION BEYOND REALITY AND BELIEVED IN THE N–N–NECKLACE'S ABILITIES. B–B–BELIEVING AND ACCEPTING IMAGINATION IS THE ONLY WAY WE SURVIVE! AND… IT IS THE ONLY WAY YOU, THE RESTORER OF GOODNESS, WILL DESTROY THE BACILLUS. REALITY IS NOT YOUR WEAPON OF CHOICE, IMAGINATION IS!"

"I think we owe Nicholas our gratitude!" Gandomine's female side advised.

Gandomine nodded, switching from a snarky voice to a genuine tone. "THANK YOU, RESTORER… TRULY!"

The Chrysalis of Winter Solstice

The Embedded Forest was once a green and lush woodland, abundant with wildlife and covered in vibrant flora. It was now a place of desolation and disease, polluted with a diabolic stench. Many of the trees had fallen, while others leaned on family members, spreading the infection from limb to limb. Beneath the bark were eggs– tiny younglings infected by the Bacillus– that hatched into larva and fed on the tree's nutrients in exchange for the evil sickness. Once developed and mature, the insects emerged through the bark and morphed into destructive monstrosities that many referred to as the embedded beetles. Pines that had once perished now glowed with a deathly purple hue.

Nicholas' breaths felt heavy and deep. Was it because of the colder temperatures or was he bewildered by the environment? His thoughts scattered as he questioned the dangers ahead. He wasn't trained to fight, nor was he proficient in protecting himself. Perhaps his only line of defense was primal instincts: at the end of the day, all humans were animals, especially when threatened with their livelihood. Maybe quick annihilation was the easier way out, versus the fulfillment of the critical role he was assigned to. Supposedly his pouch was full of items that would help his cause. "But how can I be the Restorer of Goodness if I do not know how to use them?" Nicholas asked himself as the early morning's dark sky shifted into tinges of daylight. "We appear lost and running out of time! Do you know the way?" he asked Gandomine with frustration.

"Sorry... I do not know, nor does he," Gandomine replied.

Nicholas was skeptical. "Are you certain?"

"YES... CERTAIN! WERE YOU NOT GIVEN SPECIFIC TOOLS TO ACCOMPLISH YOUR TASKS?" the cardinal asked.

"I have no instructions of each one's use. I'm hoping you might have insight?"

No advice was given as Gandomine flurried away like a busy sparrow, switching from one tree to another, and Nicholas soon lost track of the cardinal. "Maybe the primordial tome has answers?" he thought, then was startled as a branch fell on his shoulder. Glancing upward, he noticed Gandomine rustling above him.

"APOLOGIES... IT BROKE! SHE CANNOT STAY CALM! THIS PLACE SPOOKS HER!" Gandomine explained.

"You mean US... this place spooks US"!

"YES... FINE... I MEANT US!" Gandomine snapped back.

"Shh! Lower your voice! It will alert the beetles!"

Gandomine's inner conversation reminded Nicholas of the frigorific wafers he received at Bity Bitey's Baker's Bake. Realizing he was vulnerable, he removed a wafer from his pouch and tossed it into his mouth. "Frig… frig… care for a wafer?" Nicholas offered the cardinal, struggling to remember the name. "It helps prevent frig… frig… a… frozen jaw."

"Will do me no good," Gandomine replied.

Nicholas removed *The Delineation of a Magnanimous Toymaker* from the pouch and placed his hands around the cover, mesmerized by the glowing title. "Feýhañdsel taught me the use of this tome," Nicholas explained. "I'm hoping it will be able to assist us." As he opened the book, a familiar angelic pattern created impressions into the snow. Nicholas quickly stowed the tome back into the memorizer pouch.

"I know this pattern; we will follow it instead!" Nicholas directed. He was then distracted by a falling pinecone that struck him on the forehead.

"So sorry, Restorer… this tree is extremely frail!" Gandomine replied.

Nicholas sighed and rubbed his head. "It's fine… let's move on!" Following the patterns, the Restorer's feet imprinted the snowy ground, his tracks again disappearing from behind him as he moved forth on the secret path. Nicholas felt as though he was making progress as the scenery changed, accompanied by the sound of flowing water. The angelic patterns then paused and disappeared. Gandomine whispered with caution from above. "RESTORER... DO NOT MOVE! REMAIN STILL!"

In the deep layer of the woods, Nicholas heard rapid hammering followed by a swarm of embedded beetles. Flapping their wings vigorously, they raced toward a small patch of winter-hardy flowers. Hissing and bickering with one another, they contended for the limited source of food. Nicholas had pictured the beetles being much smaller in size, but these were large, round, and intimidating. Their terrestrial-looking eyes, purple glowing antennas, and long pointed mandibles gave them a horrifying appearance, but they also looked like elegant pieces of jewelry armored under a lustrous metallic carapace.

After consuming the flowers, the beetles fluttered away, leaving the ground bland, colorless, and covered in nothing but snow. The angelic pattern reappeared, indicating safe travel. Nicholas and Gandomine continued to follow the repetitive pate, tunneled by a wall of diseased trees. Growing weary of the long-winded stroll, they eventually reached a suspended rope bridge. At the other end was a secluded skerry- a tall and rounded cliff-like platform, sanctuaried within the forest. It was uninhabited, tree-less, and protected by a moat of deep and long chasms. Hundreds of feet below, toxic water covered in an embedded mist flowed; if they were to fall, they would certainly die. Nicholas looked down at his feet as the path maker imprinted a final pattern before the wide crossing. He nodded in comprehension. "Thank you Icyln; we couldn't have found this without you." The pattern responded, changing its shape to a smile before disappearing entirely.

Nicholas maintained focus as the morning drew near. He turned his attention to the long and worn-out bridge while his mother's words filled his head. *"You will be more than capable, my son, and when you do- others will thrive."* Taking deep breaths, Nicholas encouraged himself. "Time to cross! Face fear and leave doubt behind!" He gripped the strap on his pouch and pulled it tight, tugged the brittle ropes of the bridge, and carefully crossed each creaking plank. The crossing swayed left to right and whipped up and down, taunting him to go back. Nicholas stayed true, maintained his posture, and prevented himself from tripping or falling sideways. Gandomine stayed behind, watching each step that Nicholas took. "HE'S GOING TO FALL, WE ARE DOOMED!" Gandomine said. "He's the Restorer- he will succeed, I believe in him!" Gandomine argued in a female voice.

After a long struggle, Nicholas safely made his way across, thankful he hadn't plunged into the deep chasm. He was also surprised to see the rickety bridge still sturdy and upright. Reaching the secluded skerry, Nicholas' woes of evil and disease diminished, and, sensing a presence of goodness and unusual magic, he no longer felt endangered or frightened. Below him was unfrozen ground, covered with a rich and loamy soil. Nicholas kneeled and ran his fingertips through the cool, wet dirt, recalling the many times he had touched the dry and hot sand on Patara's beach. The soil glimmered with glittering specks of red, green, silver, and gold, as if each grain contained thousands of tiny sapphires. Astounded by the result, Gandomine quickly stormed across the chasm and landed on the ground next to Nicholas. "IT'S THE SACRED GROUNDS OF THE PRIMORDIAL NOBLE FIR!"

"You know of the noble fir?" Nicholas asked, surprised.

"NO! I ONLY KNOW OF THE SACRED GROUNDS IN WHICH IT GROWS."

Nicholas grew irritated. "Do you intentionally choose what you do or do not know?"

Gandomine snapped back. "I ONLY KNOW WHAT I KNOW!"

"Then do you know of anything else?!"

"NOT AT THIS TIME. I DO NOT KNOW. SHE MAY KNOW!"

Nicholas sighed heavily. "Can you please ask her if she knows?"

Gandomine mumbled and whispered. "SORRY, SHE DOES NOT KNOW!"

Nicholas lost his patience and reached for the tome, grasping it tightly with his hands. Gritting his teeth with frustration, he thought of home- of Patara, how he was raised, and everything he we taught. He looked to the sky, falling back on family roots of piety and faith "Lord! Please hear my prayer! Nourish me with guidance and answers! I mustn't fail these people!" Nicholas slammed the book open and gazed blankly into the empty compartment. He shrugged, disgusted with himself. "I haven't a clue! NO CLUE AT ALL!"

Feeling useless, he wanted to give up. "Appoint this role to someone worthwhile!" he thought. But suddenly, across the suspended bridge, it was as if the suffering pines spoke out to him. As Nicholas stared at the branches- diseased, discolored, and bare- an unexplainable intuition snuck up from behind, kicking him square in the ass.

"Autumn's dead pine needle!"

Nicholas stirred his hand inside the memorizer pouch and located the needle, removed it, and placed into the tome's empty compartment. The tome replied promptly with a pop-up story of a perfect-sized pine tree, decorated and glowing brightly with lights. At the bottom of the tree, two hands appeared, wearing gloves white as snow, and quietly placed a gift underneath. A new riddle appeared before Nicholas:

The pine needle, broken into two
Buried beneath the ground- through and through
A sapling sprouts but for only a moment
The noble fir grows as the final component

Another riddle followed; the same that Nicholas had seen when visiting Feýhañdsel's Hamlet:

My tangled limbs, they must be separated
Thus, then the bauble can be decorated
I alone, cannot provide the cure
But joined together, the disease cannot endure

The pop-up illustration faded and the tome again displayed the storage compartment, holding the dead needle. Nicholas' mind became razor-sharp; he felt as though the solutions were right in front of him. Using his fingernails, he dug through the soil, creating a small but deep hole. He snapped the needle into two pieces and covered it properly. The reaction was quick- a sapling thrust out of the ground as if in a triggered spear trap, then wiggled, stretched, and grew into a healthy pine that stood at exactly 12 feet tall. It was powdered in sparkling gold snow that melted and dripped to the ground.

"Great job, Restorer! Do not stop!" Gandomine's female side encouraged.

Nicholas recited the second riddle. "Tangled limbs... bauble decorated... tangled..." He scoped in on the newly grown noble fir. "Perhaps these tangled branches?" He wondered. "It must be!" Working from top to bottom and front to back, Nicholas straightened and untangled each branch, doing his best to even out the whole circumference of the tree. He stopped momentarily, hoping to see a reaction, but nothing happened.

Gandomine's feathers shrugged. "APPEARS UNTANGLED TO ME."

Disappointed, Nicholas ran the second riddle in his mind. "Bauble... cure... joined together, disease will not endure... bauble... decorated. Both riddles are somehow relevant."

The next task revealed itself, slapping Nicholas across the face. Somehow, it made perfect sense. In the pouch's front pocket was the special bauble enchanted by the Faithlife and encouraged by his own father.

"I believe I know what to do!"

"YOU ONLY THINK YOU KNOW?!" Gandomine mocked.

"Naturally, he knows! Don't discourage him!" Gandomine's female side argued.

Nicholas opened the front pocket and reached inside, but quickly pulled away; it was unbearably cold, even more than usual. Inside, the Chrysalis of Winter Solstice was extremely reactive, furiously clouded in frozen condensation. Building up courage, Nicholas reached in a second time. His hand stung and his wrist tightened as he pinched the red ribbon and carefully pulled out the artifact. The bitter coldness urged him to let go and drop it, but he persevered: he reached out and decorated the noble fir, looping the red ribbon around one of the branches. Hanging from the tree, the ornament activated and pulsed, and the bauble became unsettled, trembling and shaking. Inside, the hairline crack extended further, making its way down the icicle pupa, then like a sea turtle hatching from an egg, a butterfly blasted from the protective coating. It had beaming tones of blue and turquoise and a long tail with white spots. Tiny snowflakes fell from its forewing and hindwing, the veins of which were shimmering in gold. Fluttering inside, it looked as though it were knocking on the ornament's outer shell, shouting "Let me out!" Both Nicholas and Gandomine stared with wide open mouths, struck by its beauty.

"Oh my! A snowflake dragontail. It's gorgeous!" Gandomine commented.

"Very," Nicholas replied in awe.

"YEAH, YEAH... NOW WHAT?" Gandomine interrupted, ruining the moment.

Fortunately, Nicholas did not have to determine his next move, as the next event was already set in place. The red ribbon untied itself and the ornament fell to the ground, shattering into a spectacle of stars. Freed, the snowflake dragontail batted its wings and its long tail swayed like a war banner in the wind. Skeptical of the butterfly's intentions, Nicholas paced backward toward the suspended bridge, but it continued to follow him, staring at him with its beady eyes. "Hello there," Nicholas greeted with a wide but concerned smile. The butterfly quickly stormed away and out of sight. "Where has it gone?" Nicholas asked, bemused.

"Nicholas, behind you!" Gandomine yelled.

Out of nowhere, the butterfly appeared and jolted into Nicholas' vertebrae. The Restorer groaned in pain and bowed his chest outward. It felt as though he had been struck in the back by a venomous snake. His eyes rolled in the back of his head and his mouth began to foam and drool. He gurgled and stuttered words of nonsense.

"Gan... Gando... what... is... is... happening?"

"I KNOW NOT, RESTORER!"

"GANDOMINE!" Nicholas yelled as his body shivered and shuddered, using all his might to keep himself standing. Nicholas pleaded. "GANDOMINE! PLEASE hel... hel... HELL WITH ME... HELP ME!"

"YES, ONE MOMENT, I AM ASKING HER!" Gandomine replied, flustered.

Nicholas now had an overwhelming urge to fall and lie face first on the ground. "SHE KNOWS! SHE KNOWS WHAT TO DO!" Gandomine replied, excited. "SHE SAYS YOU MUST ACTIVATE A MELODY!"

"Mel... Melody... what... melancholy?" Nicholas stuttered, looking like a white-eyed demon that was staring into a holy light.

"BLEH! YOU LOOK TERRIBLE, RESTORER; THAT IS SOME BUTTERFLY!" Gandomine replied in disgust. "Forget about that... stay focused!" Gandomine intervened in a woman's voice. "Quickly, Nicholas! Say the word that activates the Caroler's Melody, and it will settle the butterfly's injection!"

"She's right. It's best you hurry– wait too long and it will kill you!"

"It will?"

"Yes! At least I think it will."

"Oh no! You can do this, Nicholas; do not perish!"

Through his pain, agony, and delusions, Nicholas recapped, trying to remember the word Gasper had used. His memory served him well and he shouted "Melovocal!" in a spray of foamed saliva.

The voices of a hundred men, women, boys, and girls sang together on top of the secluded skerry. Nicholas grunted, responding to the intriguing melody of the choir. He bent over and placed his hands on his knees, spitting the remaining foam and drool from his mouth. With the help of the carolers, his infliction started to calm, and his body relaxed. Startling him, a herald of bugling echoed in the near distance. He glanced toward the noble fir; standing next to it was a tall and stout elk–like beast. Its yellowish–green antlers hung from its head, diseased and infected.

"The Foredoomed Fallow!" Gandomine shouted.

Nicholas stood up straight, still weak but feeling more wholesome and pure. He now understood what had happened. The Chrysalis of Winter Solstice had injected a unique ability into him– he was now capable of releasing the mystical animal from its sickness.

With full confidence and bravery, he crept toward the noble fir, maintaining a slow tiptoeing pace. *Crunch, crunch, crunch* was the sound as he proceeded further. He soon realized that not every crunch of the snow was of his own– the fallow too was creeping closer, but with extreme caution. Nicholas' eyes shifted upward, staring into the twinkling eyes of the mystical beast. He had expected a creature of evil, a prowler swayed by embedded evil, or simply an animal who was scared and defensive. Instead, the eyes of the fallow showed warmth– yet a feeling of worry, a feeling of distrust, a feeling of pain– and a willingness to be helped. Taking a risk, Nicholas reached out his hand to offer companionship, then spoke softly. "It's okay, it's okay... I understand your pain... I can see you have pain... please... it's okay... it's okay..." Still skittish, the Foredoomed Fallow bugled, screamed, and slowly stepped backward.

"No! No! Please don't stray... let me help you... I'm destined to help you... do not be afraid... you and I... we are meant to be together... everything is fine."

As the fallow crept closer, Nicholas felt rare characteristics coming from her. He gently placed his hand on the front of her head, showing a gesture of comfort and kindness. An awkward sensation of happiness and joy resided between the two of them. Soon, an amazing aura of white light lit up the woods. Nature painted a silhouette of a man and a cured fallow. The huge antlers that were once broken, hanging, and discolored changed to crimson red and spanned out like wings of a dragon. The light and silhouette faded to darkness- but not for long, as the morning of the winter solstice had arrived. Rays of light shone directly on the Primordial Noble Fir as it sparkled in the sunrise. The embedded mist in the chasm below was removed and the toxic water purified. The sick and dead trees of the embedded forest were restored, green in color and full of needles. The stagnant stench of evil changed to a pleasant piney smell, complemented with a clean and crisp morning air.

Gandomine shed an enormous cardinal smile. "Nicholas has done it! He has rescued the Foredoomed Fallow!"

"I KNEW IT ALL ALONG!" Gandomine replied smugly.

"WE! WE knew it all along!"

"YES! WE KNEW IT ALL ALONG!"

Amongst a rousing forest and sun-lit noble fir, the Restorer of Goodness and the Primordial Fallow were brought together, united by the sacred powers of the ornament- The Chrysalis of Winter Solstice.

"Resurge!" Revisited

The Restorer of Goodness stood before the primordial creature. Her glossy-brown eyes fixated on Nicholas, expressing signs of trust but still leery of any abrupt actions. To ride such a divine beast required patience, friendship, and most importantly, partnership. Having raised Paloma, Nicholas was experienced in horsemanship. Using his skillset, he maintained a comfortable distance and sighted in on her movements and reactions. She had been through a lot, and adding additional pressure could convince her to flee.

Throughout the series of events, some rather more hellacious than others, Nicholas had managed to keep the stiff-coiled rope tied to his waist. He untied the line and created a large loop, then, like a wrangler pursuing a wild mustang, he swung it over his head and launched it toward the fallow. The loop missed her neck and instead tangled in her velvet-red antlers. Frightened, she jerked and pulled her head side to side with remarkable strength, competing in a fierce game of tug-of-war as the friction of the rope burned the Restorer's hands. Instead of contending, Nicholas remained calm and was able to untangle the mess he'd created. He retrieved the loop and increased the size once more, then gave the rope another good swing and threw it forward with all his might. His second attempt was successful, clearing the fallow's antlers and lassoing her neck. Nicholas pulled the knot snuggly, but not so tight that it would displease her.

His next move was to pull her in, tug... and wait... tug... and wait... until she was at terms with him. "Riding her bareback will also be a tough feat," Nicholas thought, since she was not equipped with an appropriate saddle. What he did not anticipate was that the stiff rope provided by Gibben Gubbin Gizmo's was more than just natural fibers- it contained pre-set abilities with unthinkable measures. The rope's end suddenly ignited, and sparks flashed, stinging the Restorer's fingers. He quickly released the rope and it burned toward the fallow like a lit fuse.

"This cannot be good! What have you done?!" Gandomine responded.

"It's meant to do that!" Gandomine argued in a female's voice.

"What?! No! Are you certain?"

"Yes! I'm certain. Well... almost certain."

Nicholas and the cardinal cowered and flinched as the burning rope approached the fallow's neck, scorching the tips of her tan and shaggy hair.

"WELL! SO MUCH FOR THAT! SHE HAS BECOME A FOREDOOMED TINDERBOX!"

"You are right! What have I done?!" Nicholas asked anxiously.

"PATIENCE! I assure you it WILL NOT harm her!"

Gandomine assumed correctly, as the fallow did not go up in flames. The spark of the burning rope stopped and detached itself from around her neck. What was left of the burning debris fell to the ground. From her neckline to hind end, golden primordial symbols illuminated on her body and an assortment of riding tack appeared, automatically attaching itself to her stocky build. Applied to her face was a decorative bridle and golden reins. Her back was equipped with a saddle and saddle blanket, red with white trim and the Emblem of Goodness ingrained into the material. Pleased with her new equipment, she bugled and chuckled in short grunts, flaunting as if she were dressed in a lovely new outfit.

"Amazing!" Nicholas replied. "If only it was that easy to equip Paloma at home."

"CAREFUL! SHE'S COMING YOUR WAY!" the cardinal warned.

Nicholas remained still, almost petrified, as she edged closer. Uncertain of her intentions, Nicholas responded with soft eye contact but was caught off guard as she rubbed cheeks with him.

"She recognized you as the Restorer of Goodness. Before she accepts you as her rider- she needs a name," Gandomine advised.

"A... a name... I am to name her?" Nicholas asked.

"Yes, the appointed Restorer of Goodness must give her a name."

Nicholas thought long and hard, recalling the honor of naming Drusus' freighter. He gazed upon the primordial creature- she was stunningly elegant and beautiful. Her stout body structure and velvet red antlers reminded Nicholas of the moment when he opened the satchel, unleashing hundreds of caribou as they pranced with great force and pierced through the mass of embedded hounds. Finally, an appropriate name came to mind.

"We will call her- Xalibu."

Unexpectedly, a decorative noseband appeared and attached itself to the bridle. It sparkled and twinkled, scribing Xalibu into the leather. Approving of her new name, she lowered her head and rubbed cheeks with the Restorer a second time.

"Excellent, Nicholas! She now accepts you as her rider!" Gandomine's female voice replied excitedly.

Nicholas nodded and glanced at the saddle high above. How would he reach it? There were no stirrups to use, and the fallow was much taller than Paloma. Gripping the reins, he pulled himself upward, attempted to climb what felt like an enormous mountainside with fur. The fallow became unsettled and disapproved of his technique. She kicked her back legs and bucked, throwing Nicholas to the ground. "Blast! Not again!" Nicholas complained, lying on his back for the fourth time. He snapped at Gandomine "If you know of a solution, please share!"

"I KNOW NOT! SHE IS YOURS TO BREAK, NOT MINE!" Gandomine replied bluntly. "REMEMBER, THE RULES ARE DIFFERENT HERE! A REALISTIC MINDSET WILL NOT HELP YOU!" Taunting Nicholas, Gandomine perched on Xalibu's rump. The presence of the cardinal did not seem to bother her.

"SEE? MOUNTING IS SIMPLE!" Gandomine stated smugly.

Nicholas rolled his eyes. "Simple for a snarky cardinal perhaps!"

The Restorer centered himself and switched to an open and imaginative mind. He thoroughly evaluated the situation, then thought of Kiffy, his musk oxen, and the command he had taught Nicholas as they rode to the Arena of the Frozen Demilune. Without hesitation, Nicholas hollered *"Resurge!"* To his surprise, Xalibu obeyed and lowered her dragon-sized body to the ground.

"It worked!" Nicholas grinned, receiving a nod of approval from Gandomine. Working slowly and carefully, he saddled up and took hold of the reins. Just like Booth and Eucera, the fallow lay low, still waiting for further command. Nicholas knew exactly what to say. *"Resurge!"* he hollered again.

Xalibu followed directions and began to rise. Nicholas felt as if he had been harnessed in the arms of an angel, lifted to the tallest mountain with a sky view of the world beneath him.

"Let's start off easy, girl," Nicholas instructed as he gently tugged the reins. They were off to a good start as he and his new mount trotted toward the bridge, but Xalibu was in no agreement to cross.

"WHY AREN'T WE MOVING?" Gandomine asked.

"She's intimidated by the bridge. Paloma always hated them. It took some time to break her of that fear," Nicholas explained. He patted Xalibu on the torso and pulled the reins. "One step at a time," he said, but Xalibu still refused to cross.

Gandomine's male side grew irritated. "SHE MIGHT AS WELL BE SCARED OF HER OWN SHADOW! AND... WHOSE BRILLIANT IDEA WAS IT FOR HER TO APPEAR ON THE SKERRY? SECONDLY, HOW DID SHE GET THERE IN THE FIRST PLACE?!"

"CALM... down and guide her!" Gandomine female side intervened.

Grumbling and groaning in a male's voice, Gandomine fluttered off and landed on the bridge's walkway. Xalibu's full attention was drawn to the little angry bird who was waving her down.

"HEY YOU! OVER–GROWN REINDEER! IT'S RATHER SIMPLE! SEE! IF I CAN DO IT... YOU CAN!" Gandomine shouted persuasively. "NOW CROSS!"

No longer reluctant, Xalibu trotted toward Gandomine as her large-rounded hooves stamped on each weathered and worn-out plank. Struggling to support her weight, the suspension ropes twisted, stretched, and snapped, causing the bridge to spring up and down.

"Slow and steady, girl," Nicholas encouraged, taking care not to fall in the chasm below them, while Gandomine continued to perform the circus act of guiding her across the tightrope of death. Throughout the long-winded process, Xalibu wobbled and cautiously put one hoof in front of the other. It was as if Nicholas and Gandomine were teaching a newborn fawn how to walk for the first time.

Working together as a team, they reached the other side and reacquainted themselves with the embedded forest. Sections that were still diseased and withered were now mixed with recovering pines and thriving winter fauna.

Behind them, the rickety bridge broke loose and crumbled, plunging into the deep chasm below. Nicholas questioned if it had destroyed itself intentionally or just collapsed because of the stress they had put on it when crossing. On top of the secluded skerry, the ten-foot Primordial Fir continued to sparkle and bask in the pleasant warmth of the sun.

Nicholas stroked Xalibu's shaggy neck and commended her for her accomplishment. "Good work, girl, you crossed well."

"Another task completed effectively!" Gandomine's female side expressed optimism. The cardinal's counterpart scoffed "EFFECTIVELY? PFFT... PULLED IT OUT OF OUR KEISTER! WOULDN'T YOU AGREE?" The question was directed at an insect with a shiny carapace that appeared unexpectedly and stared Gandomine down with its evil and buggy eyes.

Gandomine's eyes were now just as big as the beetle's. "You dimwit! That is an EMBEDDED BEETLE!" The beetle hissed and its antennas lit up, indicating its intention to attack.

"Restorer...? Might I suggest we start riding now? We are about to become Winter Solstice breakfast!"

Nicholas responded by pulling the reins and clicking his tongue, but Xalibu refused to move. "Please girl... help us!" Nicholas begged. Gandomine pitched in, pecking at her back. "YOU STUBBORN MULE. MOVE! NOW!" But the cardinal's sharp beak did not seem to faze her. Again recapping on Kiffy's commands, Nicholas hollered *"Cele Huit!"*

Xalibu complied and grunted in excitement, then, trampling the snow with her hooves, she gained traction and blasted forward with a burst of speed. The Restorer's head was flung backward from the extreme acceleration and Gandomine's feathers flurried like a blustery snowstorm. The embedded beetle failed to keep up with the chase and was left behind.

Outraged, it hissed and screeched in a horrid manner, calling out for assistance.

What began as one beetle soon changed to two, then fifty, then hundreds. They ambushed Xalibu and her riders, creating a cloud of embedded fog that conflicted visibility and plagued the trees that had recovered earlier on.

To prevent frigorificitis, Nicholas snatched another wafer from his pouch, chewing and swallowing as quickly as possible. He then pulled out a bag of Kiffy's traveling mix. Remembering its odd magical effects, he dumped it on the ground, where several sneezing shadblows grew instantly, enticing many of the starving beetles. Feeding on the attractive morsel, they released a snappy sneeze-like hiss and plunged into the snow with a thud, reducing the army of hard-shelled aviators to half. Beetles not lured by the delicious petals swarmed like angry bees and pummeled into one another, combining their exoskeleton structures. For every three beetles, one enhanced beetle was formed, now tripled in size.

"They are bonding into embedded super beetles!" Gandomine cried.

"I'M CERTAIN THAT THEY ARE MEANT TO DO THAT!" Gandomine's male side argued.

"You knew this all along?!" Nicholas snapped.

"Apparently he did!" Gandomine replied. "You could've mentioned this earlier!"

Having improved strength and velocity, the embedded super beetles were now able to catch up to Xalibu's group. Blinding them in a spectacle of purple flashing antennas, much longer than before, they began their assault. Their legs, sharp as fishhooks, grappled on to the Restorer's neck, and their mandibles inflicted pain with each exasperating bite. Nicholas groaned, slapping and swatting them away. His face turned pale blue and his jaw swelled and locked. Fortunately, the magical ingredients from the frigorific wafers were in his system, quickly reversing the effects of the freezing ailment. Gandomine's small crimson antlers rotated and thrusted, dissecting the beetles one by one.

"Restorer… proceed forth!" Gandomine instructed. "I will distract them; they mustn't hurt the fallow."

"Please stay! We can outrun them!" Nicholas pleaded, but noticed Gandomine was no longer riding. "Whoa girl! Niah!" Nicholas commanded and stopped Xalibu dead in her tracks, causing her to lose traction and slide across the slippery ice. With a fierce shift of direction, the beetles focused their attention on Gandomine. Although old, the rare bird gave them a run for their money, dodging each attack with a series of twists, spins, and rolls. The chase soon became a grueling battle for Gandomine.

"I… CAN… CANNOT… FEND THEM OFF MUCH LONGER!" Gandomine huffed and puffed.

"Don't quit now!" Gandomine encouraged. "Strong wings!"

"THEY ARE TOO MANY!"

"Please try! I do not wish to die!" Gandomine begged.

"I'M TR... TRYING!" Gandomine groaned, exhausted but still taking great lengths– it was no use, as the cardinal became consumed in a thick layer of embedded fog.

"I CAN NO LONGER..."

"Yes, you can keep moving! I beg of you!"

"I'M... I'M... UGH... SO SORRY..."

"Noooo, please! Unnngh!"

"GANDOMINE!!!" Nicholas shouted, losing sight of his friend except for two feathers that whirled in the breeze, one tan in color and the other bright red. The beetles remained relentless, thrusting from the evil cloud. Combining their bodies for the second time, they reformed into hideous monstrosities, staring Nicholas and Xalibu down with killer instincts.

The Restorer's blood boiled as he challenged them. "YOU THINK SIZE MATTERS?! DO YOU? THEN COME! CATCH US IF YOU CAN!" The reformed beetles roared loudly, instead of the usual hissing, determined to destroy the Restorer of Goodness. Their antennas, even longer than they were in the second phase, lit up like sparklers as they bolted toward them.

"Xalibu! Cele Huit!" Nicholas shouted. The contest continued as Xalibu galloped in unbelievable momentum. The Restorer's eyes teared and his face burned; this was the fastest creature he had ever known. The enhanced beetles struggled to keep up and their wings batted up and down rapidly like heavy rain clapping on a rooftop. Suddenly the Bacillus appeared and growled in its mysterious form, further challenging Xalibu's capability with rumbling grounds and ghastly winds that caused the tallest of the pines to fall. Xalibu shuffled left to right, avoiding one tree after another and dodging each impact by only a split second. They soon reached a long straightaway, and Nicholas heard himself shout, "YA! YA! YA!" He lowered his center of gravity and Xalibu's massive legs switched to even more enormous strides. A hue of golden entrails streamed behind her, just like it had with Mortimer, the Aquanaut of the Sea.

Angered, the Bacillus roared and taunted them. "Run, frightened mouse of goodness... RUUUNNN! TORMEEENT, WAAAKE!!!"

Ignoring the evil surroundings, Nicholas closed his eyes, envisioning himself riding Paloma across the warm beach of Patara while lightning flashed in the summer skies and struck down on the Mare Nostrum. His eyes re-opened to an environment that had gone silent except for a whoosh of air upon his face and a mysterious ringing in his ears. The embedded beetles were gone. Instead of galloping, Xalibu was prancing– she wasn't going to stop, nor did Nicholas want her to. Around them was a nebula containing colored clouds of cosmic dust and stars as bright as the sun itself. Ahead of them in the distance was an archway much like the one in Patara. Try as they may, they could not reach it; the path before them seemed like an endless interstellar tunnel.

Nicholas suddenly felt weak and empty, as though the atmosphere were a giant sponge absorbing every thought in his mind and every molecule of his body. Soon, everything around him turned to darkness.

The Brigade of Righteousness

Free–Booter soared high above the barren and foggy icefields, prospecting the enemy lines. Having exceptional night vision, he also wore an enchanted head cap that improved his field of view in the thick fog and enabled him to record the formation of the embedded creatures. Completing his assignment, the gyrfalcon returned to the encampment and swooped down into a hold–out tent. "I trust you've scouted the enemy well?" Mazielle asked as he landed on her gauntlet. Sitting alongside Mazielle was Bolo, feeding Clawclapper. "You lost us the championship; I expect better performance in battle!" he growled at the wolverine, throwing chunks of meat to enhance his craving for flesh. Also sitting with the group was Harold as he continued to scold Jaegar. "I told you! Stay in your pocket! We have not yet begun!" The best of pedagogs had joined together in support of the cause. They were equipped in the same attire they had worn at the arena, representing the animals that they tamed and trained. Outside, Kiffy sat near a bonfire with his wolves, his hunting champion, and the Restorer, equipped in his trapping pelerine and fox-themed cape. Nicholas maintained closeness with Xalibu, attempting to keep her at ease. She was still adjusting to a busy environment of people.

"Pedagog with the bird!" a lieutenant shouted through the entrance of the hold-out tent. "The commander demands a scouting report!"

"Time for tactical talk," Kiffy commented to Nicholas, overhearing the lieutenant. "I shall return, friend… I will leave you to your fallow." Having no intention of moving- not even the fox- Kiffy's animals stayed with Nicholas, resting near the warm and roaring bonfire.

As Mazielle and Free-Booter entered the tent, they were impatiently questioned by Quilo. "We are out of time! Has the bird determined our enemy count and formation?" Mazielle nodded. "Yes, I will retrieve what he knows." She removed the enchanted head cap from Free-Booter's head. "*Nark espial!*" she commanded. The gyrfalcon repositioned himself on Mazielle's arm and stared deep into her eyes. She stared back and became hypnotized as Free-Booter downloaded his findings into her mind. Everyone around remained silent, watching as the two of them synced together.

Arvel shook his head. "Wha' in hell is this, a starin' contest?" he whispered.

"Shh! Allow them to do their work," Lizabet advised.

"That's right; respect the pedagog," Kiffy teased with a smirk.

Arvel saluted Kiffy with his middle finger. "Here's my respect!"

"Brother! Be silent!" Quilo demanded, eyeing Arvel with anger. "If you do not, I will attach your tongue to a frozen blade!"

Kiffy leaned in toward the commander. "There's a sword just outside," he suggested.

Norrick rolled his eyes. "If we could, please?!"

Scattered on a square table were several scribbled battleplans and a blank sheet of parchment. Mazielle had again braided her long hair, tied together with the same bee-sized hummingbirds. As she obtained information from Free-Booter, the hummingbirds became unsettled and restless. The birds chirped loud, then louder, soon detaching themselves from Mazielle's hair. Like bullets fired from a gun, they fled toward the planning table, bumping off others standing inside the planning tent. They splattered into the parchment and plotted a portion of the enemy's formation. After the last and final hummingbird had landed, the shape of the enemy formation was clear.

Norrick spoke to Quilo, showing terror in his emerald-colored eyes. "I'm afraid it's what we expected." The commander further analyzed the parchment.

Frustrated, he slammed his giant hand down, removing a chunk of the table.

"What is it, Commander?" a lieutenant asked, concerned.

"They are in Torment's Formation!" Quilo hollered in anger.

"It can only mean they are beginning the ritual," Lízabet added.

"The embedded evil are sanctioned at the entrance of the Strain," Norrick explained to the group. "They are protecting access and include three powerful gashgobs."

"We must invade and attack them promptly!" the lieutenant suggested.

"Wrong!" Quilo growled. "Our brigade remains stationary. We garrison below the nunatak and before the fog line. I am not sending the brigade into an embedded fog of death!"

"How do we intend to interrupt their operation?" Norrick asked.

"We take bites at a time," Quilo advised. "We will assign provokers to sway them across the ice fields."

"Those are strong tactics, Commander. It should work," Norrick agreed.

Quilo continued. "When the fog line depletes, we will march forth toward the Strain. Until then we do not move an inch!"

"And who is to provoke them to our side of the icefields?" the lieutenant asked. The group then turned and glanced at the old artificer and the pedagog.

"Oh, for muklukin' sakes!" Arvel replied.

"Fair enough." Kiffy nodded, accepting the role. "If I am to provoke them, I wish to have Nicholas by our side as well."

"Negative!" Quilo snapped. "The foreigner will have no part of this! He remains here at the nunatak!"

"I'm sorry Quilo, but I disagree!" Kiffy argued.

The commander approached Kiffy and stared down at him. "You dare to undermine my tactics?!"

"No! But I undermine your lack of faith in the Restorer of Goodness!" Kiffy replied. "He and the primordial fallow will be useful to our cause! The fallow is swift and can help sway the enemy to our side of the icefields."

The commander's face turned red. "Neither the foreigner, NOR THE FALLOW, will be part of our Brigade! Now step aside or I will cut you up as meat and feed you to your wolves!"

Kiffy did not move and remained unintimidated. He gripped his weapons and stared down the commander twice his size.

"Easy, Animal Lover, he'll kill ya; move aside!" Arvel advised as he nudged Kiffy away. "Now listen careful, brother!" Arvel shouted. "Listen good! We are usin' Undertow! He's gonna help us! And if ya say one more word 'bout it! One more! I... ME... won't attach yer tongue to a frozen blade; I will scoop it out with an ice pick!"

Angered, Quilo drew his great axe and struck at his brother with great fury. With experienced finesse, Arvel drew Leonora and parried his brother's attack. Suddenly, both weapons were flung from their hands as Gasper entered the planning tent, breaking up the dispute. "Everyone! We are all together in this. The Bacillus is our enemy... NOT EACH OTHER... yep... yep... yep!"

Norrick clasped Quilo's arm. "Commander, I know you are tired and on little sleep. But please keep an open mind with the Restorer. Stick to your battleplan!" Still angry and discouraged, the commander spat on the floor and continued to stare his older brother down with temporary hatred. "Quilo... we all will die today without your support," Norrick added.

The commander calmed himself and nodded. "Lieutenants! Prepare the squads! When the enemy attacks, we will tear the embedded disease right from their carcasses!"

Below the nunatak, the Brigade of Righteousness aligned themselves on to the icefields. Facing the embedded fog line, they grew anxious that embedded creatures would quickly jolt out at a moment's notice.

"Nicholas, today you and Xalibu get the chance to grow with one another. Best you keep her speed minimized and her hooves on the ground," Kiffy advised from his blitzkrieg sledger.

Nicholas nodded. Kiffy then presented Nicholas with a mysterious candy. "Take this, friend. It's a Yuul Licorice Clover. It was made for the fallow by the Yuulnavvies."

"Thank you, but I still have the carrots you gave her last night," Nicholas reminded Kiffy.

"She's a big girl; she will definitely eat those. This candy– it has a different purpose." Xalibu could smell the attractive aroma of the Yuulnavian treat and tried to snatch it from Kiffy as he handed it to Nicholas.

Kiffy grinned. "You've eaten these before, haven't you, girl?"

The Restorer accepted the candied clover and placed it in his memorizer pouch. Just like all the items he'd received during his journey, he questioned its use.

"Now remember, friends– this includes you, ol' man!" Kiffy shouted at Arvel. "We all ride together, we all taunt the enemy together, and we all return together!"

Suddenly, Kiffy's confidence was crushed by extreme nervousness. It wasn't because he was going into battle or the fact that he was about to provoke an army of the Bacillus. It was the spontaneous presence of the woman he deeply desired and cared for. The hairs on the back of his neck rose from the presence of Lizabet's tender smile and the loving nature that she shared with his wolves. She stopped by each wolf, petting them and wishing them luck. Lízabet crouched down near Bechstein and caressed his nose. "May your sense of smell be strong." She lifted his front leg and rubbed his paw. "And may your feet lead us to our enemy."

Kiffy felt a lump in his throat as Lízabet approached the blitzkrieg sledger. She slouched and whispered into Hooley's ear, "Take care of him, champion; take care of my Kiffy." She then stared into the eyes of her super pedagog, dressed in his pelerine and cape. Kiffy suddenly forgot where he was and what he was doing as he stared back into her gradient brown eyes.

"You aren't wearing your rucksack," she teased.

"It would only wrinkle my cape," Kiffy teased back, not mentioning that the rucksack was tied down to the sledger. "I have everything I need and everyone important to me- they are all here." Kiffy squeezed Lízabet's hand and stared into her eyes. "Including you." Kiffy followed with a Salute of Degomble but was interrupted as Lízabet lowered his arm and pressed her lips on to his. Kiffy followed through, extending and enhancing the passionate kiss.

"Oh! For muklukin'! Enough of this crud, this ain't a romantic picnic… it's battle," Arvel jested.

Kiffy and Lízabet's lips separated. "Are you certain you want to team with that crank?" she asked.

"I'm certain... no better man by my side," Kiffy replied with a smirk. Lízabet smiled and kissed Kiffy's cheek.

"Please be safe- all of you." She rejoined Gasper, protected at the back of the brigade and on top of Booth.

The commander analyzed the battle strategy one last time. He thought of his wife, little Urie, and his son. Lyman had grown up so fast and was becoming a man. He feared that he would never see his family again.

His two lieutenants double-checked the formation of the battalion. "Update! Both squads!" Quilo demanded. "Everyone is equipped, eager, and ready," the first lieutenant replied. "Squad is aligned," the second lieutenant confirmed.

"Very good! Pedagog, when you are ready!" Quilo shouted.

Kiffy nodded, took a deep breath, and prepared for his pre-battle oration. In the immense fogging of corruption, they would soon encounter the embedded evil, prone to protect the Bacillus and release the deadly variant. He glanced down at his loving fox and massaged her ears, then looked to his fellow people standing before him— a brigade of malificus, embedapists, pedagogs, soldiers, heroes, union brothers and sisters, mothers, fathers, aunts, uncles, grandmothers, and grandfathers. Kiffy respected and cherished every one of them.

"We have reached winter's beating heart! On this day of winter solstice, I see wonderful individuals and amazing animals– each of us with unique talents, skills, and roles. We have faced many hardships, and we can face a million more! Strong as they might be out there, they will not outweigh the righteous!" Kiffy raised his hand and passionately swiped his face. Among the icy battlefield, a brigade of hands raised, then swiped downward in the Salute of Degomble.

"These sickened monsters, they may be embedded, but we too are embedded! NOT in evil, NOT in vain of terror, NOT in disease– BUT in kindness, in loveliness, and of GOOOODNESSSS!"

The Brigade of Righteousness stirred and shouted in battle cry, while war drums thumped and thundered. Banners flapped in the cold arctic wind as the Emblems of Goodness illuminated brightly. Legionnaires banged their swords to their shields, archers shook their bows above their heads, and malificus raised their fingertips, casting fireworks high into the starlit sky, painting the polar night in a canvas of blasts and sparkles.

"Alright, Undertow! Let's see what that beast can do!" Arvel shouted.

Nicholas nodded. He noticed a urine stain in the snow, just beneath Eucera. Laughing to himself, he now knew what the artificer meant by 'yellow snow.'

Kiffy hollered to his honorable team of wolves.

"Bech, are you ready?!"

Bechstein replied with barks of excitement.

"And ol' grope, you ready?!"

"Fuckin' muklukin' right I am!" Arvel confirmed with a wink.

Kiffy nodded with a wide smile. His teeth tightened, and his eyes grew stern and focused. He snapped the reins, up then down, up then down, and hollered: "Now Bechstein! Now Marriam! Now Oken! And Lillian!" He raised his battle hammer and pointed it toward the embedded fog. "Tele Huit! FOR THE SAKE OF GOODNESS!!!"

The 'Ye Olde Warmonger,' the champion pedagog, and the Restorer of Goodness rode side by side and vanished beyond the embedded fog line. With hopes held high, the Brigade of Righteousness cheered them on. "Ho, Ho, Rah! Ho, Ho, Rah! Ho, Ho, Rah!"

"HO, HO, RAH!"

Bechstein earned a hero's recognition as he followed the scent of hare tracks and fresh droppings. Consumed in a dense fog and glowing rime, the team relied on the wolf's training in hopes he would lead them in the right direction. Each team member equipped a glitz twiglet for sufficient light, including the fox and the wolves. As they sprinted and pulled the sledger, Bechstein, Oken, Marriam, and Lillian looked like glowing pixies with bright dog collars, tails, furry ears, and four legs.

For Nicholas and Xalibu, keeping up with the others felt like an easy task, especially compared to outrunning the enraged beetles of the embedded forest. Knowing that Xalibu was a lightning bolt waiting to strike, Nicholas kept her at a canter and restricted her excitement.

Proceeding deeper into the fog, Hooley started to whine, giggle, and cower behind Kiffy's leg. "Let's slow down," Kiffy advised, translating the fox's behavior. "Hooley is spooked; that tells me we are close."

"Pfft! She's scared of 'er own shadow!" Arvel bantered.

The team slowed and was soon met by a massive number of purple glowing eyes and the towering seracs that lit brightly behind them. Drawing close to the Strain, they were up against an assembled army, loyal to the Bacillus and swayed to protect the ruins at all costs.

"It's Torment's turd-mation, al' right," Arvel commented.

At the front of the formation were embedded hares with diseased fur and beady eyes of anger. Behind them were creatures much fiercer- ice banshees with long arms, large wings, wrinkled bodies, and decayed skin. Hovering in the air, the banshees screeched and screamed, warning the invaders to stay away. Displaying a toxic aura, embedded hounds drooled and snarled as their long-pointed tongues hung from their mouths. Kiffy's wolves competed with them in a contest of testy growls. At the very back were the strongest and most brutal- three of the four polar bears, overtaken by the gashgobs and closely guarding the entrance of the Strain.

"Quilo was correct," Kiffy commented. "They are in a defensive strategy. We will certainly have to provoke them."

Arvel pointed at the enemy. "No provokin' needed."

Kiffy had assumed wrong- a drove of embedded hares was easily persuaded and raced toward them in a zig-zag motion. "Well... that was easy! Time to go! *Diverto and Huit!*" Kiffy shouted as the wolves shifted and pulled the sledger in the opposite direction. Nicholas clicked his tongue and repeated Kiffy's command as he and Xalibu followed along.

The sudden pursuit of hares had confused and frightened Eucera. "Ya dumb wool blanket, turn 'round… move already!" Arvel yelled at the musk ox. "Eucera! *Diverto and Huit!*"Kiffy commanded.

The Brigade of Goodness waited in readiness as the provokers blasted through the embedded fog line. Kiffy and Arvel split ways and distributed the embedded hares amongst the battalion. They remained in the vicinity until they were no longer pursued and clear to return to Torment's formation. Nicholas and the fallow maintained a safe distance from the fight, which prevented them from being attacked, while keeping Xalibu calm.

Anxious to swing their swords, frontline legionnaires rushed toward the fog. "Halt! Stay in position! I will remove the legs of anyone that places one toe beyond the fog line!" Quilo threatened.

Three hares continued to hassle Arvel. Eurcera quickly pitched in, stomping one with a loud thump. "Now yer gettin' it!" Arvel smirked, as he swiped the other two with his great sword Leonora.

"Ready fer 'nother run, Undertow!" Arvel shouted across the battlefield. "Let's see if that mystic beast can outrun hounds and banshees!"

"Yes, I'm ready, Arvel!" Nicholas shouted with full confidence.

"Animal Lover! Ya done screwin' about yet?" Arvel teased.

"One moment! Incoming!" Kiffy replied, gripping his double-edged dagger and thrusting a forward stab into an airborne hare.

"More turds headin' toward Lillian!" Arvel warned.

"Why is it always Lillian?!" Kiffy asked himself. "Lillian... beside you, girl!" he hollered in warning.

Lillian had no time to react but was saved by Clawclapper as he sliced through the pelted flesh of each hare. Proud of his kills, Clawclapper boasted and flashed his sharp crampon-claws, growling in a wolverine's battle cry. "Well done! Now back to the line!" Bolo demanded.

Kiffy snapped the reins and shouted "Tele huit!" He nodded to the former champion with gratitude. Bolo nodded back in respect as Kiffy and his provoking team reunited and disappeared into the fog.

The remaining hares kept full attention on The Brigade of Goodness. Outnumbered two to one, legionnaires on the frontline faced their enemies with bravery, perfectly timing their shields in parry. Each hare bounced backward and rolled on the ground, where, stunned, they met their demise from stabbing swords. Fighters more experienced and seasoned slashed the hares in mid-air while other contenders worked together, crushing them between two shields. Fighters not as responsive lay on the ground and groaned in injury.

"Second and third lines! Do not engage!" Quilo ordered, standing beside them on the secondary line. "Save your energy and arrows!" The brigade followed direction as archers, malificus, and legionnaire reinforcements stayed in position. At the very back of the brigade was the primordial malificus and his protege. Norrick stood nearby, assigned to protect both Gasper and Lízabet if the brigade were to fail, for the two would soon be appointed a very important task.

With the help of their trained animals, the pedagogs provided frontline support. Jaegar, Free-booter, and Clawclapper joined together, forming a battle strategy of their own. Jaegar started with a taunting series of tumbles, rolls, and dances, and was soon chased down. His tiny feet and legs ran a mile a minute, but he could not outrun his foes.

"Leap, Jaegar! Don't run! Leap to me, damn you!" Harold cried. Jaegar obeyed, leaping in six-foot distances, and dove into Harold's front pocket. Clawclapper slashed with great might, tossing the hares back into the fog, while Freebooter chased after them, striking a finishing blow with his sharp talons.

"Who needs weapons when you have trained killing machines!" Bolo chuckled as Clawclapper returned to his side. "Agreed– good work, Jaegar!" Harold praised as he patted the ermine inside his front pocket. Mazielle shed worried eyes since Freebooter had not yet returned from the embedded mist. "He's coming; don't worry," Harold encouraged. Just as Mazielle was about to lose hope, her friend arrived– with slightly bloodied, scuffed, and ragged feathers, but still in good shape. "Good work, my love!" Maizelle complimented with a relieved smile.

With the first wave of enemies slain and the battlefield silenced, the embedapists took time to heal those bitten and scratched. Casualties remained low and the brigade was still strong in numbers.

"Good work on the battlefront!" Quilo commended. "Embedapists, be ready and vigilant! Next round will be much worse than the first! Archers, prepare bows for aerial attacks! Malificus, the same!"

With the swarm of embedded creatures reduced, the brigade marched to the new fog line, gaining one step closer to the Strain and Torment's formation.

Kiffy, Arvel, and Nicholas returned, staring eye to eye with the enemy. The number of diseased creatures had depleted but were still a deadly force. Provoking embedded hounds and ice banshees would be far more challenging. They were much smarter than hares and more compelled to defend the gashgobs who were protecting the entrance to the Strain. Kiffy and Arvel edged closer, quickly receiving warnings to keep away. The motion of the army remained at a standstill until Arvel grew impatient and grasped a throwing knife from his chest holster. With finesse, he tossed it forward and struck a hound right between the eyes. It yelped in pain and distorted into ice shards.

"Excellent throw!" Kiffy complimented.

"Didn't help! They ain't budgin'... stayin' put!"

"I have an idea!" Kiffy replied.

"What idea? Speaking sweet nothin's and pettin' their happy places? That ain't gonna help us!" Arvel bantered.

Kiffy reached into his rucksack and removed a silver instrument. It had a large mouthpiece and an adjustment lever that controlled the pitch. He blew into the instrument and slowly adjusted the lever outward. Baffled, Arvel and Nicholas did not see any movement of the embedded creatures, nor could they hear any sound coming from the instrument.

"What good will that do ya?!" Arvel asked, unsettled.

"Patience, ol' grope! You cannot hear it, but those drooling hounds and wrinkled banshees can! They despise the sound; it will get them coming!"

Arvel rolled his eyes while Nicholas watched with interest. As Kiffy blew into the instrument a second time, the embedded hounds shuddered and howled. The banshees screeched, covering their ears with their hands and flapping their wings irritably.

Kiffy inhaled, filling his lungs with air. Then, blowing harder into the mouthpiece, he adjusted the lever further outward, releasing a taunting and high-pitched sound that only the embedded creatures, who sang back in anguish, could hear. Many of them could no longer handle the dreaded hum and were persuaded to attack. Outraged, the front draft of hounds and remaining hares jolted toward Kiffy and Nicholas. Hovering above, a few banshees joined the assault, focused on killing the musician with the terrible tune that had stung their eardrums.

"They're peeved now!" Kiffy hollered with a smirk. "Time to prance, friend! Remember, we ride together!" he told Nicholas.

Eucera and the artificer remained unapproached. "Mukluk! Ya can't have all the fun!" Arvel shouted in frustration. He removed two more knives from his chest holster, throwing them toward a banshee. One knife whizzed through the air, missing the target, while the other sliced its hand. The banshee shuddered with a scream, convincing some of the hounds and hares to chase after Arvel and Eucera.

"Better! This way, ya gomble-brained turds!" Arvel taunted. "Now run, wool blanket!" he commanded Eucera, who responded much more quickly than the previous time. Rejoining with the group, Arvel was greeted with a beaming pedagog.

"What the hell ya smiling 'bout?" Arvel asked, annoyed.

"Who would have thought that you and your wool blanky would become the best of allies?" Kiffy teased.

The provokers were back into the race, chased down by foes with overbearing mobility. Up until this point, Nicholas had kept Xalibu at a moderate stride but was now tagged by quick-footed hounds and banshees with snappy aerial maneuvers. It seemed he was reliving the run-away escapade he had faced in the Embedded Forest. When he felt the fallow was moving too quickly, he gripped the reins and pulled them slightly. Xalibu understood his intentions and obeyed accordingly. Through the utter chaos, Nicholas and his fallow were growing together as one.

The brigade waited patiently and stared into the fog as their adrenaline slowly dwindled. They were restored and ready but would have to relight the flames of rage inside, for the second wave of angered assailants would soon be knocking at their door.

Over the howl of the arctic wind, Quilo Serdar heard sounds of sledger rails, wolves barking, hounds howling, banshees screaming, hooves clomping- and to no surprise, shouts of profanity coming from his brother.

"First and secondary lines! Shields up, swords in ready! All engage!" he ordered.

The first and secondary lines banged their swords on their shields. "HO, HO, RAH!" they shouted.

"Archers! Aerial support! Fling arrows to the sky!"

The archers complied with the commander, wielded their bows, and pulled the strings. "HO, HO, RAH!"

"Malificus and embedapists! Be on the ready for range and healing support!"

"HO, HO, RAH!" they hooted as the malificus clapped their hands, creating a magical spark, while the therapy staves of the embedapists illuminated.

Two supporting Yuulnavies, Çœlrite☒ite and Tensîle, placed their hands near their holsters, ready to test their specialized weapons.

Like a sudden sting of a bee, the provokers arrived, and the Brigade of Righteousness was consumed in embedded evil. Hounds pounced, tearing and piercing the heavy armor of the legionnaires with their sharp fangs. Banshees swooped downward like falling meteors, swiping at the already thwarted front and secondary lines. Archers reacted, congesting the starlit sky with arrows. Several banshees twirled and spun, dodging the attacks, while other arrows punctured their withering hearts, causing them to explode into flurried ice shards. Malificus overlapped with magical spells, twisting and breaking the bones of the embedded creatures, limiting their movements and agility.

"Brother, you have provoked too many!" Quilo shouted.

"Don't blame me- blame that Kiffy and his animal-lovin' toys!" he argued.

Kiffy and Arvel fought alongside the brigade, while Nicholas faced challenges of his own. Pursued by both hounds and banshees, he could not maintain a neutral position. Working as one, Nicholas and Xalibu dodged each assault as they trotted from one side of the brigade to another, playing a game of cat and mouse. Between his own kills, Kiffy made attempts to intercept the enemies that were fixed on the Restorer of Goodness.

"It's stuck– I can't pull it out!" Quilo's lieutenant shouted from the secondary line.

"Pull what out, Lieutenant?!" a nearby combatant asked.

"My sword, it's frozen!"

"Make haste! Pull it out NOW! Before it's too late!" the soldier advised as hounds sprinted toward them.

"I cannot... shit!" *Bamm*! The lieutenant was knocked to the ground as the hound pounced on him. Using his shield, he parried each snarling attack from its mouth. Soon, Quilo's big hand picked up the infectious dog by the mane and tossed it across the battlefield. The hound shook itself and charged toward the commander. Quilo growled and, with a great tug, pulled the stuck sword from the lieutenant's hilt, slashing the embedded varmint into oblivion.

"Thank you, Commander, it was stuck... I could not pull it out in time!"

Quilo helped the lieutenant stand and handed him his sword. "That explains all your young ones at home!" he teased "Seek a Malificus! And have that goddamn hilt re-enchanted so it doesn't freeze!"

"Yes, sir!" the lieutenant replied.

Two banshees struck downward. Like the beetles in the embedded forest, they quickly fused together and re-shaped to the size of a wyvern, then struck the commander and put the hulking man on his knees. Quilo curled up and relied on his sloth-headed pauldrons to protect his body and head. With arms much longer and stronger, the banshee slapped at his helm, knocking him around senselessly. His second lieutenant and a few legionnaires struck with their swords attempting to help their commander but were easily swatted away.

Still on his knees, Quilo grabbed his warming trinket, a thick ribbon tied to his arm. Stunned, his mind muddled inside his helmet and a past memory of his little girl appeared, mixing with the events of the battlefield.

Urie stood before him and wrapped her arms around his heavy armor. "Don't let the monsters poison the fluffy cotton, Daddy!" she said as she removed a ribbon from her hair and tied it to Quilo's arm. "This will keep you warm and safe!" Quilo caressed the ribbon and Urie's hand.

Slowly, she faded away and his mind cleared as he returned to his regular scheduled battle. Screaming loudly, the banshee continued to slap Quilo across the head, elevating his anger and hostility.

The commander finally had enough and wielded his great axe. He grumbled and shouted, "YOU dare attack me? HUH?! MY TUUUURN!" Rising to his feet, he swung at his rival, removing an entire wing from its double-sized torso. It screamed in pain as it tried to escape but crashed on to the icy fields. The commander showed no mercy as he placed his foot on the banshee's body and struck the tip of his axe into its head.

At the frontline, the pedagogs maintained defense on the ferocious hares. Using weapons of choice, they participated in hand-to-hand combat while Jaegar, Free-Booter, and Clawclapper repeated their trained duties. Working together, Jaegar taunted and teased while Free-Booter and Clawclapper hunted and destroyed.

"Yuultoy testing time?" Tensîle asked her fellow Yuulnavian.

"Yes, 'tis time!" Çóalrite replied as he drew his Yuulskyta, a specialized toy revolver constructed of four large chambers and a long barrel. He then pulled a Yuulfastr from his holster, a leather bladder with a pour valve at the top. Çóalrite squeezed the tube, speed-loading all 4 chambers with shiny red and silver pellets. He spun the gun's cylinder, locked it in place, and cocked the hammer backward. As he tapped his snow goggles, a crosshair appeared in his vision and synchronized with the revolver. He aimed the crosshair at two approaching hounds, pointed the weapon, and fired. Two long and shiny bullets, with a shiny red casing and a silver hollow point, rocketed from the barrel but stopped in mid-air as if the laws of physics were cheated by magic. The hollow point puked sparkling glitter onto the incoming hounds, followed by an explosive acre-wide spread of evil doggy parts. "Two rounds left! Careful- the weapon heats very quickly!" Çóalrite advised.

Excited, Tensîle quickly drew her revolver and loaded it with a *Yuulfastr*. Tapping her snow goggles, she aimed true and fired all four rounds at once. The brigade cheered as flying bullets and glitter tore the wings from each banshee's torso.

"Yaaaooouch!" Tensîle cried, dropping the weapon. "You are right; they do get very hot!"

"Great accuracy and powerful toys but need more Yuulgineering," Çóalrite commented as he pointed and fired his last two rounds, blowing up a hound who was only seconds away from gnawing his face off.

Pressure on the brigade quickly escalated, overwhelming embedapists as they nursed the rise in casualties and injuries. "Malificus! The pace is too swift! Both lines need enchanted shields!" the commander requested.

"We are short in number! We cannot do both!" a supporting malificus argued.

"Stay focused to the sky! We will help!" Norrick offered from the back, then glanced up at Gasper, who was sitting with Lízabet on top of Booth.

"The brigade is being vanquished! I must help them!" Lízabet offered.

"NO! Protect your mentor; do not stray from him!" Norrick demanded. "Gasper... can you help us?" he asked the primordial malificus, sensing a confused look on the face that was hidden under a long-tailed stocking cap.

"With what, I might ask?" Gasper responded.

Norrick calmly pointed to a fused banshee as it picked up a legionnaire then dropped him to the ground like a rag doll.

"I'm afraid we cannot echo the pace of the embedded—especially the fused," Gasper observed as a hound opened its large mouth and swallowed an archer whole.

"Oh dear! Yes, I see the trouble now. It is simple; we must stint the pace by leashing the hounds and clipping the wings of these flying serpents with our magic."

"Are you capable? It will take both of us to cast such a spell."

"I may be withered and senile, but I still have a few hidden tricks under this primordial robe," Gasper assured him.

Norrick smirked and nodded. "One last time together?"

Gasper agreed. "One last time together... yep... yep... yep."

Norrick stroked his beard, causing the flame-shaped tips to flicker and waver. Rubbing his hands together, he breathed warm air on them and pointed his palms outward toward the brigade. "HO, HO, RAH!" he cried. Gasper snapped his finger, retrieving the crutches that were tied to Booth. The armbands tightened around his wrists, and he raised them high, hailing in his raspy voice. "Ho, ho, rah! Yep... yep... yep."

As the two unleashed the primordial magic, the hairs of Norrick's beard blazed like a roaring bonfire, while the spheres attached to Gasper's crutches blustered in a blizzardy bliss. Prismatic curtains lit up the dark skies with solar light, and the fast and overpowering attacks of the embedded switched to a state of slow-motion. The brigade now had adequate time to react, as they were not impacted by the ancient incantation. Enemies could no longer fuse together, eliminating the advantage of combining themselves into beastly monstrosities.

Legionnaires slashed away at each hound one by one. Others easily blocked incoming assailants with their shields. Flying arrows increased in accuracy, hitting the air-borne targets instead of whizzing past them. Having fewer distractions and encounters, the malificus were now able to exploit spells more clearly and distinctively, while pedagogs and their animals fought with valor, depleting each hare to zilch.

Gasper wheezed, coughed blood, and lowered his crutches, struggling to contain the power of the spell. Norrick's fingertips started to curl and ache as the weight of the magic fell on his shoulders. "Bear with me, malificus... only a moment longer!" Norrick encouraged him. Lízabet quickly placed her embedapist staff on Gasper's shoulder to ease his struggle. With her help, Gasper regained his strength and raised his crutches again. Norrick also re-centered himself by rubbing his hands together and breathing warm air a second time. Properly reinforced, Norrick and Gasper upheld the spell's duration as the fighting force outlasted the second wave of embedded enemies– except for the artificer who was still in the fight.

As the supportive spell wore down and the fast momentum returned, Arvel misjudged the timing of a banshee's attack. Quickly reacting, he thrusted Leanora's tip into the winged serpent but was knocked from his mount in the process.

Sliding a great distance, Arvel scraped his face and chewed on chunks of snow and ice. He stood up, staggered, and spit bloody teeth from his mouth. Eucera bolted away in fright but was stopped just in time by Nicholas as he and the fallow arrived. They quickly became surrounded, a pack of hounds circling around them, drooling and flapping their long pointy tongues.

Arvel stared at the pack with anguish. "That'll learn ya to try to help, Undertow!" he jested.

"*Tele huit*!" Kiffy commanded as he rushed in to help his fellow provokers.

"Stan' back, Animal Lover! Toxic stools are mine!" Arvel growled.

"*Niah*!" Kiffy commanded further, adhering to Arvel's request and halting his sledging team.

"What are we to do?" Nicholas asked from inside the circle of death.

"Firs' I'm gonna take Leonara's hilt and stick it in that hound's keister! It'll piss off its petty friends and they'll fuse inna one. When they do... I'm gonna remove its front legs, grab its tongue 'n SLIT ITS MUKLUKING THROAT!" Arvel snapped.

Nicholas and Kiffy watched in amazement as Arvel did exactly as stated. The first hound made its move and was diminished by Leanora's hilt. The second and third hound circled in hesitation, then fused together just as predicted.

"Go on, ya plop a poop!" Arvel taunted his foe, slapping his stomach beneath his plackart. "Eat me! RIPE SCRAPS!"

The fused hound dug its claws into the snow, then lashed out with a sharp snarl. "That's right, ya smelly dogpie! Din din time!" Arvel grumbled as the beast beelined toward him, ready to indulge in a wintertime snack. Arvel gritted his teeth and held his great sword tightly with stern hands. "TO HELL, YA DROOLIN' PLOP!" he shouted as he lacerated the hound's front legs. It yelped in agony as Arvel grabbed its tongue and hung it like a fish on a stringer. Its over-sized mouth and fangs chomped on Arvel's hand and arm which were protected by the high-quality armor he had crafted. Taking his last knife, Arvel sliced through the creature's neckline and toxic steam exited the throat.

The chins of both Kiffy and the Restorer dropped to the ground. Even the supporting animals seemed impressed.

The Brigade of Righteousness exhaled frozen breaths of relief, while dirtied in embedded blood that was made up of shards, ice shavings, and crystalline particles. The overbearing battle had turned placid and silent.

In the sky, the prismatic curtains remained vivid and bright as they settled between the high mountain peaks surrounding the ice fields. Most of the embedded evil had perished, as had the fog line that once prevented the brigade from moving forth.

"Embedapists! Heal those that are wounded! Those not capable of fighting or who have been slain- retire them to the nunatak! Pedagogs and Yuulnavies, your service is no longer needed!" the commander instructed.

Arvel limped and approached his brother with blood dripping from his lips, nose, and forehead. "Gashgobs- I want 'em! Every mukluking one of 'em!" he demanded with killer instinct in his eyes.

Quilo clasped Arvel's pauldron with empathy. "My brother, you have been great help to us. Rest and recover! Retire to the nunatak with the others!"

Still in a rage, Arvel grabbed his blade and pressed it against his brother's chest. Quilo Serdar could feel the sharp blade slowly pierce his armor and slightly touch his skin. "I'll rest when I'm dead! Resting is overdid! Ya got that?!" he growled.

"Ol' grope would rather bleed all over himself," Kiffy remarked.

Quilo sighed but agreed as he diplomatically pushed the blade away. "Brother– I love you… but an older sister might have been much more pleasant than an OVERZEALOUS OX!"

"SPEAKING of ox– let's try to stay on dear Eucera, shall we, ol' man? Now ride with me!" Kiffy stressed as Nicholas returned Booth to the artificer. He turned to the Restorer. "Friend– we will need you and your fallow more than ever now."

Nicholas stared out into the battlefield. With great sorrow, he observed the embedapists as they helped those hurt, sickened, and diseased. He thought of home, of his people, the well-being, and the suffering. A few legionnaires wielded their swords and picked up banners that had been dropped by the fallen. They raised them upright and honored the Emblems of Goodness as they flapped in the wind. The Restorer patted Xalibu's furry neck and nodded in allegiance. "Whatever it is we must do, we shall do it!"

The commander took a moment to address his lieutenants and his legion. Although battle-worn, every legionnaire and archer that stood on two feet showed grace and compassion. They were willing to put their lives on the line once more.

"You all should be prideful for what you have done! Now we march! No creature crippled in disease will remain in the Bacillus' stead! Torment's formation- we will destroy!"

The brigade cheered on their commander. "Ho, Ho, Rah!"

"There will be NO VARIANT on this day!" Quilo declared.

"HO... HO... RAHHHHH!" the brigade roared as Quilo pointed his finger toward the ice fields.

"TO THE STRAIN!"

Leonora

"*L*et's go for a walk, Father!" Leonora suggested.

A younger, more clean-cut, and slimmer Arvel glanced out the window of his dwelling. The creek that ran alongside his family's home was filled with the winter's runoff. The morning's sunlight nourished the meadow, waking it from dormancy and enriching it with tulips and sunflowers.

"Yah... all right! Looks like the weather nice'd up," Arvel replied.

Heading outside, Leonora and her father begin their stroll. The migration of new birds enlightened them as they sang in a pretty springtime choir.

"Where are we going?" Leonora asked as she held on to her father's hand.

"We're goin' to our playtime place!" Arvel answered. "It'll keep the rottin' filth out. Expect fer tha' tickle disease I have. Can't stop that, ya know!" he chuckled softly.

Leonora laughed. "It can't come with us today!"

A happy father and his daughter played together in a grove of poppies and wild grass, so soft and lush one could walk barefoot. They skipped together– they smiled together– not a worry– not a fret– not a soul of concern– expect for Arvel's particular blight. To medicate himself, Arvel had to move his fingers very quickly. Leonora always feared her father's disease– the side effects of the medication always resulted in a sudden tickling sensation on her stomach, followed by uncontrollable laughing.

"Are you... ha ha... ha... bet... ha... ha ha... better yet? Ha! Ha!" Leonara struggled to ask.

"Almos' cured! Jus a l'il longer!" Arvel kept teasing her with a huge grin.

Leonora's warm and pleasant laugh was suddenly interrupted by another's– much darker and more sinister. That wonderful day of playtime changed to that dreadful day of poisoned purple snow drifts. Arvel's one and only child lay on the ground in tattered clothing and spoke with labored beaths. "I... I'd rather be tick... tickled... F... Father." Arvel sobbed with grief as he lifted his child and hugged her lifeless body. Looking above, he stared into the eyes of the gashgob who was laughing at him with sick pride.

Arvel stroked his warming trinket and grinded on what was left of his teeth. He glared with eyes of hatred– more atrocious than those of the gashgobs that stood before him.

"Okay friend, it's best you feed the fallow now. Give her the Yuul Licorice Clover," Kiffy advised the

Restorer. Without questioning, Nicholas removed the special confection from his memorizer pouch and placed it near the fallow's nose. With little hesitation, Xalibu gladly accepted the treat.

"Now remember, we encounter them as a trio– separate them individually! Understood?" Kiffy demanded. "That will stray them from the entrance."

Hidden in the remains of embedded fog, Quilo Serdar, two lieutenants, and twelve of his strongest legionnaires tightly positioned themselves into a square formation. Protected inside was Norrick, the Spirit of Loveliness, and her respected mentor. Quilo Serdar proclaimed his courageous team to be the *Legion of Asepsis*. As one faction, they would wait for Kiffy's signal indicating safe clearance to the Strain's entrance.

The purple glow of the Strain's towering seracs reflected off Arvel's blood-stained face. "I WANT 'em! I WANT 'em NOW!" he growled.

"Revenge is altering your mind!" Kiffy argued. "Refrain from seeing red! You are already masked with such a color!"

"I WANT 'em!" Arvel growled again.

"Stay wise! We face them as a trio! They are stronger together!"

"Don't give a muklukin'!" Arvel further argued.

"They will fuse! You know that as well as I!" Kiffy stressed.

"I want 'em... all of 'em," Arvel repeated under his breath as his heart thumped rapidly. He raised the warning trinket, kissed his wife's wedding band, and placed the ring on the tip of his great sword. Leonora reacted, shining brightly and glowing in primordial symbols of goodness.

"I KNOW YOU HEAR ME, OL' GROPE! REFRAIN!" Kiffy hollered, knowing exactly what Arvel's intentions were.

Arvel removed the ring and tightly gripped Leonora's hilt. Trying to resist temptation, he was taunted by the screeching laugh of a gashgob. He grumbled hatefully as haunting memories drew him back into vengeance. All logical thought escaped as he raised his great sword and kicked Eucera with his toes. "Forward, wool blanket! FOR MY WIFE! AND FOR LEONORA!"

"Damn it, Arvel! NO!" Kiffy cried. "Bech! Tele huit! Charge forth! Nicholas! Please help! We must stop him!"

Both the pedagog and the Restorer chased after the stubborn man, but lost sight of him as he and the musk oxen disappeared into thin air. Several seconds later, they re-appeared and positioned themselves in front of the gashgob. In Arvel's hand was a mighty spear; Leonora had reforged into a powerful primordial weapon. She had an ice-hardened shaft and contained mystical properties that were identical to the armor that slept in the catacombs. Her grip was wrapped in glistening green and red material, and her tip contained a long-pointed and ragged-edged head that could pierce through a stone wall.

Eucera had also changed. She was still the same brute ox, or "wool blanket" as Arvel called her, but was now outfitted in chivalric attire. Like a royal knight in a jousting match, Arvel positioned the spear and focused firmly on his target while Eucera trotted like a prizewinning destrier. The spear sparkled and shined brightly, as if the spirit of Leonora had blessed it herself. Aiming true, Arvel thrusted the spear through the gashgob's transparent chest cavity. Its purple-glowing heart remained attached to the spear's tip as it ripped through the gashgob's spine. It screamed, screeched, and snorted, while the bear beneath moaned and bawled, afflicted just the same.

"Can't laugh no more, can ya?!" Arvel mocked as the embedded creature shattered into shards of ice.

Consequences intervened, just as Kiffy had warned. The fight took a turn for the worse as the two remaining gashgobs became hostile and fused together. Arvel and Eucera were now ants, waiting to be squashed by a one-ton predator. The artificer shifted his eyes upward to a behemoth with white fur, standing at twenty feet tall. Its ugly aquatic master screeched in amplified tones, revealing its long, over-sized fangs.

"Back up, ox! Back up!" Arvel demanded, but it was too late. Arvel plummeted from his mount as the bear cupped

Eucera with its paw and tossed her away. From afar, Arvel could hear the snap of the oxen's leg followed by deep grunts of anguish. He re-planted his feet and wielded the primordial weapon. "Double the size! Double the fall!" he shouted with confidence.

The bear roared and breathed noxious disease from its mouth. Fortunately for Arvel, his arctic helm could filter the toxin. Locating the bear's weakest point, Arvel re-positioned the tip of the spear to the appropriate spot, but black spots suddenly altered his vision while loud ringing stung his eardrums. He had lost a lot of blood from his prior wounds, causing him to feel faint and feeble. Leonora became very heavy, and he struggled to keep her steady. The embedded bear took advantage of Arvel's weakened state and struck him across the head, removing his helm and stunning him. His body rocked back and forth, and he dropped Leonora as he inhaled the putrid scent of the bear's toxic breath. He placed his hands on his knees, coughing and retching, reminding him of the times he'd drunk too much ale. Bested and beaten, Arvel raised his head and stared– this time in fear instead of hate.

"FINISH ME! YA GOMBLED STOOL CLUMP!" Arvel screamed, swiping his finger across his neck. "STRIKE HERE! REUNITE ME AND MA L'IL ONE! NOW!"

The bear lowered itself on all four legs. Eye to eye, face to face, nose to nose, and toe to toe, Arvel and the animal stared each other down. The bear lightly growled and sniffed the artificer. For a split second, the furry beast seemed to show mercy. It was as though it had temporarily removed itself from the gashgob's control.

Arvel raised his hand and slapped the bear across the head. "FINISH! NOOWWWWW!" he screamed. The bear stood tall and roared in defense, ready to deal the finishing blow and end the primordial warrior's life.

Just in the nick of time, Kiffy stormed in and commanded his team to shift to the left. Jumping from his blitzkrieg sledger, he tackled Arvel, knocking him to the ground, and shielded him with his body. The bear's knifelike claws sliced through Kiffy's pelerine and slashed into his back. Kiffy groaned as his shredded cape blew away in the winter wind. The bear growled, stood back on its hind legs, and swiped with its left claw. Dodging the assault, Kiffy rolled away and thrusted with his double-edged dagger. The attack, merely a puncture wound that felt like a tiny insect bite, had little impact on the fused anomaly. Kiffy reached for his double-headed war hammer and whacked the bear's foot. It reacted and roared in anger as the pain distributed to the gashgob, who screeched, clicked, and snorted, ordering the bear to improve its performance. The bear obliged and pinned Kiffy down with its bloody and injured foot. It latched on to Kiffy's arm with its large jowls, and the pedagog gasped as sharp teeth dug into his existing scar.

As instructed, Nicholas remained at a distance, but felt useless, heeding the dwindling defeat of his fellow patriots. Arvel was knocked out as cold as the frozen ground he lay on. The pedagog was shouting in terror as he was dragged into the icefields. Determining that quick action was the right course, the Restorer commanded Xalibu to chase after Kiffy.

Regaining consciousness, Arvel crawled toward Leonora and picked her up. She had returned to the great sword she once was. He struggled to his feet and hobbled toward the blitzkrieg sledger, where he attempted to calm the wolves who were confused and concerned about their missing pedagog. The skittish fox whined, giggled, and hid underneath Marriam. "Easy! Ain't gonna hurt ya!" Arvel assured her, but Hooley showed little trust as she rushed toward the ice fields, picking up Kiffy's cape with her mouth.

Arvel opened Kiffy's rucksack and removed a *finger-flicker-flutter*. He pointed it upward and shot a signal into a clear, cold, and starlit sky. Colorful sparks ignited above, shaping into the Emblem of Goodness.

Using a freshly-cracked glitz twiglet, Nicholas and Xalibu followed a trail of smeared blood. The red-stained pathway soon came to an end, dashing any hope of finding the animal trainer. "Blast! Which direction are we to go?!" Nicholas questioned himself. He contemplated the situation- perhaps Kiffy had been thrown, as Eucera had? Or worse- had the embedded bear gorged on his flesh?

The fallow stirred, distracted by an incoming wildling. An indistinctive figure ran toward them- it had four legs, a bushy tail, a pointy face, and odd-shaped wings that flapped from its cheek bones. "Prepare yourself!" Nicholas warned the fallow. "It may be an embedded life form- perhaps fused." Fortunately for them, the monster with facial flight gear was the gentle fox, who was clinching tightly on to Kiffy's cape. Determined to find her pedagog, she dashed past them, expressing little acknowledgement of their presence.

"Tele huit! Follow!" Nicholas commanded. Hooley appeared to have an accurate sense of direction; they soon encountered pieces of shredded garments and droplets of blood. They stormed past Kiffy's two-headed war-hammer, his double-edged dagger, and the warming bracelet that had been detached from his wrist. "Niah," Nicholas quickly ordered, shocked by what he was seeing. "Resurge!" Xalibu lowered herself as Nicholas dismounted and crouched next to Kiffy.

"Af... afraid I'm not in a 'beary' good condition, friend," Kiffy joked feebly. Nicholas examined Kiffy's significant injuries. "No... I'm afraid not- you are terribly wounded."

Kiffy's trapping pelerine had been torn to shreds. Losing his warming trinket had exposed him to the elements. His skin and face were frostbitten and the scar on his arm was torn open. Hooley dropped the cape from her mouth and covered Kiffy's mangled body.

"Th... thanks, girl. It... it's good to see you ag... again!"

"What can I do to help?" Nicholas asked urgently as an aggressive growl of the bear echoed nearby, followed by a vile snarl of the gashgob. "Flee!" Kiffy advised. "Take her- take the fox past the archways."

"The fox? Archways? This will heal you?" Nicholas inquired.

"No, I cannot be helped, friend. Realign, and finish what we came here for- preventing Torment."

Nicholas didn't understand, and once again had little opportunity to seek answers. "As swift as the fallow was, we could not reach the archways," he stressed.

Kiffy shivered and groaned in pain. He tried his best to speak clearly and locked his jaw tight, to refrain from chattering. "The fallow... *unnnh!* She will listen- but only to you. Flee as you did before in the Embedded Forest. Stretch her legs and let her prance. When she races against butterflies- she will seek your permission. When she does- let her fly!"

Thick ice crunched nearby, crushed by the mighty embedded creature as it loped toward them. "Fl... flee, Nicholas!" Kiffy warned again. Nicholas quickly returned to Xalibu and hollered *"resurge"* as she stood up to her towering height. Like an excited horse, Xalibu shook and flicked her mane, ready for action. Nicholas sensed an extraordinary energy coming from the fallow, as if a supernatural ability screamed inside her, ready to release itself.

Hooley tucked herself closely to Kiffy's body, determined to stay by his side. He was her treasured companion; he had rescued her and had always taken care of her. Kiffy's fingers shook vigorously as he softly stroked Hooley's face and reinforced the knot on her scarf. "All is... *unnnnh...* in order... it is up to you to help us now." Refusing, Hooley yelped, whimpered, and caressed Kiffy's face with her pointy nose.

"Y... you ha... have to go now! You are my special lady– and my champion. Be my champion once more. I... love... you! P... pono! Restorer of Goodness!"

Hooley continued to hesitate; she did not want to leave her pedagog but somehow knew she had to obey him. Taking a long leap, she positioned herself on to Xalibu's back, impressing Nicholas, considering how tall the fallow was. "You can trust me," Nicholas said as he attempted to bond with the fox. He peered down at Kiffy with saddened eyes. "I am very sorry for what has happened to you. Helping Arvel as you did... you are a saint of *kindness.* And– you have been a great friend to me."

Kiffy nodded with a grateful smile. "Flee, Restorer! Realign!" The "Animal Lover'" listened to the distressed barks and winding bays of the fox as she rode away. Already missing his Hooley, Kiffy started to cry. He wrapped his stout arms tightly around his cape as the fox-themed silhouette opened its ocean blues and shed a tear of sorrow from its eye. Kiffy flexed his chest in extreme anguish and tightened his fists as he withdrew from his life. A burst of steam escaped from his lips as he released his last and final agonized breath.

"Petáxtei san petaloúda!"

Leaving Kiffy behind did not sit well with the Restorer. He felt terrible as Hooley continued to weep and wail for her pedagog; it was as though he had kidnapped her against her own will. The current situation ate at his emotions and flared his temper. "Why? WHYYYY ALL OF THIS?!" Nicholas questioned the Almighty, the Lord and savior that his parents, his uncle, and he himself had committed their faith to. Theopanes and Nonna had dedicated their lives to help improve the wellbeing of others. But– WHY were they deprived of their OWN well–being?

This Bacillus, this variant– Nicholas saw them as advocates of the devil who persuaded and consumed innocent creatures and beings. WHY did the Bacillus seek to destroy humankind through acts of torture, suffering, and death? Flashbacks intruded: of Gandomine disintegrated in a cloud of embedded beetles, "Nóvva" the toy ship broken into pieces on the rough cascades of the river, his mother releasing her grip from his hand as she perished from the dreaded plague, and Kiffy– a person who always put himself before others- left behind, mangled and barely recognizable.

"WHYYYYYYY?!" Nicholas screamed to his Lord above. "IS HEAVEN THIS HEARTLESS?!"

Nicholas' eyes turned as black as the polar night around him. He had to channel his temper, his anger, and his mourning. How would he release it? The same way he always did- by riding hard and fast. He had done so with Paloma along the hot and dune-filled beach of Patara, and now he could do it again with Xalibu in the cold and barren darkness of the winter solstice. He was determined to fulfill his duty and was impelled to reach the archways just as Kiffy advised. "If this is the cross the Lord hath given me to bear, then I shall BEAR it!"

Nicholas pulled the reins and tapped the fallow on her side with his feet. "TELE HUIT!" he commanded. Xalibu happily obliged as she stretched her long legs, switching her speedy gallop to a lightning-strike prance. The newly formed trio re-entered the lunar world that Nicholas and his fallow once visited. The same weakness and emptiness Nicholas had felt before struck him anew. Energized with adrenaline, Nicholas counteracted the effect, while voices of Arvel and Kiffy helped maintain his composure:

"Firs', ya gotta get that thing to listen to ya. Second, ya gotta get it to fly."

"She will seek your permission. When she does- let her fly!"

Inside the interstellar paradigm, the archways appeared and lured them to reach it. The primordial fallow pranced with all her might and ability. Configured in many shapes, sizes, and colors, a kaleidoscope of butterflies consumed them. Floating alongside Xalibu, they streamlined past her, encouraging her to catch them. Xalibu grunted in excitement- she wanted to play and move as swiftly as they did. She cocked her head backward and sought permission- approval that only the Restorer of Goodness was capable of giving her.

Nicholas smiled- he could not believe his eyes, nor could he have imagined that Kiffy's advice would result in such a striking event. He nodded and patted Xalibu's furry neck. "You have my consent! *Petáxtei san petaloúda!"* (Fly like a butterfly!)

It was as if Nicholas had spoken words of primordial magic as Xalibu propelled like a Pegasus with velvet-red antlers. A bell did not ring and Xalibu never grew wings but instead kicked and fluttered all four of her legs. Defying gravity, she propelled high into the air.

The arches that had seemed so far away and unreachable now neared closer and closer and were coming up quickly. Unexpectedly, the fallow slowed herself and hovered high above them. The trio watched as the butterflies descended and scuttled through the center arch. "What is it, girl? Is something– " Xalibu suddenly nosedived at a great rate of speed. " –*wrooooong?*" Nicholas whooped at the fox "Hooooold on to your scarf, little laaaaady!" as Xalibu glided through the archway, imitating the actions of the butterflies. The fallow tightened her legs and used them as landing gear. Touching down on solid ground, she returned to a rapid prance.

The world beyond the arches was hazy and indistinguishable. A tremendous physical pressure took its toll on the Restorer; he could no longer uphold its supernatural environment. He was concerned that Hooley felt the same way. Glancing back at her, he was bemused by her scarf, which was now glowing in symbols of goodness– passing the archway had mysteriously activated the striped neck garment. Nicholas was further confounded as a pack of wolves barked and howled to the left of them; it was Bechstein, Oken, Marriam, and Lillian being commissioned by a questionable wanderer. The apex of his bent hat flapped vigorously as he rode along atop Kiffy's sledger.

He motioned his hand to the fox. "Come to me, champion! You've work to do!" Hooley quickly leaped from Xalibu and on to the sledger. "Restorer! We will shift this burden on to us!" The wanderer snapped the reins with a mighty thrust and blinded Nicholas with a blazing white light. Startled, Xalibu applied her brakes and flung

Nicholas from her back. Departing from his dreamy state of affairs, Nicholas tumbled, rolled, and crashed into a pile of logs. He breathed heavily, aggravated by once again lying on his back. Xalibu lowered her head and nudged him in apology. "Where are we now?" Nicholas asked her. He then recognized the logged cabin that nestled before a thick and vast taiga– it was the gatekeeper's home.

Arvel raised his hand and slapped the bear across the head. "FINISH! NOOWWWWW!" he screamed. The bear stood tall and roared in defense, ready to deal the finishing blow and end the primordial warrior's life.

Just in the nick of time, the wanderer stormed in and commanded the sledging team to shift to the left. Jumping from the blitzkrieg sledger, Hooley knocked Arvel away. The bear's knife–like claws swung at the fox but could not match her fast agility. The embedded creature paced toward the artificer, who was lying on the ground unconscious. Hooley quickly chased toward it and stood over Arvel to protect him, showing her teeth and following with a threatening series of barks and giggles. The bear growled and roared while its attached master screeched at the fox. Hooley's scarf re–illuminated in symbols of goodness. Relying on her natural hunting skills, she lunged from the ground, curled her toes, and face-planted the ground with her tiny, pointed nose. The scarf appeared to give her great strength and abilities as the ice beneath her cracked and split in several directions. She gazed up intently at the bear, who stood still and stared, mesmerized, into her angry eyes. The ocean blues she once had morphed into a defined golden color, intimidating the animal who was much grander than she was. The gashgob screeched and snorted, furious that the bear was refusing to obey and attack. The horrid purple color of the animal's eyes dimmed and returned to their natural black pigment. Its master cried and shuddered in a loud demonic tongue as the two merged bears magically detached from one another and returned to their original size. The gashgob retreated, using its tentacles to crawl away. Hooley's abilities had removed the embedded persuasion and convinced the bear to attack it. It gripped the icy ground with its claws and chased down the pointy-toothed atrocity. Opening its large jowls, it grabbed the gashgob's head and tore it from its slimy body. The death of the gashgob covered the area in ice shavings as the fox and the polar bear fled into Ethe fields.

Regaining consciousness, Arvel crawled toward Leonora, which had returned to the great sword she once was. He rose to his feet and grunted in pain as he hobbled toward the blitzkrieg sledger. Opening Kiffy's rucksack, he removed a finger-flicker-flutter, a

Yuulnavian, long-tubed signaling device with a gritty film molded to the outlet. Foreign writing was was stamped on the side:

ᚦᚢᛘᛒ ᛩᚾᛚ⹁

It warned the operator to "use thumb only." Naturally, Arvel ignored the instructions and tore the film with his chipped teeth. The finger-flicker-flutter activated, filling Arvel's mouth with sparks and scorching sections of his blood-stained beard. He pointed the device upward as an enormous comet-like flare screamed into a clear, cold, and starlit sky. The Emblem of Goodness flashed high above, forming into a constellation of blazing celestial energy. It signified hope and showed the legion that the role of glory was now placed on their shoulders.

Arvel limped toward Bechstein and kneeled next to him. The leading wolf placed a sloppy kiss on Arvel's face with his tongue. "Ya dumb dog! Did good today! All of ya did! That owner a yers would be proud, good feller he was!" The warmonger's eyes turned sad. Somehow, Arvel knew that nurturing his vengeance had caused dire consequences. With little blood left in his veins, he collapsed. Bech whined and gently licked Arvel's nose for confirmation. The "ol' grope" was still breathing- and alive.

Arvel's signal reflected in the eyes of the legion. No longer bound in embedded fog, they proceeded forth with crystal-clear visibility. "Expand formation!" the commander ordered as they neared Eucera, lying on her side and grunting in misery. The legion's protective square widened and surrounded the injured musk ox.

Lízabet dismounted from Booth, receiving a stern look from Norrick.

"Lízabet! Stay with your–"

"Grandfather! Hush! The ox requires my help!" The embedapist examined Eucera and applied pressure to her leg. She groaned and twitched, reacting from the slight movements.

"Shh! Shh! It's okay… shh!" Lízabet responded in a gentle tone. "Her leg is broken. She is rather shaken up but will be fine." The chivalric armor Eucera once wore was no longer equipped, but still appeared to have protected her. Lízabet rubbed the oxen's large hump. "You were thrown a great distance, weren't you? 'Tis surprising your ribs and neck were not broken." To her surprise, Lízabet noticed that a piece of the armor had broken off and was tangled in the oxen's hair. Although the armor had vanished, it appeared a shard of steel had remained. "This is what protected you... Arvel's?" Lízabet muttered but retained focus and placed her embedapist staff on the oxen's leg. Eucera bellowed loudly as her bones realigned, set, and then instantly grew back together.

"Commander, could you please return her to her feet?" Lízabet requested. Using his legs, Quilo lifted the heavy brute. She was a hefty girl, even to the stout commander. As Quilo tied her to the other musk ox, Booth expressed signs of happiness as brother and sister reunited.

After a long-fought battle, fluctuating strategies, and primordial spells, the Legion of Asepsis had finally reached the Strain's entrance. Quilo felt a lump in his throat, seeing his brother lying underneath Bechstein. The legion expanded formation a second time, surrounding Arvel and the wolves. Quilo placed his ear on Arvel's chest, relieved by the sounds of sharp breaths and a heartbeat. He picked his brother up, threw him on his back, then placed him on Eucera. Arvel sat upward while his head drooped downward, periodically mumbling nonsense. He opened his eyes for a split second, realizing he was back with Eucera. "Wool blanket? Yer alive? Cheated death too, did ya?"

"What of the pedagog?" Quilo quickly asked, attempted to obtain information from his brother. Arvel drew back into his catatonic state and did not provide an answer.

Norrick observed the emotional reaction of his granddaughter as she stared at the empty sledger. "I know that you deeply care for him. But you must remain studious with your mentor; he needs you. Let us hope he and the Restorer are safe."

"I... I know... we must have faith," Lízabet responded with a tear.

"My help has concluded; I will make sure the pedagog's wolves and sledger get back to the nunatak safely," Norrick assured her. Lízabet grabbed her grandfather and hugged him tightly. Norrick closed his eyes and embraced her loving spirit. "I am proud of you! You mother- she smiles upon you on this day."

Norrick helped Gasper dismount from Booth. "It has been some time since we have faced such troubles," he commented. "Yes... it has... yep... yep... yep- sorry, what troubles do you speak of?" Gasper asked, confused.

Norrick pointed to the sudden winter storm. Embedded snowflakes fell and covered the ground's icy surface with infected purple powder.

"Oh! Yes, right! Not good at all, Norrick. Not good at all!"

"You are certain you wish to continue?" Norrick asked.

The primordial malificus nodded confidently. "It must be contained- we cannot set Nicholas up to fail."

Norrick agreed and gave the Salute of Degomble. With saddened eyes he clasped Gasper's shoulder. "For the sake of goodness, my old and dear friend."

Gasper returned a Salute of Degomble in front of his hidden face. "For the sake of goodness... yep... yep... yep..."

Norrick addressed the commander. "The Primordial Malificus and the Spirit of Loveliness are in readiness."

"Legion! Unsecure the formation!" Quilo Serdar ordered. He saluted Gasper and Lízabet. "Luck and goodness to you both!"

Once blocked by a powerful and deadly force, the Strain's entrance was now unguarded and accessible. Not the best of tactics, nor the strength of the greatest armies, were capable of combating what was inside, for only the elderly man and his prodigy were destined to such a feat. The task before them had no rite of passage, no tunnel with a light shining at the end, no colored road made of bricks, no road untraveled that would make a difference. In the abode of embedded snowflakes, the Bacillus remained in its vulnerable and weak state. Threatened, it trembled the ground with intermittent quakes. But with each shake and shift, it meant those of goodness still had a fighting chance.

There was still a ray of hope hanging onto a finite window of time. Beyond the Strain's walls, hell was in labor and ready to give birth.

Winter's Beating Heart

The Strain- a ruin built in peril, upheaval, and chaos. Its rigid serac walls and inner grounds were destained in disease. Infected snowflakes, or "sick fuzzy cotton" as Urie called it, fell to the ground in thick layers of embedded snirt- natural snow blemished by embedded and fiendish filth that glowed in dark purple hues. Its presence indicated that the Bacillus was in a reactive state. Hard at work with its invisible hands of impurity, it strived to create a nemesis of goodness- a ruthless variant.

Through the work of Nicholas, the release of Gandomine had angered and threatened the Bacillus, while the rescue of the Foredoomed Fallow had greatly stunned and curtailed its potency. In battle, the commander had executed well-planned tactics, and the Brigade of Righteousness had flushed away the embedded guard force of the Strain. But to the victor there were no spoils, as the death of each embedded creature nourished the Bacillus and helped recapture its strength. Regardless, the actions taken and the intentions of goodness were crucial building blocks of a wonderous phenomenon, capable of destroying the impenetrable enemy.

Lízabet eyed Gasper with concern. "Mentor– my neck, head, and shoulders ache. My throat feels coarse as if it were scratched by a wolverine's claw. I... feel confused... as though... I'm being offered something sweet, a candy that I simply cannot refuse to taste."

"Ignore the savory temptation; this is not a candy store," Gasper snapped back as he raised his Crutches of Winterstorm and cast a primordial spell to protect himself and Lízabet. "The Bacillus is aware of our presence, yep, yep, yep... it will do what it can to embed us."

Gasper stepped on a slimy substance beneath the embedded snirt. "Oh my! Rather mushy." Using the magic of his crutches, he lifted the carcass and shook the dirtied snow from its transparent skin. Its ugly pointy teeth and long tentacles revealed it to be a gashgob. Unlike the first three, the fourth and final gashgob would not instigate a challenge or cause a ruckus. The embedded creature had been persuaded to sacrifice itself and would be used as a more significant component.

The innocent polar bear had detached from its master. Its robust frame, except for its head, was buried and frozen under the embedded snirt. Lízabet frowned at the bear's adorable round ears and broad nose that left a deathly expression of pain and anguish.

Horrible noises of sick children coughing, whooping, hacking, moaning, and whining echoed off the Strain's towering seracs. Severe gusts screamed and howled, cutting through Lízabet and Gasper like a knife. The inner grounds quaked and rumbled as wet snow packed itself into a large ball, which rolled away and placed itself in the middle of the Strain. Another snowball, slightly smaller, packed together and rolled, lifting itself on to the first. Finally, a third and even smaller snowball formed and rolled, rapidly placing itself on top of the others. Small pebbles attached to the top, creating a mouth with a devilish scowl. Two large rocks shaped into eyes, glowing in embedded purple, then two dead branches, as though they came from the pines of the embedded forest, came from out of nowhere and created arms.

"I highly doubt the Bacillus is intending to create a snow ally who enjoys warm hugs," Lízabet said.

"Right you are, yep, yep, yep," Gasper replied. "Remain vigilant!"

A little human boy appeared dressed in an oversized coat, a long-tailed stocking cap, and puffy gloves. He picked up more embedded snow and packed it between each section of the snowball-stacked figure. "Hmmm..." the little boy pondered. "It needs a nose." He bent down near the deceased gashgob and broke a long, pointy tooth off from its mouth. "This will work perfectly!" the little boy exclaimed with a big smile. Without skipping a beat, Gasper engaged the child. "Boy! Halt!"

Startled, the boy turned around. He had a face covered in freckles, with vivid emerald-green eyes, and his peculiar appearance stunned Gasper with realization. "What is your name, child?" he asked.

"My name? I... I don't have a name... not yet." The boy returned to his project but was interrupted again just as he was about to place the nose.

"You have built a fine creature indeed- yep, yep, yep," Gasper lied. "But a nose from a gashgob would make it ugly and mean. Use a scarf instead!" Gasper nodded to Lízabet. "Your scarf?"

Lízabet stared, confused, since the scarf was her warming trinket and removing it would expose her to the elements. Having faith, she cautiously pulled the scarf from her neck and handed it to Gasper. To her surprise, she felt fine and wasn't freezing to death. She assumed the spell her mentor had cast substituted for the warming trinket.

"Why have you given me a scarf?" Gasper asked her, baffled.

"You requested it, mentor," Lízabet replied patiently.

"I did, and for what may I ask?"

"For this child- to dress his creation," Lízabet reminded him.

"Oh yes! Right! For the boy with no name, yep, yep, yep." Gasper presented the scarf. "Dress your creature with this garment."

The little boy grabbed the scarf. "But it instructs me to give it a nose... not a scarf," he argued.

Lízabet was skeptical, but as much as she loved scarves, she found herself playing along. "But a scarf is much more comfortable and cozier. Don't you want your friend to be warm?" she asked.

Flustered, the boy sighed and nodded hesitantly, then placed the scarf around the creation's neck. The child suddenly felt chilled, and his teeth chattered. A tickle in his throat developed and he started coughing aggressively. "It does not like the scarf! It wanted a nose instead! It says it must punish me," the little boy cried. The child's fair skin turned pale, and his forehead reddened. Sweat dripped down his face as he broke into a fever. He covered his mouth with one hand as he whooped in long lingering coughs, holding the gashgob's tooth in his opposite hand.

Lízabet became concerned and saddened by the child's sudden illness and sickly appearance. "Mentor, I don't understand... what is wrong with this child?"

Gasper eyed Lízabet. "Whatever happens, do not show empathy for this boy!" he instructed firmly. Lízabet glared back in frustration– she did not understand or agree with her mentor but would stand by him.

"Remove your hand from your mouth, boy! Speak your name!" Gasper demanded in his raspy voice. The child refused, shaking his head vigorously. He whined and moaned in his suffering and continued to cough inside his palm. Gasper leaned on his crutches to support himself and grabbed the child's hand, jerking it from his face. "Now tell us who you are!" Gasper demanded again.

The boy hunkered over and whooped a third time. He gazed up at Gasper with his freckled face and teary emerald-green eyes. "Please! I just want to build a friend that will play with me and my toys. Please?" A pair of wooden crutches attached to the boy's arms. Displeased, he cried and shouted. "I can't get sick!" The little boy pointed to Gasper, "YOU... and ME... we always wanted to walk and run, jump and climb– play with our toys!" Further realization and sadness struck Gasper like a ton of bricks. "I... I know, child. I know..." he replied.

The boy's illness worsened, and he started screaming at Gasper in a ferocious fit. "Now WE can never play with our toys! NEVER!"

"I know, child, I know," Gasper replied gently. "WE never wanted it this way, but life did not choose this path for us." The child quickly broke out in tears as he drew the malificus into his current woes. As Gasper watched the little boy weep and rely on his wooden crutches for support, he could understand the child's struggle and limitations. He gently placed his hand on the little boy's shoulder. "I'm afraid you are confused, child; you are not who you think you are."

"Mentor... remember... no empathy!" Lízabet reminded Gasper from behind.

Gasper nodded. "I demand you tell me who you really are."

The boy choked back on his tears and attempted to answer. "I... I'm G... Germ–"

"Enough!" Gasper interrupted, suddenly angered. "Your name is not Germana!" he shouted. He swiped the wooden crutches out from underneath the child and they vanished in a magical sparkle, causing the sick little boy to fall face–first into the infected snow. Gasper lifted the boy's chin with the foot of his own crutch and exposed his embedded purple eyes. "I know what you really are! Now... tell... me... who!" Gasper implored. The boy whooped and gasped for air, spewing phlegm and mucus from his mouth and down his chin. He stuttered his words "T... t... tick... tick... tick...!"

"WHAT VARIANT ARE YOU TO BECOME!" Gasper hollered.

"TOR... TORMEEEEEEENNNNNT!" the child screamed.

Watching in disbelief, Lízabet readied herself and tightened both hands around her embedapist staff. She knew that drastic measures were about to take place.

The little boy shrieked at Gasper. "You FUUUU... you useless malificus... SHITLESS cripple! I wanted to give it a nose, and you tricked me! It did not want a nimble-knitted scarf! I was going to play with my toys!" The boy pointed at Gasper again. "YOU... ME... WE COULD'VE PLAYED WITH OUR TOYS!"

The child rose to his feet, growing stronger and more powerful, then blasted Lízabet with an embedded snow squall, consuming her in an intense blizzard of infection. He shifted focus, determined to complete his assignment of placing the nose on the creation of stacked snowballs, but was thrown to the ground by the malificus, briefly shunting the Bacillus' persuasion. Driven to obey, Torment picked himself back up- for once the nose was attached, the little boy would shape into its final variant form.

"ONCE I PLACE THIS NOSE, I WILL HAVE THE TOYS I ALWAYS WANTED! I CAN PLAY WITH THEM FOREVER! EVERYBODY WILL WANT TO PLAY WITH MY TOYS!" Torment screamed.

Lifting his crutch, Gasper threw the boy to the ground a second time. "Nobody wants your toys! They are afflicted tools, meant to plague humankind and its well-being!"

The little boy was relentless as his purple glowing eyes bloomed brightly. He picked himself up again but was quickly heaved in the opposite direction. "Stay down, boy! YEP, YEP, YEP!" Gasper hailed. Lízabet's scarf on the child's creation began to glow, melting the embedded snow on which it was placed.

"NOOOO! STOP!" the child screamed from the ground. "You're killing my one and only friend!"

Gasper performed well, constraining the child with his remarkable skills, until sudden sensory changes conflicted him. His mind became sluggish, his motor functions slow. The complexity of his magical task became confusing to him; his awareness became stormy and fickle. He then realized his time was up, that old age had finally dominated him and that his primordial abilities were becoming callused. The Bacillus' potency was quickly restoring itself. The little boy picked himself up a third and final time, brushed the embedded snow from his pants and big coat, then bolted toward the malificus, now capable of overpowering him.

Lízabet continued to struggle, consumed within the embedded snow squall that had greatly ailed her with sickness and confusion. She stirred her embedapist staff like a big spoon, relieving her symptoms and eliminating the aggressive storm. Her visibility cleared just in time for her to see the little boy thrust the gashgob's tooth into Gasper's chest.

"Meeentoorr!" Lízabet shouted in despair. Gasper gagged and choked, dark red blood blasting outward from his hidden face. Torment thrust the tooth into Gasper's chest a second time. The malificus leaned on to his crutches for dear life but could no longer hold up. He quickly snapped his fingers as his crutches vanished, then collapsed facedown into the embedded snirt.

The little boy fell back on his hands and knees as his eyes returned to the rich emerald green they once were. He breathed heavily, starting up at Lízabet, feeling helpless and sad for what he had done.

Tears ran down his face. "I don't want to be sick... please, just toys... just toys." Lízabet was drawn to the suffering child as her face switched from an expression of hatred to one of pity. Although she had never borne a child, a mother's intuition swayed her to kneel and embrace the boy, even though she knew his true form– and intention.

Lízabet gulped, holding back emotion. "I'm, I'm...very sorry... but you cannot be– Torment cannot exist."

Torment changed quickly, squeezing Lízabet's arms with enormous strength and discontent. He growled lowly and clamored in a dark and vile voice as though he had just gone through demonic puberty.

"I will destroy Goodness, Kindness, and Loveliness, then! The Magnanimous Toymaker will NOT be born– ONLY MY INTERGLACIAL ARMY!"

Lízabet pushed the boy away and maintained a tight grip on her staff as it reforged into a new weapon of immunity. At one end a large globe was attached, and inside the glass, golden snow fell gently and peacefully.

At that exact moment Lízabet understood her mentor's motives. His unique abilities and his appointed task were now hanging on her shoulders; this was not just another training session. Dread and negativity filled her heart while fear tried to overcome her confidence. She thought of Nicholas and the great strides he had taken to create this opportunity. The Bacillus was still stunned and vulnerable from the Restorer's actions but was only seconds away from breathing life into an ungodly creation. Lízabet realized the great trauma her fellow people: her friends, her grandfather, and her mentor had faced. In this fine hour of winter's beating heart, the embedapist wasn't going to hesitate, NOT at this moment, NOT EVER AGAIN.

"NO! You are going back to where you came from! NOW!" she hailed. Her unique spirit of loveliness cultivated her as she pointed the Staff of Snowstorm toward Torment. The golden snow inside the single globe blustered as words of primordial magic released from Lízabet's lips:

"Svaaaaal baaaaaaard! Errreeeeee venk haaaarr! Toymaaaaaaaker Klaaaaasss!"

The entire ruins of the Strain were pelted with dragonflies and ladybugs that purified the embedded snirt and dimmed the eerie purple lighting of the towering seracs. The scarf gleamed, melting the variant's sculpture down to nothingness.

As Torment withdrew, it roared in a tone of children coughing, whooping, hacking, moaning, and whining. The roar ranged near and far, entering the ears of the Legion of Asepsis in the icefields, including those of Norrick as he raced Kiffy's team toward the nunatak. Norrick snapped with a broad smile. "It is done! The variant is toilworn!" His happiness quickly turned bittersweet when the champion fox and her new polar bear friend appeared and ran alongside the sledger. While Norrick was pleased to see them, he also felt a deep sadness, as he understood the true meaning behind the animals' sudden presence.

Resting and recovering atop the nunatak, the Brigade of Righteousness reacted to the roar and chanted loudly. "HO, HO, RAH! HO, HO, RAH! HO, HO, RAH!"

Jaeger jumped from Harold's pocket to see what all the commotion was about. Instead of scolding his ermine, Harold shook Jaegar's little hand. "Good work! We did it, Jaegar!"

Mazielle smirked and caressed Free-Booter's feathers. "Success, my love! Success!"

Even Bolo, the prior hunting champion, commended his wolverine. "You fought well! I am proud!"

Vibrations of the variant's roar traveled even further, reaching the town of Degomble. "They have stinted the variant! I can hear its roar!" a stronghold watch claimed.

"Yes, I hear it too. Quick, ring the bell loudly! Let everyone know of our victory!" a fellow lieutenant instructed.

As the Golden Bell of Trepidare chimed in a euphony of hope, the soldiers, stronghold watchers, and supporting residents swiped the front of their faces with the Salute of Degomble.

Inside the Strain, Lízabet attended to her mentor. His skinny chest inhaled and exhaled in injured breaths, while his withered body shook aggressively. "Your mother would be proud of you... Spirit... of... Loveliness, yep... cough... yep... yep," Gasper acclaimed in his raspy voice.

Lízabet returned a sorrowful smile and removed the long-tailed stocking cap, exposing her mentor's hidden face. Underneath the cap was an aged man with wrinkly skin, grayish-black hair, and vivid emerald-green eyes. Lízabet placed her hand on his cheek and stroked his beautiful, freckled face. Gasper wheezed and panted weakly as he spoke his last dying words: "For... for... the sake... of... goodness, my fare shield maiden." He released his final agonized breath as it traveled away on its own journey.

Sobbing, Lízabet kissed Gasper's forehead. "For the Sake of Goodness, mentor." She redressed his head with the long-tailed cap, hiding his face again. "Now rest– my sweet Germana."

Strong in Mind, Body, and Soul

The enfeebled returned safely to Ethereal. Using his ability to hear the carolers, Nicholas guided them through the protective walls. The sick and injured lay on wooden stretchers, carried by those healthy enough to lift them. The fallen were respectfully covered and pulled by musk oxen on wide and long sledgers, which were designed to switch from rails to sturdy wheels when needed over muddy or rocky terrain. Weary themselves, fellow embedapists kept sight on those less fortunate, attending to their wounds and maintaining their vitals until they reached the care facility in Violet's Agora. Citizens of Ethereal cheered and applauded as their beloved heroes returned home. Before departing to their families and loved ones, many thanked Nicholas for his service. Others gave him the Salute of Degomble, which Nicholas had grown accustomed to and easily responded to. The warmth and presence of each person surrounded him, filling his heart with happiness.

Nicholas and Xalibu parted from the group and returned to Atka's Flume. "Resurge!" Nicholas commanded, and Xalibu lowered herself, putting him back on solid ground. He stroked the fallow's face- to him she was still an entity of unique beauty. "Let's rest awhile, shall we? I'm sure you are exhausted too," Nicholas advised as he sat along the bank of the plunging pool beneath the falls. The ribbon-like curl and sway of the cascades were just as remarkable as the first time he'd seen them. His thoughts returned to the battle and his rescue of the Foredoomed Fallow. He grieved for Kiffy- his kind nature, his witty sense of humor- and even missed Gandomine and the cardinal's constant bickering.

Xalibu nudged his shoulder, interrupting his thoughts. "I'm sorry girl, I know not how to care for you. I have no stable for you to rest in and no food for you to eat except for these carrots of Kiffy's." Nicholas removed the leftovers from his memorizer pouch and threw them to her. "I will have to request double shifts at the Cardinals of Joy just to feed you," he teased. "We can only hope someone in Ethereal can provide guidance."

Nicholas became distracted by his reflection in the pool's water. His hair had grown long and messy, his face scattered with stubble. He looked deeply into the haggard eyes of the man staring back at him. Nicholas saw a man still lost, confused, and scared- a man placed in a world he still didn't understand, given abilities beyond his greatest imagination and comprehension. "Restorer of Goodness" was what they all called him, but did his support bring them closer to prosperity?

Nicholas spoke to his reflection. "So 'friend,' as Kiffy called you, where do you go from here? Seems you still have much to learn." He then shouted at himself. "And YET... you still know not your true purpose!" Nicholas shook his head in frustration, picked up a rock, and tossed it at his reflection. The water rippled, distorting his reflection and then quickly clearing itself, now showing two other men sitting next to him. To the left of Nicholas was the wanderer with the dirty grey beard, wearing the tall conical cap with a bent apex. And to his right was the same man dressed in an exquisite velvet red coat with white trim. Below his thick and bushy eyebrows, the jolly fellow's warm eyes stared back at Nicholas. He reached out and clasped the Restorer's shoulder and smiled gently underneath his snow-white beard. Oddly, Nicholas did not feel the touch of the man's hand, nor see the two of them as he quickly turned his head in both directions. The only physical appearance was Xalibu behind him, happily chewing on the last of her carrots.

Over-tired, Nicholas decided to ignore what he'd just seen, and he buried his head in his knees. From within the rowdiness of the Curling Ribbon Falls, a whispering voice spoke out to him.

"Nicholas... Nicholas...?"

The Restorer lifted his head, taunted by the voice and the sudden glistening of the pool's water.

"It... is... time... Nicholas. Time to... pull... the... sea!"

Nicholas sighed. "It's best I clear my mind for a while. Perhaps a swim will do me good." He eyed Xalibu with concern. "You won't wander off, will you?" he asked. Xalibu nudged him with her nose and Nicholas smiled. "I'll take that as a yes. I will only be a moment." He safely stowed his memorizer pouch under a large boulder and stripped down to his undergarments. Although it had been a long time since he had last been swimming, he was able to maintain a steady rhythm of well-placed strokes. The sunlight and lukewarm water of the pool was most refreshing after a frigid adventure of embedded fog, polar nights, bitter cold, and blizzards. Taking a deep breath, he dove to the bottom, rubbing the smooth bed of rocks with his hand. Already his mind felt more at ease. Suddenly he was bumped by a most familiar creature, a shelled reptile he had often seen back at home.

"Sea turtles... here? In Ethereal?" Nicholas questioned.

A dozen more sea turtles lunged by, and Nicholas suddenly lost control as an unseen force siphoned him toward them. He worried that he would eventually reach the other end of the pool and smash into a rock face, or worse, be dragged underneath the falls. Like wings of a hawk hovering in a summer wind, the turtles spanned their legs outward and jetted forward, pulling Nicholas with them. Golden trails streamed behind them as the warm and shallow pool changed to a cold and deep sea. For a split second, the seafloor showcased a sunken freighter with the name "Nóvva" scrawled on the angelic figurehead. The drowned bodies of Drusus, Otho, and the crew floated above the freighter, all curled up like a dead fetus in a mother's womb. Stunned by the sight, Nicholas did what he could to maintain his oxygen but began to choke and gasp, consumed in the clutches of the dark blue brine.

At the Restorer's favorite spot- the perfect rock- a woman and her reunited friend sat, overlooking the falls.

"Sending him back, are we?" Gandomine asked.

"How do you mean?" Gandomine asked her.

"I'm certain he's meant to go home. At least for now!" Gandomine confirmed.

"What?! No! You are sure?" he argued.

"She is correct," Violet intervened. "There is no need to question her."

"Suppose he'll drown?"

"What a terrible thing to say!" Gandomine scolded.

"Nicholas will be fine! We can only wish him safe travels," Violet assured them.

From below, Xalibu grunted and bugled loudly, concerned and anxious for her missing rider.

"And the primordial brute- what are we to do with her?"

Violet grinned. "I have determined the perfect caretaker."

"I'm finished, Mother!" Urie cried. "I completed all my chores today. Savage was hungry again, so I fed him... AGAIN! He's getting puddy... pudgy! Oh! And I didn't let him escape this time!"

"Well done!" her mother replied, as she led a cow to the barn. "What's the matter, dear?" she asked, noticing a large frown on Urie's face.

Urie sighed. "I did it again this year! I was so busy with my erran... err... errdads... I forgot to request a gift from Fey... Freyhadsel!"

"I'm sorry. There is always next winter."

"I guess so," Urie replied, pouting. "It's just... just that I wanted to request that Daddy stay home... that he STAYS home and never leaves!"

"That is very thoughtful of you to put others before yourself. We all wish the same thing, dear."

"I hate it when Daddy leaves! Do you think that one day, Daddy will never come back?" Urie asked.

Her mother attempted to remain unemotional but honest. "We can only pray that day never comes. Your father is a true warrior– he loves you and misses you just as much as you miss him." She then smiled widely. "Come, I have an additional task for you. It's inside the barn and it will cheer you up."

Urie sighed and muttered under her breath. "O... kay... Mother. Work... work... work... Urie do this... Urie do that...!"

Urie's mother cracked open the barn's door. "Now, before I show you what's inside, you need to know that you must approach her slowly and carefully. Understood?"

Urie folded her arms and lifted an eyebrow curiously. "Yes, Mother. I will." As she peeked into the barn, her chin dropped and her eyes sparkled. Inside, Urie's "horse" was resting comfortably in a spare stable. The barn contained quarters that were wide and high enough to compensate for Xalibu's tall body and massive velvet-red antlers. Ignoring her mother's instructions, Urie jolted toward the fallow.

"Ugh! Urie! Please slow down! Approach carefully!" her mother warned.

"It's you! Hello again! You're not sick anymore! And you are SOOO beautiful!" Urie stroked the fallow's mane as Xalibu caressed her hand. "But who made her better, Mama?"

"Remember the stranger you mentioned- the one who helped you retrieve Savage?"

"It was Nicholas?!"

"Yes, Urie," Violet replied, entering the barn. "The kind and gentle person you met is the Restorer of Goodness."

"Wow! He is?! Uh... what's the Restrictor of Gladness?" Urie asked but jabbered on. "I can't believe Nicholas BELIEVED me! No one else does, ya know! Everyone says I have a dangerous imaggonation."

Gandomine suddenly thrust through the barn's entrance in distress. "LOUSY, HIGH-STRUNG, OVER-FLAPPING, LOUD-HUMMING VAMPIRE SUCKERS. I STILL CANNOT FEAST ON THE SERDAR'S FEEDER!"

"Mind your beak! A young lady is present!"

"Gandomine! You are free?" Urie replied excitedly.

Gandomine calmed and perched on a stack of hay. "That's right, child. Nicholas believed in your story—he believed in you. If you hadn't had a 'dangerous imagination,' he wouldn't have released me from my cage, and we wouldn't have worked together to rescue this magnificent creature."

"MAGNIFICENT CREATURE? OVER-SIZED GRUNTING BEAST IF YOU ASK ME!" Gandomine's male side replied, winking at Urie.

"Quiet! Be kind!" Gandomine's female side demanded.

Urie smiled and giggled. entertained by the cardinal's inner arguments, while Violet kneeled and spoke to her with her tender emerald-green eyes. "Urie, you must listen very carefully. This fallow has distinct abilities. Nicholas will need her to remain healthy and strong. We leave it up to you to take care of her, groom her, feed her- keep her nourished and happy. Can you perform these tasks for him?"

Urie looked to her mother for approval. "You will have to work hard and be dedicated to her," her mother warned. "I TOO will have to work equally hard explaining this to your father." Xalibu lowered her head and nipped at Urie's hair.

She giggled, then hugged the fallow's neck tightly. "You protected me once! Now it's my turn to protect you!" Urie turned to Violet and accepted the responsibility. "You chose the right girl!"

Inside the Serdar's barn, a mutual relationship between the little drift keeper and the primordial fallow began. Nicholas' loyal mount would reside with her new friend until the time that the Restorer of Goodness would return to her.

The drome branch remained empty, concluding the day of cardinals assigned to the care facility. "Phew! Busy today!" Linde expressed as she locked the shutter tight on the departing window. "With the return of the brigade, many are needing help and treatment. Hopefully the cardinals we sent will bring them joy in their recovery."

"I'm sure the embedapists are equally overworked," Duggle commented. "Any word from Nicholas?"

"I've heard that he returned, but I haven't seen the whites of his eyes." Worried, Linde glanced at the empty, unlocked cage. "Gandomine's either."

Inside the aviary, a service bell chimed like the loud sound of birds chirping and singing. A customer had arrived at the front of the store.

"Do they not know it is nearly closing time?" Linde complained, exhausted.

"Not the first time we've been whistle–bit. I will go help them," Duggle offered.

"It's fine! I will let you clean this remaining cardinal dung instead," Linde instructed.

"By golly, thanks!" Duggle replied sarcastically.

Linde threw Duggle a dirty look and made her way to the front counter. The service bell sounded a second time, a third time, and a fourth, and Linde grew more irritated with each push. "Yes! Yes! I'm coming! I'm coming!" she hollered as she entered the storefront. "I'm afraid it's nearly closing time! Perhaps this can wait until tomm–" Linde stared blankly at the customer in shock and awe; her eyes quickly teared up with happiness. "Mother?!" Violet nodded, showing equal tears in her emerald–colored eyes. With little hesitation, Linde struck Violet with an enormous hug. "Oh, Mother! It's been too long. I've missed you so much!"

Later that evening in Violet's Agora, the community of Ethereal gathered in a crucial town meeting. The crowd stirred with mixtures of emotion and negativity as Norrick, Quilo Serdar, and Violet stood before them, prepared to address their concerns.

"Ring of Sonant," Norrick chanted, quieting the crowd, then spoke through the smoky ring. "People of Ethereal! Our long wait has come to an end; the divination of the Restorer of Goodness has been completed. Our time of reckoning has begun!"

"Reckoning, what reckoning?" a lady from the crowd asked.

"The Restorer of Goodness has completed several daunting yet required tasks," Norrick replied.

"What tasks?" another asked.

A local farmer belted out. "What of the quakes? They are happening every day! I question the survival of my crops!"

"Are our businesses and livelihood in danger?" a store owner questioned.

"Although the Restorer's tasks were necessary, they have aggravated the Bacillus. I'm afraid the quakes will continue to harass us," Norrick explained. "We must put faith in the engineering of the Yuulnavvies- that our structures and buildings will stay standing, that our water will remain pure and our soil fertile."

"So many have come home sick, injured, or DEAD!" another expressed.

Norrick continued. "Yes, the Brigade of Righteousness has returned from a long-fought battle at the Strain. The release of Torment has been contained; the variant is toilworn. But I must warn- the Bacillus will continue to strive for its release."

"My God! Torment?!" one yelled out.

"Are we no longer safe?"

"Will many of us get sick?"

"Ethereal's magical walls will still protect us," Quilo Serdar confirmed, his voice amplifying through the clouded ring. "I have also recruited additional military units to serve and protect our town."

Norrick returned to the magical microphone. "We all will face many struggles and challenges, and YES, unfortunately our potential of getting sick or dying will rise. But we must stand together, help each other against the Bacillus, and follow the tasks that map us to our day of reckoning."

An aggressive question came from the crowd. "Did the Union of Goodness approve of this battle- are they even aware of these actions?"

Quilo quickly snapped back. "Your question is unnecessary! We did not simply piss in the wind! These tactics were discussed in the Union Hall and approved. Each step we take going forth will be reviewed in our council!"

The crowd grew rowdy and unsettled and continued to overwhelm the group with further questions and concerns. Several others blurted out in anger.

"What good is a Restorer who can't restore!"

"That's right! Should the Restorer be at fault?"

"Plague, drought, and destruction are all I see!"

The master embedapist stepped forward. With respect and sincerity, Violet spoke out over the ruckus of the bewildered townsfolk.

"At one point in our life, every one of us has sought to define who we are! The same applies to Nicholas, who was defined as the Restorer of Goodness. We all wake each morning in hopes to thrive and make a difference in our lives. But sometimes, even at our best, it seems that we are merely surviving. Therefore, we must clench our fists and sock our hardships right in the BLINKER! Our fists are our day-to-day contributions. Tonight! We must bask in our accomplishments as a community. Tonight! We shall light our building tops... showing appreciation to those that risked their lives on the battlefield and prevented Torment's arrival. We reflect on what the Restorer of Goodness has done for us, and most importantly- we commend ourselves and what DEFINES... US! The Restorer of Goodness and the coming of the Magnanimous Toymaker is our reckoning! They will be the hearty fruit of our future."

A few hopefuls in the crowd shouted out randomly.

"Then we must work together."

"Let us thrive!"

"For our families, for our children, and our beloved!"

"Yeahhhhh!"

Violet responded. "Ethereal! Let our town shine brightly! Gandomine- if you would, please?"

"Certainly!" Gandomine replied.

"WHAT? NO! WE KNOW HOW?"

"Yes! Of course we know how! Now focus!"

The meeting grounds became silent as Gandomine's feathers quivered and shook, releasing a singing trill of musical notes. The cardinal repeated the tune, but everyone remained confused- nothing was happening. Gandomine trilled a third time while Violet gleamed at her amazing songbird. "You mustn't forget?" she hinted.

"Oh yes, right!" Gandomine replied.

"WHAT? NO! I'M SURE THAT IT IS BROKEN NOW."

"It will work!" Gandomine argued.

In a momentous occasion, Gandomine and the entire crowd worked together as one, humming the bird's song simultaneously. With all the cardinal's will, Gandomine followed up with a closing melody and slapped the bell with a mighty wing. At the Cardinals of Joy, the Chrysalis of Winter Solstice re-formed itself and hung inside Gandomine's cage. The icicle cocoon cracked and broke into pieces. The wings of the Snowflake Dragontail fluttered, enchanting the surrounding cardinals who were resting peacefully in the aviary. Like a shooting star, the butterfly bolted into the departing window. The shutters unlocked and flew open as many cardinals stormed out into the night, lighting the building tops in Atka's Flume, Eilor's Croft, and Violet's Agora. All sectors of Ethereal shone with bright and festive colors. The cardinals reconvened near the embedapist care facility and flocked together toward the building for the final spectacle, illuminating it in an amazing aura of gold and silver that beamed high into the dark sky.

As if a miracle had occurred, the worry and fret of the community vanished. On this night, the cardinals had created a display of lights so remarkable that it warmed the hearts of every man, woman, boy, and girl with a most extraordinary feeling– one of hope and joy.

Nicholas' eyes flung open, followed by urgent coughing and hacking as sea water blasted from his mouth and nose. He lay flat once again in what had become an overly repetitive and disfavored position. Thoughts of Arvel entered his mind once again.

Well bein'? I would question yer well bein' lyin' on yer back.

Yer the pick a the litter, Undertow!

Fortunately for Nicholas, there was no knife pressed to his throat this time and the ground beneath him did not feel frozen and rigid, nor was he hurt and being carried to a distant stronghold. He felt warm, relaxed, and calm as he stared above at a clear blue sky, where the seabirds soared freely through the air. He carefully sat up, shook his head as if he were removing a million spiders from his plugged ear canals, and gazed at his surroundings. It appeared he had returned to the beached dunes of Patara. He spotted three peculiar angelic patterns printed in the sand that were trailing toward a well-known spirit. As he observed the little girl wading in the tide, he heard the sudden sound of cracking and crumbling. Sea turtle hatchlings burst from their eggs and raced toward the sea with all their might. One of them lost direction and collided with the girl. Icyln picked up the hatchling and beamed at Nicholas with her entrancing smile.

The wind picked up, blowing sand into Nicholas' eyes and clouding his vision. As he attempted to remove the debris, a delicate hand gently brushed and swiped the hot and gritty gomble from his face. Still unable to see, he heard a most familiar voice. "I love you, Restorer of

Goodness. You have become strong in mind, in body, and in soul. Always remember- in life you must pull the sea." His vision finally cleared, and the person standing at the shoreline came into view. It was no longer Iclyn, but a mysterious grown woman. With her back turned to Nicholas, she was still holding the distressed hatchling. The woman carefully placed the turtle into the water and the aquatic newborn swam forth into the Mare Nostrum, beginning its new life. She then turned around and faced her son, beaming the same entrancing smile. As his mother faded away, Nicholas realized that *Nóvva* had given him that special present, a gift underneath the primordial cedars, that would forever define his true meaning and purpose- **The Chrysalis of Winter Solstice.**

In a blinding spiritual light, one agonized breath spoke to another. "Kristopher? Kris? It seems you are lost, young man! This sign- it is not for you to follow. You are a Klaas, your sign is different. It points in another direction- toward a pivotal destination."

"This sign, is it the right one for you?" Kris asked.

"Yes," the agonized breath replied. "I am fulfilled- I have done what I can do in my lifetime. I must follow the direction in which it points."

"And my sign, where do I find it?" Kris asked again.

The Faithlife surrounded Kris. "We all shall help you... yep... yep... yep..." the agonized breath replied.